PRESS PLAY

PRESS PLAY

OFF-LIMITS LOVERS
Book Four

LORE TOWNSEND

Press Play
Paperback Edition

Love N. Books Press
An Imprint of Wolfpack Publishing
1707 E. Diana Street
Tampa, FL 33610

www.lovenbookspress.com

Edited by My Brother's Editor

Press Play was originally published as Scandalous Lover in 2024 by Lore Townsend

Paperback ISBN 979-8-89567-637-0
Ebook ISBN 979-8-89567-636-3
LCCN

For anyone struggling with boundaries in this digital world.
I see you, girl.

Before we begin...

A content note: a couple of my early readers suggested that I include a warning about a potential dub-con issue in the first half of the book. I saw the opening scene with Sam and Naomi as more boundary pushing, where she seduces him into letting go of his hang-ups around getting it on with someone so forbidden, but other people have read this differently. If you're sensitive to content like this, skimming over the first steamy scene, or skipping this novel might be your best choice.

Another note: There is discussion in this book of parental loss and loss of life during childbirth (in the past). If you are sensitive to those issues, this might be one to skip. *care emoji*

Love to you!
Lore

Welcome to Faraday Island

If this is your first time checking into The White Sands Resort, you're in for a tearjerker. Sam and Naomi's story is not the easiest to read but has the greatest happily ever after. Please make sure to check the author's note with content warnings before proceeding! Here's a series cheat sheet, just for fun.

The owners of The White Sands Resort:

- **Dominic:** The chef
- **Sam:** The general manager
- **Ben:** The lawyer
- **Avery:** The wild card

- **Reina:** Dominic's fiancé. You can read their love story in *Off the Menu*.
- **Franzeska:** Avery's girlfriend. You can read their love story in *Shameless*.
- **Victoria:** Ben's fiancé. You can read their love story in *Lying For Keeps*.

Places you'll go:

- **Faraday Island:** a fictional tropical island with the climate and geographic features of a small island off the coast of Belize (where I was when I started writing this series).
- **Saubry Village:** The town on Faraday Island.
- **Merit Island:** The small island next to Faraday where the guys own a house.
- **The White Sands Resort:** the four guys purchased the abandoned resort over a decade ago and reopened it as a high-end beach destination.
- **Raft:** The high-end restaurant located inside the lobby of The White Sands Resort.
- **Reef:** The casual fare restaurant located poolside on the lower level of the resort.

PRESS PLAY

Rule #1

HOLD ON JUST A LITTLE BIT LONGER

NAOMI

> **Naomi**
> I know, I know. It's stupid. But apparently you can't get by just making fun of online dating anymore. Women want real solutions to the problems of loneliness in the city. So, off I go.

> **Angela**
> Well, message me when you're done and let me know how it goes. Who knows, maybe you'll meet someone.

My current Instagram bestie is supportive, but not exactly able to commiserate. She found her way into a clean eating niche early on in her career, therefore missing most of the humiliating stunts we lifestyle influencers have to put ourselves through.

I laugh out loud into my phone screen, attracting the attention of a group of men standing together near the front door of the bar. Avoiding eye contact, I quickly type my reply.

Naomi
Don't count on it.

Slipping my phone into my purse, I inhale and exhale trying to bring my confidence back up to normal levels, which has been getting harder and harder these days. Back in my twenties, I could walk into any room and own the damn place. I suppose I still look like I own most rooms—and I better with how long it takes me to get ready—but I don't feel it anymore.

I just have to get through this month.

A few more long weeks of chasing content and likes, and then my big launch will be here, and I'll be set. I'm almost giddy dreaming about all the accounts and licensing deals I'll be eligible for once I pull off this epic content for PassionFly. It's a career maker, and I'm lucky to be the one they chose. I'm sure there were a ton of other mid-level influencers like me vying for the chance.

A deal like this will give me all the visibility I could ever dream of and all the perks that come with it. Not that I've been doing terribly…but it's a bit of an uphill battle for market corners these days, and it's getting harder with every birthday.

The dating event I'm attending tonight, while pretty much guaranteeing me fantastic views and engagement, is hitting a bit close to home. It was one thing to walk my followers through the process of setting up online profiles and screening out potential first dates—none of which I went on. It's quite another to be out here in person, throwing myself to the god of mingling singles.

Especially when I've resigned myself to being one forever.

One more month. Just one more month.

I pull open the heavy wooden door before I can talk myself out of it. The place is cheerfully lit, with yellow walls and dark wood tables. In true Austin style, the tables are long and communal with benches on both sides.

Perfect. Not only do I have to lower myself to speed dating

like some kind of 90s sitcom character, I have to do it sitting at the same table as all the other losers.

I shake off the thought.

I'm not like them. I'm here for research. To get a story and some cute pics of myself having the time of my life for my channel.

I approach the bar with swagger I've learned to fake like a pro and order myself a margarita. Might as well have some fun while I'm here. I snap my first selfie with the cute cocktail—the little pink paper umbrella contrasting nicely with the yellow walls. I give a big smile for the camera before ditching the flimsy paper atrocity in the closest trash can before it can leach red 40 into my drink.

"Five minutes, everyone. Please come make yourself a name tag. If this is your first time, let me know, and I'll give you a rundown of the rules."

Booze in hand, I make my way over to the organizer's table. "Hello, I'm Naomi. I emailed about doing a piece on this event for my channel."

The woman in charge—Bev or Barb or something—I can't read the cursive on her name tag—matches my dazzling smile. "Of course, welcome. Is this your first time at a speed dating event?"

I laugh mid-sip and cough. "Yes. I wasn't sure it would be my scene or my followers' scene, but there are quite a few people in the right age group. Now we'll just see if they're the quality my channel will be looking for."

Barb or whatever gives me a knowing smile, like she's heard it all before. "You're going to have a great time. If you're a little nervous, just know it's normal, and all the guys are nervous as well."

I narrow my eyes at her as she deftly sidesteps my whole comment about how I'm not here for myself and offers me advice as if I'm going to be searching for the love of my life in this cheesy, western-themed bar.

I respond with a tight-lipped smile that I hope displays all my annoyance and more, and set down my drink to write my name on a red and white sticker name tag.

"Perfect. Now, I recommend sticking it to…" She trails off as I peel off the plastic backing and stick the paper to my left boob.

I look up to find her grimacing. "Most women feel more comfortable with their tag stuck somewhere besides…you know."

I look down at the red and white rectangle perched on the tip of my perky left tit and back up at the woman, giving her a shrug. "I think I'll be okay."

Bless her heart, she just plows right on with her welcome spiel. "The dates last for five minutes. Everyone will have a chance to chat with everyone, so don't worry about where you sit when you start. This event is specifically for men seeking women and women seeking men, so we separate the group by gender. When the first buzzer goes off, the ladies will sit down on the bench facing the bar. When the second buzzer sounds, the guys come out in alphabetical order and sit down in front of the ladies. After five minutes, you'll hear another buzzer, and the guys slide down. You'll stay in the same place for the whole event."

She shuffles through her bag and produces a thin notebook and a pen with the name of the event on it, passing them to me. "You can take notes on the guys you like, and you're welcome to take any numbers you want. The guys know not to ask for phone numbers, and we ask that you don't offer yours. Just take their number and decide later if you want to shoot them a text."

"Well, I'm not really here for that, so I guess…" I trail off as I see her face. She thinks I'm completely full of shit. I clench my teeth and gesture with the notebook and pen. "Thanks. I'll just go find a seat."

Her pageant queen smile is back in full force. "Perfect. We're getting started in two minutes."

I set my drink down at the very end of the long table and

pose for another pic with the notebook and branded pen before finally allowing myself to glance around at the people. The women all look as tired and over it as I feel—and I'm not even here for a date.

The guys, however, are just plain adorable.

I can see the optimism in their eyes and smell their longing from here. It makes me hope they find someone willing to take their number tonight. I vow to take every single one even though there is zero chance I'll be calling anyone.

I'm lost thinking about if it would be better to take their number and never call or refuse their number and not get their hopes up when the first timer dings.

Here goes nothing.

I slide onto the bench in front of my cocktail and set my notebook down, only to be tapped on the shoulder by a prim, type-A-looking woman with flat, straight hair and glasses.

"First time?" she asks, not in the friendliest tone.

I nod and smile.

"Scoot on down. We can't all climb over you."

"Oh," I say as I look down the table at the entirely empty bench. It seems like it would be easy enough for them to step over it and get seated, but drill sergeant Barbie over here is waiting impatiently, with other women lining up behind her, so I scoot. Women are scooting in from the other side too, so before long I'm stuck in the very center of the table, with one sweater-clad hopeful smashed into me on either side.

Fantastic.

I snap another selfie, trying to get the shoulder proximity in the frame.

It's not my intention to hit the internet and make fun of the event—at least not entirely—but I do want to give a proper representation for my followers. Who knows, maybe I'll inspire the organizers to opt for private tables in the future.

The second buzzer sounds, and the guys start sliding down the bench. I try not to make eye contact as they go by, which is awkward and not like me at all, but this whole thing has me a bit off kilter. Jammed in here with too many bench mates has my oxygen levels waning and the heat rising. I haven't even started my first date yet, and I'm already starting to sweat.

I decide to occupy myself by jotting down a little intro in my notebook.

> *9/23-Saturday-The Swing Inn-Downtown Austin.*
> *Speed dating event set up by The Hopeful Howdy*
> *First impressions: should have single tables rather than cram us onto this bench.*

After all the men are seated, the buzzer goes off, signaling the start of our first date.

I look up and straight into a familiar pair of baby blues.

Rule #2

YOU'RE NOT A KID ANYMORE

NAOMI

"Oh!" I exclaim, the sound leaving my lips entirely on its own volition. My brain short circuits, offering no help with closing my gaping mouth.

Sam smiles and shakes his head. "Of course this is how this would go for me. Sorry to drag you into my bad luck."

I laugh, blinking myself back into the present moment. "No, no. It's not bad luck. I'm happy to see you. It's been forever."

I realize with a start where we are and hold up my phone as a defensive shield. "I'm just here to do a piece for my Instagram channel. Being single in Austin, that kind of thing. Women go crazy for it. I'm not actually..." I trail off as I realize how badly I just stepped in it. "Not that there's anything wrong with being here looking for someone. I mean...I'm going to shut up now."

Sam laughs in the easy, good-natured way I remember from spying on him and the others from behind my book, pretending not to hang on their every word as I created worlds in my little girl mind with those guys at the center.

He's aged well—like, so well—and I can't take my eyes off

him. His dark brown hair now has salt and pepper at the temples, and charming smile lines crease his eyes and cheeks. He's…gorgeous.

Shit, how long have I been staring?

I look away quickly and suck down my drink.

"It's okay. I know what you mean. It wasn't my first choice to be here either, but I'm finding it pretty difficult to meet anyone on the island. One of our vendors lives in the city and set me up with this event, so I figured, what the heck. At the very least, I might get to talk to someone who isn't my employee for a few minutes."

He cocks his head and tosses me another disarming smile. I can feel myself leaning forward just to get closer to him and try to stop…but I can't.

"And what do you know? I run into little Naomi."

The blush that shoots across my face is so hot I nearly fan myself.

Did these sweater ladies get closer in the last minute?

"Well, I'm happy to have run into you. Are you in town for a while? I'm a bit of a local expert. I'd love to take you around and show you what Austin has to offer." I can almost hear the desperation in my voice.

Look at me, I'm an adult now. Hang out with me.

If anything could ever bring back the feeling of growing up lonely on the big New York estate, it's this feeling right here. The *please pay attention to me* feeling.

Sam just shoots me that smile again.

I'm dead. Literally.

"I fly out of Houston tomorrow, but I don't have any plans for tonight. Well, other than this."

I pull my notebook out so fast I elbow not one but both sweater ladies, earning me matching glares. "Give me your number, and I'll text you when it's over."

"We'll both be here when it's over."

"Just in case." I've got to keep it together but try telling that to the little girl I've become. I can almost feel the hot sun of a New York summer, smell the grass, and feel the cool lake water as it dries on my skin.

I'm definitely sweating.

Sam pulls the notebook across the table and jots his number down. When he slides it back, I grip the flimsy pages to my chest like a treasure.

The timer goes off, and I jump a foot, earning more glares from either side. "Dang. That was really short."

"Speed dating, I guess."

I'm not ready to say goodbye, not with the way he's been looking at me, but he's already sliding down the bench to the next lucky lady. With his eyes locked on mine.

"See you later," I mouth silently.

He just grins and gives me a wink before turning his attention to his new date like a perfect gentleman.

OH. MY. GOD.

Sam freaking Griffin. One of my brother's best friends and business partners. What are the odds? I'm about to pull my phone out and start doing what I do best—googling him and posting all about my fantastic speed date blast from the past—when a voice cuts through my ecstatic celebration.

"Hi, I'm Mike."

I look up from my phone and reality comes crashing down on me like the stupid ice bucket challenge I got talked into.

I steal a quick glance down the bench, trying to count how many of these "Mikes" I'm going to have to suffer through before I get Sam back.

"And you're Naomi, I see."

I snap back to center. "Yes, sorry. Naomi. It's nice to meet you, Mike."

And so it goes. Each new guy is a blur of pleasantries and job titles. I smile politely and offer as much information as is strictly required before allowing the guy to jot his number down on my growing list of digits I'll never call.

It's truly amazing how much guys think we care about their jobs. I make a mental note to chat with Bev about giving them a better pep talk. We want to get an idea of their income level—hell, that should be on the damn name tag—but the last thing we want to do is spend five minutes hearing about residency rounds or sales calls.

"Nice to meet you, Steve. Have a great rest of your evening."

"The night is young if you want to grab a drink here or at another bar. You're my last date and favorite woman I've met tonight."

I can feel the side-eye from his previous date next to me as I try to manage an apologetic smile. "Sorry, not tonight. But I have your number." I hold up my notebook as proof.

"Well, be sure to use it."

I smile just long enough for the guy to wander off before letting it drop like a stone.

"You sure did well," the lady next to me says, eyeing my list of numbers.

"I guess I did." I glance at her much shorter list and bite my lip. "Do you want them?"

"Your list of numbers?" she asks, incredulous.

"Yeah. There's only one I want." I tear the paper neatly, so my notes and Sam's number are safe at the top, offering the rest of the sheet, with the whole list of guys' names and numbers, to the stunned blondie.

"Thank you. Wow." She tucks the paper into her purse like I just handed her a hundred-dollar bill.

"Do you want to take a selfie?" I ask, already planning the caption for the photo that shows just how generous I am for helping this poor lady out.

I find Sam at the bar, talking with some random woman. I try to exude enough "get the fuck out of here" juju to scare her off, and it works.

Still got it.

"There you are. Any luck with the guys?"

I blush as laughter rises up from my belly. I've got to get this under control. I'm turning into a puddle every time this guy opens his mouth.

I may have had a teeny crush on him growing up, but I had crushes on all my brother's friends. They were like idols to me. Untouchable, so cool, like characters in a movie I wasn't allowed to watch.

But there's no reason to still be stumbling over my words all these years later.

"Not exactly. I got plenty of numbers, but none I'm going to use."

"Ouch," Sam offers good naturedly.

"Oh, I didn't mean yours. I'm definitely going to use yours."

His eyebrows raise, and I suppress another giggle.

"So, Miss Austin expert. Where to now?"

I tap my chin and consider. I was planning to just go home, but this opportunity is too good to pass up. "You hungry?"

"Always."

"How about tacos?"

"My love language."

Oh god, Naomi. Do not swoon.

"Great. Perfect. Well…" I glance around the bar at the people milling about. "It's over, right? Can we just leave?"

I look back at Sam, and he smiles. "I doubt they're going to try to keep us here."

"Right. Okay. Tacos."

And just like that, I'm leaving the bar arm-in-arm with an adorable ghost from my past.

Rule #3

SHE'S NOT A KID ANYMORE...

SAM

Of all the women I imagined sitting across from at a bar in Austin, Naomi wouldn't have even crossed my mind long enough to make the list.

I try to think back to the last update I heard about her life or whereabouts, but I come up blank. To say it's been a decade since I saw the woman would not be an understatement.

And woman she is.

I still have an image in my mind of the little sister who always followed us around and demanded to be included in things Dom had zero intention of including her in, but I see none of that little girl sitting across from me now.

What I see is a bold, smart, confident woman.

One who I'm pretty sure is trying to get me drunk.

Not that I mind. I can't remember the last time I felt free enough to relax like this. Or the last time I was in the presence of a woman who lit my insides on fire quite the way Naomi does. Every look from those sparkling green eyes makes my breath catch. Every glimpse of her tongue darting out to trace her lower teeth as she grins makes my heart beat a little faster.

I'm on shaky ground here, but somehow, all I want to do is dance.

Just the thought makes me feel like an old man, considering how long it's been since I actually did dance. With a woman or not.

I'm forty-two, not exactly ancient, but my job requires me to be on call all the time, and I wasn't the biggest partier even before I started managing The White Sands. The other guys would always let loose, but I had so much to lose, it never felt like the right move.

Even now, when we're all part owners and theoretically on even footing, I still feel like I have the most to prove. It didn't help when the guys fell in love, one after the other over the last few years, leaving me to be the actual odd man out at every gathering.

They all managed to find someone on the island, but I just don't see how that's possible for me. I have an image to maintain —the trustworthy, approachable general manager of a multi-million-dollar property in the Caribbean. No matter what the guys say, I can't shack up with one of the employees or guests.

"I got you a hibiscus, or as the locals call it, Jamaica."

"Thanks." I accept the much too tall cocktail from a grinning Naomi.

She's starting to get a bit pinker in the cheeks, so I know she must be feeling the alcohol. And yet here we are, settling down to our drinks and not nearly enough food.

"I think this might have to be our last stop. Maybe we should order a few more tacos and chill for a bit."

Her mouth drops open in indignation. "Last stop? I have, like, eight more taco places I want to take you to. And it's only…" She lifts her phone to her face. The sparkly pink device never leaves her hand. "Eleven? Dang. How did it get so late?

Well, regardless, I know a couple of the places are open till midnight. There's still time."

She's adorable in her eagerness to show me the city she so clearly loves. And she's getting more and more eager as time goes by and drinks go down.

I've considered a handful of times over the last few hours whether I should be doing more to dissuade the fervent looks and smiles that I see her shooting my way.

Because all I'm doing is returning them.

She smiles. I smile.

She giggles. I bite my lip.

She leans against me as we stroll down the sidewalk, and I pull her arm into mine.

It's a slippery slope, and one I've been on since we walked out of that first bar together.

There's no way around it—this woman is sexy as hell.

Her long, curly brown hair, loose and wild over her creamy tanned and freckled shoulders seems to be begging me to run my hands through it. I find my head tilting to the side, imagining what it would be like to tuck my face into the curve of her neck and the angular ridge above the swell of her breasts. The desire to be closer to her churns through me. I lose focus while she's telling stories as I watch her tip her head back and laugh.

I'd like to blame the alcohol on this sudden rush of passionate feelings, but I can recall very similar ones when I first saw her at speed dating. The mere presence of her does something to me, and I can't pass it off as booze induced.

But there's no doubt it's the alcohol making me consider things that otherwise would be out of the question.

I look down at my hands, flexing my fingers to bring myself out of my completely inappropriate fantasies.

"I'm going to go order us a platter of tacos to soak up all this booze. Let's just hang here. It's quiet." I cringe, sounding like an old man. "And we can talk."

Naomi narrows her eyes but doesn't protest. When the feast

arrives, we both dig in. I feel better immediately. More stable, more clear-headed.

But somehow, I still feel like taking this woman back to my hotel.

It's a bad idea, right?

"I can't believe I haven't made it to The Sands since opening week. You guys have owned it for what, a decade?"

"Just about." It's crazy to think about it like that, but time has flown by. From our meager beginnings as a bunch of clueless city boys to the savvy, island business owners we've become, it's been a wild ride. "You should come visit. Hit me up anytime. I'll get you the best room in the resort."

Naomi raises her brows and smirks. "Maybe I'll do that." Her attention drifts to her phone momentarily before her eyes come back to meet mine. "I bet my followers would love a full spread on the hottest getaway just a short jump from Houston."

"Exactly," I offer, although all the follower talk has me a bit confused. I've never been a big social media guy. I have a woman on our front desk staff who manages the accounts for The Sands, and my own personal accounts are dusty, deserted roads, complete with tumbleweeds.

Naomi seems to have combined the personal and professional, creating a business of…well, herself.

"So, what do you tell your followers? How does picture-taking translate into a job?"

Her face blooms open in a way I haven't seen before, the subject clearly lighting her up. "It's not a hundred percent my job, you know, most things are paid for by the family, but I'm growing my personal brand from local Austin influencing and general lifestyle influencing to sustainable fashion influencing for women in their 'business and family years.'"

A shadow passes through her bright eyes as she makes the air quotes, but it's gone before I can identify it.

"It's been getting more and more challenging to keep up with the younger influencers." She rolls her eyes when I scoff at that.

"You know what I mean. I'm thirty-two, almost thirty-three. That's a whole different demographic from when I started. I need to be able to have broad enough appeal to stay in the game. Women who are in their thirties have different considerations and interests. Things like family, careers, and houses. And if they don't have those things, they want them. I'm going to have to figure out a way to stay relevant as a single, childless woman in her thirties."

"Hence the speed dating."

"Exactly. For the last few years, it's been easy to slide by on commiserating about how much online dating sucks, but that content isn't getting results like it used to. Women want solutions."

She breaks off and looks down at the device gripped between her hands, although she doesn't flip the phone screen to face herself.

"It's hard getting older and not being sure if all the dreams you had for your life are ever going to happen," she says softly.

When her eyes rise once more to meet mine, I nod. "I get that. If someone told me at thirty-two that I'd still be single at forty-two, I would have called them crazy."

She narrows her eyes. "Why are you single? Isn't that island covered with bikini babes?"

I shrug. "I suppose, but it's complicated as the GM. Honestly, I'd prefer finding someone who didn't have a connection to the resort at all, so I could have a home life and a work life that were separate."

"Hence, the speed dating." Naomi mimics my earlier words with a smile.

I nod. "Hence the speed dating. I know it's a little far-fetched to think I'm going to talk a woman from Austin into moving to Faraday to live with me, but…I don't know."

Naomi's eyes widen in surprise. "Are you crazy? Any lady would jump at that chance."

"No one has yet."

Her mouth opens and then closes again. I wait eagerly for her to turn her thoughts into words. I find myself on the edge of my seat waiting for her opinion on things, especially things about myself. Not something I'm used to feeling with anyone, not even the guys.

She's perceptive and insightful, offering her views on the world in the kindest ways. I hate to say it, but she's nothing like I would have imagined when I thought of little Naomi all grown up. She seems to have avoided a lot of the spoiled rich girl entitlement attitude I see every day at The Sands.

She's...great.

Too great.

I should probably get out of here.

"Wanna get out of here?" she asks, reading my mind.

"I was just thinking that. I've had a really good time tonight, Naomi, I hope—"

"I mean, like, with me."

I just stare.

She laughs at what must be an incredibly stupid look on my face. "Do you want to come back to my place? It's pretty nice. Could be nicer than your hotel room. Definitely less lonely."

Oh, dang. Here it is. The moment of truth. "I..."

She waits.

"I'm not sure that's—"

"I'll never tell anyone."

And there it is.

Once those words leave her lips, I have no choice but to face the hard truth. The only thing preventing me from jumping on this opportunity like a kid at Christmas is the idea that someone might find out.

I can't risk it.

"Naomi," I start, but the woman's already ten steps ahead of me.

"I get it. It would be weird if anyone found out. Maybe it's kind of weird anyway. You probably remember when I was born…not that anyone could ever forget that." She glances down at the back of her phone again as if considering checking it before bringing her piercing gaze back to mine. "But that's ancient history. We're adults. We're single. We're in a city where no one who knows anything about our past is going to barge in. It's totally safe."

I must not look convinced because she blazes on. "I'm not even suggesting that anything is going to happen. I'm just inviting you back to see my place. As friends. We're friends, aren't we?"

I want to hold out a bit longer, just so I can tell myself later that I did, but part of me is concerned she's going to bail if I don't agree soon.

And, while that would be preferable, it's not what I want.

"Okay."

Her face lights up. "Okay." She does check her phone then, tapping quickly, before placing it face down on the table. "I just called an Uber. They'll be here in," another quick peek at the screen, "three minutes."

I nod, impressed with the efficiency of the transportation system here in the real world. It's easy to forget how normal people live when you spend all your time in la-la land.

When a silver Prius pulls up, I take a deep breath and follow her into the back seat.

Rule #4

SOMEONE HAS TO KEEP THEIR PANTS ON

SAM

The car drops us off in front of a tall, white building surprisingly close to where we were just eating.

"We could have walked."

Naomi shrugs. "I didn't want you to have enough time to talk yourself out of coming over."

I'll be damned if I'm not completely flattered by the way this woman is trying to get me into her apartment. It's been a while since I was pursued like this.

Who am I kidding? I've never been pursued like this. Maybe I've never been pursued at all. I was never exactly the most eligible bachelor of my close-knit friend group.

It feels as warm and fuzzy as it is terrifying.

Because this girl is as off-limits as they come.

Naomi unlocks her door, and I follow her inside. The place is immaculate, just as I expected it to be. Chic, modern bohemian with a flare of...something. Maybe Texas? I wouldn't be surprised if the culture rubbed off on her a bit. Hell, I've only been in town for a week, and I'm already talking myself out of a new pair of boots.

"Do you want a drink?"

I shake my head. "I think I've had enough for tonight."

She starts to walk into the kitchen, and I call after her. "You've had enough, too. If you plan on anything happening."

She turns at the doorway and tosses me a flirty, incredulous look. I grin at her dramatic acting skills. "Why, Mr. Griffin. Was that you telling me what to do? I'm not sure at what point this evening you got the idea that I take orders from anyone."

Her tone is heated and seductive. My cock responds, eager to play with the vixen.

"You can do as you please. But my limits are hard and fast."

Naomi puts her hands on her hips and struts toward me, pouting adorably. "Do I need to pass a field sobriety test?"

She keeps walking until her chest is pressed right up against mine. With all our heated stares and arm holding over the last few hours, this is the first physical contact that feels intentional. I force my breath to steady as I look down at her fierce, green eyes, peering up at me from between her lashes.

"That's not a terrible idea," I manage.

She takes a step back, and the loss of her body heat sends a chill through me. I actually shiver.

"Shall I walk a straight line? Stand on one leg and touch the tip of my nose? Recite the ABCs backward?"

"Dang, girl, how many field sobriety tests have you been given?"

She tosses a flirty smirk that goes straight to my cock. All this waiting, all these games, they're killing me. But I have to be careful. I could be putting my whole life and livelihood on the line here. There's no way I'm going through with anything if she's drunk.

"I just watch a lot of TV."

"Stand on one leg and do the nose touching."

I watch as Naomi obeys my command, enjoying the sight of

her bending to my will far more than I was expecting. When she brought up the field sobriety test, it made me feel a bit like a manager. Now that she's balanced there a foot away from me, tapping her fingers against her nose without breaking eye contact, I feel like a different kind of boss.

"Did I pass?" she whispers, still hovering on one leg.

I nod and close the distance between us.

This could be the biggest mistake of my life, but there's no fighting it.

My lips touch hers, and it's instant fire. She leans into the kiss, eyes tightly closed, and I watch her for a long moment before surrendering completely. My hands finally get their way, landing on her shoulders first and sliding down the soft skin of her arms to her hands.

She gives me a little squeeze as my fingers graze her palms, and I take that as encouragement. As my hands make their way around her luscious hips to grip the ass I've been watching all night long, I press my tongue into her mouth, forcing her to open for me.

The taste of her is better than I ever could have imagined. Sweet and salty, like a dessert. The feel of her warmth beneath my hands as I run them down her back and over her ass, giving her full booty a little squeeze as I make my way down to the bare skin of her thighs and then back up, trailing my fingers up her bare legs and under her short, tight skirt.

When she pulls away, I'm almost expecting it.

Almost relieved.

"Wait," she says breathlessly.

I meet her eyes but don't find the hesitation I was expecting. If anything, her gaze blazes hotter than ever.

"Let's go to my room."

And I want to, of course.

I should say yes.

But I can't make the words come out.

"Naomi, I…I might need to take this slower."

Her face slides into a sly grin as she takes me by both hands. "I get it. I promise I won't make you do anything you don't want to do. Let's go in there, and we can make out a bit more. No pressure. You can keep your pants on as long as you need to."

"I'll be keeping my pants on all night," I say, but my argument has little tooth since I'm allowing her to lead me down the hallway.

Her bedroom is like walking into a page in a magazine. Soft shades of pink and cream wash over the walls and windowsills, mixing with the golden light from a couple of floor lamps creating a feeling of warmth. At the room's center lies an enormous bed, draped in cream and jewel-toned blue. It's a layered cake of textures—plush throws, delicate lace, and bold, patterned pillows all carefully arranged. A vintage, distressed dresser stands against one wall, its surface adorned with trinkets and treasures that sparkle under the glow of string lights artfully draped above.

On the far wall, a cozy loveseat covered in floral and geometric prints echoes the room's eclectic spirit. The small sofa sits under a large window, framing views of Austin's vibrant cityscape, while green, vining plants perch on the windowsill, adding a burst of freshness and a hint of the tropics. If I didn't already feel right at home, that little touch would have pushed me over the edge.

She tries to lead me to the bed, but I finally find my brakes. "How about over here," I say, leading her instead to the loveseat. The Texas sky is clear tonight, and I can see the full moon through the white sheer curtains.

"Wherever you're comfortable."

She seems agreeable enough as she flops down on the sofa and leans toward where I stand, but I know she's humoring me. She knows damn well she's going to get what she so clearly wants.

Because how am I going to turn down those eyes? That body?

I slide in next to her, and we fall back together as if pulled by a magnetic force. Those velvety pink lips of hers—magically pink and yet not smearing all over as I lick and suck on them. It makes me want to try harder, pressing forward until I'm nearly on top of her, driving my tongue into her open, willing mouth as my hands continue exploring her soft, sumptuous body.

I'm nearly lost in the moment, suspended in time, when I feel her fingers slip down and take a firm grasp of my achingly stiff erection on the outside of my jeans.

I gasp, surprised, and Naomi takes it as an invitation to grip me harder with both her hands, one on the back of my neck, holding my head in place, the other sliding up and down my length.

When was the last time a woman touched me like this?

I won't even try to do the math.

The last thing I want to do is think about other women right now, even if they are so far in the past, I can barely recall their faces.

I want to be fully present with this woman. This perfect, gorgeous, totally and completely off-limits woman.

I pull back suddenly, and Naomi loses her grip on my neck.

As I sit up, the sight of her disheveled before me, lips swollen and eyes hooded as her mouth drops into a surprised O…well, it almost sends me diving right back in, consequences be damned.

Alas, I'm nothing if not responsible.

"I should go."

"Sam—"

"No, I get it. It's totally safe and secret."

"But…" I can hear the smile in her voice as she teases me.

"But it's a lot. I'm going to know it happened."

"Yeah, you're going to know that you had a hot night with a woman who, if history serves, you'll probably never see again. So ,we have a little backstory. I think that makes it even hotter."

I shake my head, but I'm smiling in spite of myself. "Don't

tell me you had a crush on me growing up. That might make it too weird."

She slaps my chest playfully. "Don't be ridiculous. I had a crush on Avery like everyone else."

I laugh and shake my head again before tilting it back to rest on the soft cushion of the sofa and consider the full moon outside the window above me.

She's totally right. I have no reason to feel so hesitant.

It's just...

I place a lot of weight on being the responsible one in the group. The one who always does the right thing. The one everyone can come to for solid advice or help in a tough situation. I'm the predictable one, and I like that about myself. It makes me trustworthy. It's why I'm such a great manager.

What would it mean for me to go so completely off the rails like this?

"I can hear you thinking over there," Naomi says, snuggling in until her head is curled in the crook of my neck and shoulder. I wrap my arm behind her warm body and pull her close, forcing back my moan at our heartbreakingly intimate position.

If I'm not careful, my longing for a life that includes endless hours in this very position is going to start to show.

"It's not you, gorgeous. It's me." The words come out sounding strained, but at least I managed to force them out. Every fiber of my being is battling the idea that I have to get up and leave this woman.

Naomi just laughs and snuggles in closer. "You did not just say that."

"Sorry. I wish I could give you the good time you deserve."

"You deserve it too."

Do I really, though?

I came to this city tonight with one goal—meet someone who might be interested in starting something long-term on Faraday Island. I know that's an insane goal to have for a speed dating event, but it hardly seems like giving in to a one-night stand with a woman who I could never be in a relationship with would be a successful end to the evening.

I want to, though. There's no denying that. But I'm an expert at denying myself things. It makes me a better person to make the right choice, even when it's hard.

My self-control, however, is waning by the second, especially now that Naomi's lips have found the sensitive skin of my neck and are grazing upward toward my jaw. I close my eyes and sink into the feeling, allowing my hands to roam once more. She moans in pleasure as I touch her and…well…I may have lost the battle.

Or won.

It's hard to say at this point.

Her lips find mine, and it's over. She can feel my resignation, I know she can, because she slides one leg over until she's straddling my lap.

Now that I have her full body in my arms, pressed against my chest, settling down on my hard cock, it's everything. She's everything. I can barely remember my own name, let alone why I was trying to fight this in the first place.

She's soft and smooth under my hands as they graze down her arms. Even softer in the places I find when I push her top up a bit. I can't get enough touching, and it seems like she's feeling the same.

Naomi pulls her mouth off mine, and I lean forward like a baby bird.

I'm distracted enough that I only notice my shirt coming off when it drags over my face, blocking her flushed cheeks from my view.

Naomi falls on my bare chest like an animal.

"Oh my god, you're so fucking hot. I knew you would be," she whispers against my skin as she drags her lips and tongue up my stomach and over both nipples.

I grip her ass tighter to me, grinding her center along the hard ridge of my erection.

When her lips hit mine again, my life is complete. Between her tongue pressing into my mouth, her hands sliding over my bare chest, shoulders, and stomach, and the way her body feels as we grind together—this may be all I need to survive.

I lose her mouth again and battle to keep from moaning in despair.

"Okay, so I know I said you could keep your pants on as long as you wanted…"

I can't help but smile. "But…"

Naomi perks up as I play along, sitting up straighter. I take advantage and grip both of her large, perky breasts in my hands.

"But…what if I kept my pants on instead?"

My eyes lift and meet hers, my brow furrowing. "What do you mean?

"I mean, I know you're maybe not comfortable with the full meal deal." She grinds into my cock as she says the words, sending my mind reeling. "But I also know it's only a matter of time before my tits come out." She bites her lip and leans into my hands on her breasts.

Without thinking, I slide them down to the hem and pull the top right off.

Naomi laughs and shakes her chest at me. "Yup, just like that."

She reaches behind herself, unhooking her bra. I get both of her naked, perfect breasts in hand and lean forward to capture a nipple in my mouth.

Whatever she asks for now, she's going to get.

"I need to taste you," she says softly.

I glance up from sucking her nipples.

"I'm taking these jeans off so I can get your cock in my mouth."

My mouth falls open but not a single word comes out.

"And in return, I'll promise you that my pants will stay on unless you take them off. Deal?"

"I..."

Naomi groans in frustration, gripping me by the shoulders. "Whatever it is you're so scared of, Sam, you have to let it g—"

"Okay," I say quickly before I lose my nerve. Or come to my senses.

"Okay," she repeats, smile growing wider.

Then she's sliding off my lap, taking her warmth, softness, and glorious tits with her. My mouth falls open to protest, but she's already pulling me up to stand with her. I wrap her back in my arms and follow, holding tightly as she walks backward across the room. When we reach the far wall, she spins and takes another step so my back presses against the cool wall.

She pulls away and places a hand firmly on my chest to keep me from following. "Stay put."

I can't complain, can't form a coherent thought as I watch her drop to her knees in front of me. I still have my jeans on, and my erection is very visible through the thick material. Naomi drags her fingers down it, followed by her teeth.

"Is this guy going to be as beautiful as the rest of you?"

My eyes roll back in my head as her teeth find my tip, nipping it through my pants. "You can..."

I look down to find her gazing up at me from under her lashes.

"I'm sorry, what was that?" she teases me sweetly.

"You can take them off."

Her face twists into an adorable smirk. "Oh, really. I can take them off, can I? You've really come around, haven't you." Her fingers land on my belt buckle, and I suck in a breath, the anticipation shooting sparks through my torso.

"I feel like I should make you beg," she says as she starts to slide my belt open, torturously slow.

I would.

"But to be honest, at this point I feel like begging myself," she goes on as the buckle finally falls open.

And I lose my mind. "Do it."

"Do what?" she says, still holding my loose belt in both hands.

"Beg." The word escapes my mouth in someone else's voice. I'm possessed.

Naomi bites her lip and flutters her eyelashes. "Oh, you'd like that, would you?"

I nod.

"Okay..." she says slyly, sitting back just a bit, still holding my belt.

If I'd kept my damn mouth shut, my pants would probably be on the floor right now, but whatever this is, I can't seem to stop playing along.

"Sam...I really want to take those pants off, what do you say?"

"No."

Naomi's face transforms into a pout, and she lets out a huff. "Please?"

I shake my head. I have no idea what to say. I'm so sure I'm going to say something completely stupid and ruin this, so I stay quiet.

"I want to play with your cock so bad." She lands a hand on the outside of my pants, dragging her fingers up said cock for emphasis as she coos the words at me. "It just looks so delicious in there. Don't you want me to suck it?"

"Beg."

Her breath catches, and I can see the effect this game is having on her as well. "Please, Sam. Please let me suck this beautiful cock of yours. I promise you'll like it."

"Play with your tits."

She obeys with gusto, lifting the lovely ladies into both hands and tweaking her own nipples as she blinks up at me.

"Now beg again."

"Sam...don't you want my hot, wet mouth on your cock? I'll suck on your tip and play with your balls just like you tell me to. I'll do anything you tell me—"

"Do it."

Naomi squeezes her breasts and looks up at me innocently. "Do what?"

"Get my cock out and suck it. Right now."

"Oh god, I thought you'd never ask." She has the button and fly of my jeans down so quickly I barely register it before I feel my pants around my ankles. I lift each foot and allow her to pull them off entirely. She pulls my boxers down next, not bothering to get them all the way off before catching my bouncing erection with one hand.

"I fucking knew you would be so beautiful." She's not even talking to me, totally lost in her own little world down there.

I bite my lip and lean my head back against the wall as her tongue touches down on my tip. She swirls it there lightly, tasting me. I feel my boxers being pulled the rest of the way off and lift my feet obediently without even looking down.

Once I'm completely naked, Naomi really goes at me with a gusto. I hang my head in amazement, watching as she holds my shaft in both hands and starts feeding me into her mouth. Her tongue feels incredible sliding over the underside of my shaft, and I steady my breathing, wanting to make this feeling last forever.

I can't take my eyes off her. She's the sexiest thing I've ever laid eyes on, breasts bouncing as she sucks my cock. I've had blow jobs before but never one that felt like this.

As if she can read my mind, she slips me out of her mouth and looks up at me with the most adorably eager smile. "Tell me what you want."

"Take my balls in one hand. Yeah, just like that. Holy shit." I drift back into mute territory as she cups me in one hand and drives my shaft back into her waiting mouth with the other. I feel my tip hit the back of her throat, and her teeth graze softly down my length as she draws me back out.

A few more minutes of this, and I'm going to blow.

"Baby, I'm getting close."

She pulls out suddenly, still working me firmly with her fist. "I want you to come in my mouth."

"Are you sure?"

She sounds very sure, but I still want to check. None of the women I've been with have ever requested it. I sure as hell want to. My orgasm is closer than ever just thinking about it.

"Hell yes. I'm going to drink you."

Fuck.

Of course she is.

She must be as turned on by my imminent orgasm as I am because she's going full speed now. Her grip on my balls stays soft as she speeds up her sucking, fucking her own face with my cock. My eyes feel like they're on fire from not blinking, but I can't look away.

"God that feels so good. I'm going to come. Are you ready?"

My tip is back against the top of her throat as she hums her agreement. The addition of that vibration is what sends me over the edge.

I buckle forward, and I careen into the greatest orgasm of my life. I hear myself cry out, but it sounds like a different person. I'm disconnected from every part of myself except for the one currently exploding into the hot, wet mouth of this femme fatale.

She sucks me dry and then sits back on her heels, wiping her face and grinning at me. "You are so fucking hot, you know that?" she says.

I shake my head. "You are the hot one. Damn it, girl. That was mind blowing."

"I know," she offers sweetly as she hops to her feet, hands on her hips. "Do you want to lay down on the bed and watch me get myself off?"

My mouth drops open, and I snap it closed, nodding quickly as if the offer is going to be rescinded.

"Go ahead and get comfy."

Rule #5

YOU MAY NEED TO BE TIED UP

SAM

Still in a stupor from my orgasm, I make my way over to the bed and crawl to the center. I turn and lean back against the headboard, knees bent in front of me. Naomi is busy in her walk-in closet, but I can't see what she's doing in there.

I don't have to wait long.

She appears wearing nothing but a lacy pink thong, her soft curves and ample breasts sashaying over to the foot of the bed. She holds up both hands, and I look at them in turn, examining the toys she's brought with her.

"Big," she says, holding up a long, hot pink dildo with another smaller attachment coming off the side. "Or small." This time she holds up a small, matte black oval with no defining features that I can see from here.

The small device looks like it would block less of her body, so I choose that one. "Small."

She tosses the large pink toy aside and climbs onto the foot of the bed where she sits on her heels. "Now, I know I said I wouldn't take my pants off, but I kinda had to for this to work.

Do you think you're going to be able to contain yourself up there?"

I shake my head honestly. I'm barely containing myself now, and the show hasn't even started.

"Do you need me to tie you up?"

My mouth opens as a surprised breath escapes audibly. "No. No, I can control myself."

Naomi laughs. "We'll see about that."

Standing there, out of reach, she slowly slips the pink panties down her thick, creamy thighs. I can't take my eyes off the way her breasts squeeze together as she bends over fully to get the garment over her feet.

I want to crawl into that cavern and live peacefully for the rest of my days.

Her perky breasts continue to taunt me as she crawls up onto the bed, perching just out of reach with her knees spread wide.

"I don't think this is going to be a long show, to be honest. I am so riled up right now."

My cock lifts between my legs, and I glance down at it, marveling at its half hard state so soon after coming into this enchanting woman's eager mouth.

"I guess I'll have to pay close attention then," I manage.

"You really are something, you know that?"

I shrug, not taking my eyes off the way her thighs come together at the peak. The way her soft stomach rounds out the triangle. I want nothing more than to open her up. To see what she's hiding in there.

But that's not my job right now.

I'm just here to watch.

I bite my lip. "You're something."

Naomi laughs, capturing the tiny toy in her hand and clicking it on. I can hear the soft buzz. "This is certainly something."

She spreads herself a bit further, and I get a peek at the pink center of her.

The wetness has me salivating.

When she touches the buzzing toy down between her legs, my eyes shoot to her face, and I watch her transform. All her features soften as her eyes hood. The tip of her tongue darts out and is captured between her teeth.

I freeze, my muscles locked tight. Every cell in my body focuses on the action happening just a foot away.

"Do you want to know what I'm thinking about?" she asks, voice husky and low.

I nod again, stupidly, even though the correct answer is probably no. I shouldn't want to know what she's thinking about, because I have a suspicion that it will test my self-control even more.

"I'm thinking about you looking down at me while I sucked your cock. You looked so in charge, like I was your little slave. I pretended I was, you know. Your slave."

Fuck. She's doing this on purpose, and it's working.

"I loved it when you made me beg. I would have made you beg if you wanted, and that would have been fun too. But when you ordered me around..." She digs her hand deeper between her legs, and I strain to get a better look from my position against the headboard.

"Do you want to see?" she asks, and the look on her face tells me she knows damn well what the answer is.

"I want to see so bad."

"What do you want me to do?"

"Turn around and get on all fours."

Naomi tosses me a wicked smile before she obeys. Once she's got her ass facing me, knees spread, she reaches back up between her legs with the little toy.

"Like this?"

I can see everything now. The full spread of her slit in shades of pink, purple, and cream. Her wet opening, where she dips her fingers and the toy before heading back up to her clit and moaning. The full, delicious view of her ass, round and supple, and so very grabbable.

Bitable.

Smackable.

"Just like that," I tell her, the words coming out a bit hoarse.

"I love it when you're watching me like this. I'm going to come so fast. Do you want to see me come?"

The answer is fuck yes...but not like this.

I can watch her come over and over in my memories for the next fifty years of my life.

Right now, I have the opportunity, the invitation, to do more.

And I'm going to accept it.

Naomi squeals in delight and surprise when I land both hands on her ass.

I slide my hands up and over the soft, roundness of her ass and grip her hips, pulling her body up to mine. "You're driving me fucking crazy, princess."

Naomi laughs. "I'm doing it on purpose."

I have to smile as I toss her onto her back on the bed. "I know you are. And do you know what's coming now?"

She shakes her head with a grin, biting her lip. "I don't have a clue what's coming next with you, Sammy. But whatever it is, I'm ready for it."

I position myself between her wide knees and capture the little toy from where it fell at the foot of the bed. It's still buzzing, and the velocity of the machine surprises me once it's in my hand. "Strong little guy, huh?"

Naomi laughs. "You gonna use it on me, or what?"

I look down at her, spread and practically begging for her orgasm. "Where do you like it?"

Reaching one, long pink-fingernailed hand down, she spreads her lips open to reveal the glorious cavern of her labia and clit. I bite my own lip to keep from diving headfirst.

"Up and around the sides of here." She shows me with her fingers, and I lean down to follow her movements with one of the narrow ends of the buzzing toy. She gasps when it makes contact, and the sound goes straight to my dick.

"And you can slide down here."

I follow her fingers as they graze down her slit toward her opening.

"And inside."

Her fingers move out of the way and allow mine to dive deep. I press the vibrator as deep as I can with my finger and watch it slide back out. I press it in again, holding it there with my finger inside her body as I glance up at her face. She's watching my hand, but her gaze shifts to mine when she feels me looking at her.

The complete unashamed, unabashed pleasure is something I never want to end.

"That feels so good, Sammy. Give me a little more clit, and I'm going to come."

When the vibrator slides back out, I let it drop to the bed beside her hip and drive just my fingers back inside. Naomi moans, and I swear to god my cock leaks a little.

It's too much. We're too close. But I can't stop.

I send in another finger, and she responds. I add another and fuck her with them, building speed as I chase her wetness in and out.

"Clit, Sammy, please."

Well, she did ask nicely.

I lower my face while continuing to fuck her hard and fast with three fingers. When I suck her clit into my mouth and hold it there, giving it little flicks back and forth with the tip of my tongue, Naomi screams and then goes silent, her whole body clenched as her breath catches. She spasms, and I work her through it, my fingers massaging the soft walls of her body as I try to keep a hold of her clit with my lips.

"Oh my god," she manages to get out.

And I have to agree. There is something completely holy about this moment.

"Sammy," Naomi whimpers as her body stills.

I've never had a nickname before, and I already know I'm going to be hearing her voice say that word in her sex-sated whimper for years to come.

Sammy.

I sit up and look at her laid out on the bed before me, panting and smiling. My hand is still inside her body, the taste of her on my lips.

I'm not ready to stop, not ready to let go of this moment, so I pump my fingers a bit more, reveling in the velvety feel of her. Her wetness comes down my fingers like a slide as I work them in and out.

Without even thinking, I pull my hand out and replace it with my other, using the hand that's drenched with her orgasm to grab my now very hard dick.

Her orgasm lubes up my skin, and I bite my lip against the searing pleasure of touching myself with her wetness.

I switch hands again, bringing my newly wet fingers up and around my tip as I plunge the others back inside her. Again and again, I sink into her depths and carry her sweetness over to rub on my tip, my shaft, and down to my balls. I'm drenched in her and pumping myself harder as I pump into her with my other hand.

The pleasure is overtaking me, and I'm leaning forward, trying to fight the urge to close my eyes. The last thing I want to do is miss a second of this.

"Sam," Naomi says, not a whisper now. Not a nickname.

Her tone snaps me back to reality. I catch the uncertain look on her face, and my eyes shoot back to my dick, which is gripped in my hand with my tip hovering less than an inch from her wet opening.

I jump up, dropping my dick to catch the bed with both hands and steady myself as my feet land on the carpeting. I'm backing away quickly, shaking my head, until I run smack into the wall. I lean on it, the solid, reassuring presence allowing me to take a breath.

"I'm sorry. I got carried away."

"It's okay." Naomi is back up on her knees, both hands raised, trying to calm me like a scared animal.

That's about how I feel right now. I can't believe how close I just came to sticking my dick right inside her. Without a condom, no less.

I have lost my mind.

"Hey, hey, hey."

I can hear in her voice that she can tell I'm freaking out and is doing her best to de-escalate the situation. De-escalation is usually my job, so I take pity on her, lowering my hands from the protective stance I find myself in and shaking my head.

"I'm okay. I…I just…"

She reaches over the side of the bed and comes back with a tiny pair of pink shorts. I watch as she pulls them on, saying a silent farewell to all her lovely lady parts.

"There. No more worries, okay. Why don't you grab your shorts?"

I tear my eyes away from the breasts that she has not put away yet and spot my own black boxer briefs tossed carelessly on the floor across the room. I walk over and pull them on. My heart rate starts to mellow out. I can finally breathe and think clearly.

I know I just made a complete ass of myself in front of this confident, vivacious woman. I don't know how flushed my face is, but I'm willing to bet it's nearing fire-engine red.

"Come over here," Naomi says.

I glance up and find her chest still bare. My gaze shoots toward the safety of the door. "I should go."

"Come here, Sam."

I walk over until I'm standing with my knees pressed against the side of the bed, arms dangling at my sides.

"It's okay to have boundaries, you know. You've made yours

very clear, and I respect that." She pats the bed next to her, and I consider sitting down but hesitate. I don't know if I can be trusted after that last bout of madness.

Naomi reads my mind. "Even if you change your mind tonight, I'm not going to." She snaps the waistband of her shorts. "Shorts on. Pussy closed for business. Okay?"

With a smile and a sigh, I sink down next to her. "You may need to put a shirt on as well."

"I'll put mine on if you promise to keep yours off," is her sassy answer.

She reaches for a tank from the floor beside the bed and pulls it on. Then she drags both hands across my still bare chest.

Her touch feels so damn good. This whole night has felt so good. And all I've done the whole time is fight against it. "Sorry I'm acting so crazy. It's not you, believe me."

"Don't be sorry. This was the most fun I've had in a long time. And I get it. I don't have a band of brothers like you do, but I watched you guys growing up, and I understand you have complicated relationships. Whatever's going on in your mind, whatever story you're telling yourself about who I am and how this could end up going badly for you, just know that it won't be because I told anyone. Okay? That will never happen."

I nod and offer her a tight-lipped smile. "In another world, I think the two of us would've gotten along very well."

"We're getting along well in this world, Sammy."

I close my eyes as the nickname hits me right in the chest. "Well, another life then."

Naomi says nothing, and I open my eyes to find her watching me with a look I can't quite place—and reading people is my job.

"Lay with me for a few minutes?" She scoots back and stretches out with her head on one of the many pillows on her colorful, fluffy bed.

"Just for a few minutes," I say, mostly to myself as I collapse beside her.

She winds her legs into mine and pulls me close. Our arms wrap and tangle until we're a tight knot of limbs and bodies, snuggled together in the center of the bed.

I close my eyes and lose myself in the feeling of being so close to another person. Trading orgasms is one thing, but snuggling? Wrapping tightly in the body of another person and just breathing together? That's quite another.

"It would be warmer under the covers..."

I suck in a panicked breath. "No, I can't really stay that long."

This woman is off-limits. Completely forbidden. I'm not staying the night in her bed.

She reaches behind herself and pulls a large, fuzzy throw over us. I sink into the warmth of the blanket and her body once more. When I feel one of her hands snake up between us and capture my hand, threading her fingers between mine, it's all over for me.

Consequences be damned, there's no way I can get up now and walk away from this feeling. It's not even the ghost of pleasure still radiating out from my dick, seeping into every cell of my body. It's deeper than that.

Comfort, closeness.

Things I've been craving for so long.

I lose myself in the moment, allowing myself to pretend. It's all very dangerous, but that danger isn't here in the bed with us. It's just like Naomi said. She won't tell. I'm safe here.

The only threat is inside my own mind.

I'll just stay another few minutes.

Rule #6

THIS IS NOT YOUR LIFE

SAM

I wake up alone, sunlight pouring in through the curtains.

With a big sigh, I roll out of bed and find my pants.

It's time to face the light of day.

At Naomi's house.

Where I stayed after I told myself I wouldn't.

Fuck.

I follow the smell of coffee into the kitchen and find Naomi there, still in the same little pink shorts and tank top, pulling out a cast iron pan and placing it on her half-size gas stove.

She turns when I walk in and smiles at me.

So much for facing reality. I'm going to live inside this fantasy for as long as I can.

She walks over and kisses me, pulling back to look up into my eyes as I hold her close.

"Good morning."

"Morning, princess."

"I made coffee, and I was just going to fry up some bacon."

She tries to turn and walk back to the counter, but I hold her tight. Her face turns back to mine, a surprised smile lighting up her features as I lean in for another long kiss.

And just like that, I'm transported to another life. One where this is my home, my woman, my family. My morning routine.

Everything I've ever wanted.

If only this wasn't so complicated.

If only choosing this life wouldn't mean giving up the one I've worked so hard for.

I end the kiss and release her. "That sounds great. I'd love a cup of coffee."

She stands, watching me for a long moment before walking over to the cupboard and pulling out a purple mug scattered with gold stars in a constellation I recognize but couldn't name. "How'd you sleep?"

"Amazing. That bed of yours is incredible. I wonder if I could fly one of them home with me."

She's not looking at me as she sets the cup down, and I wonder if my perfect morning fantasy is going to be overtaken by awkwardness. It's the last thing I want, but I'm not sure how to prevent it. This situation *is* a bit awkward.

"Cream? Sugar?"

"Cream," I say and accept the carton of half-and-half from her with a smile.

"So, when's your flight?"

I glance up at the black and white cat clock on the kitchen wall. My flight is currently boarding. I would have needed to be in Houston to get through security and customs hours ago.

"A few hours," I lie.

She looks back from the stove, wide-eyed. "Do you need to leave? You've still got to go to your hotel, pack, and get to Houston."

There's something in her voice that I can't ignore. It's desire, but not the same kind as last night.

She doesn't want me to leave.

Maybe as much as I don't want to.

"I have some time. I can stay for breakfast."

She relaxes, and I do the same, some kind of unspoken compromise having been reached.

We have this chunk of time together.

And then it's over.

My mind drifts to worrying about when I'll ever be able to get another flight to Faraday after missing mine, but I force it back to the present moment.

"Do you have to work today or anything?" I ask.

It's an obvious attempt at forcing small talk, but when Naomi turns around, she's smiling.

She'll allow it.

"I work from home on my social media channels. I go out all the time and do stuff so I have content, but I don't exactly have a schedule."

"What do you mean by social media channels? I mean," I say quickly when she narrows her eyes at me. "I understand social media, like Instagram and TikTok, but what does it mean to have that be your job? Where does the income come from?"

"I get paid when I can get people to buy things from other people. So, my job is to have enough people follow and trust me that when I go somewhere or recommend something, they also go there or buy that thing. It's a balance of creating eye-catching content, being a relatable, trustable person, and selling things."

"Influencer," I say, finally feeling like I have a tiny grasp on the meaning of the word.

Naomi smiles down at me as she scoops the bacon from the pan. "Exactly. People will buy what I suggest they buy, but only if they want to be me. So, I have to present my life in a way that looks pretty perfect but also authentic and vulnerable enough that they can relate to me as a real person." The eggs hit the pan with a sizzle.

"That sounds like my own personal version of hell."

She laughs. "Which part?"

I think about it for a long moment. "I guess the part where

you put everything you do and think online. I'm more of a work at work and home at home kind of guy. I don't like it much when the two cross over."

A perfectly cooked and styled plate of bacon and eggs, complete with an orange slice and a buttered English muffin appears before me on cheerful red pottery with a ridged rim.

"Thank you," I say in amazement. "I don't usually get such royal treatment in the morning. Or ever, I guess."

Naomi sits in the chair across from me at the small square table and leans forward on her elbows. "No one's cooking for you down on Faraday?"

I shake my head, holding my hand to my mouth while I finish chewing the first delicious bite. "Not unless you count the cooks at Reef."

"That's the new restaurant you guys opened in the basement, right?"

I cock my head side to side. "It's more of a ground level space than a basement. It's on the pool level and has a big door that opens to the patio. It's really cool, actually. The guests have been leaving the best reviews. Raft is great and all, but Reef is really what we needed for our guests and their families to get their day-to-day meal needs met."

She's quiet, and I glance up to find her grinning at me.

"What?" I can't help but smile back.

"Nothing. You're just adorable when you talk about that place. It's like your baby."

She's far from wrong. "It does sometimes feel like a dependent that I'm responsible for keeping alive."

Naomi laughs. "That's not all a baby is, you know."

I take another bite and wait curiously for her to go on.

"Your baby is what you love most in the world. What you're most proud of. What you can't stop thinking about and want to succeed and flourish so badly that you would pour your own blood, sweat, and tears into helping in any way you can."

I chew quietly and try to identify the double meaning she's clearly trying to communicate.

I come up empty handed. My usually keen intuition is failing me when it comes to this woman. Or maybe I just can't hear it over the buzzing in my ears that amps up every time she gets within a few feet of me.

"Well, when you put it that way. It's definitely my baby."

"But you work with your friends. Isn't that crossing your work/home boundary?"

Just the word boundary sends me straight back to last night when I was centimeters from plunging myself into her forbidden pussy.

I feel myself flush and look down at my breakfast. "It's not quite like that. The guys and I don't exactly work together. Dom and I do, but the other two..." I trail off with my foot in my mouth.

"The other two just fly in and out when they feel like it?" She rushes in to save me.

I smile up at her gratefully. "Something like that."

It's so much more than that, but I don't know how to put the relationship with my three best friends and business partners into simple words that won't make me sound like a complete fool.

How they feel more like family than friends.

How we've managed to set aside our complicated work arrangements as co-owners of the resort anytime we're not in meetings or doing resort-related work and just be pals.

How much it means to me that they trust me to helm the ship that is The White Sands Resort on a day-to-day basis, rarely questioning my judgment or decisions. At least not as often as they question each other.

A decade ago, when I first came to the guys with the idea to buy a run-down island resort, they balked. It took me the entirety of the five-day guys' trip to get them on board.

Dom fell first, as I knew he would, the allure of his very own restaurant being something he couldn't pass up.

I'm still not entirely sure why the other two eventually signed on. Whether it was just to make me and Dom happy, or if they truly saw something there for themselves. Either way, just ten short months later, we were rolling up to the mostly abandoned property with stars in our eyes.

And not much else.

The funny thing about taking a leap of faith is that you just never know how far down the universe has placed the net.

If it wasn't for the bottomless pockets of my three besties, as well as a group of local contractors and other tradespeople who saw some potential in our project—or just took pity on us—we would have been just another cautionary tale for other young, inexperienced, budding entrepreneurs with more money than sense.

"And you live off property?"

Naomi's question pulls me back into the present moment. "Yeah. I bought a house the first year we were there. It was a bit of a fixer-upper." Understatement of the century. "But I've put in a lot of work, and it's starting to come around."

Naomi tosses me a smirk. "Starting to come around after ten years of work?"

I shrug, chewing and swallowing before I answer. "I work at the resort a lot, so I only have my weekends to do house stuff. It was only recently that I started really getting those, and there have been some setbacks. Storm damage and whatnot."

"Oh, I heard about that storm last year. Your house flooded?"

"The inside stayed dry, but the winds took out one of my outbuildings and the yard took on some water."

"The tropics are a crazy place to live."

I nod but then shake my head side to side as I consider. "I don't know. We have the weather and the obvious limitations like transport and importing most things we want, but I don't think it's any crazier than living somewhere like here. Every time I visit the mainland these days, I feel more and more like I'm going to get hit by a car or have a seizure from all the flashing lights."

She laughs, and I absorb the sound, warmth filling my body.

What I wouldn't give to make this woman laugh for the rest of my life.

Nope. Not thinking that.

I set my fork down a bit too hard and the bang echoes through the quiet kitchen. I grimace. "I should probably get going."

"Oh, right."

We both sit for a long, slightly awkward moment, looking at our plates.

Naomi recovers first, standing and clearing the table. "Um, I guess most of your stuff is still in my bedroom."

I glance down at my bare chest in amazement. How did I manage to come out to breakfast without a shirt on?

"Yeah. I'll just go grab my shirt." I stand, and she doesn't turn, facing away from me as she rinses the plates. After a moment, I leave the kitchen and retrace my steps back to her room.

The sight of her mussed-up bed should not be sending all the blood in my body south, but it is.

How am I ever going to recover from last night?

I snatch up my tee and make a beeline for the safety of the living room where Naomi is waiting, looking as uncertain as I am about the next step.

It's comforting that she isn't just sending me off with a smile, as if I was just another one-night stand. She's visibly unsure of herself, biting her lip and shifting from foot to foot with her hands clasped.

I shouldn't do it, but I walk right over and pull her into an embrace. She relaxes in my arms. I shift slightly so she won't feel my dick hardening.

"I…I had a good time last night," she says finally, head still tucked between my shoulder and ear.

"I did too." What else can I say? I can hardly tell her how much she rocked my world. How I'm leaving here a different person than when I walked in. All the things I want to say are on the tip of my tongue, but I bite them back.

There's just no way.

"I wish things could be different," she says, giving voice to my thoughts.

I respond by putting my entire foot in my mouth. "You're telling me. I just spent the last hour pretending this was my life."

My words fall heavily into the air around us, settling like dust in the silence that follows them.

I hold my breath waiting for her to decide I was making a stupid, completely inappropriate joke and laugh, but she doesn't.

Finally, after what feels like an eternity, she pulls away and takes a step back. My arms don't let go right away but finally drop when she's far enough away.

"Let me get you an Uber."

I give her my hotel name, and she works her phone magic.

And now it's really, truly time to leave.

"You can come over anytime you're in the city," she offers as I pull open the door to her apartment.

"Thanks. I'll do that." We both know I won't.

There's an awkward pause, both of us waiting for me to reiterate the invitation for her to come down to The Sands, but I can't make myself do it. Back then, at the taco place, things were so simple.

I'm not sure what they are now, but simple isn't exactly the word I'd choose.

"I'll see you around, okay?" I say as I walk out into the hall.

Naomi stays in her apartment, leaning just inside the doorframe. She nods.

"Have a good flight."

And then I walk away.

Rule #7

AUSTIN HAS RECEIPTS

SAM

Six Weeks Later

I'm just going over my morning schedule when I hear a tap on my open door and glance up. Maria, the front desk manager, is leaning on my door frame.

"What's up?" I ask, ready to help with whatever she needs. Sure, I have a full day's worth of work lined up for myself, but that all goes to the back burner when the resort, or one of its many employees, needs something.

Which is exactly why I have a never-ending to do list and rarely get anything crossed off.

"You might want to head over to Raft. Dom called an all-staff meeting, but when everyone showed up, he dismissed people selectively. And it seems like he was sending away only the women? Anyway, there's way too much testosterone in that tiny dining room for comfort."

I'm already halfway out the door, giving her an exasperated look as I pass. "Thanks for letting me know."

It's not completely unusual for Dom, the head chef of our two restaurants, to pull something crazy without warning me. It's just been happening less and less often since he finally found the love of his life a few seasons back. I've almost stopped worrying about stuff like this.

I guess I shouldn't have let my guard down.

Don't get me wrong, I love the guy. We've been thick as thieves since grade school when my mother secured me a scholarship to the exclusive private school in the next town over and threw me to the wolves.

Dom saved me on day one from getting beat up by a bunch of jocks and brought me into his fold. Ben and Avery were quick to welcome me as well, and it's been the four of us ever since.

I make my way down the long hallway to the door that leads to the Raft dining room. The place is closed at this hour, and I'm honestly surprised Dom is here at all on a Saturday morning. He's in his kitchen until late into the night, so he usually rolls in around noon.

I nearly have a heart attack when I turn the corner and see the "meeting."

It's Dom standing in front of the bar with nearly forty guys sitting around the dining room, listening to him rant.

"...eyes on every inch of this place. Even when you think I can't see you, I can. Is that clear? And if any one of you lays so much as a finger on her, you'll not only lose your job, but you'll have me to deal with personally. Each and every one of you knows I have the resources to make you disappear—"

"Chef," I say loudly, interrupting his pointed threat as I walk quickly over to stand beside him.

He doesn't even glance over at me, raising two fingers to point at his own eyes and then points them around the room at each and every one of what looks like all of the resort's male employees.

I gawk at him for a beat before catching myself and turning to the room. "You're all dismissed, thanks for coming. Sorry for whatever this was. No one is at risk of bodily harm or job loss at this time."

Dom just continues to glare at each man as the group files out of the restaurant.

When the place is empty, I turn to him with an exasperated sigh. "Do I even want to know what that was about?"

Dom turns to walk back toward the kitchen, and I follow. "Don't start acting like I'm a crazy person. I just wanted to make sure those fuckboys know what's going to happen if they lay a finger on my sister."

I stop short as the words slap me right across the face. I shake it off quickly and hurry to catch up with Dom as he moves through the prep kitchen toward his office. "N-Naomi?"

He turns with one hand on the handle, looking at me like I'm an idiot. "That's the only sister I've got, isn't it?"

I let out an exasperated sigh. I can usually brush off Dom's antics. As long as they aren't causing real issues for the resort, it's not my problem. Especially because I have so much to worry about, and he's as much an owner of this place as I am. More actually.

But this? This is my problem. On many levels.

"What does Naomi have to do with anything?" I keep my voice level and neutral, even as my insides melt.

"She's going to be on island for a bit. I guess she got into some kind of trouble with her internet job and needs to get out of the city. My father is being less than hospitable, as I'm sure you can imagine, so she's coming here."

She's coming here.

Elation and sheer dread draw their swords and start dueling in my ribcage. "Oh."

Dom tosses another glance at me, and I catch myself once more. "Okay. She's staying with you and Reina."

He sighs. "Yeah. Next week."

Okay. I have one week to prepare myself for this total and complete shit fuck.

"Because Reina has guests at the house," he goes on. "So, until then, she's staying here at the resort. The only room available was a small second-floor one, but that's going to have to do. Maria got it all set up last night."

"Oh." The word is more of a reaction to the air being forcefully sucked out of my body. "She's here already."

"She's coming over on the eleven fifteen water taxi. I'm going to have one of the shuttles go pick her up."

"I'll pick her up," I say too quickly, and Dom turns on me once more, eyes narrowing.

"Mister I-don't-have-twenty-minutes-in-my-day-for-a-lunch-break suddenly has time to ferry my fugitive sister around?"

I take a deep breath to recover.

I am the manager of this goddamn resort.

I will not be spoken to like this.

"The shuttles run a tight schedule, Dom. They can't just be rescheduled on your whims."

"Right." He nods, unflustered by my scolding. "Thanks."

For the rest of the morning, my state of dread-filled excitement makes getting work done nearly impossible. I more or less just watch the clock.

I'm happy about my choice to go pick her up. It'll be good to have a moment alone together—outside of the resort—to get on the same page before we're thrown into the tight-knit, nosy community of The Sands.

When ten thirty rolls around, I decide to head into town, unable to make myself sit still another minute. I'm just lifting the keys to one of the resort's golf carts from its hook when my perfect plan sinks down the drain.

"Hey," Avery says, flopping his elbows down on the front desk and grinning at me. "I hear you're running a taxi service today."

I grit my teeth but force myself to stay calm. "Nope. Just picking Dom's sister up at the dock."

"Perfect. I've got someone coming on that same boat. I'm going to ride in with you."

"I can pick them up too. No need to head all the way into town."

"That's okay. I need to grab a few things at the store anyway." And with that, he snatches the keys from my fingers, taking with them any hope of getting a second alone with Naomi.

Rule #8

BRACE FOR IMPACT

SAM

Avery drives, and we fly down the dirt road so quickly I know we're going to be much earlier than I expected. He yammers on about one thing or another, but I'm barely listening. I manage an *oh* or *dang* in the right places to encourage him to go on, as I've learned to do in my years of working with people and many, many years of listening to this particular man's stories.

I can't make my mind settle. I've got the same set of questions running through my mind on a loop.

Is she okay?

What is she doing here?

How long is she going to stay?

Is she going to want to do what we did again?

Is everyone going to find out what happened?

That last one is the kicker. If it wasn't for our shared past, I would want her answer about doing it again to be a resounding yes. I would run to the top of the tower at The Sands and scream it for everyone to hear.

But that's not the world we live in.

Here in the real world, I have a resort to run with a man who just threatened our entire staff to keep their hands off his sister. I know I have a bit more standing than any of those guys but still. Ruining my working relationship with the man I interact with so closely and who holds my future in his hands is not my idea of a good time.

Even if it means giving up my shot at love?

I shake off the idea and lean my head back, eyes falling closed. She's not my only shot. I know it's been challenging to meet someone on this island, but it will happen.

All the other guys found their one and only.

I just have to wait for my turn.

If I can get through Naomi's visit without getting my entire life smashed to pieces, I'll get back on the hunt.

As predicted, we get to Saubry with enough time for Ave to hit the store first and still arrive at the dock before the boat.

"How about little Naomi coming to hide out on the island, huh?"

I turn to him, interest piqued. I forgot that there was information I wanted that could be gained from Loose Lips Avery. "What's it all about? Dom didn't really say much."

He shrugs. "I don't know the full story, but from what Fran told me, she runs some kind of lifestyle Instagram blog, and she did something that pissed off a lot of people. Now she has to take a break from posting because an angry mob jumps on her in the comments section every time. I guess she's getting a lot of threatening emails which is why she wanted to head out of the city."

I try to display an appropriate amount of shock and concern while inside, my brain is screaming. The idea of Naomi in danger has sent all my protective instincts into attack mode.

"Wow. That sounds scary," I manage.

"Yeah. The internet is a terrifying place, man. It's why I mostly stay away and let them talk about me how they will. Every time I've tried to get involved or jump in to offer the real story about something, it always goes sideways. I've learned that it's best to just use this thing"—he pulls his brand new, top of the line iPhone from his pocket and wiggles it next to his face—"as a camera and an iPod. Oh, and a clock." Glancing down at the screen, his eyebrows raise. "Speaking of which, they should be pulling in now."

We hop out of the cart and walk down to the dock just as the water taxi is tying up. We stand among a group of people waiting for the same boat, everyone craning their necks to spot their person walking down the dock.

I don't even need to search for mine. The second she steps off the boat, my eyes are drawn straight to her.

She's wearing black linen shorts and a pink tank, her signature pink lips smiling at the worker helping her step onto the dock. Her long auburn curls flow freely down her back, captured by the breeze off the ocean. The curves of her body look amazing in her summer outfit, showing off just enough skin to test my self-control.

I lick my lips, remembering how she tasted. How her body felt in my hands.

Fucking hell.

None of that.

I'm going to be professional and casual. Cool and collected.

Self-preservation mode on.

"Look who it is. Little Nay-Nay." Avery pushes to the front of the crowd to meet her as she steps off the dock into the sand. He snatches the bag from her hand before dragging her into a big brother hug. She pulls away laughing.

"How long has it been? A decade? More?" he asks.

"I was here for the opening, so yeah. About that."

I watch them turn toward the luggage cart where Naomi points out her two large, pink suitcases. Avery tips the guy who gets them down and starts carrying them across the sand, looking pointedly for me.

I snap into action, stepping around the people I was doing a poor job of hiding behind, and walk forward to meet them.

Desire churns in my veins, even as apprehension takes my breath away. I don't know what I'm going to say, I only pray it's not completely stupid.

"Hey, Naomi."

She turns to me with a big knowing smile before shaking her head and looking at her feet for a brief moment before meeting my gaze once more.

She gets it. I can see it in her emerald eyes. She's going to spare me the guillotine.

"Hey, Sammy. Been a while."

At first glance, she looks more or less the same as I remember her from the city. As I continue to search her gaze, however, I can see that something has changed. There's a dullness where before I saw her spark. There's hesitation instead of confidence.

Avery laughs and cracks me on the back. "Yeah, Sammy. Why don't you help a guy out and grab one of these bags."

I tear my eyes away from her and take the handle of the enormous rolling suitcase from Avery. It's heavier than I expect, but I try not to let my surprise show. This is more than a simple vacation if she brought all this with her.

Naomi trails behind us, calling out answers to Avery's casual questions.

Her flight was fine.

The boat ride was a little bumpy, but she had a good seat.

She's excited to be on Faraday.

I listen to her making polite small talk and worry over her words. She's saying all the right things, but something about her tone tells me all is not as okay as she'd like us to think.

I'm not sure how to ask any questions of my own, especially not with an audience. Whatever I say will come out sounding stupid—or completely inappropriate.

"Isn't that right, Sam?"

I shake myself back to the present moment as Avery tosses a question my way. "What's that?"

He raises his eyebrows at my out of character inattentiveness. "I was just telling Nay that she's got a great room at the resort."

I wouldn't have phrased it exactly like that, but I answer, "Every room at The Sands is a great room."

She laughs, loud and long. "Meaning my room sucks?"

I open my mouth to protest, but she waves me off. "I'm joking. I know this was last minute. And it's not like I was expecting the best room in the resort or anything." She mimics my words from her apartment with her gaze pointedly on me.

I can feel her eyes boring into me, begging me to remember.

I bite my lip to hold back a grin. Naomi does the same.

I'm fucked.

"Oh, hey. There's Tomás." Avery rushes back through the crowd toward the dock, shouting his friend's name.

Finally, I have the moment I wanted all along.

Don't screw this up, Sam.

"I was surprised to hear you were coming," I say.

"Sorry I didn't text you or anything. I lost that little slip of paper with your number."

I grimace. "Shoot. I should have gotten yours. What was I thinking?"

She smiles at my obvious discomfort. "You were thinking you needed to get the hell out of my apartment and never see me again."

My mouth drops open in shock. "What? No. That's not what I was thinking. I was..."

I trail off, shaking my head.

I don't have time for this. I need to get something said, and this might be my only chance. "Dom held a meeting this morning where he threatened the life and livelihood of any man at the resort who laid a finger on you."

Naomi rolls her eyes. "I guess he hasn't changed much, huh? I was hoping love would soften him a bit."

"It has, I think. In some ways." I shake my head again. I can't get derailed here. "Naomi, this resort—"

"I get it, Sam. No telling anyone what happened."

She mimes zipping her lips closed, and my cock jumps in my shorts. I shift from foot to foot, trying to keep my gaze from locking on her sweet mouth.

What the hell is wrong with me.

"Thank you."

I know there was more I wanted to say, more promises I wanted to extract from her, but I'm completely distracted by having her body so close to mine.

Avery appears suddenly behind her, a tall olive-skinned man with dark hair following him. He inadvertently hits the back of Naomi's legs with the rolling suitcase as he swings it up into the cart, and she falls forward—straight into my arms.

We both laugh as Avery apologizes, but I can't let go.

She gets her footing and tries to stand back up, but I hold her arms tightly, my body refusing to obey my mind.

I don't want to be gentle.

I want to press her to her knees and make her beg.

My hands drop to my sides as the thought shoots through my brain, causing my cheeks to flush and my breath to catch.

Naomi watches the whole thing with a knowing smirk, shaking her head and smiling back at me as Avery helps her into the front seat of the cart.

I'm stuck in the back with photographer and YouTube star Tomás from Spain, listening to him recount his travels in an accent I know would make most women melt.

I want to be included in the conversation going on in the front seat where Avery has Naomi talking at length about something I can't quite grasp with this guy talking nonstop in my ear about transfers and gate changes.

When we finally pull up to The Sands, I'm irritable and sweaty. I put on my best host smile and help unload the luggage.

"Sam, you want to take Naomi up? I'm going to get Tomás checked in."

Walk Naomi up to her room…alone? That's the last thing in the world I need to be doing. But what comes out of my mouth?

"Sure."

I snag the keys to 215 from the rack behind the counter and leave the guys there, pushing the cart I loaded with Naomi's suitcases. "Looks like you'll be staying for a while?"

She's quiet behind me long enough that I glance back to make sure she's still there. She's following me with her eyes downcast. I can see the exhaustion in her whole demeanor, and I know it's more than the long day of travel.

We reach her door, and I lean against it, cocking my head at her. "Everything okay?"

She finally meets my eyes and gives me a shrug. "It will be."

"What happened? Last time I saw you, you seemed to be on top of the world."

Another pointed look, this time with an eyebrow raise. If she's surprised I brought up our meeting in Austin, she's not the only one. "People are not always what they seem."

It's my turn to look surprised. "I guess that's true, but—"

"I don't really want to get into what happened right now, okay?"

"Oh, of course. You must be exhausted." I unlock the door and hold it open for her, following her inside with the cart.

"This room is fantastic," she says, spinning in place in the center of the tiny living area.

I glance around the room myself, seeing it through her fresh eyes.

It may be one of the smallest rooms, and on the non-view side of the property, but it's a cozy, well-designed space.

I picked out furniture that would be welcoming and easy to relax on, rather than the wicker and cushions that were here when we bought the place. This room has a teal corduroy loveseat-sized sofa with a small maple coffee table and matching end tables with seashell-shaped lamps. A rattan screen partially hides the queen-size bed, where I know a seafoam duvet is waiting for her with towels twisted into some tropical creature shape by our creative housekeeping staff.

Not that I'm going over there myself to check.

I unload her bags and stand them next to the bar that separates the small kitchenette from the living area. "I guess I'll leave you to it."

"Let me give you my number," she says, turning back from the sliding doors where she was examining the patio.

I'm tempted to say something about the room phone and how I can always get ahold of her that way if I need to. That would be the wise move here. But do I? No. I don't.

I pat both of my pockets and come up empty. "I must have left my phone back in my office."

Her mouth drops open in shock. "You don't have your phone on you?"

I couldn't have surprised her more if I dropped my shorts and did a little dance.

My heart beats a little faster at the thought.

I take a step closer to the door.

"I don't always have it. I'm pretty easy to find if someone needs me."

She's looking at me like I'm a crazy person.

"You might find yourself leaving yours behind sometimes now that you're here."

The raised eyebrow she's giving me lets me know that's not likely.

She types in my number as I rattle it off. "I'll just message you, and then you'll have mine."

"Okay." An awkward silence ensues, and I take another step toward the door. "Well, I'll see you around."

"I'll text you."

I clench my jaw, unsure how to respond. I can't have this

woman texting me when my phone is laying somewhere anyone could see it.

I have to get that phone in my pocket…now.

With a nod and a smile, I close the door behind me and jog the one flight of stairs to my office. It takes me a few moments to find my phone under a stack of papers on my desk, and I feel relieved when I do.

The notification is waiting for me—a WhatsApp message from an unknown number. I collapse into my chair, already opening the screen to edit the contact. I type in Naomi but then pause. My finger hovers over the screen for far too long.

I backspace and type Natalie.

Tossing the thing back on my desk, I lean back in my chair and groan.

How has it come to this? Fake contact names and lies and pretending. I honestly feel like one of the guys right now.

And as much as I've tried to be like them over the years, it doesn't feel as great as I always imagined.

My island life with its dream job and home I can call my own suddenly feels like a house of cards.

And Naomi is the wind.

Rule #9

YOU'RE ONLY AS SICK AS YOUR SECRETS

NAOMI

A tiny blue and black bird perches on the railing of my deck and lifts its little head to the sky, letting out a high, sweet sound.

I lunge for my phone to capture the video for my followers.

But then I freeze.

Is it even worth taking the video?

For so long I've had one focus—capturing my life and turning it into marketable content. Now I'm a bit unsure of what to do with myself. I guess I could just be storing up content to share when all of this blows over, and I'm back online.

Yeah. That's what I'll do. Perfect plan.

Way easier than trying to find a new purpose in life.

I snag my phone and head to the sliding door that leads to my deck, but the bird is gone.

And with it, my entire life comes crashing down.

"It's just a stupid bird!" I yell at myself as I collapse back onto the sofa, tears brimming in my eyes.

But I can't help it. It's not just the bird. It's everything.

My morose thoughts are interrupted by a knock at the door.

I'm on my feet in an instant, running my fingers under my eyes to fix any smeared makeup and checking my hair in the mirror beside the door.

Perfect as usual.

Figuring it's probably someone to scold me for yelling, I swing the door open with a sweet smile on my face, apology and silly story about a bird on the tip of my tongue.

But it's Dom.

My eyes drop to my feet, and I take a step back without offering him a greeting. I leave the door open and cross back to the sofa, tossing myself on it with arms folded.

What is it about my family that turns me back into a sullen teenager?

Maybe it's because you actually did something wrong this time, and you know he's going to lay into you for it?

"Not even a hello?" he asks, walking into the room and closing the door behind him like he owns the place.

Oh, right. He does.

"Yeah, well. I'm not feeling very friendly."

I should be. This guy just offered me refuge from the big, bad world. I should be thanking him and offering to help in whatever way I can. But somehow, that seems too vulnerable. I've had a lot of hits to my soft underbelly in the last few days, and I'm not sure I can survive many more.

Dom is notorious for hitting you where it hurts.

He crosses the room and sits on the coffee table, facing me on the sofa so that our knees touch. He leans forward and clasps his hands, elbows resting on his knees. "I know you've got a lot going on right now. I don't fully understand it, but you're in my home now." He holds up a hand as my mouth shoots open to protest.

I flop back and glower at him, steeling my mind against the lecture I know is coming. The same one I got from my father.

But Dom surprises me.

"And you will be treated as our guest of honor for as long as you need to stay."

My eyes narrow suspiciously, waiting for the trick. "But…" I offer.

He stands. "No buts. I'm happy to have you here. Happy to be able to help you out. When you're ready, have someone at the front desk get you a ride up to my house. Reina is looking forward to meeting you."

"Okay," I say softly, not meeting his eyes. I feel even more like a stupid teenager now, faced with his calm, gracious words. Why on earth did I think he was going to be mad at me?

I look up then, and my own question is answered. The guy could be our father, twenty years younger. He's got the same dark hair and olive skin. The eyes that seem to pierce right through to your soul.

I look back down at my hands. "It's been a long week."

"Well, when you're ready to talk about it, we'll be happy to listen."

The "we" in his sentence is not lost on me. I knew that my brother found love, but I wasn't prepared for how fully it seems to have transformed him. For the better, it would appear.

"Thanks."

"In the meantime, most people around here find talking to Sam much easier. And since you're in the hotel for another few days, you might seek him out. He's easy to find. Office next to the front desk. He's not there twenty-four hours a day, but almost."

Just the name Sam from Dom's lips is enough to get my heart racing. He doesn't know, of course. Sam made it clear that he wasn't telling anyone. And I've kept up my end of the bargain as well.

"I might just do that."

"I'm going to put a reservation for you on the books at Raft for dinner tonight."

I look up in surprise at another small kindness coming from the lips of my formerly cold, absent brother.

And then an idea begins to form.

I saw the look on Sam's face when he settled me into my room. The guy is nervous about me being here. This could be the perfect opportunity to get him alone for a chat and set things right between us.

And it will give me a chance to come clean about something else as well.

Something I should have told him back in Austin.

It's going to suck, but this has already been the worst week of my adult life. What's one more painfully awkward conversation?

Besides, if I want even a glimmer of hope for something more between Sam and me, I have to get this off my chest. I've learned my lesson about keeping big secrets and assuming no one will ever find out. When they inevitably do and it's not you who told them, it's much worse than it would have been to have fessed up in the first place.

Ask my career how I know.

"Can you make it for two? I wonder if Sam would want to join me. I think you're right about needing someone to talk to."

Dom runs his hand through his hair as he considers. "I know damn well he doesn't have any plans tonight, and that would get him out of his office for a few hours. I'll message you and let you know what time."

"Sounds good. Thanks."

Dom leaves, and I'm once again in the last place in the world I want to be—alone with my thoughts.

I pull on my swimsuit with a cover-up and toss my phone and a hat into a pink canvas bag. I decided when I got on that plane in Houston that I wasn't running away to hide. I was just taking a vacation. I guess it's time I start acting like it.

The huge crystal blue pool sits surrounded by a tan and cream tiled patio in the space between the two buildings of the resort. It's flanked on either side by rows of colorful blue and sea-green canvas cabanas, filled with lounging pool goers. The sandy beach is a few short steps away, the cerulean ocean visible just beyond.

A girl could get used to this.

I'm just settling into a padded chaise lounge and tipping my wide-brimmed hat down against the sun when a waiter in black shorts and blue resort polo sets a menu down on the little table next to me.

"Can I bring you a drink, miss?"

I tip my hat to glance up at him, grateful for my enormous dark glasses when I lay eyes on the tall drink of water.

I can see why Dom was worried if all the male employees around here look like this.

Luckily, I'm still recovering from one scandal and not about to jump right into another.

Unless it's with a certain handsome GM. I'd burn my whole life down for one more night with that guy.

Or what's left of my life anyway.

Girl, get it together.

"I'd love a gin and tonic. Extra lime."

"Coming right up."

I tip my hat back down and settle into the chair. All in all, this isn't so bad.

Sure, the social channel I've been working to build for the last ten years is burning to the ground with what I thought was my online community—my friends—fanning the flames.

But I landed here in paradise with a one-way ticket and an open invitation.

I may be officially gaga over a guy who will probably never want me.

And who begged me to keep our tryst a secret.

And who looked like he was going to pass out when I suggested sending him my number.

But it could be worse, right?

Actually, yes. It's going to be a lot worse when you tell him the truth.

Rule #10

YOU'RE DEAD EITHER WAY

SAM

I'm still staring at my phone like it's a time bomb about to explode when I hear a soft tap at my door. Glancing up, I smile at Susan, one of the head housekeepers. She's been with us since almost the beginning and has been instrumental in bringing other hard workers onto the team.

"Hey, Susan. What can I do for you?"

Her smile turns apprehensive. "It's the cart again."

I set my phone down and lean back in my chair. "Dang. What's going on this time?"

She looks at me solemnly. "My husband tried to fix it, but he thinks it needs a new part. It's above our abilities. It didn't start at all yesterday evening. I walked home and then had to walk back in."

I lean forward, elbows on my desk and regard her with eyes wide. "From Palm View?" I sigh. "That's too far. You should have told me. Please call in the future, and I'll have someone buzz you home and pick you up."

She's shaking her head. "I don't want to bother the whole resort over my own problem. We'll have saved enough for a new one in a few months. I just wanted to let you know why the cart was parked in the lot and not moving. I don't want anyone to think it's been abandoned out there. I'm sure they will tow it away when we buy the new one."

"Susan, you're one of The Sand's most dedicated employees. We're not leaving you hanging like this. If the cart's already here, that's great. I'm going to call mechanical and have them pop over and take a look. Will you head down there to give them the keys and let them know where it's parked? If they can't get it running, we'll set you up with one of the carts from the rental fleet at no charge until you and your family are able to get a new one." I tap the eraser side of my pencil against my phone and consider. "You have an older model Club Car DS, right?"

She nods.

"I bet Bucky will want that for parts if it ends up being unfixable. We've got quite a few of that same model working on the shuttle runs. We'd be happy to buy it from you."

She's looking a bit misty-eyed now, but her face is sharp with determination. "Thank you, Sam. I should have just come here in the first place, but I didn't want to bother you."

"It's no bother at all. I'm going to message Bucky now, you head down there on your next break, okay?"

With another nod and smile, she backs out the door, closing it behind her halfway like she found it.

I type out a quick message to our head mechanic then toss my phone back on my desk. I trust him to take care of Susan's cart, whether that means fixing it or buying the broken-down thing for parts. If it comes down to it, we'll be happy to give her the money for the new one, but I've learned over the years that people around here prefer to be self-sufficient. It's caused me to get very creative in the ways I offer help to the islanders. They always prefer a loan over being given money, which has developed into a whole new department of resort HR that operates like a bank. I still sneak in bonuses to hardworking employees when I can, but most often it's offers of help, food, or more hours that are the most well-received.

The expat transplants living in employee housing or rented apartments around the island are a whole different story. They work in the way I'm used to from years of running departments in hotels back in the States. When they need something, they ask for it. And money always talks.

It's a fine balance to strike between the two groups, making sure each feels supported by The Sands without feeling like anyone is being unfairly favored.

Just another day in the life of a mid-sized resort GM in paradise.

My phone lights up with a reply from Bucky, and I nod to myself. It's taken care of. I glance at the clock on the screen and notice that I missed lunch again.

With a sigh, I pocket my phone—my new constant companion—and head toward the stairs down to Reef. Everyone glances up and smiles or waves when I pass, many offering a hello or a how's it going. I return each smile and give each person a moment of eye contact as my way of letting them know they can stop me to say something if they need to. It's my job to be available for anything anyone needs here, even if my stomach currently thinks otherwise.

I make it all the way to the ordering counter at our quick service deli-style restaurant adjacent to the pool when I finally have someone take me up on my open invitation. Luckily, it's the guy taking my order, so I get to multitask.

"Hey Sam, I was just going to run up to talk to you on my break."

I offer a genuine smile. "Looks like I saved you the trip, Nat. What's up?"

Nathaniel is new this season, from the States, and lives in

employee housing. Even though he's only been with us for a few months, the kid's fitting in great, and his supervisor Marcus let me know at our last meeting that he's talking about next season like he's already decided to stay. That's what we love to hear from the seasonal staff, especially hardworking, easygoing staff members like Nathaniel.

"My mom and aunt are flying in next week."

"Oh, that's great. Are they staying at the resort?" I probably would have heard about their visit to approve an employee discount, but it's possible Maria, head of the front desk, took care of it instead.

"No. We…they…" He glances down at his hands and fidgets with the pen he's holding. "They're staying with me," he finishes without meeting my gaze.

I can feel the energy change as he considers the predicament he just got himself into. By admitting that his family can't afford to stay at The Sands, something that is understandable—it's not a cheap place to stay, even with the discount—he thinks he may now be in trouble for having guests in employee housing.

"I'm sure they'll love to see where you're living. If you need extra bedding while they're here, just ask housekeeping. Tell them I said it was okay."

When his eyes shoot back up to mine, they're shining. "Okay. Thanks, Sam. Do you think we could…"

He trails off again, and I know exactly where this is going. I pull two keycards from the stash in my back pocket and hold them out. "These keys will get them into the ladies' showers, locker rooms, and the pool area. You can access the gents with your employee card, and I'll make sure it gets activated for pool usage."

He takes the cards from me, holding them to his chest and beaming like I just handed him two golden tickets. I guess in some sense I did. Being able to bring his guests to the resort to enjoy the pool facilities is a great perk of working here—and one that isn't offered to everyone. It's earned through demonstrating respect for the property and everyone on the island.

Nathaniel certainly fits that bill.

"Be sure to shoot me a message some afternoon when you're all at the pool. I would love to come down and meet your family."

He nods again, still gripping the cards to his chest. "I really appreciate that. Did you want to order something?"

"I do. Can you have a sandwich sent to my office?"

"Right away, boss."

Dom finds me at my desk, signing department expense reports while enjoying my ham and avocado sandwich.

"You know, we've got tables down in the restaurant. You installed them yourself."

"The guy who survives on leftovers eaten while standing over the trash can is lecturing me about working through lunch?" I bite back at him good naturedly, leaning back in my chair and smiling.

He just shakes his head, returning the smile.

You learn a lot about a person when you're trapped on a tiny island running a business together, and what I've learned about Dom is that he's just as solid a friend as he ever was. The guy may be gruff and hotheaded at times, but he's got my back.

I wonder what he's learned about me?

"What's up?" I ask. Not wanting to get rid of him, but well aware that his time is spread just as thinly as mine.

"Dinner tonight. I put you and Naomi on the books at six."

What the hell?

"Why?"

The word comes out too quickly, too harshly, and Dom's forehead creases.

"Because she's here alone and needs someone to talk to. She's been through something in the last few weeks that's shook up her whole life. I'm not totally clear on what it is, but I figured if anyone can offer her counsel, it's you. You know I can't do the mushy, helpful shit."

I already know there's no way out of this, but I can't help but fight. "I don't know much about the internet scandal world."

"See? One golf cart ride and you already know more about what's going on with her than I do."

His statement is so final, like he's just realized how perfect his plan is for setting us up for dinner. He's going to leave if I don't do something.

I stand quickly, drawing another side glare as he turns to head back out the door. "Why don't you make it for four?"

I have his attention now. He turns back to me, arms crossed, eyebrows sky high.

"I'll message Reina and Fran. I'm sure they'll jump at the chance to eat at Raft with us."

Dom says nothing, so I stammer on like an idiot. "I may have a calming perspective, but getting her hooked up with some female friends on island is going to be best in the long run."

His face transforms as he considers, softening as he contemplates. "Okay. Yeah. That's a good idea. I'm sure Reina's houseguests could use a night on their own. I'll let her know. You talk Fran into it."

I smile and flop back down in my chair. "No one ever had to talk Fran into dinner plans."

Dom huffs out a laugh. "That's true." Another nod and he's back in the doorway. "See you at six."

My breath rushes out of me once he's safely down the hallway. I collapse my head into my hands.

What a goddamn mess.

Sure, it'll be better to have the girls there as a buffer at dinner, but this is only a stopgap solution. Naomi will be on the island for the foreseeable future. There's no way I'm going to be able to avoid her entirely.

Or can I?

I already work a ton, who would notice if I started working

even more? I could move into my office, pile my desk with paperwork, and finally get caught up. Hell, I could start employee performance reviews. Sure, it's four months earlier than usual, but may as well get them out of the way, right?

I'm considering printing out the entirety of last quarter's expense reports to get a head start on our tax filing prep when I feel my phone buzz in my pocket. I already know who it is before I even pull it out.

Naomi
Hey, Sam. Dom invited us down for dinner tonight.

I'm excited to try out his restaurant. See you at six!

I should tell her about the other guests, but I want to make sure they're on board first, so I punch out a quick text to Fran.

Sam
Franny...dinner at Raft at six tonight with a special guest. Say yes.

I don't have to wait long for her typing bubble to pop up.

Fran
Yes, obviously.

No Avery?

I tap my fingers on my desk considering. There's no real reason for him not to come, other than the fact that our five-star, award-winning tasting room restaurant is generally booked months out, and Dom's already going to have to drag a table out of storage to fit the four of us.

Sam
Fifth wheel

Fran

Sam
But if Reina can't make it, there'll be a seat for him

Fran
Ooh! Reina's coming? Yesss! I'll text her right now to make sure she doesn't bail.

Perfect. Let the ladies sort it out.

I type and delete four different messages to Naomi before finally deciding on one to send.

Sam
Looking forward to it. Reina and Fran are joining us. You're going to love them.

Naomi's typing bubble pops up and disappears over and over until I finally have to put my phone down as my eyes start to burn from staring at the screen. It's nearly ten minutes later when the message finally comes through.

Naomi
Okay!

I set my phone back down as dread washes through me.

This situation is completely out of control.

Maybe I made a huge mistake by not using this dinner as a time for the two of us to talk and get on the same page. I just panicked at the thought of being alone with her.

Especially under the watchful eye of the guy who knows me best in the world. The guy who happens to be her overprotective big brother and my business partner.

I consider my options.

I can come clean and get out in front of the whole thing.

Terrible plan.

I can keep pretending what happened didn't happen and lie for the rest of my life.

Not my favorite, but better than the first.

I sigh as the most likely scenario occurs to me. I keep my mouth shut and lie to my friends, knowing Naomi could somehow let it slip that something happened between the two of us. Then everyone will know, and they'll all know that I lied.

I can't let that happen. But am I brave enough to choose plan number one and put myself right into the path of Dom's wrath?

It's the ultimate lose-lose situation. I'm dead either way.

Rule #11

THE GAME ISN'T THE PROBLEM. IT'S ME

NAOMI

Reina is the first person I see when I make my way down to the restaurant just before six. I've seen a few pictures of her on the resort socials, but this is the first time we've met.

Our family isn't exactly the get together for holiday dinners type. Maybe we would be if my mom was around, but I never got the chance to find out.

"Naomi." She approaches with a big smile that I can't help but return.

Her big, blue eyes are glowing with happiness. Actual, genuine happiness. It's almost refreshing after so many years of internet life, complete with its filters and posed smiles. This woman doesn't need a filter at all, her strawberry-blonde hair, tan, and freckled skin could be a filter itself. One that people would pay to use. Myself included.

"Good to finally meet you, Reina. I can't believe it took almost four years."

She pulls me into an embrace and holds me there for so long that I relax into it and start to really, truly hug her back. We breathe together for a moment, and I catch her scent. Some kind of flower. And cinnamon maybe. Everything about her is calming and reassuring, even the smell of her shampoo.

Maybe island life is what I need after all. It looks pretty good on Reina.

She pulls away and holds me at arm's length, looking me over like a proud grandma or something. "I'm so happy you're here."

"Me too." The words surprise me as they come out feeling very true. When I first got on that plane, I wouldn't have described my mental state as happy, per se. But now? Far away from the bustling streets and self-imposed pressure to live a perfect, Instagram-worthy life? I may not actually be happy, but I am feeling happy.

Baby steps.

"Girl talk!" comes another cheerful voice from behind me. I turn, Reina's hand still on my shoulder and smile at the newcomer.

I know exactly who this is. Franzeska, the feisty beauty who snagged Avery Covington.

Her face is all over the internet, both on her and Ave's profiles and on the many celeb accounts that follow Avery and other rich, handsome men like him.

The first thing I notice about her is how comfortable she seems, just like Reina. She's dressed simply in an emerald-green tank dress that sets off her hazel eyes and long, dark hair. Those tousled beach waves look very…well, beachy. Perfect, but in that annoying way that you know damn well she didn't have to spend the last hour working for.

Unlike mine, which have yet to meet the ocean here on Faraday. And which I spent the last damn hour perfecting.

I glance down at my own outfit, high-waisted, belted linen shorts with a cream silk tank. Both items had to be steamed after the long trip in my suitcase before I wore them tonight. I know neither of these women was at home steaming their outfits or curling their lashes before coming to dinner.

I'm feeling like a total bimbo. A fake. A fraud.

It's the last thing I need before sitting down at a table with Sam.

I try to hide my apprehension behind a big smile. "You must be Franzeska," I say as Reina lets me go and pulls the woman into the same hug she just gave me.

I guess I'm not so special after all.

"It's just Fran these days. Avery made sure of that."

There's humor in her voice, and I'm sure the story she's hinting at would be funny and worth hearing, but I'm struggling to rally my excitement for this dinner all of a sudden.

I was less than stoked to hear that these two women had been invited to dinner at all. I was hoping for a few hours alone with Sam so we could get some things straight.

So I could get something off my chest.

And now I get to spend those hours sitting at a table with these two perfectly skinny, effortlessly beautiful twenty-somethings.

I know it's not a competition, but…I mean, isn't everything?

Reina takes my hand along with one of Fran's, and we walk together down the hallway toward the restaurant entrance. As soon as we pass through into the bright, airy dining room, I spot Sam leaning against the bar, chatting with one of the employees.

A male employee, my jealous heart notes with relief.

I'm going to have to get this shit under control.

That man is not mine, as much as I wish things could be different.

Even if I flew down here with the tiniest kernel of hope that maybe, just maybe, he'd be interested in hanging out a bit. Hooking up a few times in secret. That possibility gets less and less likely every hour that goes by in this place.

From the perspective of a city girl, a secret affair seems easy to pull off. Now that I'm here, on this tiny island, in this small resort, communing with this tight-knit group of friends, I can see his hesitation.

Hell, we'll be lucky to get through this dinner without throwing off some kind of vibe that everyone in the room picks up on.

I wait by the hostess station while Reina crosses over to the bar and lays her hand on Sam's shoulder to get his attention. He turns and smiles down at her and then his gaze lifts to mine.

Even across the room, I can feel the impact of that gaze like a shot to my heart. My mind takes this opportunity to flash a few choice images from that night in Austin across the movie screen of my mind, and I lose the ability to breathe for a moment.

I pretty much have the whole night memorized, from the first touch on my love seat to the adorable way he curled around me in bed while assuring me he was going to get up and head back to his hotel. And every hard, wet, orgasmic moment in between.

I'm startled back into the present by the hostess saying something, and I smile over at her, nodding, even though I missed the words. She leads Fran and I toward a table near one of the windows overlooking the beach. Reina and Sam follow.

The table is set for four, and I choose a window seat, arranging my bag to hang on the back of the chair within reach. I don't want to be involved with the decisions about where everyone else sits, so I busy myself checking my phone for a moment until everyone else is seated. When I glance back up, I find Reina across from me and Fran to my right. Sam is diagonal.

As far from me as he can get.

With a quiet sigh and forced smile, I turn to Fran, determined to make this evening fun—even if my heart is aching for the man across the table. "I had the biggest crush on Avery when I was a little girl."

Fran and Reina both laugh in surprise, their faces lighting up at my admission.

Fran leans in conspiratorially. "I am here for all the embarrassing childhood stories. Don't hold back."

I smile back at her, happy to have broken the ice, but I'm grateful for the interruption of our server with the first wine of the evening. While it's true that I idolized Avery and all my brother's friends, I wouldn't say I was privy to many of their embarrassing stories. Or any stories, really. They were all ten when I was born, coming into the world and leaving it irreparably changed. By the time I was old enough to really hold a conversation, they were all packing for college.

I distract myself from unwanted feelings from the past and present by arranging an artsy shot of my wine glass against the backdrop of the window, complete with rising colors from the impending sunset. I try out a few filters before capturing the moment, and when I look up, I find everyone watching me. And none of them have their phones in hand.

I glance quickly around the table and don't see another phone at all.

In the city, it's considered perfectly normal for everyone to have their phone face down on the table in front of them. As a matter of fact, if I joined someone for a meal out and didn't see their phone on the table, I would worry they had seriously bad news, or I was about to get dumped or something.

That doesn't seem to be the case here. I put my phone down beside my napkin again and smile at everyone. I'll try to keep my phone time to a minimum if that's what everyone else is doing, but I'm hardly going to put it away. This meal is bound to be photogenic as hell. And I have content to create.

"I guess you guys all have phones full of tropical sunset wine glass shots already, huh?" I try to lighten the mood with a joke, and the girls smile, but I can tell I missed the mark.

"Naomi, you're going to love Raft. It's a foodie's dream, and every plate is worth a picture." Sam's words of familiarity, as if he knows me, are a surprise, and not just to me. The girls both glance over at him as silence falls over the table for a moment.

Reina jumps in to pick up the pieces. "I checked out your Instagram, and he's totally right. You'll have so many great pictures to post after tonight. And between Sam and me, we know just about everything about where the food came from and the small, local purveyors and fishermen who deliver it every day. Local sourcing and sustainability are important to the Raft dinner program."

A now all-too-familiar dread mixed with sadness falls over me at the thought of my channel, but I shake it off. "I'm not posting at the moment, but I'm still gathering content for when I get back to it."

I know they're all dying to ask, so I wait. The silence turns awkward, and I glance down at my phone again, craving its familiar weight in my hand.

"You don't have to talk about it, if you don't want to," Fran offers.

I smile over at her in gratitude. The last thing I want is to ruin this meal with my own sob story.

"Maybe when I have a few drinks in me."

"Well, that won't be a problem here," Sam muses as the server comes to top off our wine glasses. We haven't even gotten the first course yet, and we've all already made it through the first glass of wine.

I lift my glass in a cheers. "Nowhere to drive, right?"

After a few courses and a few more wine pairings, I'm settling in. Gone are the self-conscious worries from earlier. Gone is the dread over my future in the influencer scene. I'm just a girl, enjoying a super fancy meal with friends in paradise.

It feels good to let go. I still take pictures of every dish like they're my newborn babies, but I also let myself enjoy the food and company.

It might be the best meal of my life, in both regards.

Reina is glowing with wine and more than happy to entertain us with stories about her and Dom's early days. "The next morning, I get a knock at the front door, and it's two delivery men bringing me a brand-new mattress. Sweet gesture, but everyone was watching, and it was difficult to explain why I was getting a brand-new bed and no one else was."

"You couldn't just tell them that you were banging one of the owners, and he needed to replace it for his old man back?" Fran asks, and we all crack up.

"Nope. So, I told them that everyone was getting a new one."

"You didn't." I'm alive with the energy of the table now, happier than I've felt in years.

Reina's nodding. "I sure did."

"And the next day," Sam cuts in, laughter lighting up his beautiful face, "we went to town, and Dom was on a secret mission to get over a hundred mattresses imported to the island the following week."

My mouth drops open in a wide grin. "So, he told you about sleeping at Reina's?"

"Of course not. He claimed that his kitchen staff wasn't well rested enough so he needed to get them all better beds," Sam says laughing.

We're still cracking up when the man in question strolls over to our table, arms crossed. "I'm getting noise complaints from the other guests about you four. Mind keeping it down?"

Even in his gruff scolding, I can see the soft edge of humor in his features. When Reina jumps up and throws herself into his arms, Dom's face breaks into a contented grin.

I won't say it's the first time he's ever smiled, but it might be the first I've witnessed. He doesn't even try to hide it as he shoos Reina back to her chair and settles his attention on me. "Did you enjoy your meal?"

"It was incredible. I got some great pictures. I can send them to you if you want."

"Send them to Sam. He's the one in charge of advertising."

My spirit falls a few notches, and I gaze back down at my plate.

"Stop, Dom," Reina chimes in. "You're not fooling anyone." She grabs one of my hands across the table. "Send him all the pictures. If you don't, he's just going to be in Sam's office first thing pouring over them."

"Sure," I say. "No problem."

"Why don't we head down to the bar after dessert, and we can all look at them?" Fran pipes up. "Naomi promised to spill her drama once she got some drinks in her, and I'm guessing it's getting pretty close to that time." She turns to me, sly smile in place. "Am I right?"

She's right about the drinks part. The story? Not so much.

I'm not sure I'm ever going to be ready to talk about what happened, but that's not an option. I'm going to have to get comfortable talking about all this if I ever have a shot at restarting my channel and making amends to my community. I may as well start practicing.

And maybe after Sam hears my plight, he'll be more inclined to overlook certain other transgressions.

"One more drink will probably do it," I say, and the girls squeal in delight.

I only glance at Dom for a moment, catching his slightly disapproving glare and looking quickly away—straight at Sam.

I wouldn't call Sam's look disapproving. He looks worried for me. Sad, even. It's not exactly what I want him to be feeling toward me, but I suppose it's better than angry.

Offended.

Exploited and objectified.

I let out a sigh and try to cover it with another big smile. "What's this I hear about dessert?"

Rule #12

TELL IT ALL, EVEN THE UGLY PARTS

NAOMI

Fran texted Avery as we were finishing up at Raft, so by the time we reach the beach bar, we're a crowd of couples.

Only Sam and I aren't holding hands.

He settles himself a few seats away on the bench at the long, wooden table and orders a soda water when it's his turn.

I should probably do the same. Thirteen courses with wine pairings, no matter how small, is not a normal night of drinking for me, and I'm feeling a little fuzzy.

The girls seem to sense that and take full advantage, pouncing on me as soon as the server drops off our drinks.

"Okay, spill it. What do you have to do to get shunned from the internet?"

I take a long sip from my sangria, trying to figure out where to start.

People don't understand what I do, and more often than not, when I start explaining it, all they do is look for ways to make fun or belittle my work.

I get it. I live fabulously and document the whole thing in

pictures and sassy captions for my seven hundred and ninety thousand followers, who then take my advice and buy things. It's not a normal job. But I love it.

At least I did.

Back when I was on top of the world, fielding message after message in group chats with other mid-sized influencers and even some newbies who ate up my advice like candy.

Back when just the sight of me walking through the door would have small restaurant owners and boutique clothing store managers falling all over themselves to bring me taco spreads or their best new styles.

Back when I was on the invite list for every event in Austin, big or small, and had to prioritize my own self-care time rather than overbooking myself—a decision-making process that was content gold for my followers, who often chimed in to help me choose.

It's wild to think that life was mine less than two weeks ago.

I glance around at the moonlit beach, the tiki torches, and the smiling faces of my older brother's friends. Here goes nothing.

"Well, I don't know how much you know about influencer culture, but the gist of it is that I have followers on my platforms who trust me to bring them the best of everything in Austin and beyond and who are willing to go places or buy things based solely on my recommendation. It's a lifestyle channel, so I'm selling my own lifestyle. My life, my looks, and my habits are the product. And people want what I'm selling. Or they did anyway."

But will they still? That's the question. The one I don't add to my little spiel about what I do. Because in the end, it was my community of fellow influencers who took me down, not my followers.

My sweet, loyal followers, who posted so many lovely, supportive comments. Most of which I didn't get to read before I had to shut off commenting on my recent posts due to trolling.

Trolling by my friends.

"I think I get that. We all have one of those people who we follow and would buy anything they wear or eat or read, right?" Fran asks.

Reina nods quickly, an encouraging smile on her lips as usual.

The guys all look like they're about to be lined up and shot.

I can't help but smile at their reactions. I've learned over the years to stay positive in the face of confusion and disapproval. It's the only reason I'm sitting here right now, considering myself on a break, rather than straight-up fired from my channel.

"One of the things I do a few times a year is rep a big brand who has a launch or some kind of big product promotion. I've done content spreads for Sephora, Hilton Hotels, and Uber. Influencer marketing is a huge new area of interest for companies because it's essentially one friend recommending something to another, and people trust that way more than ads the company makes."

"But they pay you to post them?" Sam asks.

I smile over at him. "Oh, yeah. They pay a ton for posts where I use their service or stay in their hotel and tell my followers how great it is. For Sephora, I got a full in-store makeover and was sent home with all the products to do mirror videos. People watch me using stuff and know they want to buy it."

"I've had brands wanting me to do stuff like that. I don't check my Instagram messages much anymore, but they're always full of companies wanting to send me stuff to wear in pictures and whatnot," Avery chimes in.

I nod to him. "Exactly. So, I was working on a collab with a company called PassionFly, which is one of those clothing box services where you get a package once a month put together by a stylist and get to keep the stuff you like and send back the rest. Their platform was sustainability, which is really big right now with my followers and with my demographic in general, especially in the Austin area. They source from ethical companies, use green packaging, purchase carbon offset credits for shipping—"

"I'm sorry, carbon offset credits?" Avery asks.

"Ave, she was just getting to the good stuff. Don't derail her. You can just google that." Fran moans beside me.

I glance over with a smile. "It's no problem. I can explain pretty quickly. Imagine every time a company does something that pollutes the air, like flying planes or running factories, it's like they're putting a bunch of balloons filled with bad gas into the sky. To make up for the mess, companies buy what's called 'carbon offset credits.' Think of these credits like eco-friendly deeds or actions somewhere else. For example, planting a forest or investing in wind farms that create clean energy. Each credit is like a promise that somewhere, an amount of pollution equal to what the company made will be taken care of, either by sucking it back out of the air or by preventing it from happening somewhere else. So, when companies buy these credits, they're basically saying, 'Hey, we made some mess here, but we're helping clean up an equal amount of mess over there.' It's like trying to balance the scales to keep our planet enjoyable for everyone. This way, they can work toward being more sustainable and less harmful to the environment."

Dom laughs and not in the friendliest way. "Sounds like you've rehearsed that one a few times."

I offer him a tight-lipped smile. I'm still getting used to this guy as a fellow adult, rather than any kind of authority figure in my life, so I want to give him the benefit of the doubt here. "It's a concept that a lot of people struggle to grasp at first, so I do find myself explaining it often."

"It's hard to grasp because it's total bullshit," he bites back.

"Anything could be looked at from alternate angles and be found lacking." I shrug, meeting his eye at last. This guy is not going to intimidate me. Not tonight. Not with this fancy wine swirling in my veins.

"The actual 'sustainable' thing to do would be to not produce the pollution in the first place. Polluting all you want over here and then buying some pollution cleanup over there is not a way to cancel out pollution. The way to cancel pollution would be to not pollute. And pay to clean up other pollution as well. Then you could call yourself sustainable and ethical and not be a complete lying shit."

As a person who is currently canceled as fuck, I try not to flinch as he throws the word around.

Never let them see your weaknesses.

This man was one of the reasons I grew up with that as my motto.

"Well, it's the system we have in place, and one that's widely accepted as being good for the planet."

"What would be good for the planet is stopping all the shipping and fast fashion in general. If people could buy things from the store in their own town and re-wear the same outfit a few damn times, we—"

Reina slides her arm though Dom's and pulls him close, using her lips to quiet his ranting. Then she glances at me apologetically. "Sorry. My parents got us a subscription to *The Atlantic* for Christmas last year, and somebody," —she tosses a look at Dom—"is feeling very well informed."

Dom huffs. "It's true."

"Dom, stop. She was just getting to the part about her. You can soapbox later. We want to hear Naomi's story," Fran cuts in.

Dom raises his hands in surrender. "I'm just saying."

I jump back in, happy to be handed the floor once more. "What you're saying isn't totally off base, Dom. There are plenty of people who agree with you one hundred percent. But it's the best system we have right now, and it provides funding for a lot of great projects that otherwise wouldn't be able to exist, so we all just go with it."

Dom looks like he has more to say about that, but he keeps quiet.

"So, PassionFly. There are a lot of these subscription clothing boxes these days, and each one needs to find their niche market in order to be viable. PassionFly went with sustainability and ethically produced clothing. It's a great idea. Fast fashion is killing the planet, as Dom was saying. So, they got in touch with me a few months ago, and it sounded like a good fit. They sent boxes of their upcoming line, and I made unboxing videos and try-on videos with the clothes. I had them all scheduled to start posting at the beginning of this month when the service was scheduled to go live."

I glance down at my lap, smoothing my hands over my linen shorts, remembering how excited I was when I pulled a similar pair out of my first PassionFly box. All that stuff ended up at Goodwill.

"It was a big jump for me. It was my first ever large-scale company launch. Before that I was just doing sponsored content and posts for existing brands. It looked like the beginning of a long-term relationship between myself and the company, which would have been great for my channel because everyone would get to see the new clothes before they hit the site, and I would get boxes of new clothes every month. Pretty great. On top of that, they paid really well."

"But..." Fran leads me, feeling the climax of my story coming.

I offer her a sad smile. "But it turns out that they sent these collab invites to lots of influencers at my level and higher, and one of them saw the company and decided it was too good to be true. She started investigating and waited until the week the company launched to release her investigative series about how the company created shell clothing companies that looked small and sustainable while sourcing their clothes from sweatshops in China."

The table waits for me to go on in expectant silence.

"She had photographs of the addresses of the so-called sustainable companies which turned out to be abandoned warehouses and vacant lots. She had pictures of the same clothes I had in my videos coming off the lines at the factories."

I pause and think back to the most damning—and most shared—of those pics. It featured a girl who couldn't be more than ten years old piling clothes into boxes with a bloody hand wrapped in a towel and rubber banded.

When that picture first hit my inbox, I was wearing the same sweater the poor kid was packaging.

"What does that have to do with you, though? I get that it's bad for the company, but it's not your company." Reina quickly comes to my defense.

I nod and offer her a sad smile. "I spent the three days she was posting horrific pictures and stories from sweatshops posting videos of myself excitedly opening and trying on the clothes. Recommending that my followers get a subscription right away. A lot of them did, and when it all came out, they were pissed at me. The company folded and disappeared. No one got any kind of refund. They wanted my blood to make up for their lost money."

"Brutal," Fran says.

"The worst part is that the woman who broke the story knew. We weren't close friends, but we ran in the same circle. She knew damn well that I'd taken on the company launch. She chose not to say anything about the piece she had to have already been investigating at that point. She just let me do my launch and then took me down."

"Do you think it was intentional?" Reina is on the edge of her seat.

I shrug. "Probably not intentional toward me in a personal attack, but when there are people to direct blame at, and inflammatory content to share, drama spreads faster and farther on the internet. They were able to use my name and my content to fuel the fire against the company. And I was the collateral damage."

"But people must know that it wasn't your fault?" Reina looks like she might cry at any moment.

I wish I had something comforting to offer. "Outrage is the number one driver of content performance on socials. If you can create content that makes people feel outrage, it links into some primal part of our brains. We just have to share it. We have to tell everyone. That's why shit like this goes viral so quickly. People love to be the first to tell everyone about a new scandal. Everyone loves a good car wreck."

I finally look away from the rapt attention of the two women and laugh at the emotions on the faces of the guys. They range from confusion—Sam, to disbelief—Ave, to absolute disgust—Dom. All three of them are silent, mouths hanging slightly open as they consider how on earth to respond.

I jump in to save them. Or to save myself from whatever they might say.

"So, anyway. That's what happened. For the five days or so it was going down, it was pretty ugly. I had to shut off commenting on my entire channel. I hired a PR firm to handle my emails and inboxes for the time being. And my whole life is on pause while I wait to see if it's going to blow over, and I can start again, or if the trolls are just waiting for me to come back so they can shit-post again." I finish off my drink.

"Damn," Fran says finally, and the rest of the group murmurs in agreement.

"It's okay." It's not okay, and I can't believe I made it through the whole story without crying, but I can't stand the pity pouring off these people and raining down on my head. "It comes with the territory. I put myself out there as the face of a channel, and the internet is not a safe, friendly place. This kind of thing is always possible. I've seen it happen to tons of other influencers."

My gaze falls back down to my hands, and I fiddle with my straw as I think back to all the scandals I've gleefully shared myself. All the times my fellow influencers were being roasted for something ridiculous, and I fanned the flames instead of helping them out.

"And none of your friends stood up for you?" Reina voices my thoughts, and I cringe.

"That's the thing about cancellation. It's very contagious. If anyone speaks up in favor of the person being canceled, they're immediately canceled themselves. I would never expect anyone to do something like that for me."

Because I would never, ever, do it for them.

Avery blows out a long breath. "Wow. I had no idea how cutthroat the world of ladies trying on clothes on the internet was."

I let out a grateful laugh as he breaks the tension. "Yeah."

"Is there anything we can do to help?"

I look over at Sam for the first time since we sat down. His face is the picture of concern. "Just harbor me until I can go back to the real world, I guess. This is just a wait and see kind of situation. I'll post something in the next few days when my PR people tell me that the waters seem to have calmed down a bit."

"Like an apology?" Reina asks. "I've seen those floating around, videos of people apologizing for saying or doing something wrong."

I give her a sad smile. "And what were people saying about those videos?"

She cringes. "Nothing good. They're never genuine enough or too little too late or something like that."

I nod. "A written statement went up on my channel as soon as this all went down, but I'm probably not going to be encouraged to post a tearful apology video. Those do far more harm than good."

"The internet is awful," Reina says, tears brimming in her eyes now. Dom pulls her close and places a gentle kiss on the top of her head.

I have to look away from the adorable show of affection.

I could've used this side of him growing up in the battlefield that was our home.

"We're happy to harbor you for as long as you need," Sam offers.

I look back at him, and I think we share a meaningful look. It might just be the drinks, though. "Thanks, Sam."

He holds my gaze for another moment, and I definitely see something there.

Maybe this thing between us isn't quite over?

I double down on my decision to get him alone at some point this evening so we can talk...and maybe do some other stuff.

I don't have to wait long for my chance.

He pushes up off the bench. "I'm going to hit the gents."

Perfect. I wait just long enough to not be suspicious and then excuse myself to the ladies' room.

I'm not even out of my seat, however, before Reina is up, looping her arm through mine.

"I'll show you the way."

"Oh, that's okay. I'm sure I can find it," I protest uselessly as she leads me away from the table. "There are signs."

"Girls gotta stick together, am I right?"

I want to like this woman so much. I do like her. She is the closest thing I have to a girlfriend right now, and I should be embracing every bit of attention she wants to give me, not trying to lose her around every corner.

By the time we make it back to the table, Sam's already in his seat.

I'm just scheming how to hotwire a golf cart and follow him home when the party starts breaking up. We crowd into the small bar area while the guys settle the tab.

"You did the right thing coming here, Naomi," Fran says, leaning tipsily against the bar. "This island is the ultimate refuge. And if you want to put those content creation skills to good use, we've got a wedding next week that would be perfect for promos for our company, Paradise Events."

My eyebrows raise slightly at the kind-of job offer. Not that

I'm looking for one, but it would be great to have something to do. "Sure. I'd love to help out."

"Let's talk soon, yeah?"

I nod with a smile.

"We're going to go pull around the carts," Avery says, kissing the top of Fran's head. "You and Reina head up to the lobby. We'll see you in a few."

He and Dom disappear down the beach and around the corner of the resort.

"I'll walk you ladies up," Sam says, wrapping an arm around Reina's shoulders as the group turns to head to the steps leading up between the two buildings to the street-side lobby.

They're two steps away when I jump into action. "I'll walk up too."

Sam glances back at me, eyebrows raised, and I know my voice was too loud. I'm going to have to get this buzz under control if he's going to take me seriously when I finally spill my secrets.

Even more so if I convince the guy to come up to my room.

I flash back to the field sobriety test he watched me perform for him in my living room in Austin and feel my face growing hotter.

Get it together, girl.

I hurry to catch up, falling in step alongside Fran.

"Who's the wedding for next week?" I ask her, mainly to have some reason to be with the group, rather than excusing myself to my room just upstairs.

Her face lights up just like it did when she mentioned it earlier. She really loves this wedding stuff.

"It's an older couple flying in from Monaco. They have serious money and want to spend it on this party. One of the things they requested was gold-plated silverware, which Avery had to fly to LA to pick up and then fly back to the island in a briefcase with a wrist lock."

My jaw drops. "Oh my god. Do you still have it?"

"The case? Yeah, it's at our house."

"We should stage that homecoming. Avery pulling up to the resort with the case locked to his wrist. That would make such epic content."

Fran shoots me a sly smile. "I never would have thought of that. You're a keeper. Come by the house tomorrow morning. We have great coffee, and I'll give you the full rundown."

"Sounds great. I'll be there."

"Ride's here," Sam calls as Fran and I follow them into the lobby and toward the large double doors leading to the street.

"See you in the morning," Fran says as she leaves me standing in the center of the lobby and heads toward the doors.

Sam and Reina are right behind her.

"Sleep tight," Reina calls.

"Sam, wait." I hadn't meant to be so obvious, but he's leaving with them, and I can't let him go.

He turns to me with his head cocked to the side. "I'm going to get them settled and then head home. See you around the resort tomorrow?"

I grit my teeth. No. No, no, no. "I just..." What reason can I possibly offer to get him to stay without giving away everything in front of these women?

"Night, Naomi," he says, opening the front doors and letting a rush of warm night air into the room.

"Sam," I say, but my voice is too quiet. He's going to walk out of here.

"I..."

I can't think of anything to say.

Except for the truth.

"I filmed us."

Rule #13

YOU BROKE THE RULES. NOW SHE'LL BREAK YOU

SAM

It's the last thing in the world I expect her to say, and it takes me a full moment to process.

Fran gets there quicker than I do.

"What?" she asks, looking over her shoulder at Naomi standing in the lobby.

I look at Naomi myself and see the truth of the statement written across her face.

I've got to get Fran and Reina out of here right away.

"I think I'll walk Naomi up to her room after all."

I mime taking a drink to insinuate that the woman's a bit tipsy. Reina smiles in understanding, but Fran's eyes narrow at me before she glances back at where Naomi stands in the center of the lobby.

I usher them out without another word. Dom and Ave have the carts waiting in the pickup loop, arguing about something stupid. They pause and walk toward the women as they exit the building. I close the door and lean against it, finally face-to-face with Naomi.

"What did you say?" I ask. Surely, I misunderstood. Hell, maybe she is drunk.

"I...I'm sorry. I didn't mean..."

Relief pours through me at her words. I almost laugh. I can't believe I let myself think that she—

"I didn't mean to say that with other people around. I've been trying to get you alone all night so I could figure out a way to tell you..." She trails off again and dread creeps up my spine.

I've been avoiding her, worrying that she was going to say or do something that would give us away. I guess I should have let her get me alone.

"Why don't we head up to your room? I'll get you settled." Whatever's going on here, it's not going on in the lobby of my resort, where anyone could be listening.

I walk down the hallway and up the stairs without waiting for her to acknowledge what I said. When I glance back from the top of the stairs, she's trudging up them, head hung low.

The sight of the usually confident, vivacious Naomi, reduced to this silent, sullen woman scares me more than anything she's said so far. I haven't even started to process the implication of her words. I just need to get her alone and get her talking.

After she lets us into her room, I close the door and lean against it, inhaling deeply. Preparing.

"Okay. What on earth did you mean down there? It sounded like you said you filmed us?"

She nods, and I start to panic but force myself to remain calm.

"At your apartment in Austin?" Gotta get the facts straight here, so I know what I'm dealing with.

Another nod.

That's when I lose it.

"Why?" I shout the word and then look around myself frantically, cringing at the walls to other rooms mere feet away.

When I look back at Naomi, she's cowered even further,

perched on the arm of a chair, looking at the floor, wringing her hands.

"Naomi?" I can't stand the silence.

"I just…film things. It's what I do." Her voice is desperate, and for a moment, I almost move to comfort her.

But then I remember.

"You film things for your social media channel. Is that what you did?" I can hear the panic in my own voice as I try to keep it down. "Did you post the video somewhere?" The last words come out as a hissed whisper.

Naomi jumps to her feet, meeting my gaze for the first time in what feels like an hour.

"No! Of course not. I would never post it anywhere. I would never show anyone."

I let my head fall back and close my eyes. That's a relief. I calm down enough to take a deep breath and let it out slowly. When I look back down, Naomi's eyes are begging me to understand. To forgive her.

But I'm not sure I'm ready for that.

"Then why? Why would you do something like that?"

She offers me a guilty smile. "I like to watch."

My eyes widen and then close at this new bit of information. It's a lot to process.

"You watch the video?"

"Over and over and over."

A new feeling rises up from my stomach, mixing with the dread and sending my whole nervous system into chaos. It's not a bad feeling. If anything, it's kind of…curious.

"But we didn't even have sex."

I try to imagine her, alone in her room, watching a video of herself giving me head, but my brain starts to short circuit.

Naomi just stares. Some of the timidness from a moment before lifts, and she's standing straighter, looking at me more directly. "I watch what we did, and then I close my eyes and imagine you fucking me."

Her words send a shockwave through my entire system, like all the water in my body is gathering into a tsunami.

I can't think of a response fast enough, so Naomi drops another bomb on the smoldering ruins of my mind.

"It's really hot. If you ever want to watch it—"

"I don't," I say quickly, before anything else can sneak out of my mouth.

The last thing in the world I want is to curl up on that sofa with this woman and watch a video of us fooling around on her phone.

Right?

Naomi just shrugs, as if she offered me a soda and I turned her down. I feel alarm starting to rise again at her nonchalance.

"I would be far more comfortable with you deleting it off your phone."

She cocks her head to the side, watching my unease with narrowed eyes. I marvel at how quickly the tables have turned. Not two minutes ago, I was the one standing tall while she cowered. Now, I'm starting to feel like I might crumble.

"It's not on my phone. I have a secure server. Heavily encrypted. You have nothing to worry about."

Her dismissive tone sets something off in me. "Says the woman who just got taken down by the online community for untrustworthiness." It's a low blow, but I haven't got much else to work with here.

I watch my words hit her.

She flinches slightly, not dignifying my words with a response.

"I should go," I say, finally coming to my senses.

"Sam, stay."

She reaches me as my hand hits the door handle, her firm touch on my shoulder making me pause.

"Why?"

"I don't know. This could be fun. We had fun before, right?"

I can't go down this road with her, so I just shake my head. She tries to remove my hand from the knob, but I don't let her.

"That's a big, fat lie," she says, her voice unnervingly calm. "I know you had fun because I watch you almost every night."

I close my eyes and wish I was anywhere else. "You did not have my permission to film me."

Naomi lets out a sigh and takes a few steps back, her hands hitting her sides with a soft thud. "I know. And I shouldn't have done that. That's why I'm telling you now."

I grip the door handle like a life raft. "What? Why?"

"Because I want to ask for your permission."

"My permission for what? You already did it."

"I want your permission to keep watching it."

"Why?" I ask again, apparently only capable of one-word questions in this headspace.

"Why do I want to keep watching it? Because it's the hottest thing I've ever seen."

I can't force my lungs to take a breath as I white knuckle the door handle.

"I watch it with my phone in one hand and my little black vibrator in the other."

Images of that very vibrator in my own hand flash through my mind. My breath finally comes, but it's audible, like a gasp.

Naomi laughs softly from right behind me, and I jump.

How did she get so close again so quickly?

"You remember that vibrator, right?"

I pull the door open and practically run into the hallway instead of answering. My dick's going to get me in trouble if a certain iPhone-wielding voyeur spots it.

"Sam, wait."

I don't wait, hurrying down the hall toward the stairs as quickly as I can without flat out running.

"Let me send it to you. You can watch it, and if you think it's crap and want me to delete it, I will."

I whirl to face her. "What?" The question comes out too loud, and I look wildly from side to side at the hotel doors next to me, praying I didn't wake anyone.

"Let me send it to you."

"No. I don't want it anywhere near me." I take a few steps toward where she stands in the hall. "This could ruin me. Do you understand that?"

Naomi stands her ground. "If you watch it and still want me to delete it, I will. Deal?"

I shake my head and turn back down the hall. "No way."

"Aren't you at least a little bit curious?"

The real answer is too frightening to be allowed in my own mind.

"No."

"Say you'll watch it."

"No."

"Fine," she says before turning to head back into her room.

Madness overtakes me as she starts to disappear from view.

"Fine." My voice comes out sounding far more confident than I feel. "Send it to me."

Her head pops out of the doorway, a devilish grin on her face. "Coming right up."

Rule #14

CRY, PRAY, BEG—IT STILL WON'T SAVE YOU

SAM

I feel my phone buzz in my pocket as I cross the dark lot to my cart, but I don't dare check it.

It's not until I'm safely in my house, curtains drawn, settled on my couch that I finally click the link Naomi sent. It's a downloaded file from a web hosting site that does, in fact, seem secure. She's set up a passkey linked to my information, and it makes me jump through several hoops before the file is delivered.

I grab myself a beer while I wait for the enormous file to buffer enough to play with my slow island internet.

When the video finally starts, I cringe at the sound of my own voice coming too loud from the tinny phone speaker. I hit the button to turn it down to almost silent as I watch myself walk onto the screen.

The camera was set up on the tall dresser in Naomi's bedroom. From this vantage point, I can see the love seat, the bed, and the wall where I stood perfectly. The door to the walk-in closet is just to the left of the frame.

We enter her room and stumble, hands on each other's still clothed bodies, over to the loveseat. I watch us fumble and laugh for a few painfully awkward moments before jumping the video forward.

I'm standing and walking across the room with Naomi close behind. My back hits the wall, and I get a full view of my own face for the first time. I look nervous, a bit uncertain, with flashes of what could only be called recklessness passing through my eyes as I watch the gorgeous woman on her knees before me.

I click the volume up just a bit and listen to our words, even though I have them memorized from playing it over and over in my mind since this all went down.

"Do it."

"Do what?"

"Beg."

"Oh, you'd like that, would you?"

With those words, I watch my face change. Gone is the timid man. The man who knows damn well he should be anywhere but here. He's been replaced by someone fierce. Someone who has the power in this situation and is greedily giving it away to get what he wants.

She has my pants down, and I step out of them. When her hands reach up to grip my prominent erection on the screen, I can't help but reach down and set my hand on the front of my pants, knowing I'll find a similar situation in real life.

I stroke my palm firmly down the length of myself from the outside of my jeans as Naomi sucks the tip of my cock into her mouth. I can't tear my eyes away from the screen, can't take a breath as more and more of my length disappears through those pink lips.

Losing the battle, I hit pause, set my beer down on the table, unbutton my jeans, and lower the zipper. I only make enough room to get my hand inside and grip myself, my palm clammy, my jeans too tight, phone balancing precariously on my thigh.

I'm not ready to commit to full-on jerking off while watching myself get head on my phone screen.

I'm not sure what that would say about me, but whatever it is, I don't want it said aloud.

Naomi has both hands on my body. One gripping my cock, feeding it in and out of her lips. The other hand grips my hip, her nails curling into my flesh as she uses my leg for balance. I grip my own hip in the place I remember, the place I watched those fingernail marks fade from for days after finally catching a flight back to Faraday.

With a resigned sigh, I go with it, stroking myself in long, firm grasps, eyes glued to the tiny figures on my phone screen. She's pulling away now, and I know what comes next.

She tells me to come in her mouth.

I lean my head back, allowing my eyes to close for a millisecond before snapping them open once more.

She's got my cock in her mouth. I can see on my own face that I'm close. Back is the uncertainty in my face, and I know why. I haven't made a habit of coming in women's mouths. I've always pulled out, assuming that's the right thing to do.

I'm nervous for myself just watching, but I can't look away. On screen, I have one hand twisted in Naomi's long, auburn curls, not moving her head, just holding on for dear life. I don't take my eyes off my cock in her mouth as I start to contract at the core.

I watch my face crumple into my orgasm, eyes squeezing involuntarily closed, bottom lip clenched tightly between my teeth. Naomi tilts her head upward, following the movement of my cock as my body spasms, keeping as much of it in her mouth as she can manage.

She licks and sucks as my cum fills her throat. I can see her swallow over and over as my hips start to move, plunging my length deeper into her hot, wet mouth.

I don't remember doing that, and I watch with my mouth open as my face transforms once more. The uncertainty once again replaced by lusty desire. I glare down at her with dark eyes, fisting her hair and pumping into her mouth.

The stranglehold on my cock not giving me what I need, I slide my fist up to massage my tip, dragging my other hand down into my boxers to pull my balls gently. Fuck, it feels so damn good.

Am I really going to come, alone in my living room, watching homemade porn starring myself?

Naomi sits back on her heels on screen when I release her hair, and I soften the grip on my cock, amazed I managed to watch that whole scene without coming. I can't hear what we're saying with the volume turned down so low, but I know what happens next. She puts on that little pink number, and I choose the black vibrator.

I'm dying to watch her little show again, but I'm too wound up right now.

I snatch up my phone and hit pause, giving myself three long, deep breaths to get ahold of myself before using one slightly shaky finger to move the play bar forward slowly, scrubbing through the video until I watch myself launch forward and capture the vibrator from Naomi, tossing her on her back on the bed.

I stop moving the video forward but keep it paused as I get up from the couch and head to my bathroom. Snagging the bottle of cocoa butter lotion from my counter, I avoid meeting my own gaze in the mirror.

Fuck it. If I'm going to do this, I may as well do it right. Doesn't mean I'm going to be able to look myself in the eyes as I do though.

Unless those eyes are on-screen.

I breathe out a nervous laugh as I head back to the sofa, cock still bouncing out of my undone jeans. I drop the damn things to my ankles and flop back down, lotion bottle at the ready.

I turn the volume up much higher than I dared before and hit play.

I've got my hands on her body, moving quickly from her hips to her breasts and back again as if I can't get enough.

I can't see my own face from this angle, but I can see Naomi's. Her eyes are open, watching me with desire and surprise. I can't blame her for that. I remember feeling exactly the same way that night as I let my lizard brain take over and ravish her in all the ways I'd claimed I wasn't going to.

Well, almost all the ways.

My cock is slippery in my hand as on screen I press her legs open further and touch the little toy down on her clit. She cries out, and I nearly come just from that sound alone. I relax my grip and let my strong hand slide lightly up and down my shaft. I need to last through this whole thing like I've never needed anything before in my life.

Just like Naomi said earlier in her hotel room, I'm going to watch this as foreplay and then close my eyes and stick my raging hard cock into that sweet pussy. In my mind, I'm going to come deep inside her while she screams my name.

For now, I keep my eyes glued to the screen as I slip the little black vibrator into her body and catch it as it pops back out.

"You're driving me fucking crazy, princess."

"I'm doing it on purpose."

I'm fisting myself on screen just as hard as I'm fisting myself now, using the juices from her pussy to lube myself up, switching hands as I drench my fingers in her and smoothing the luscious liquid over my cock. I imagine that's what I'm lubed up with now and have to lighten my grip once more to keep from blowing too soon.

My hand is inside her, thumb on her clit as she moans. My cock is a living, breathing thing in my hand, telling me to drive it home. I can hear it screaming at me as if I'm in that room again.

A loud chime from my phone shatters my little fantasy world, and a text notification flashes across the screen.

I can't focus quickly enough to read it before it's gone, but it does its job.

I'm caught.

I fumble to pause the video with my lotion-covered fingers, turning the volume on my phone down all the way and closing out of the file hosting site, swiping up to close every open app on my phone just for good measure.

I toss my phone back on the table and collapse backward into the sofa, wiping my hands on the towel I had set next to me.

I lost my mind there for a moment.

What the fuck was I doing jerking off to that?

She videoed me without permission and then forced me to watch it so that she would agree to delete it.

How did that turn into...this?

Rule #15

AGAIN...AND AGAIN AND AGAIN

SAM

My phone buzzes again, and I snatch it up, angry at the interruption, but angrier at myself for even being in this compromising situation.

Two texts from Naomi.

> **Naomi**
> What do you think?

> Tell me you're enjoying it.

I almost throw my phone across the room. But in the end, I set it gently back down on the coffee table and rest my head in my hands.

It buzzes again.

> **Naomi**
> Are you watching?

I snatch it up and punch out a reply.

Sam
No.

She sends a laughing face emoji, but I'm not feeling one bit like laughing.

Naomi
I can see that you are. You're logged in as yourself.

Damn technology. I should have known she would be able to tell I started playback.

Naomi
You even made your username your own name. Very James Bond of you.

I groan and set the phone back down.

What am I going to do now? She knows I'm watching it.

I've been caught red-handed. Literally.

Before my rational brain can come up with a plan, another brain takes over.

I pick my phone back up.

Sam
I'm watching it.

Naomi
You've gotten pretty far. Enjoying yourself?

Sam
Yeah.

Naomi
Are you touching yourself?

How am I supposed to answer that? I flop back on the sofa, phone still in hand. I don't know how to do this. I've always been a terribly shy flirt. It could be what's to blame for my lack of a romantic life. But this is on a whole new level. Sexting? Admitting to a woman over text that I'm jerking off to our homemade porn?

She texts again while I'm ruminating.

Naomi
I am.

Damn it.

My fingers move with a mind of their own.

Sam
Tell me.

Naomi
Ooh, he's going to play. I wasn't sure there for a moment.

I don't respond to that, and her typing bubble appears a moment later. My cock is screaming at me, so I fist it lightly as I wait for her response.

Naomi
I love the part where you come in my mouth. Your nice guy act falls away, and you start fucking my face as you come. Did you see that part?

Sam
Yeah. I like that part too.

I'm not giving her much, but it's apparently enough. Naomi takes it and runs.

Naomi
And I love the part where you lose control and throw me back on the bed and start touching me. Have you made it that far?

My fingers don't want to type the next words, but I force them to, one letter at a time.

Sam
I like the part where I'm lubing myself up with your juices.

My cock jumps in my hand, and I hit send with a smile. Naomi responds immediately.

Naomi
Tell me you're fisting that cock right now.

Sam
I am.

And before I can stop myself, I type another.

Sam
Are you touching yourself right now too?

Naomi
Oh yeah. I have my little vibrator on low, and I'm feeding it in and out of my pussy to get it nice and wet. When we start the video, I'll put it on my clit and come again.

Her typing bubble hovers as I try to process that last text, pumping my cock harder.

Naomi
And again and again.

Damn.

Naomi
Have you come yet?

Sam
Not yet.

Naomi
Are you waiting for a certain part?

I'm not sure how to admit the truth, that I was going to wait till the end and close my eyes and imagine fucking her, so I lie.

Sam
I was just getting there when someone interrupted me.

She sends a hot, sweaty faced man emoji, and I smile.

Naomi
Well, let's get back to it. Tell me what time you're starting at, and I'll start at the same place.

I close my eyes briefly, shaking my head. There's no way I'm going to be able to say no to that, not with my dick calling the shots.

I only hope I don't wake up tomorrow regretting this.

With a deep breath and a heavy sigh, I pull the file hosting app back up and get the video to the place where I start touching her clit with the vibrator. The action can't last much longer than ten minutes after this point, and I'm sure my cock won't last even that long.

Sam
25:32

Naomi
Ooh, getting right to the good stuff. Give me just a second.

Naomi
Okay. I'm hitting play.

I do the same, clicking the volume up before settling the phone back on my knee. Naomi's beautiful voice cries out, and my fist tightens. My own voice follows, a moan of pleasure so deep and rich with longing that I wouldn't have recognized it as my own if I hadn't seen the video evidence.

Naomi
Sometimes, I skip right to the place where you make that sound.

Naomi's comment pops up in the small comment section at the bottom of the screen, right in the video app.

I guess we're doing this now.

I click into my own comment box.

Sam
I don't recognize myself.

Naomi
As the brilliant fucking sex god you are? Well, there's no way to deny it now.

I laugh softly at her sass, eyes glued to the screen. I'm slipping the little black vibrator deep into her body now, holding my hand out to catch it as it slides back out.

Naomi
I do that to myself all the time now.

Naomi
After you did it, now I can't keep it out of myself. Somedays I carry it in my purse so I can sneak into the bathroom and get myself off just like you did.

Well, maybe I won't last two minutes. Not with this new commentary.

Sam
Are you touching yourself, princess, or typing?

Naomi

I'm doing both. Talk-to-texting with two fingers in my pussy.

What I wouldn't give to see that.

I fix my gaze on the screen, watching her writhe and moan as I work her clit.

Sam
Are you touching your clit?

Naomi
Always.

Sam
I'm so close.

Naomi
Which part do you want to watch while you come?

Sam
I want to close my eyes and pretend I'm fucking you.

Naomi
Oh god, please tell me what you're doing in your mind.

Sam
I don't know if I can do both.

Naomi
Can I call you?

I clench my teeth and consider. I can feel my orgasm floating away as I go through the pros and cons, so I decide to hold off.

Sam
Not tonight. I'll talk-to-text you through it.

Naomi
Vibe on high. Ready for you.

I click into the comment box and hit the little microphone button to turn on talk-to-text. After another deep breath and long sigh, I re-up the lotion in my hand and start to speak.

Sam
This part at the end where I'm lubing myself up with you?

I think about it all the time.

You were so fucking wet.

Naomi
I'm that wet now.

A surge of pleasure hits my brain, and I try to keep it together, loosening the grip on my cock as I make long strokes from root to tip. I've never wanted to delay my own orgasm more than I do right now.

I want this to last forever.

Sam
Are you at the part now where I almost put my cock in you?

Naomi
Yes. You're like one inch away.

Sam
I wanted to do it so badly.

Naomi
I wanted you to.

I still want you to.

Sam
Pause the video right there.

A short pause and I wait with my breath held.

Naomi
Done.

I pause my own, the image on the screen one I already know I'll never forget.

Naomi is splayed out before me, arms stretched long above her on the bed. I've got my cock in one hand, my other is resting on her body, my thumb just grazing her clit. I'm bent over, having just sat up from licking her and the tip of my cock is dangerously close to her entrance.

Sam
Can you imagine what it would feel like if I put it in you right then?

Naomi
Yes

Sam
Tell me.

Naomi
you're so big, and your cock is so hard. I'm wet, but it still takes you a moment to work your way inside, inch by inch, stretching me open.

Fucking hell.

I release my cock altogether and try to steady my breathing, reaching down for a soft pull on my balls.

Naomi
I can feel your tip sliding into me, deeper and deeper.

I take my tip in my fist, sliding my hand down slowly, imagining burying myself in her body.

There's no calming down my breathing now. One pump, maybe two, and I'm a goner.

Sam
You better come for me, princess.

Naomi
Now?

Sam
Right goddamn now.

After an excruciatingly long pause, my phone buzzes with a WhatsApp notification. I click the banner to switch apps and find myself looking at the play button of an audio note.

I fumble to hit the button so quickly I nearly drop my phone, catching it at the last second and setting it down on the sofa beside me just as Naomi's voice lights up the room around me.

I close my eyes and pretend she's there.

"Oh, Sammy, I'm going to come."

She moans and whimpers for a few moments, and I hold my breath, working myself right up to the edge.

"I'm going to come on your cock. Are you ready?"

"Yes," I say aloud to the empty room.

All I can pick out are a few choice expletives mixed in with moans as I listen to Naomi send herself into oblivion. I keep my eyes closed and follow, bellowing out a moan of pleasure as my orgasm explodes inside me—and outside me, landing somewhere in the living room.

I can barely make myself care about the mess I'm making as I spasm and gasp, matching the volume and pitch of the breathy voice coming from my phone speakers.

The audio clip ends with her giving a little giggle, the sound piercing through my chest like a hot poker.

I want her here.

I need her here.

I drop my still throbbing cock and flop back on the sofa, fully and completely spent.

My phone buzzes, and I glance down at the screen.

Naomi
Did you get there?

I don't reach for it, instead closing my eyes once more. Now that I got myself off, the mist of insanity that lowered over me the second I hit play on that video is starting to lift.

What am I doing?

I can't be doing this.

My phone buzzes again.

Naomi
Do you still want me to delete the video? 😉

Reality hits me upside the head in full force.

This is Dom's little sister.

Dom…whose money allowed me to have the life I have.

She's got a video of us fooling around.

It's my job to tell her to delete the video so I can protect my life and friendships.

But there's no way in hell I'm going to do it.

Rule #16

YOU DIDN'T FALL, YOU JUMPED

SAM

I don't respond to any more of Naomi's messages that night, but they don't stop. By the time I get up for work the next morning, I have four unread messages, and not one of them is an important work-related message that I left my phone on all night for.

> **Naomi**
> That was so freaking hot
>
> Thanks for playing
>
> Night, Sam
>
> Let's talk tomorrow

I close the app without responding, but I know she can tell I read her messages. Damn technology.

I get two blissfully quiet hours in my office in the morning to deal with scheduling and HR issues that were sent my way the day before. It's nearly ten before my phone buzzes.

Naomi
I'm heading to Fran's house to talk about wedding stuff in a few.

I vaguely remember her and Fran discussing the wedding at the bar. It'll be great to have her out of the resort today. I can't think knowing she's close.

Knowing I could climb one flight of stairs and do in person all the dirty things I was imagining last night.

Sam
Sounds like fun. Let the front desk know if you need a golf cart, and they'll set you up with one.

Naomi
Ooh. He lives! I was starting to wonder if I needed to go check on you.

I smile down at the screen, feeling a bit sheepish for never returning her messages. It's not like me to leave someone hanging.

Sam
Sorry, I had an early morning.

Naomi
No problem. You just disappeared on me last night. 😉

Shame starts to creep up from my gut. I had no right to ghost her like that. I've been thinking a lot about how this whole thing affects me and my life, but there's another person involved. One who has feelings and deserves my respect.

Sam
I should've said goodnight. Sorry. I was feeling a little...uneasy

Naomi
About the video?

Sam
About the whole thing, really. It was my first time doing anything like that.

I wanted to be pissed about the stupid video.

But I wasn't.

Naomi
You did great. 

I laugh out loud just as the door to my office opens.

Dom.

I tuck my phone in my pocket and clear my throat. "Morning."

He narrows his eyes at me but huffs out a good morning before jumping right into business.

"The produce truck is late. Would you mind calling down to the dock to find out if the barge made it in on time?"

"Sure thing."

"And we've got a full tasting for next week's wedding couple at noon today if you were planning to come down."

"I've got it on my schedule."

"I'm moving Naomi up to the house today. Her room has a check-in at four."

I cough in surprise at the mention of her name but recover quickly. "Let me know if you need help."

As if his words summoned her, my phone starts buzzing in my pocket. I reach down to hit the button without taking it out.

Dom just watches me. "I think we can handle moving a few suitcases."

My phone buzzes again, and I jump, reaching down quickly to silence it.

"You gonna get that?" he asks, eyebrows raised.

"Oh, it's not…I mean, yeah, of course. But I know who it is." I stumble through the words. "Nothing important."

Dom just stares at me for another long moment before turning and exiting my office without another word.

I flop back in my chair, relieved, as I pull my phone out.

Naomi
Seriously. It was like the second-best night of my life. 😉

I'm moving up to Dom's house today.

Sam
I heard. He was just here.

Naomi
So much for privacy…

I should be grateful she's moving out of the room above my office. Out of my building and into the watchful home of her protective brother. Maybe that'll finally force me to move on from this crazy dream.

Instead, all I want to do is reassure her, and myself, that everything will be okay.

Sam
Dom and Reina work a ton.

Naomi
And I can always hide you in a closet if one of them comes home unexpectedly.

I laugh in surprise and feel myself blush just a bit.

Sam
I didn't say anything about coming over there.

Naomi
I'm going to talk you into it eventually.

I don't know how to respond to that, so I just set my phone down. It buzzes again almost immediately.

Naomi
I'm very persuasive.

Again, I set the phone down without responding. And again, it buzzes.

Naomi
Can't decide what to wear...

I smile at the message, which is not the reaction I expect from myself. I want walls between myself and this forbidden woman, but I also melt because she knows me. Knows what I'm thinking and feeling. Knows when to push and how to get me to do things I never knew I wanted or needed.

When was the last time a woman really knew me? Maybe never. And this woman is just so...perfect.

My phone buzzes again.

I glance down at the screen and see that it's a photo message. I click into the app so quickly I almost send the phone flying across my desk.

She sent a picture of herself kneeling on the floor of her room in front of the full-length closet mirror. She has on a short skirt and her knees are wide, giving me just a hint of red panties at the apex of her thighs.

The phone covers most of her face. Her long, wavy hair is down around her shoulders, looking wild, like someone was running their fingers through it.

She apparently hasn't chosen a top yet, because those

gorgeous tits I've been dreaming about are covered only by an arm draped across her chest. I can't see either nipple, but I've got a full view of the soft swell below her arm.

What is it about her skin and her softness that sets me off the way it does? I stare at that picture long and hard, imagining myself leaning down to bite her soft, tan flesh.

It doesn't take a full minute before I'm dealing with something else long and hard.

Sam
You know I'm working, right?

Naomi
😂

Sam
What are you trying to do to me?

Naomi
😇

Sam
I might have to shut my phone off, princess

I hit send before I can talk myself out of it. I shouldn't be using that sexy pet name when we're texting from my office.

Hell, I shouldn't have a sexy pet name for Naomi at all.

This woman is nothing but trouble.

Unfortunately, she seems to be exactly the kind of trouble I want.

I shake my head, trying to clear some of the images from the video session last night from my brain, but it doesn't work. Instead, I close my eyes and lean into them.

Her soft body in my hands.

The taste of her on my tongue as I licked my way over her skin.

The sound of her voice calling my name.

Sammy.

This little fling, or whatever it is, could be my ruin, both personally and professionally. Is it really worth it? My logical brain leaps onto its soapbox and starts shaking its head. No, no, no, it says. Cut this shit out.

But my body thinks differently.

The feeling that's been lingering in my chest since that evening at Naomi's apartment back in Austin officially has a name after last night. And it's not desire or lust or horniness… although I'm certainly feeling all those things.

No. The feeling is hope.

This woman has me thinking maybe I'm not a lost cause after all. That maybe the quiet, happy home life I've always dreamed of is possible.

That maybe someone could love me.

I've never admitted out loud, or even to myself, that I'm unlovable. I know in a logical sense it's not true. My mother loves me. The guys love me. My employees have a respectful adoration toward me that's some flavor of love.

But the warm, intoxicating, all-consuming kind of love? Love that fills the holes in your heart and makes you want to spend the rest of your days keeping the car filled with gas and the cap on the toothpaste? That kind of love always seemed like it was meant for everyone but me.

When I was younger, I searched for what was missing about me. What I needed to improve or purge to be able to connect with a woman at that level.

I never found it.

Eventually, I came to the silent conclusion, never admitted to anyone, not even to myself, that my dream was just impossible. That, for whatever reason, I was incompatible with love.

Everyone liked me. I was everyone's friend. I was a great boss.

I just wasn't husband material.

Until now.

I know it's stupid to have decided, after one night together and a completely inappropriate porn texting session, that I'm somehow fit to be a husband. And it's not even that I'm really thinking that. It's just…

A woman likes me.

A woman wants me.

And it's a woman I can see myself being with. I did, as a matter of fact. When I sat in her kitchen in Austin, it felt like a premonition of some kind. That I was seeing my own future, as crazy as that sounds.

Hell, this whole thing sounds crazy.

Is crazy.

But I'd rather burn alive than give it up.

Sam
Send me another one.

Naomi
You waited too long. I'm dressed now.

Sam
Get undressed.

Naomi
I thought you were working.

Sam
I am.

Naomi
Alone in your office with the door closed?

I glance up at the door, which is cracked just enough for me to see the teal hallway outside. My door is always open. It's a promise I make to my employees.

One that might have to change a bit.

They can knock, right?

I get up and walk over, closing it as quietly as I can before returning to my seat.

It's still unlocked. Anyone could stroll in at any time. But it feels different. I pick my phone back up.

Sam
Yup.

Naomi
Prove it.

I laugh out loud at her text, even as the meaning sends chills down my spine.

Sam
You asking for a dick pic, princess?

Naomi
God, you say the sexiest things.

Another laugh bursts out of me, but it fades away as I start to consider.

Sam
I don't know if that's a good idea.

Naomi
You've quite enjoyed my bad ideas so far...

I set the phone on my desk and glance down at the tent in my pants. The one that seems to respond to the sound of my phone vibrating these days.

Can I really take it out and shoot a picture of it? Right here in my office?

A sound out in the hallway makes me jump an inch out of my chair, and I sit for a long moment, still as a statue, waiting for the door to fly open.

It never does.

Eventually I regain the ability to breathe, but it comes with the renewed ability to think clearly.

There's no way.

But what if…

I climb to my feet, adjusting myself in my pants just in case, and make my way over to the door. I stand with my back pressing against it and look down at the phone in my hands.

Then I look up toward the corners of the ceiling, scanning the room for security cameras that I know damn well aren't there. I scan my bookcase for teddy bears with hidden nanny cams like a madman.

When I look back down at my phone, I break out in a cold sweat.

Sam
I can't. I tried.

Naomi
That's okay!

Don't freak out.

I smile as I'm able to take the first breath in what feels like ten minutes. I let the oxygen calm me. She gets me.

I'm so fucked.

Naomi
Try this—slide one hand down and touch yourself over your pants, then take a selfie of just your face.

The thought of doing what she asks makes my heart race but doesn't induce nearly as much panic as the thought of getting caught in my office with my pants down and phone in my hand.

Slowly, I slide one hand down until it's cupping the bulge in my pants. It's all I can do to hold in a gasp as the screaming nerves finally get some attention. I grip myself firmly and open the camera app.

Switching to front facing, my own face fills the screen. I can't watch myself do this, so I close my eyes and hit the shutter button.

When I'm brave enough to reopen them, the image waiting for me takes my breath away once more.

It's my face, but the expression there isn't one I've seen in the mirror. My eyes are closed with my lip clenched just a bit between my teeth, revealing a flash of white. My cheeks are flushed, but it looks good on me. I look healthy and alive. I look happy, as if underneath that mask of poorly restrained desire is a smile. A genuine smile.

I hit send quickly before I can talk myself out of it.

Naomi
Damn.

Sam
I don't know that guy.

Naomi
You keep saying that.

Sam
It's true. I'm predictable. That's my personality. No surprises here. Except with you.

Naomi
Good.

She's right, of course, but I can't help the flare of anger that rises in me at her flippant response.

Sam
Being predictable and trustworthy is what makes me such a good manager. It's what makes me a good boss and a good friend. It's what makes me...me. I don't know what all these surprises mean for my life.

Naomi
You're wrong about that, Sam. What makes you a good boss and great friend is your big heart. And that will always be there, inside, no matter what other changes you make.

Sam
You don't know me well enough to say that.

I regret the text the second I hit send. I stand with my jaw clenched tight, waiting for her to respond so I can follow up with an apology.

The text bubble never comes.

I walk back over to my desk and sink heavily into my chair.

Sam
I'm sorry. I didn't mean that and never should have said it. This whole thing has me a little on edge.

My office door swings open so fast it hits the opposite wall with a bang that makes me jump and drop my phone to the desk.

"Why's your door closed?" Dom demands.

I take a deep breath to keep from screaming at him for such a rude interruption. The last thing I want is to act out of character and draw attention to myself.

"The air conditioning kicked on a second ago, and it closed. I was just getting up to reopen it."

Dom crosses his arms over his chest. I'm dying to read his

expression, but if I look straight at him for too long, he'll read mine.

"Is that so?"

"What's up, Dom?" I feel like regular Sam would just brush off his hostility and offer my help, so that's what I do.

Even though I'm no longer regular Sam.

"Just wanted to check on that produce delivery."

"It's on the way. You could've texted me."

His eyes narrow as I toss out the accusation, and I realize my mistake right away.

"I would have texted anyone else, but you." He takes a step forward, still looking pointedly at me. "You don't always have your phone on you. So I always walk over here to talk to you."

I nod. "You're right, and I appreciate that." I keep my tone calm. Soothing the aggressive animal in my office.

"But you seem to have your phone on you more now."

He knows. My entire life is about to crumble into the sand. I try to keep my cool. "Yeah, I was just…working."

Dom cocks his head to the side. "Worked through breakfast, I assume?"

I relax slightly and manage a small smile. "You caught me."

He just rolls his eyes, turning back toward the door. "Come down to Raft a few minutes early, and I'll make you something. The last thing you need to do is show up to the tasting hungry."

He walks out without waiting for my answer, knowing damn well I'm not going to turn down a meal cooked for me personally by our head chef.

The guy has a gruff exterior, but he's not all bad. He's still a nurturer at heart. All chefs are.

I blow out the breath I've been holding and drop my head to my hands. Nurturer or not, he's going to freaking kill me.

My phone buzzes, and I jump to grab it, all worry over the interaction with Dom gone instantly as I hurry to read how Naomi responded.

Naomi
I want to know you.

I drop the phone and close my eyes. It might have been better if she responded in anger, telling me what a dick I was and that she never wanted to speak to me again. This? This I don't know what to do with.

I don't get a full minute to process before my phone buzzes again.

Naomi
If you'll let me.

Rule #17

WOMEN DON'T GUESS. THEY KNOW

NAOMI

I pull up to Fran and Avery's house and let out a long, low whistle.

"Who would ever know this jungle mansion was hiding out here?" I mutter to myself as I climb out of the cart and crane my neck to see the second floor. "Holy crap, there's a rooftop deck?"

I'm already picking out the perfect outfit in my mind for a photoshoot up there.

"Morning," Fran calls as she crosses the front porch. I climb the few steps up to meet her, and she and I exchange a loose hug. "Big bro let you loose in your own golf cart, huh?"

I shrug and smile. "Sam offered it."

"Did he now? And when did he do that? Last night at the bar? Or were you two talking this morning?"

Uh oh.

"Um, I ran into him in the lobby, and he offered."

Fran folds her arms over her chest and regards me with amusement dancing across her face.

I'm so fucked. I panic and start rambling.

"We're just...I don't...Sam and I..." I trail off as I realize I walked right into her trap.

"Okay, then," Fran says with a conspiratorial smile. "Looks like we've got all sorts of things to talk about."

She leads me through the open front door into her wide open, sun-filled living room.

"Like wedding stuff?" My voice gives away my nerves.

I clear my throat and try to get ahold of myself as Fran tosses me a look over her shoulder.

"Wedding stuff, sure. But I want to know about you and Sam."

And there it is.

"What do you mean?"

Fran just laughs. "Girl, please."

She walks into the open kitchen and pulls two brightly colored ceramic mugs from a cupboard. "Coffee?"

I just nod, unable to form words as my brain swirls with possible excuses I can offer for whatever Fran thinks she knows.

She pours coffee and sets it on the bar with cream and sugar. I sip nervously, waiting to be grilled.

"Spill it," she says finally.

"I don't know what you're talking about. Sam is just...Dom's friend. Some guy. He just offered me a golf cart to borrow. He's known me since I was born."

"And last night at dinner when he sat as far from you as possible but never took his eyes off you?" she asks.

I shrug. "I—"

"And at the bar when he jumped in to defend you at every turn?"

"Well—"

"And what about when Reina and I were leaving, and you blurted out something about a video, and all of a sudden you were so drunk he had to walk you upstairs to your hotel room. Alone."

"I guess I had too much to drink."

"Bullshit. I talked to you the whole way up to that lobby, and you were far from too drunk to walk up a flight of stairs."

I twist the mug nervously in my hands and consider my options. She obviously knows and denying it further could make it worse. Whatever scenarios she's imagining are probably far wilder than the truth.

Or…maybe not.

I take a deep breath and let it out. Fran sits back in her seat with a smile, knowing she's won.

"Okay. Well, you have two options here," I start, making up my game plan as I go along. "I can make another stupid excuse, and you can decide to believe me and let it go, or you can ask me one more time, and I'll tell you the truth."

I hold up my hand to stop her as she starts to speak. "But once you know the truth you can't unknow it. And you might not like what you hear."

Fran's smile turns feral as she sits forward and leans her elbows on the bar. "I regret nothing. Spill it."

I sigh and take another sip of the delicious coffee for strength.

"Okay," I start, and then come to my senses, glancing around the house. "Is Avery here?"

"No, he went kiteboarding."

I droop slightly, my last remaining defense shot down. "Sam and I fooled around in August when he was in Austin."

Fran's smile turns to a grin. "I knew it. He came back from that trip all smiles and avoidance. He wouldn't tell me a thing about his time there and why he was so late coming back. I know for damn sure it's the first time that man has ever missed a flight."

My mouth drops open, but I snap it closed, tucking that little tidbit of info away for later.

I need to focus here.

I know Sam's going to freak when he finds out about this conversation, so I need to minimize the damage as much as possible. I'll tell her the basics but leave out the incriminating details.

"We didn't talk at all after he left. He was pretty freaked out about Dom finding out and swore me to secrecy."

Fran mimes zipping her lips closed.

"When I got to the island, I could tell it made him nervous. He's a freaking catch, and I wouldn't mind seeing how things went between us, but I'm not sure he's going to go for it."

"So, no secret island hookups yet?" she asks, on the edge of her seat.

I roll my eyes. "The guy avoids me like the plague."

"But you've been talking."

I toss her a sly smile. "We've been texting."

Fran's mouth drops open. "Hot texting?"

She's loving this so much, and I wish I could feel the same.

I just feel like a traitor.

"Yeah."

Fran sits back in her seat and crosses her arms. "We've all been trying to get Sam hooked up with someone, but it's not an easy task. He's a particular guy, and he seems to have an idea of exactly who and what he wants. Finding that person on this island has proven impossible."

"All the other guys imported their ladies, right?"

She tosses me another smile. "That's right. And you're an import. You could be just who he's been waiting for."

I shake my head. "I imported too much baggage."

Fran's face twists as she considers. "Yeah, Dom's going to be a mountain to move. But every relationship has challenges."

"It's not just Dom. It's Sam and Dom. I'm not sure about the specifics of their relationship, but it's almost like Sam's afraid of the guy. Not that I don't understand that. I spent my whole life terrified to be alone with Dom. But that's little sister stuff. Sam shouldn't be afraid of him, right? Aren't they all partners in this business? Dom can't fire him."

Fran looks pensive. "I'm not a hundred percent sure of the

setup with all that, but I'll do some digging. Avery will spill just about anything if I have my top off."

Panic floods back in.

"You're going to tell Avery." It's not even a question. I know how this goes.

"Nah," Fran responds.

I narrow my gaze, pinning her with a questioning stare. "What do you mean, nah? Don't partners tell each other everything?"

I cringe as I let out a secret of my own. I don't know how these things work because I've never been in a relationship. I've had plenty of flings and dates and whatnot, but no one's ever stuck around.

Fran's either oblivious to my slip-up or decides to let it pass. "I tell him most things, but for something like this, I know for damn sure he wouldn't want to know. If presented with the info and the option to know or not know, he would choose to not know. Just to keep life at the resort less complicated. So, no. I'm not going to tell him."

I feel relieved, which turns out to be short-lived.

"But he's going to find out," Fran adds.

"What do you mean?"

Fran just laughs. "Everyone's going to find out. It's hard to keep a secret here."

I bite my lip and try to pretend I hadn't already come to a similar conclusion the second I set foot in that resort.

"The secret is really important," I say. "To Sam."

Fran's eyebrows lift. "But not to you?"

I shrug. "I don't have to live here and work with a pissed-off Dom every day."

Fran nods thoughtfully. "But you could. Live here, I mean."

I let my eyes wander around the airy, Spanish-tiled kitchen while I consider. "I guess. My Instagram is really Austin-based, so that would be a transition." I shake my head. "No. It would be starting over."

"Maybe a fresh start is what you need. It doesn't sound like things were exactly sunshine and rainbows in your old community."

It's certainly not the first time I've considered what she's suggesting. How could I not consider wiping the slate clean and starting over after such a huge blow? But it just feels like letting them win. If I disappear, tail between my legs, the bullies will have gotten their way. And I will have let them get away with it.

"Don't want to let them win?" Fran asks, reading my mind.

When I glance back up at her, I'm surprised to feel a rush of emotions that mist my eyes. I nod. "They shouldn't have done what they did. It wasn't fair. And if I never come back, if I disappear, they will have gotten exactly what they wanted. It almost seems like an admission of guilt."

"I get that. But you can't live your life trying to prove things to other people. How would that even work with your job? Can you truly create content from your heart if you're only doing it to spite a couple of mean girls?"

This woman is wise beyond her years. I suddenly feel even luckier to have landed here when my life crashed and burned. "I've thought about that for sure. And whether it's ever going to feel the same to hit publish on a post when I'm constantly worrying about whether it's going to be taken down by trolls." I drag my hands down my face. "The PR people told me to get a few posts ready to go for next week, but I can't even imagine what they'll be. All I can think about is how people could react poorly to whatever it is I choose to post. You're right. It's not going to work if that's how I feel."

Fran lays her hand on mine sympathetically. "That doesn't sound like a sustainable way to go on."

I close my eyes as the tears rise to the surface.

"But," she goes on, giving my hand a squeeze, "maybe it won't be like that. Maybe time will do its job and settle this mess into the past where it belongs."

I nod, not looking up. "Maybe."

"Until then, you're here, and you may as well make the best of it." Her tone brightens, and I lift my head to see her smiling encouragingly at me.

I wipe my eyes. "It feels great to be here. I feel safe, which is not how I felt in the city for the last week I was there."

"And we've got an absolutely insane wedding next week to help with the distraction."

I'm finally able to return her smile. "Tell me everything."

She wasn't kidding about the insanity. The couple has pulled out all the stops planning a lavish party fit for royalty. From the armored vehicles carrying vintage wines being brought over on barges, to the African tiger refuge that's having ten years of operating costs covered in exchange for bringing a few cubs to the island for pictures, the wedding plans Fran lays out for me are unreal.

"This is a content creator's dream come true."

She's grinning at me. "So, you'll do it?"

"Oh, yeah. You couldn't keep me away from this party if you tried."

"Fantastic. I've never had someone specifically looking for ways to capture a wedding as content, so you'll really be on your own. There will be a Sands photographer, and the couple has their own photographers, of course, but my thought was that you could just put on a party dress and let your inspiration guide you. I'll share some of the stuff you shoot with the couple, as a bonus, but they signed a waiver allowing us to use the images from their celebration in our own promotional materials, so I'll be holding back the best of the best for our own socials."

"Sounds like a blast."

"Anything you need? Camera-wise or anything else?"

I shake my head and my phone. "I've got the whole package right here."

Fran glances down at her own phone. "Shoot, I have to get to The Sands for the tasting. Do you want to come?"

I smile and shake my head. "I'll follow you back, but I have to get packed up. I'm moving up to Dom's this afternoon."

"Oh, that's right," Fran says as she gets up and starts packing the wedding notes in her portfolio. "No more private room to carry on secret affairs."

I laugh. "Not that there was all that much carrying on happening, but yeah. Moving into the belly of the beast is going to put a damper on any possible future trysts."

"Have you been out to Sam's place yet?"

"We're not exactly on going to his house together alone terms."

Fran looks at me like she's scheming. "It's pretty private."

I sigh. "I'll be waiting for my invite."

Rule #18

PRETENDING WORKS —UNTIL YOU ZOOM IN

NAOMI

We part ways in the resort lobby, Fran hurrying off to Raft and me slinking up to my room to pack. I didn't fully settle in over the last few days, knowing I'd have to move, but I still have items strewn from one end of the room to the other.

I'm just tossing my last bikini from the porch railing toward my suitcase when I catch my own reflection in the mirror. I smile at the girl there, tossing my hair and posing.

There's no denying it—island life looks good on me. I left my hair to dry naturally this morning after an early swim in the ocean, and it's dried into soft, beachy waves. I gave up on makeup, so my only highlight is my lash tinting, giving me a slightly glammed up natural look that I'm absolutely loving.

Even my curves, which I adore but still try to smooth out with flattering cuts and colors, look voluptuous and sun-kissed, from the tan lines on my shoulders to the new smattering of freckles on my chest.

I feel like a goddess.

Snatching up my phone, I do what I do best, capturing just the right angles, creating some really stunning images.

I can't post it to my socials yet, and somehow…I don't even want to. I've spent a lot of years dolling myself up in the freshest styles and hippest filters, trying to match my own face to the aesthetic of my perfectly curated channel.

The girl looking back at me from the screen doesn't fit the look at all, but somehow, I like her more.

On a whim, I pull off my top and run the hand not holding my phone over my bare breasts, enjoying how the cool breeze from the patio door sends goose bumps up my arms and pebbles my nipples.

I snap a couple shots that only include slivers of my face, focusing on the bare skin of my chest and the shadows cast by my fingers.

Glancing through them, I'm struck by the bold contrast and edgy rawness of my own image. I scroll back up a few weeks to some of the shots I took of myself in Austin. Meal prepping in a matching two-piece sweat suit. Sipping perfectly foamed matcha in front of a living green wall in a café down the street.

I pause on that picture in particular, zooming in to look closely at my face.

This was taken when I was happy.

Full days before I knew my life was about to come crashing down.

My hair and makeup are perfect, my outfit portrays the ultimate afternoon out with the lady friends vibe I was going for, even though I was completely alone. I'm smiling, like I always am, mouth open just slightly as if I'm laughing at something one of my besties said.

I scroll up even more, a frown spreading across my face as I see photo after photo with that exact same expression.

How could I not have ever noticed this before?

My signature look is just me pretending to be happy.

Pretending to be hanging out with my friends.

I scroll back down to the images I just took of myself, alone in my hotel room.

Most of them have my face cut off, but a few show my full expression. I zoom in on one and inhale sharply. There's no fake happiness. No pretending to be someone or somewhere that I'm not.

It's just Naomi. Real and raw and completely unfiltered.

Sam's face comes to mind as I'm looking at myself. I close my eyes and remember how it felt when he was looking at me. When he was touching me. I open them again, and the girl I see on the screen is exactly her.

I finally have words for how I felt when I was alone with that man.

Purely and completely in the moment.

It's how Sam lives his life, and when I'm with him, I feel like I could learn to do the same—if he would only let me.

The text conversation this morning went better than I expected after Sam's radio silence since the night before. When his line went dark after we'd both gotten off, I thought for sure I'd lost him.

Now I don't know what to think.

He's on my mind even more than he was in the weeks after he left Austin, and back then I was getting off to that video on the daily. Now that I'm here, and he's in on my little secret, the whole thing feels bigger. Meatier. Not like something shameful that hovers over my head, but something alive and growing.

Does he feel it, too?

I know I probably shouldn't send him topless pictures of myself while he's at an important meeting with Dom, Fran, and the wedding couple, but somehow the idea of him looking at me, thinking of me, in such an inappropriate setting makes it even hotter.

He doesn't have to look if he's too busy.

I literally have nothing to lose anymore.

I choose the best, most anonymous of the bunch and toss it

into our message feed, biting my lip in nervous anticipation as its status shifts to sent.

When it changes to read mere seconds later, I'm unable to contain my squeal of excitement. He's looking at me with Dom sitting right there. Maybe sitting next to him.

I shouldn't have sent it.

I could get us both in big trouble.

Why does that feel like the best part?

Rule #19

YOU CAN'T BE EVERYTHING WITHOUT LOSING SOMETHING

SAM

"And then we'll do the scallop course, paired with the Krug Clos," Fran is saying, gesturing to the artfully plated dishes of seafood, vegetables, and sauce Dom sets in front of the wedding couple.

The two smile up at him, eyes wide with delight.

This tasting has gone a lot smoother than I expected. Often, when you get people who are spending the kind of money these two are, they come with a lot of expectations and demands.

Not this couple.

They've been nothing but polite and gracious throughout the whole process. They have requests, sure, but they are happy to let Dom and his crew work their magic in the kitchen.

I've sat through enough tastings with picky couples, or worse, picky parents of young couples, to appreciate these two smiling faces.

My phone buzzes in my pocket, and I slip it out enough to peek at the screen, already anticipating what I'm going to find.

But she surprises me. It's not a text, it's an image.

I used a how-to on the internet to change my phone settings so message previews don't show on my lock screen anymore, so I can't see what the picture is, but I can imagine.

After that racy pic she sent me in my office this morning, I've been wondering when she'll send me another.

I'm in deep, deep shit with this girl.

Because there's no way I'm going to walk away.

I push my chair back silently and make my way to the bar where a water pitcher is set up with crystal tumblers for palate cleansing between courses. I pour myself a small glass and take a sip while I try to nonchalantly slide my phone back out of my pocket.

It slips from my fingers and crashes to the wood floor, making the whole table jump and look my way. I bow my head and retrieve the offending device, holding it up sheepishly.

"Sorry about that."

They all turn back to the tasting except Fran, who keeps me pinned with her knowing glare.

I'm not sure what, or how much, she knows, but she's onto something. She heard too much in the lobby last night when Naomi blurted out about the video. She's too smart to let something like that go.

I hold her gaze for a moment before casually glancing down at my phone screen as if I wasn't breaking out in a cold sweat under her glare.

I flip through a few emails, scrolling until I feel her turn back to the table. Checking just to be sure, I find her once again engaged with the wedding couple.

I shouldn't do what I'm about to do, but I'm doing it anyway.

I click to open the message and hold my breath.

It's Naomi, topless again, in front of the mirror. The sun is coming in at a sharp angle, casting her body in sepia stripes as she holds her fingers up against the glare. Her face is angled so I can't see most of it. To most casual onlookers, this could really be anyone, but that doesn't make me feel any safer about holding it in my hands right now. I'd know those curves anywhere. The soft swell of her breasts. The line of four freckles running from her left collarbone up toward her ear that I ran my tongue across while she moaned in my arms.

I'm sure the guilt of it is written right across my face.

I glance from the gorgeous, erotic, image of the woman who's been on my mind nonstop for the last few weeks up to the table where her brother is sitting.

And back down at my phone.

I let out the breath I'm holding as slowly and quietly as I can, shifting so that I'm facing the bar. It's dangerous to angle the screen so anyone from the table could come up behind me and see, but I can't very well stand facing them with my cock swelling in my pants.

I click the screen off and set the phone on the bar, taking another long drink of water. I have to get back to the table, but all I want to do is run to the elevator.

After a moment, I gather myself enough to return to my seat.

"Sorry," I say to the guests. "Employee emergency."

The bride smiles warmly at me. "You must be very busy running the whole resort."

I return her smile, slipping my phone back in my pocket. "I have plenty of help."

It buzzes immediately, and I try to keep my face calm.

Fran's hand lands on my arm, but I don't dare look over at her. "Sam's just being modest. He's the only one who can properly satisfy the guests."

My mouth opens slightly in shock, but I force it to morph into a smile. "Thanks, Fran."

My phone buzzes again in my pocket.

I'm not sure if Fran can hear it or if she's just trying to give me a hard time, because she doesn't let up.

"There are only a couple courses left, Sam. We can probably finish up here if you need to take care of something."

I offer her my best GM smile. "It's nothing that can't wait."

Dom sets out a new round of dishes, and everyone's attention shifts. I use the distraction to slip my phone out and open the message screen, carefully angling it away from Fran, who is sitting awfully close to me all of a sudden.

Naomi
Moving day.

I have exactly one hour left in this private room.
I wonder what I'll do with my last bit of freedom.

An image comes through as I'm reading the last message, and I cough in surprise, once again drawing the suspicious eyes of the woman next to me.

"On second thought, I think I have to go take care of this," I say, starting to rise.

"Employees getting out of hand?" Fran asks.

"They're just—"

"Needy?" Fran adds before I'm able to voice my lame excuse.

I offer her a tight-lipped smile as I push my chair in.

"Enjoy the rest of the tasting. We'll talk soon about guest check-in times, okay?" I say to the couple, who smile and nod.

I nearly collide with Dom as he's approaching the table with two new plates in hand. "Leaving?" he asks.

"Yeah," I say, backing away from the table, motioning with my phone. "I have to go deal with something. Employee stuff."

He raises his eyebrows but says nothing.

I keep backing away until I hit the doorway to the hall that leads back to the lobby, then I spin and make my escape.

I'm sweating.

My heart is racing.

Since when do I get the third degree every time I need to leave a room?

It's only then that my rational brain takes back over and offers me the sad truth.

It's probably all in my head.

Dom didn't say anything about me leaving.

Fran didn't call me out about Naomi.

My guilty conscience is blowing the whole thing out of proportion.

I've got to get it together.

But I don't know how.

I've never done anything like this before. I've never done anything bad in my life. I've never lied to anyone, let alone my closest friends.

It's only a matter of time before I fuck this all up.

It's gotta end.

I repeat the phrase over and over in my mind as I climb the stairs to the second floor and approach Naomi's room, glancing over my shoulder every other second to make sure I'm not being followed.

By the time I knock, I'm determined.

I'm going to end it.

Rule #20

FUCK IT

SAM

Naomi swings open the door wearing a sexy red lingerie set that leaves very little to the imagination.

I rush into the room, pushing her inside and closing the door quickly. "What are you doing? I could have been anyone."

She just laughs. "No one else is coming up here."

"I could have been your brother."

She huffs and rolls her eyes. "If that asshole was knocking on my door, I would have known it deep in my bones and probably gone to hide somewhere."

That catches my attention. "Why are you so afraid of him?"

Naomi's eyes raise until she's got me pinned in her piercing gaze. "I could ask you the same question."

I open my mouth to answer, but the words stick in my throat. The last thing I want to do right now is admit the truth of my situation. Not when she's standing there, looking at me like I'm worth something. "What do you mean?" is all I manage to stammer out.

She just waves her hand at me. "Never mind. I don't want to talk about my brother right now."

Her gaze falls to the floor, and she turns from me, walking over to the far wall where her suitcase is still splayed open and bursting with colorful articles of clothing. She lifts a pair of tiny pink shorts and bends over to start putting them on.

My reaction is automatic, instinctual.

I walk swiftly across the room, catch one of her wrists in my hand, and stop her before she can get her foot into the shorts. She gasps softly in surprise, almost losing her balance. I step in closer and steady her with my body pressed behind hers.

She straightens until she's got the full length of her smooth back pressed to my chest.

For a long moment, we just breathe together like that.

I don't remember telling my hand to slide from her wrist up to her shoulder. Or telling my fingers to trail softly over her skin, leaving a spray of goose bumps in their wake. Her breath catches when I graze my fingertips over her collarbone. I'm sure mine would catch as well—if I was breathing.

She doesn't stop me, so I continue my silent exploration of her nearly naked body, letting the softness of her curves speak to me in braille as I close my eyes and let myself enjoy the feel of her.

When my hand reaches her hip, I tilt my head down so my lips rest on the top of her shoulder, allowing my tongue to escape just enough to get the taste of her in my mouth. I feel her feel it. Feel her suck in a breath and lean into me just a bit harder. I tighten my grip on her hip to hold her to me.

I can't do what I want to do, which is throw her on the bed and claim every inch of her body. I can't take that kind of risk...

But what if all this holding back is the real risk? What if I lose my chance with her forever? Losing her seems like the worst idea, even if breaking it off was my plan not ten minutes ago.

"Sam," she whispers, and I realize my grip on her hip is

steadily tightening until my fingers are digging in, not wanting to let go. I relax my hand and feel her relax in my arms.

"We don't have to do anything. I know you're nervous," she whispers, causing my eyes to drop closed in shame.

She's not wrong. I'm nervous as hell.

But now that she's in my arms, I can't hear my logical thoughts over the sound of her soft breathing.

"Do you know how long I've waited to have my hands on your body again?" I ask.

She nods, and I smile. "I guess you do, don't you."

"I think about you all the time," she whispers. "At first, it was like I was obsessed. I watched the video every night and pretended you were there with me."

Her words hit the deepest parts of me, and I nearly buckle at the knees. If only I could tell her I was feeling the same. That I still am.

But as soon as I say those words aloud, as soon as I tell her how badly I want this, there won't be any way to hold back. So, I try to keep my response surface level. "I've never been much of a porn guy."

"But..." she responds, and I can hear the smile on her lips.

"But last night was incredible. I don't know what came over me. It was like I was under a spell or something."

"A spell you put yourself under?" Humor still dances through her tone as I let my hand drift back up to trace her navel.

"A spell you put me under, princess."

Naomi surprises me by spinning quickly in my arms until we're face-to-face. "That reminds me. Did you miss your plane that morning? You told me you had plenty of time. That you could stay for breakfast."

My mind reels wondering how she found that out. Who was she talking to about me? Who might know?

The answer comes to me quickly. "Fran."

Naomi cracks a guilty smile. "I didn't tell her. She just knew."

I let my arms fall to my sides, taking a step back. "This is a tough place to keep a secret."

"She's not going to tell anyone. Not even Avery."

I offer Naomi a small smile, even though the truth of the matter is far more complicated. This was always going to be a dangerous game. "I don't know what to do."

Naomi reaches down and pulls on the pink shorts, followed by a black tank top. I watch her in dismay. I'm not sure what I hoped would happen here, in a room at my resort with her brother on his way up, but it's definitely not happening now.

"We don't have to do anything. I know it's scary that someone already found out, but I didn't tell her much. And I didn't make it seem like it was an ongoing thing."

I'm equal parts relieved and heartbroken at her words.

And fully and completely fucked.

"Yeah, okay," I respond, just to say something.

"She's going to play it cool. So, we just play it cool, too, okay?"

I nod.

"Speaking of playing it cool, though. Seriously, Sam, you missed your plane?"

I shake my head as I feel heat rise to my cheeks. This wasn't something I ever planned on telling her. "I didn't want to leave."

Her smile, like the cat who caught the canary, is worth all my embarrassment. It twinkles up to her eyes and dimples her cheeks. "So, when you were sitting in my kitchen, telling me you still had a few hours…"

"My plane was probably boarding."

Her mouth drops open. "You never should have come over at all. You should have gone back to Houston that night."

"I had a car scheduled to pick me up at four that morning from my hotel."

"You blew off your whole trip home to hang out with me? Not even knowing what would happen in my bed?"

I shrug. "Is that so hard to believe? You're...you. Beautiful, smart, fun, and everything I've ever wanted."

She looks away quickly, and I follow her face with my gaze, trying to read the expression she wants to hide. When she doesn't respond or look back up at me, I take a step closer and catch her chin in my hand, turning her face to meet mine. The look she holds there is poorly masked sadness and regret.

My hand falls away, and she takes a step back.

"I wish you'd stayed longer," Naomi says finally, meeting my gaze. Her eyes are fierce, brimming with emotion.

"Yeah. I wish I'd stayed longer as well."

We stay locked in the heated stare for so long that I lose track of time.

When Naomi finally looks away, I'm almost grateful. I have no idea where that would have gone.

"What time is it?" she asks.

I slip my phone out of my pocket and grimace as the screen lights up. "Shit."

Naomi just turns back to the suitcase, throwing things in by the handful. I try to be helpful by gathering a few items draped over the desk chair. I should leave, but once again, I don't want to. Especially not when she told me she wished I'd stayed that morning. All I want to do is stay, even if it's the stupidest move right now.

I watch as she uses her full body weight to press the top of the stuffed suitcase and runs the zipper easily along its track, standing the roller up on end. She glances around the room, and I do as well.

"I'm not going too far if I forgot something."

She's not looking at me, so I surprise her just a bit when I come up behind, pulling her back to my chest once more.

"Naomi, I..." I trail off, resting my head on the top of hers. I watch her hair ripple gently with my breath, unsure of what to say.

"I know, Sam," she says quietly.

I'm sure she's just trying to make me feel better about this whole thing. The last thing I want to do is leave with so much unsaid, but it's hardly the time for whatever we need to talk about. Dom will be here in less than five minutes. He's not the kind of guy who runs late.

"What do you know?" I ask, refusing to allow her shifting body out of my tight grip.

"I know that this whole thing has to be kept secret, can't be anything more, and I'm stupid to get attached."

I close my eyes at her words, spoken so matter-of-factly.

"I'm an adult, Sam. I get it."

It's the resignation in her voice that breaks me. "Naomi, I've never wanted anything in my life as much as I want you to be mine."

I feel her knees go soft and her breath catch as my words land.

"But?" she offers, and I can hear the bitterness in her voice.

I relax my grip and take a tiny step backward, creating enough space between us that I can turn her around and look down at her. When she refuses to look up, I tilt her chin up with one finger. Our gazes lock, and I can see the war of emotions she's fighting.

"But this is complicated. There's no doubt about that," I say softly.

"Because of my scary brother?"

I cock my head to the side, considering. "Because of choices I've made over the last decade. Ones that involve your brother, yes."

Her eyes cast downward, and all of a sudden, the only thing that matters to me is not leaving this room with her thinking she's somehow not good enough.

"I get the feeling that you don't always feel as strong and amazing as you portray yourself to be. As you are," I start, and it's all I can do to speak the words, knowing what they will cost me. "But I see you, Naomi. And I know how amazing you are. So, if you forget, you can always come ask me."

She groans against my chest. "Why do you have to be so perfect?"

Her words are muffled but still surprise me enough that I laugh softly. "Born this way, I suppose."

She looks up at me then, not laughing. "I want you. I want this. I'm not going to pretend I don't."

I let my eyes close for a moment, the weight of her words heavy on my mind. "I want it, too, Naomi—"

I don't get to finish my thought as a booming knock echoes through the room. Luckily, I suppose. I have no idea what I was going to say.

Naomi laughs nervously and wriggles out of my arms. "Now that's a Dom knock."

"I guess I can hear the difference," I whisper.

"Fuck. You should have been long gone by now."

I follow her gaze around the room, knowing damn well there's nowhere to hide a fully grown man in here. I doubt I'm going to be able to shimmy under that bed.

"Coming!" Naomi shouts, tossing me a conspiratorial grin that I return with a shake of my head.

Two more bangs make us both jump a foot.

Then there's a beep, followed by the sound of the lock clicking open. Naomi and I both rush over to the door as it starts to open. Thankfully, I put on the chain lock when I came in, so it catches after opening only a few inches.

I stand with my back to the wall, a foot to the left of the door, as Naomi comes face to face with an angry Dom through the gap.

"Why do you have the chain on?" he demands, rattling the door against the restraint hard enough to be intimidating, but not hard enough to risk breaking it. He is one of the owners of this building after all.

"For safety, Dom. You never know when some guy is going to try to break into your room."

"I don't have time for this, Naomi. I need to get back to work."

"I'm almost ready, just give me a second. I'll meet you downstairs."

Dom huffs but backs off when he realizes she's not going to open the door. I watch with pride as she confidently stands her ground.

Not like she has a choice right now. It would be awfully hard to explain why I'm in her room with the chain lock on.

"I'm leaving the luggage cart here," Dom says, and I cringe at the condescending tone of voice. "I'll go pull the golf cart around. You better be down there in five minutes."

And then he storms back down the hallway, leaving the door ajar.

Naomi takes a full moment to calm down her breathing with her eyes closed before looking over at me and nodding. "Okay..." she starts but trails off when she sees my face. "What?"

"I can't believe he talks to you like that."

She rolls her eyes and turns back to start rolling her suitcases toward the door. "Oh, yeah. That's Dom. I used to call him Dinosaur Dom in my head when I was a kid. Still do sometimes."

"He's fairly short with most people, myself included, but I've always considered it to be just his way of being efficient." I shake my head, pushing away from the wall. "But that was just him being a dick."

She shrugs. "He's a dick, for sure. And not the good kind."

I watch her fumble with the retractable suitcase handle for a long moment before I catch myself and hurry over to help. Our hands touch on the plastic handle, and I should just pull away. I should drag the heavy luggage to the door and make my escape while I still can.

Instead, I pull her to me and do the thing I've been thinking about almost constantly since our night together in Austin.

Our lips meet, and I can tell she's a bit surprised by the sudden kiss, but she relaxes into it, parting for me to taste her. I close my eyes and savor her mouth, allowing my hands to drift down her body once more.

We stand in the center of the hotel room, in the eye of the storm that is our problematic secret tryst, and disappear into each other. Or, at least, I allow myself to disappear into her. Gone is the weight of my lies. Gone is the stupidity of wasting the incredible luck I was offered in the form of escaping from here undetected.

The only thing that exists is this woman's body. Her soft skin and the taste of her and the little noises she makes as I touch her everywhere all at once.

And even though I am the responsible, studious GM of a multi-million-dollar resort, it's Naomi who pulls away first.

"You have to go."

I close my eyes and rest my forehead against hers, not loosening my grip on her one bit. "I know."

"Go. I'll see you later, okay?"

"Okay," I respond, even though it's not okay at all. I came up here to get things settled, but they feel more unsettled than ever.

I came up here to tell Naomi this couldn't happen, and this thing between us had to end.

I almost laugh at how ridiculous that idea seems now.

This may be a terrible plan. It might mean the end of all I've worked for, all I've helped build here. But I'm not strong enough to walk away.

Rule #21

THE CRACKS BEGIN TO SHOW

SAM

"Sam, do you have a minute?"

The voice stops me in my tracks as I step into my office.

The answer is no. I'm just here to grab my keys before escaping to the oasis in the jungle that I call home for the rest of the day and my day off tomorrow.

"Of course, Maria, what's up?" I pocket my keys and lean back against my desk, trying to show her a calm, welcoming face.

She comes in and closes the door behind her.

Bad sign.

Maria has been dealing with some medical issues this season, and this isn't the first time we've met behind closed doors about it. The resort has been helping out with the bills from the local clinic, as insurance isn't a thing on this island, but deep down, I knew this day was coming.

"I'm…" Maria casts her eyes down as emotion overtakes her after only one word.

I take a step forward and lay my hand on her shoulder. "You're safe here, Maria. Take your time."

She brushes tears from her cheeks without meeting my eye. "I think it's time for me to go stay at my sister's house in the States."

I nod, even though she isn't looking at me. It was only a matter of time before she was going to need care that just isn't available at our little island clinic.

"I'm really sorry to hear that. I'm glad you have somewhere to go, though. Your sister is ready for you to move in?"

"Yes," she says, finally meeting my eye. "She's been trying to get me to move for months. She lives in a city, close to hospitals where I'll be able to start treatment if that's what I need."

"Well, I'm sad to see you go, but I'm happy to hear you'll be getting the treatment you need to stay healthy."

She nods sadly. "I know I'm leaving you in a bit of a lurch, Sam. I just took over the social media management this season, and already I'm having to quit on you."

I shake my head and start to speak, to tell her that nothing is more important than her health, but she waves me off. "I can still do the posting for as long as you need if someone can just send me pictures. I'll get that set up with the other front desk workers. Everyone can send a few pictures a week, and I'll still be able to make posts from the States."

"I'll rally the front desk in a meeting next week, and we'll come up with a plan, okay? You worry about getting yourself back to the States safely. Let me know how we can support you. I'll arrange the taxis and even the flights if you need."

Her smile is sad, but genuine. "Thanks, Sam. I'll be back just as soon as I can."

I return her smile, trying to keep my emotions in check. The last thing she needs is to see her own failing health reflected back to her in my eyes. "You'll always have a job here."

With pursed lips and damp eyes, she turns and leaves my office.

I drag my hand down my face. Between the incredible kiss upstairs and this terrible news, I'm feeling on the edge of becoming overwhelmed. I check my desk one last time to make sure I'm not forgetting anything and then make my escape.

Rule #22

HONESTY ISN'T THE PROBLEM—CLARITY IS

SAM

My house is three small buildings, in a low-lying area in the jungle on the north end of the island. It was built as employee housing for the estate further down the road but was sold off by the new owners when they turned the mansion into a vacation home. I was lucky enough to snag the property for a song the first year we moved to the island to start renovating The Sands.

The largest of the buildings is my main house. It has a large open room on the lower level with a finished bathroom and ladder loft. I've arranged the main room to function as a living room with a couch and small TV, as well as a kitchenette of sorts with a coffee maker and mini fridge. The actual kitchen is in the next building, separated from the main house by a short path. Last fall I installed a slanted, a-frame corrugated metal roof over the walkway, so I can stay out of the rain when heading over to cook in one of our many tropical rain showers.

It's a bit unorthodox, as the guys like to tease me about from the comfort of their mansions, but it's more my style. I love the feeling of living in a house that really could only exist in a place like this. All three of my friends and co-owners live in houses that could easily be in the States, or anywhere else, with imported furniture, central air, and massive refrigerators.

It's all so unnecessary and so out of place. Buildings like that exist at odds with the natural beauty of the tropics. My property embraces it.

I've upgraded a bit every year and finally reached a place where I can say that I have all the comforts I need. The covered walkway was a big improvement, and a few years back I installed a mini split AC unit in the main house, something everyone was amazed I went without for so long. I shrugged them off, but the hard truth of the matter is, I'm just not here all that often, and almost never in the hottest part of the day. I work long hours giving The Sands and its employees everything they need to thrive.

The upgrades I've completed over the last few years haven't been for me. They've been done with the future in mind. I would never admit to my friends that I was trying to get this place ready for a family, but I know they know. You'd have to be blind not to see it. The guys are a lot of things—spoiled, stubborn, arrogant—but they're far from unobservant. And they know me well.

The last of my three buildings has been the focus of my time and energy this season and will continue to be until I get it just the way I want. The single-story, one-room hut sits between the main house and the kitchen, forming a triangle. The covered walkway between that house and the main house is almost completed and when it is, I plan to finish the bed and build a shelving unit, as well as a window seating area in front of the large picture window that takes up most of the south-facing wall. It looks out over my small garden and the orchard of fruit trees planted by past residents.

The sleeping loft in the main house has been fine for me, but a proper bedroom is what's going to make this place a home.

I toss my keys on the counter and pull a bottle of light, local lager from my mini fridge and snuggle it into a blue foam koozie to take with me out into the yard. I glance at the couch and consider flopping down there, but there are too many usable hours left in the day to give in already.

I grab a rake and head down to the lower side of the north end, where the jungle is always trying to reclaim the land. I cut back the plants here yesterday morning, leaving the branches and palms in a neat mound. Using the rake and a broad, wide shovel, as well as thick leather gloved hands, I load everything into the wheelbarrow and push the thing down the narrow path into the jungle where I have my brush pile.

Looking down over the now clear area, a feeling of pride comes over me, bringing a smile to my lips. There really is no greater satisfaction than seeing the finished product of your own hard work. I wish more people understood that.

I peel off my shirt and use it to mop sweat from my brow. It's a hot time of day to be out here working, but I use the time I've got. I spot a project I've been putting off in a shady part of the yard and head over there.

Three hours later, the shadows are growing longer, and I get my first mosquito bite. I guess it's time to call it a day. Outside, anyway. There's plenty of work to be done in the house after I relinquish the yard to flying insects.

In the outdoor shower connected to the main house, I close my eyes and let the refreshing water wash away the day. It was one for the records, that's for sure. I've been keeping the thoughts at bay with grueling manual labor, but now that my body's at rest, they all come flooding back.

Naomi is incredible. Every moment with her is incredible.

And incredibly stupid.

I had plenty of time to come to my senses after our night together in Austin, and I let it all go at the first sight of her. I was defenseless from the moment she stepped off the boat with her rolling suitcase and bright smile.

And then she ambushed me with that video, something I

should still be pissed about, but anger toward her for taping our private moments is the last thing I'm feeling. Just the thought of the video, ready for me to hit play at any moment, has my cock stiffening, cool water be damned.

I should check my phone.

I laugh to myself as I duck my head under the water, rinsing off the last of the soap and dragging my hands down my face. That damn plastic rectangle is on my mind all day. I'm honestly surprised I left it in the house during my afternoon of yard work.

I hit the faucet, water conservation always at the front of my mind, and dry off with a towel still warm from the sun. When I get into my living room, striped towel tucked around my waist, I walk straight to my phone like it's a beacon calling to me.

No messages.

Okay. That's fine.

When I left her, she was loading her suitcases into the cart to be taken to Dom and Reina's house. I'm sure she's busy unpacking and getting reacquainted with her brother after many years of little to no contact.

I bite my lip as I think back to the conversation we had when I first entered her hotel room earlier.

"Why are you so afraid of him?"

"I could ask you the same question."

I know damn well why I'm apprehensive about putting my relationship with Dom on shaky ground. But, while it would make my life more challenging, I'm not exactly afraid of him.

Not like Naomi seemed to be.

I've known Dom my whole life. I know the guy isn't violent or abusive. But he does lean toward controlling, and he's stubborn as hell. I frown, imagining her growing up with him and their father as the only family she had to lean on.

Naomi's mother died right after she was born, some kind of complication with the pregnancy or birth that was never explained to me. I have a memory of her funeral so vivid it almost feels like a scene from a movie. The whole family in dark clothing with somber expressions stepping up to the grave to toss white roses onto the lowering casket.

After that day, their mother was never mentioned again. It was an unspoken rule, but one everyone obeyed. Granted, I didn't spend a lot of time around Dom's younger sister, so it's very possible she had other support systems in place, kinder ones. But if she did, I never saw them.

I only remember hearing about the tragedy of Naomi's birth mentioned one time after that, passing by their father's library on my way up to Dom's bedroom one day. He was speaking on the phone, and I distinctly remember hearing the words, "Nothing but trouble, since the day she was born."

When I got to Dom's room, I asked if his sister was okay, and he told me she had been in trouble at school again for skipping class and dress code violations.

That memory haunts me now. The idea that she could have been told over the years that her mother's death was somehow her fault. That the man of the house considered her a sorry replacement for the woman he loved dearly. I don't know how I could ever ask her about it, but I hope someone did. I hope there's someone out there who tells her she deserves to be here, no matter how her birth changed the family.

But I doubt Dom is that person.

Somehow, my phone is back in my hand. Or possibly I never set it down to begin with. I stare at the screen for too long, finally shaking myself out of the trance it seems to have me under. I check to make sure the ringer is on, so I'll know the moment I get a message, and leave it on the counter to get dressed.

Another hour with no messages, and I'm officially concerned. I sit on a stool at the kitchen bar and watch the reflection of the ceiling fan in the dark phone screen.

I should go over there.

No, that's crazy.

I should send a message.

But what if she's in a place where someone sees her phone and reads the message?

I don't know what to do. My eyes drop closed as the impossibility of the situation starts to make my head ache.

The phone chimes so loud I nearly fall off the stool. I snatch it up and stand, wider awake in this moment than I've been in hours.

A photo message from Naomi. It's her standing in what I know is Dom's living room, the panoramic view of the ocean and sky behind her. I can tell from the color of the sky that it was taken at least an hour ago, her face partially shadowed by the back lighting of bright sun.

She's smiling.

I text back immediately.

Sam
Settling in?

Naomi
I'm officially canceling my gym membership.

A wide grin spreads over my face. I know exactly what she means by that.

Dom bought his island mansion while we were still in New York, haggling the sale price of the resort with the brokers. At the time, it seemed to me a show of optimism on his part that was wildly out of character. We didn't even own the resort yet, and he was already buying a house. He was the most excited about the prospect of the new resort, second only to me, and the idea of finally getting his own kitchen to create the restaurant of his dreams.

When we showed up on the island to sign the paperwork and Dom got to take possession of his new house, what we found there is the stuff of legends. Of all the squabbles and actual fights we've had as a group of four guys, never did I worry for the safety of my two friends as much as I did when they stood at the base of the hundred white stone steps that led up to Dom's new house.

The only way up to Dom's new house, we learned.

Avery and Ben had a riotous time poking fun at him while I tried to help him make the best of it. When he finally snapped and turned on the guys, it took all my strength to hold him back from pummeling them.

Over the years, we've all gotten used to it, but it's still a sight to behold for anyone new to the island or Dom's house. One hundred and six steps up and one hundred and six steps down. Each and every time.

He installed a handrail when Reina moved in, which I'll never admit to being grateful for.

Sam
It's pretty incredible, huh?

Naomi
Yup. He told me he prefers it this way. 🙃

While it feels disloyal to be making fun of my friend behind his back, I can't help but smile again at that.

Sam
I'm sure he did.

How's your new room?

Naomi
Huge. Gorgeous, of course. I'm sure I'll feel right at home here...

I bite my lip and consider her statement. Being relatively new to extended text conversations, I still struggle with discerning tone. I decide to change the subject.

Glancing around the room, I look for something in my own house that feels worthy of sharing with her. This place is no hilltop mansion, but I'm proud of it. I decide on the window over the sofa, where the sunset is just visible through the trees and the white magnolia flowers just outside glow almost golden in the warm light.

I snap the picture and send it. Naomi responds right away.

Naomi
Beautiful! I heard you have your own property somewhere. Can I see it sometime?

I glance back at the cozy green sofa, cast in slanted light from the window. I can imagine her there, smiling up at me as she curls her bare legs beneath her. I have to close my eyes as a pang of longing hits me so hard it takes my breath away.

Sam
Of course.

I don't know how it'll work, but I'm not about to deny her anything.

Naomi
I'm having dinner with Reina tonight while Dom works. I'll be down at the resort tomorrow helping Fran with wedding stuff. See you then?

The thought of waiting until tomorrow to see her, then seeing her only at the resort, surrounded by people, is not what I was hoping for.

Sam
Sounds good.

Naomi
Well, I guess this is goodnight...

The three dots at the end of her sentence nearly give me a heart attack. What does she mean by that? Does she mean that it's actually not good night, and there's more coming? Did she hit the extra punctuation by accident?

I'm once again baffled that people use this as their main form of communication. It's no wonder the world is splintering into disarray.

Sam
See you tomorrow

I purposely leave my sentence open, with no period, just in case she wants to keep messaging. I grind my teeth at the sloppy look of my sentence fragment as it hangs in the conversation thread. I quickly add a smiling sun emoji and hit send.

Naomi sends back a palm tree.

I've never been so confused in my life.

Rule #23

THE BATTLE LINES ARE DRAWN

NAOMI

I wake up in the big, soft, unfamiliar bed and lay still for a long time, looking out at the view of the hills behind the house that are visible from the parted curtains in my room.

I guess this is home. For now, anyway.

I can hear movement in the house, wooden chair legs on tile floors, and voices drifting softly in the warm air.

Getting dressed in soft shorts and a cropped bathing suit top, with every intention of spending my day in the sun and water, I head out to face my new roommates.

Reina and I had a great time at dinner the night before. She's an incredible person, genuinely kind and open. Thoughtful and observant.

How she ended up with Dinosaur Dom I'll never understand.

Big bro worked until long after I went to bed, pink wine lulling me to sleep after Reina and I got the kitchen cleaned up. It was a big day for a lot of reasons, my move being the least interesting of the lot.

Every time I close my eyes, and even sometimes when they're open, my brain tortures me with flashing images of that kiss in my hotel room. The feeling of Sam's hands on my body.

I can still smell the man on my skin.

I hear his words like the soundtrack to my life.

I see you, Naomi. And I know how amazing you are.

I spent the whole evening with Reina distracted and inconveniently turned on, the brush of my thighs together mixing with the memories of him sliding his hands over my stomach and hips, his strong fingers gripping me there. As much as I enjoyed my time getting to know my future sister-in-law, it was often a struggle to focus.

I would have loved to tell her. To tell anyone.

I bite my lip as tears swell in my eyes for the millionth time at the thought.

There's no one left. Even my so-called best friend, the woman who I spent the last decade sharing everything with, turned out to be just as fair-weather as the rest of them.

My phone, after years of being the melodic, disco-ball center of my universe, sits still and dark on my bedside table.

I shake it off as I reach the end of the short hallway that leads into the kitchen. I'm fine. This is going to be fine. It's a tough period right now, but time will smooth things over.

Besides, I do have Fran. I just need to get to her.

I smile at the tiny rush of excitement that blooms in my chest at the thought of how thrilled she's going to be by this new development.

Sam wants me as much as I want him. Even though the whole thing is complicated, seemingly impossible, he said the words.

"You're looking awfully chipper this morning," a gruff male voice says, wiping the smile from my lips.

"Morning, Dom."

"I was just starting to wonder when you'd make an appearance."

Anger flares in me hot and bright. "It's not even eight o'clock. Are you seriously going to start this day by criticizing how late I slept?"

Dom holds up both hands in surrender, as if my defensive response was completely out of line.

"Good morning," Reina's singsong voice comes around the corner, and I look at her gratefully.

Maybe I can just ignore the guy. It's worked fine for most of my adult life.

"Grab a cup of coffee and join us on the patio. We want to talk about a couple of things."

I like the sound of that about as much as I'd like the idea of a trip to the gallows, but I don't see any way around it.

I take my time stirring cream and sugar into my cup in the now silent kitchen before marching out to the patio like a woman on death row.

The two of them sit side-by-side in deck chairs facing me. Dom's arms are crossed, his signature scowl in place. Reina's hand rests on his forearm, and she leans forward slightly, face kind and welcoming. I wonder for the millionth time what she's doing with my brother.

"Is this some kind of intervention?" I joke as I settle into the chair one of them arranged directly across from where they sit.

Reina's face softens, and it looks like she's about to speak, but Dom beats her to it.

"We just want to have a chat about what's going on with you. What your plan is."

This is more or less exactly what I expected, so I just sigh and shrug. "I'm just laying low for a bit, and then I'm going to get my life back on track. I won't be here forever."

"That's not what we're worried about."

I open my mouth and close it. If they aren't concerned that they just gained a permanent houseguest, then what is this?

"I'm just confused about what your plan is for the rest of your life."

My eyebrows shoot up, but I say nothing. There's no point. He's just getting started.

"You're thirty-two years old, still three years away from the stable income the trust is going to provide you."

I bristle at the mention of the trust, something that's been the topic of discussion at many, many family meals in our household growing up.

My grandparents built a financial empire capable of supporting us all for the rest of our lives. Hell, it could have supported a small country for a decade. But they were concerned their children and grandchildren would turn into a bunch of lazy, do-nothing people, like so many of their friends watched happen. So, they added stipulations to the trusts. Thirty-five or graduated with a master's degree before you could access any of the fortune set aside for you.

Dom did his MBA right after college, while he was still stringing our father along about joining him at the family firm. But the second his trust account was unlocked, he was gone, and he never looked back.

I remember those years vividly. I was a teenager, struggling to find myself and my place in the world, when Dom dropped the news that not only would he not be joining my father at work, he was headed to Europe to work in restaurants. He told me I could come with him, but I assumed he was joking.

To say that my father gave up on life would be a sorry understatement.

Dom was his plan. His legacy. There was no chance I was going to replace him, so my father didn't even try. He allowed me to follow my passion for photography and art and pursue a degree in visual arts, even though Dom had to get his in finance or risk being cut off.

My father shrank into himself, spending more and more time at the office until it reached the point where he didn't come home from the city for weeks at a time.

Our house became even more of a tomb than in my early years, when the family was in mourning over my dead mother.

And I learned just how unimportant I was to them. Invisible. Non-existent.

My junior year of high school, I would spend hours setting up artsy shots for social media, building my life into a rich, happy place like a diorama for people to scroll on their phones.

The internet became my family.

It was all so much simpler than my real family. Instead of having to show up and be someone these stick-in-the-mud men thought I should be, I could show up exactly as myself, represented in whatever way suited me best, and everyone would follow right along. They would see me and like me.

I learned to curate my life for the tiny screen and found that I was really good at it. I ran a lifestyle blog through college when that was popular, followed by Tumblr, and finally Instagram.

No one could control me because I was completely in control of my image. They saw what I wanted them to see.

And people were always watching.

It's addictive, that kind of attention. I watched myself transform from an artsy teen posing with flowers and graffiti art to a polished, confident authority on how life should be lived. When I spoke, people listened. When I did something, they all wanted to do it too.

I had no idea what a house of cards I had built for myself. Blinded by the little hearts into believing that I was important to those people.

"I got a call from our father last week."

My attention shoots back to Dom as he drops this bomb. "What? He called you?"

He hasn't called me. Not since I called to let him know that I was leaving the city for a while and why. I wouldn't have bothered, but again, I'm not thirty-five, so I needed him to bolster my accounts more than usual for a while until I could get things back on track.

He refused.

"Apparently he wants to start taking part in his children's affairs again, and he's decided to take his last few decades of failure out on you," Dom says, and I almost feel a hint of camaraderie from him as I consider how similar our positions are right now.

I let out a sigh, having exactly nothing to say about our father. Turns out, Dom has plenty.

"I had no idea things were still so bad."

I take a full moment to process the words while running my finger along the rim of my pale teal and cream porcelain mug before the possible meaning sinks into my mind.

I want to be angry at his intentional ignorance, but the wave of emotions is too exhausting.

"Yeah, well..." It's not meant to be a statement, simply a filler.

"I thought you were doing well. I follow you, you know."

I glance up at that, into his calm, curious eyes. The same dark eyes that I've been trying to get to see me for my whole life finally are. Or maybe I'm just now brave enough to look into them.

"You follow me on Instagram?"

"Yes. I have an account to follow The Sands and you."

I catch movement out of the corner of my eye and find Reina there, nodding, signature smile in place.

I can't help but smile as I shake my head, still processing this information. "What's your username?"

He looks to Reina who just rolls her eyes. "It's whatever they gave me. User 6537 or something. Reina wanted to help me upload a photo of our sunset as my profile picture, but we never got around to it."

"You're a bot," I joke, even though I feel more like crying.

Dom shrugs. "I guess so."

"Well, then you know more about what I've been up to than I do about you, I guess."

He sits forward, elbows resting on knees, and pins me with those intense eyes once more. But again, the longer I hold his gaze, the more welcoming and human it becomes. Is it possible I missed the real person in there for all these years?

"I thought you were doing pretty well. Your pictures and the things you type really make it seem like you're on top of the world."

My eyes fall down to rest on my hands where they cradle my mug. "Well, that's the idea."

"If things were going badly, you should have said something. Should have reached out."

My defenses fly up to greet him. "Everything was going pretty well. Until it wasn't. It happened so suddenly. I'll get back on track."

He sits back in his chair, arms crossed. "I thought a lot about what you said at the bar the other night. About how your job works and how everything went wrong. Then I compared that with the image of you I had from watching your Instagram for all these years. I can't shake the feeling that it's all fake, and I should be worried about you."

I sit up straighter as anger rises from my belly to my lips. "You have not contacted me in years." The last word comes out as a hiss.

Dom refuses to back down. "I told you already. I thought you were doing okay."

The audacity. "And the only reason you would ever need to call your little sister would be if she was not living up to your standards? What about just to say hi?"

"The phone works both ways."

I nod, holding back the tears that threaten to brim in my eyes as emotion overtakes me. "I suppose that's true enough. I just chose to use mine to call people who support me. People who give a shit about my life enough to be there for me."

"Oh, you mean your internet friends who won't be associated with you now because it might hurt their follower count?"

I drop my head to stare directly into my lap as the first tear falls. Because yeah, I did mean those people. Those were the only people I had. And he's right, I ~~have~~ no one now.

Even when this whole thing eventually blows over, I'll never be able to go back to the way it was. I'll never be able to trust that community or feel like I'm a valued friend.

It hits me right now for the first time. It's really over. I have nothing.

Even if I get my channel back, it was always about way more than the channel. It was my life.

And now it's over.

"Yeah. You're right." I nod, still not looking up to see whatever smug look is on his face at having so successfully taken me down a peg. "I put my trust in people, and they betrayed me. Sorry to be such a disappointment."

"Naomi, what Dom's trying to say is that he's—we're—concerned for you. We want to help in any way we can."

I look up then, straight into the earnest, eager eyes of my brother's twenty-something fiancée. What the hell does this woman know about me and what's going on with my life? The only reason she's sitting here right now, in a position to be offering comfort and advice is because she snagged herself a rich boyfriend.

Would they still be so worried about me if I was hooked up with a multimillionaire?

I sit up straighter as the thought hits me.

I am the fucking multimillionaire.

I don't get to skewer her with my cutting new insight, however, because Dom jumps in first, doing the thing Dom always does.

"I wouldn't be so worried if you were in some kind of a relationship. You're thirty-two years old. Have you thought about trying to settle down? Get married?"

I knew it. My mouth drops open, all confidence sucked out of my chest, replaced with impulsive stupidity.

"Sam told me that you threatened all the men on this island to stay away from me or risk bodily harm."

Definitely shouldn't have said that...

Dom narrows his eyes at me but says nothing. I can almost see his mind working. I need to distract him and quickly.

"Maybe I'll go find myself a nice pool boy to hook up with. Would that make you happy?"

Dom's face remains impassive. "Like *Sam* said," the inflection he puts on Sam's name sends a chill through me. "There isn't a pool boy on this island who will touch you."

I throw up my hands in exasperation. "Which is it, Dom? Do you want me to settle down, or do you want no guy to ever touch me?"

Again, he refuses to allow me to rile him. "Don't you want to find someone?" He glances sidelong at Reina, who's smiling at him like he hung the damn moon. "It's pretty great."

My mouth drops open at the uncharacteristic display of affection, as subtle as it was, but I snap it shut.

I'm on my feet before I realize it's happening. "Of course I do!"

My shout falls on two surprised faces.

"Of course I want to find someone. It's just...not that easy. I'm not exactly the kind of person people want to date."

The truth is far more complicated, but my words have already done their damage—to myself. I spin and escape into the house before anyone can try to comfort me with empty words.

I have to get out of here.

Collecting my few essentials into a canvas bag, I start the asinine journey down all one million steps to the sandy road below the house. I know they can see me from the porch, so I keep my pace quick but steady. I keep my face stern but calm.

I'm not used to making such public admissions of my own shortcomings—or admitting that things aren't perfectly the way I want them. Everything I do in life is intentional. If it's not, I find a way to make it look intentional for my channel. Or I hide it away.

I have no idea what to do now that one of my deep, dark secret feelings is out in the open like this.

I only make it about twenty feet down the sandy path before Reina catches up to me. I startle and glance back at the house, wondering if there's some secret elevator they failed to mention.

Maybe the woman just has calves of steel after living in that house for so long.

"That got a little off track, Naomi."

"Sorry to bum you guys out with my loser life."

She easily keeps pace with me as I huff down the sandy road. "That's not what I meant. Dom…well, he can be stubborn and overprotective, but he really does mean well."

I stop short and turn to face her, planning to give her a piece of my mind about how that man thinks he can just say whatever he wants and then send his girlfriend down to smooth things over, but she just looks so…nice.

I grind my teeth and say nothing.

She must see the indecision on my face, because hers softens further. "He wants you to be happy."

There's no stopping the eye roll that statement produces. I shake my head and keep walking.

"I'm serious. This whole situation really threw him. I've never seen anything like it. He worries about you, you know. Always has."

"No, Reina. That may be what he told you, but it's far from the truth. When you worry about a person, you check in on their well-being. You speak to them more than once every five years. He had my whole life to look out for me when I was living on that estate, being raised by nannies and trying my best to stay out of the way of my father who blamed me for all his problems. Instead, he ignored me completely when I was a kid and continued to ignore me for my whole life. And now, he somehow thinks that he has a right to step in and tell me that how I choose to live isn't good enough?"

I shake my head again, trying and failing to keep the emotion out of my voice. At least it's just Reina who's about to watch me cry. I'd rather throw myself off the bluff than break down in front of Dom.

Reina lays her hand on my shoulder, and I slow my pace until I'm stopped again, staring down the path in front of me.

"That is all valid and true," she says in her soothing voice. I brace myself for the but. "But Dom lost his mother that day, too. He—"

That's the end for me. I shake her off and spin around on the sandy path, unconcerned about how I look or how emotional my voice is going to sound.

"Reina, that man has had my entire life to play siblings and commiserate over the loss of our mother. He never even tried. And now, now that he's so worried about my future? You heard him. He's only worried that I'm not married and popping out babies. He doesn't care about who I am or what I want in life. You can go back and tell him to drop the fake worry act. I didn't believe it before, and I don't believe it now."

I spin once more and head down the path as the tears break free and careen down my cheeks in rivers. Reina doesn't follow.

I reach The Sands in record time, wiping my face and hoping people will assume I'm just flushed from the morning heat, which is already making me sweat. It was hot in Austin, but this hot is different. It surrounds you like a fog anytime you step away from the ocean breeze.

The front desk lady solemnly informs me that there isn't a single room available, and won't be for weeks, but lets me sweet-talk her into handing over the keys to a golf cart.

I sit on the vinyl seat, grateful for the shade of the roof, wondering what on earth to do next. While it's true that my father blew his top and refused to fund my little island getaway,

I'm by no means broke. I could rent myself a room somewhere and move on with my recovery—alone.

I don't even know why I chose to come to this stupid island. I could have gone anywhere in the world. There must be a thousand tiny islands just like Faraday I could have chosen. Probably much cheaper ones. Did I really think that Dom was going to be a different person all these years later? That he would welcome me with open arms and be excited to hear about what I'd been up to in the years he missed?

I snort at the thought, shaking my head.

No, that wasn't it. Sure, heading to Faraday was a questionable choice, but when I needed somewhere safe to land, it was the first thing that came to mind. But the reason wasn't Dom.

It was Sam.

I jam the keys into the ignition, decision made but hesitate before clicking the cart on. I know where I want to go, who I want to be comforted by. But things between us have gotten more complicated over the last week. I'm no longer the blast from the past who he hooked up with one time on vacation. We're teetering on the edge of stepping into "something more" territory, even though neither of us understands how that could work.

Like Fran said, it's not like you can have a secret relationship on this island. No one would be dumb enough to think that. The fact that we've gotten away with it for this long is amazing.

I grip the steering wheel hard as I consider my next move. I know what I want to do. I know that I don't give a damn about furthering the damage to my already smoldering relationship with my brother. But I also know how Sam feels about it. He's so sure that this thing between us will fracture his working relationship with his business partner, ruining a lifelong friendship. As a recent scandal survivor, I can certainly understand his hesitancy to burn his whole life to the ground. And as a recent survivor of Dom's wrath, I know that Sam's probably right about how the whole thing will end up.

But there's another side to this coin. There's the side that becomes increasingly hard to ignore every time we're together. It was lit up like a neon sign when he was in my hotel room yesterday.

"I get the feeling that you don't always feel as strong and amazing as you portray yourself to be. As you are. But I see you, Naomi. And I know how amazing you are. So, if you forget, you can always come ask me."

And that settles that.

Rule #24

IF THIS ISN'T REAL, DON'T WAKE ME UP

NAOMI

Reina pointed out the tiny road through the jungle that leads to Sam's property the first time she took me to town, but that was apparently not enough information to find the place.

I spend nearly an hour going back and forth on the road I'm sure is the one she pointed to before I finally see the little turn off marked with a green wooden palm tree sign that leads down the next tiny jungle road.

I pause at the head of the driveway and try to gather myself a bit, not wanting to show up flustered and sweaty.

I want to get flustered and sweaty after I show up…

No. That's not why I'm here. It might be a happy side effect of showing up, but the reason I came is to talk this over with the only person on the planet who knows enough to understand.

When I finally get up the nerve to pull my cart in beside his, Sam's standing on the porch, hands on his hips, grinning at me. My heart leaps, and relief pours through me. I'm not sure where I got the idea that everyone's always going to be disappointed when it's me showing up, but it was probably my childhood where everyone was always disappointed it was me showing up. I'm always braced to smile in the face of their dismay.

"I was just about to come looking for you," Sam calls as he comes down the steps toward where I parked. He gathers me out of the cart and into his arms, and I swear to god I almost fall apart.

"What do you mean? How did you know I was coming?"

I glance up and watch his smile turn into a sly grin. "Reina called Fran, who called me. I called The Sands and learned about your golf cart heist."

He's holding me tightly as he says the words, his voice filled with kindness and humor and worry. I'm beside myself with the feeling of belonging. Something I've watched other people feel my whole life but never quite figured out for myself.

"The front desk lady was a total pushover."

He laughs, and heaven and earth move.

"Come on, you must be hot after all that driving."

"I got lost."

"It's easy to do. Next time, just call me, okay?"

"Oh, okay. I just didn't know if you'd...you know. Tell me not to come."

I can feel his body stiffen, and I hold my breath, waiting for him to agree. Waiting for him to tell me he's going to grab me a bottle of water and send me on my way before I ruin his entire life.

"These days, all I think about is having you here."

My brain repeats the words three times silently to itself before finally accepting them. I can't even begin to form a response, so I just lean heavily into his side as we make our way up the few steps to his front porch.

He lets me go to open the door, and I turn in a full circle on the deck, really seeing my surroundings for the first time.

We're in an oval-shaped clearing in the jungle, large enough that I can only just see the far end from here. There are three small buildings in a little gathering, all painted ocean blue. I stand on the threshold of the largest one. I can see two smaller structures off toward the far end of the property, maybe sheds.

The three larger buildings have sandy trails connecting them, neatly lined with large, smooth rocks and covered with tin roofs. As I glance around, I see fruit trees, heavy with ripening fruits that I don't recognize from here. There's a grid of raised beds filled with squash vines and tomatoes in green wire cages.

This is incredible.

And not in the Instagram "take a picture and post it" kind of way, but in the "I want to stay here and live quietly for the rest of my life" kind of way.

"I thought your place was—" I break off, putting my foot directly into my mouth as I try to find a way to soften the harsh way I've heard people describe his house. "A work in progress?"

Sam steps over to stand shoulder-to-shoulder with me with his arms crossed and cocks his head, following my gaze out into the yard. "It's definitely a work in progress."

"Yeah, but..." How to put into words what I'm seeing right now? What I'm feeling? "It's amazing."

Sam slides his arm around my shoulders and pulls me in tight to his side. I melt.

"I'm glad you like it. Come see inside."

The tour starts in the main house, as he calls it, which is the largest of the three small buildings and is essentially the living room. My eyes fall on the sofa, and I flush a bit imagining him there, watching the video I sent. Or was he in his bed?

I need to see his bed right away.

He follows me up the wooden ladder to a sleeping loft that he explains is his temporary bedroom until he gets the other building finished. It's simple, in a bachelor pad kind of way, with forest green sheets and a small yellow lamp painted with faded flowers that looks like it could have come with the house.

It's clean, though, and that's what matters. I can almost smell the warm breeze that dried his sheets on the line outside.

I crawl up until I've got my head on one of the pillows,

kicking my sandals off before curling up and closing my eyes. When I open them and glance back to find Sam, he's still on the ladder, watching me.

"No afternoon nap?" I ask, trying to bring lightness to the moment that's starting to feel heavy.

I meet his eyes, and the heaviness grows. There's something there. Something about the way he's watching me, arms folded at the top of the ladder, chin resting on his forearms. Like I'm a mirage he's waiting to watch disappear.

"It's hard to breathe when you look at me like that," I manage finally, not lifting my head from his pillow. It smells like him, and I want to take it home with me.

"Like what?" Sam asks, chin still resting on his arms, eyes pinning me to the spot.

"Like..." I know what I want to say, but I also know I have to soften the blow. No point in ruining all the fun we've been having with a wet blanket of sad feelings. "Like you're glad I'm here."

"Is that so hard to believe?" He sees right through my statement and into the darkness of my heart.

I close my eyes again for a moment before answering. "It's just not a look I'm used to getting, I guess."

"How can that possibly be true?"

I shrug, officially regretting saying anything and needing this moment to end before I end up in tears. "Show me the rest of the property?" My voice betrays me, and I watch Sam consider, taking a deep breath in and then out, his eyes searching mine the whole time.

Finally, he reaches out to touch the only part of me close enough, the heel of one foot. His fingers are like electricity, heating me with sparks straight to my core. "Come on, then."

I follow him down the ladder and out the side door, where he leads me down the short, rock-lined path to the second largest of the three blue buildings. I glance up and smile at the tin roof, tacked together in neat, straight lines, but obviously recycled or reclaimed metal sheeting. He passes through the white wooden door and holds it open for me. I meet his eyes, and finding that same loving look still there, I quickly glance down at my sandals.

I don't know what to do with this. These looks are sending me signals that our situation can't support. Does he want me or want me to stay a secret? How can it be both? Secret love? Is that a thing?

I shake it off and walk past him into the mid-sized roundish room.

And stop dead in my tracks.

From the outside, this looks like any other small, octagonal building. But inside…

It's not quite finished, as Sam said, but I can see the vision. He whitewashed the walls and hung sheer white curtains on all eight of the tall, narrow windows. The floors are sanded and polished mahogany, something I recognize after being told about the natural mahogany forests on the nearby islands and shown how it was used for much of the flooring at The Sands. I wonder if these pieces were left over from that. They come together across the room in small chunks, fitted expertly end to end. The slight variations in color give the room a rustic, woodsy feel. I bet if the curtains were all pulled aside, lying in here would feel a lot like being in a tropical forest.

In the center of the room is an almost finished bedframe, mahogany as well, with four sturdy posts and ladder-like head and footboards. I glance up at the vaulted, circular ceiling and see a skylight at the very top, the brilliant blue sky smiling down at me from above.

"That thing used to leak like crazy, but I got it sealed."

Sam's voice drags me out of my stupor, and I glance over at him.

"It'll be amazing to weather the big rain showers in here. Once it's all done, of course."

"It's fantastic. You did all of this?"

He looks down, and I can tell he's about to go humble on me. "The building was already standing, but..." He smiles as I roll my eyes at him. "Yeah. I've been working hard to get this room to match the vision I had when I first saw it. And I'm very nearly there."

"It looks perfect to me. You just need to drag that mattress out of the loft, and we could sleep here." I stop short as I realize what I just said. When I dare to look back up at Sam, he's grinning at me. I can feel myself blush, something I've never done so much in my life before meeting this man.

"Come on, I'll show you the kitchen and then put you to work."

He's out the door before I can process that.

And protest.

Rule #25

IT'S NOT ABOUT THE PHONE

SAM

Having her here is just as perfect as I imagined it would be, even if it's not exactly the cozy nesting I've been fantasizing about. It's something. After our shared admissions in her hotel room yesterday, I'm glad she seems willing to take this slow.

Or, as slow as we can take it when we've already shared almost every part of ourselves.

Knowing that she wants me as much as I want her, and that she understands why this is so difficult for me, has proven to be both comforting and terrifying. I've openly acknowledged the reasons why this is crazy and could never work but we do nothing to distance ourselves from it.

Talk about a shared fate.

I only hope it's not the disaster I've been imagining every second that I'm not imagining her lush, naked body in my bed.

"I'm a pretty good cook, if that's the kind of work you had in mind."

Naomi comes up behind me in the main house, walking

straight up to my back until her cheek presses against my shoulder blade. I smile and reach back to catch one of her hands, bringing her around to the front.

And I almost kiss her right then and there, but something holds me back. Maybe it's knowing that if I start kissing her now, I'll never stop.

And this tour is far from over.

"I was thinking more along the lines of yard work," I reply with a grin.

Naomi oohs and ahhs over my little kitchen, complete with the gas stove that I had barged over—one of only two things I purchased new from the outside world. I'm especially proud of the kitchen, with its hand-built, sanded countertops and deep, stainless-steel sink that I salvaged from the wreck of a restaurant that we transformed into Raft.

When I started building this property into my forever home, I designed the kitchen with a family in mind. Big meals shared at the outside table, cooking and eating together.

It hasn't gotten nearly as much use as it deserves, mostly offering a single burner flame for me to reheat food from the resort or boil water for coffee. Someday, though. I keep making the little room big promises. Ones I hope I'll be able to keep.

Once we've toured the whole living space, Naomi lets me help her into a wide-brimmed sun hat that was left here years ago during some all-hands-on-deck work party that makes her look the part of adventurous homesteader in the tropics. My heart aches.

"Why don't you drop those straps and let me sunscreen your back?"

The mischievous smile Naomi tosses me has my dick coming to life. As do her next words.

"Maybe it'd be easier if I just took it off."

I smile and stalk toward her, bottle of SPF 50 under one arm. "It's best to limit sun exposure to your more…sensitive parts." I run my hands up her torso and stop just before I have one breast cupped in each hand on the outside of her shirt, running my thumbs down the sides of luscious, bitable breasts. "Especially this time of day."

Not that I don't want her to strip off this tiny shirt and let me get my mouth on her skin, but again, I know I can't be trusted once I begin.

"Well, we can't have me getting my nips sunburned, now, can we?" She's playfully egging me on, and I'm both excited and terrified.

I take a step forward, allowing the now stiff situation in my pants to brush up against her hip.

Naomi's eyebrows raise. "Oh really? It's the sunscreen and funny hat that's doing it for you, isn't it?"

"It's the woman in the hat, actually."

"Well, farmer, you know where I stand on this."

Her words send chills down my spine because I do, indeed, know. She would let me strip her bare right here and have my way with her.

I steady my breathing to keep from diving headfirst into the ocean of gorgeous, smooth skin before me.

"Maybe just the straps for now," I manage to get out, voice surprisingly even.

Her smile turns sly. "Sure, sure. Let's not get carried away or anything. I hear there's plenty of yard work to do."

I take my time rubbing the sweet-smelling lotion onto every exposed inch of her body, from her ankles to the tip of her nose.

"Jeez, Sammy. I never imagined sunscreen could be so erotic. I'm going to be thinking about that in my bed later."

Unless you end up in my bed…

I give her a little extra dab on her chin, which she playfully rubs off.

Water and Bluetooth speaker in hand, we head out to the corner of the yard where I was working the day before. It's a partially shaded, mostly flat patch of earth where I envision housing handmade wooden compost bins as soon as I can get the vines cleared.

And build the compost bins.

The projects of homeownership never end.

"What's the plan, boss?"

I smile over at Naomi, who stands with her hands on her hips, surveying the site. "I'm going to cut back these vines." I gesture to the now wildly overgrown section of flowering vines that I cut back the season before. "And you can rake them into a pile. We'll haul them out in the wheelbarrow."

I watch as she turns in a full circle, rake in hand, evaluating my plan.

"You know what?" she says finally. "This will make for some excellent pictures. I'm going to go grab my phone."

I laugh softly and nod, not a bit surprised by this proclamation. The only thing that's a bit curious is the fact that her phone isn't already on her. I can feel the weight of my own phone in my fifth pocket, my now constant companion. "Run on up and grab it. I'm going to get started."

She runs off, and I drag the weed-eater out of the small shed near our worksite. I'm checking the line and oil when I hear her cry out. I drop everything and bolt for the house.

I fly through the back door just in time to see Naomi rushing out the front door toward the driveway. I follow. By the time I get out to the front porch, she's already finished her search of the golf cart's floorboards and is collapsing into the driver's seat.

I walk over and slide into the passenger seat beside her. "Everything okay?" I ask, even though the answer is obvious.

She just groans and rests her forehead on the steering wheel. "I forgot my phone."

I bite my fist to keep from smiling, and I'm grateful Naomi isn't looking at me. This is clearly a devastating situation for her, so I want to be supportive.

"Why don't you head back to Dom's and grab it? You know the way back now, so it will only take a few minutes."

After the quick, third-hand conversation I had with Fran about Naomi being on the run from Dom's, I have a feeling I know the answer, but I still want to give her the space to talk about it in her own time.

Naomi just shakes her head again. "I can't go back there yet."

My forehead creases with concern. This sounds like more than just a little sibling annoyance. "Why not? What happened?"

She flops back in her seat and lets her head drop backward to rest on the metal bar behind her. "Just a stupid fight."

"Tell me."

She sighs and finally looks my way. "It's why I came over here in the first place. To talk to you about it."

"But you changed your mind?"

"Once you started showing me your house, I just loved being here, the last thing I wanted to do was ruin it with my petty problems."

I reach over and slide my arm around her shoulders, pulling her closer to me. "Let's hear it."

"They wanted to talk this morning, and it was going okay—"

"They?"

She huffs out a laugh. "Yeah. Dom and Reina. My new parents, I guess."

"Okay..." I'm nervous about where this is going. My loyalties have been solidly in the corner of those two people up until very, very recently.

"Seriously, at first Dom was all nice about everything and told me he followed me on Instagram, which I had no idea about. But then he started in on this stuff about how it wasn't his fault he hadn't called in five years because he saw on my feed that I was doing okay. And I was like, you can still call someone just to say hi, and he was like, phones work both ways."

She lets out another sigh, nestling closer to me. I hold her tightly, waiting for her to go on. It's incredible to me, now that I have this perfect, interesting, kind person in my life, how little Dom actually mentioned her over the years. I never gave it much thought, but it's all I can think about now. I guess I'm about to learn a lot more about the reasons behind his behavior. I try not to kick myself for not asking him sooner.

"That was the beginning of the end. He claimed he would worry about me less if I was in a relationship, and I told him I knew he threatened every man on the island against touching me. It went really downhill from there. He told me I needed a plan for my life, as if the entire career I built for myself was nothing. I stormed into my room and grabbed my bag and..." Her voice drops as a sob escapes her lips. "Forgot to grab my phone. I'm sure I would have noticed before I got too far, but Reina chased me down the path trying to get me to feel sorry for him."

"You can use my phone?" I offer stupidly, still trying to process the back and forth of her and Dom's argument.

She sits up, wiping her face with both hands. "It's not the same. And it's not even about the phone. I don't even need it, really. It's just..."

I wait patiently for her to get wherever she's going.

"It's always been my whole life, that phone. My community, my brain, my entertainment, my map. Hell, it's my credit card. How could I have forgotten it?"

"You were upset."

She deflates right before my eyes. "I guess."

"Sounds like you're upset about losing things that the phone represented, is that right? And that happened before this morning, but you've been putting off processing the feelings you're having about the losses of those things? Your community, your job?"

Naomi turns her head slowly to face me, pinning me with her intense stare. Her mouth is open slightly, and I can almost watch her mind working. She stares at me for so long I start to get nervous that I said something wrong and screwed up any chance I had of ruining my entire life with this woman.

Finally, though, she turns her gaze back to the house. "Yeah. You're right."

I reach for her hand, and she doesn't pull away, but she doesn't squeeze mine back either. I'm still in this limbo, waiting for whatever she's about to say next.

"I don't know what to do."

Her words fall heavy in the hot, dusty air between us. I listen to them fall, wishing I had a magic wand I could wave to make this all better for her.

"I ran. I packed a bag, okay, three bags, and got on a plane. I didn't see any other options. There was no one to call. No one to help me."

She turns her gaze back to me suddenly, and I can see her holding back tears. I want to pull her close once more, but I can tell she needs to get this out.

"I have almost a million followers but not one friend."

I squeeze her hand firmly as her deep, dark truth surfaces. I know it must be painful for her to admit that, but it's the first step in healing. "Well, you have me."

Her head drops, and she looks down at where I hold her limp hand in mine. Her silence speaks volumes.

She doesn't have me, and she knows it. She has me right now, when no one can see us. She has me, a guy who would deny any connection to her if asked. A guy who's too chickenshit to stand up and tell the world he wants to be with her.

"I'll tell him," I blurt out before I lose my nerve. It's the only thing to say. "I'll tell everyone."

Naomi sighs, still not looking at me. "No, it's okay. This isn't really about that. This is my own shit, and I don't think it's going to be helped by you firebombing your whole life, which is the only safe place I have right now."

She looks up at me then, eyes sad but dry. "Let's just play it cool, okay? Just like we decided. At least for now. And I,"—she takes a big breath and blows it out—"need to learn how to live without my phone. Without anyone watching. Except you."

And that is how, after telling myself I wouldn't, I find myself in a secret relationship with my best friend's little sister.

Kind of secret, anyway.

For now.

"You want to see how I solve most of my problems?" I ask, grateful to finally have something to offer that I'm sure will work.

"I'd love that."

Rule #26

SWEAT IT OUT

NAOMI

It's not long before my tears are long forgotten. Dry, or possibly just indistinguishable from the rest of the liquid now pouring down every inch of my body.

"It's freaking hot out here," I say, taking a break from raking to wipe my sweaty brow with my sweating, sticky forearm.

Sam grins over at me, setting down the weed-eater and stretching. As I watch, he peels off his own sweat-soaked shirt, tossing it over the side of the wheelbarrow.

"Totally unfair," I chide, even though I'm not a bit displeased by my new view.

I start to rake again with gusto.

I officially love raking. Who knew it could be so fun to move piles of plant matter from one place to another with a giant spiny fork? I can't even explain the satisfaction of it. One minute the ground is covered in the remains of vines Sam butchered into little pieces, the next—clean.

I pause for a moment and lean on my rake as a thought occurs to me. I wonder if housecleaning gives this same kind of satisfaction. I've always heard people talk about stress cleaning, but I always assumed they were just getting the benefits of the exercise. Endorphins and whatnot. I certainly never gave more than a passing thought to my own clean house after returning from lunch each and every Thursday to find it thoroughly scrubbed and organized by Sara, my housekeeper.

The thought that I've spent my whole life letting someone else claim the satisfaction of turning my tornado of a room into their own personal Mt. Everest is sobering. No wonder all the rich people I know are so unhappy.

Because right now, I'm on top of the world. Sure, I have shirtless Sam to feast my eyes on, with his long, lean frame and knee-length shorts sagging low on his hips, not a colorful hipster tattoo anywhere in sight. I'm practically drooling as I imagine running my hands up his strong back, the lube of his sweat making my skin glide over his—

He turns to look at me, eyebrows raised, and I snap back to work, raking like my life depends on it.

We load the brush into the wheelbarrow wearing leather work gloves. Mine are at least two sizes too big, causing me to smile whenever my freakishly large hands come into view.

Sam dumps the load back in the jungle, down a trail to where he tells me his brush pile is. I wait at the edge of the forest, unneeded, but not ready to stop helping.

This was so much fun.

We walk back over to the worksite to gather up the tools, and I stand back and admire how great it looks.

"Pretty nice, huh?" Sam asks, coming up beside me and leaning his shoulder into mine.

I nod up at him. "You were right. That was just what I needed."

The truth of my words don't hit me until I've spoken them. I feel so much better. Not just cheered up or having forgotten my problems temporarily. I'm a new person.

Covered from head to toe in sweat, dirt, and plant matter which, in itself, is another new experience.

"Why don't you grab your rake, I'll show you where it goes in the shed," Sam says, tucking his clippers and gloves into his pockets.

"Sounds good," I respond, just as the sky gives an ominous boom.

My head whips around to Sam, who's grinning at me, eyebrows raised. "Looks like we finished just in time."

As if timed to his words, the universe opens up at that very moment and what feels like an entire ocean's worth of water starts to pour down on our heads.

I let out a scream, and Sam grabs my hand, pulling me behind him toward the safety of the nearest outbuilding at least fifty feet away. We run through the pouring rain, avoiding where the water is already puddling, laughing as we get thoroughly drenched.

When we finally reach the tin overhang, I fall into his arms, exhilarated, dripping, and so, so happy. Sam holds me tightly to him, and I can feel his chest shake with laughter. When I glance up, he's looking down at me, raindrops sliding off the ends of his lashes.

"I think this is the first time I've given a rake such a big hug," he says with a smile.

I glance down and see that I never set my rake down. I've got it pinned between us in the embrace. I let out a laugh so pure and joyful that it almost brings tears to my eyes.

Have I ever, for a single moment in my life, been this happy?

"I really love my rake," I manage and Sam's grin just grows wider.

I start to lay my head against his chest, to curl into the warm, glowing feeling of this moment, this perfect embrace, but Sam's fingers catch my chin, turning my wet face back up to meet his.

I see his lips coming and close my eyes, allowing the kiss to hit my other senses. I feel the softness of his skin against mine. I smell the rainstorm mingling with the earth and the jungle, the fresh scent of being washed clean. I taste the salt of our hard work, the clean water from the sky, the perfect sweetness of Sam as he deepens the kiss, pressing into my mouth.

I let the rake go, dropping my arm to let it fall to the side and rest against the building. Before I realize what's happening, I'm pressed against the hard wood of the shed myself, Sam's hands on either side of my shoulders as I relax onto the solid surface.

He's kissing me so deeply, and I'm chasing every swipe of his tongue, eager for more of this man in any way I can get it. I finally get to live my dream of running my hands up his wet torso, the rainwater mixing with sweat and dirt, creating a slick, gritty feel to him that I can't get enough of. I grip the meat of him and pull him closer.

I know I'm just as wet and dirty, but somehow the thought of it doesn't make me shy away, exactly the opposite. I want to co-mingle our messy bodies. Right here and now.

"Sam, take my shirt off," I say into his cheek as I manage to slide my lips away for a brief moment before he recaptures them, groaning into my mouth.

Our lips part for another second as he obeys, pulling my soaked tank top and bra together up and over my head, gently freeing them from the tangle of my wet hair. I don't see where the garments land, my eyes still closed, every nerve in my whole body bracing itself for the moment when his hands finally touch down on my sensitive skin.

I swear to god fireworks go off when he takes my pebbled nipples between his fingers.

Thunder booms so loud we both jump.

Sam recovers first, dropping to his knees in front of me, all attention focused on getting my nipples in his mouth. I decide if he's not worried about the storm, I'm probably safe out here and allow myself to relax into it. He's sucking and biting me in the most delicious ways, and I almost don't realize how low his hands have slid on my hips, or how my shorts and panties seem to be coming down with them.

He doesn't pause to ask permission, and I give no resistance, biting my lip and watching as he abandons my damp clothes around my knees and reaches both hands up to spread my thighs and touch the tip of his tongue down on my screaming clit.

I can't help but laugh in surprise. "Jeez, Sammy. Just going for it, huh?"

His intense gaze meets mine, mouth still hovering centimeters away from my core. "This is all I ever think about."

"Well," I manage as he lays into me, tongue flat and broad, swiping the entirety of my slit. "Don't let me stop you."

I don't think I could if I tried. Sam's strong hands grip my hips as he feasts on me like a dying man, my moans of pleasure being periodically drowned out by a boom of thunder or the pounding of rain. I'm a whimpering, begging mess by the time he releases one hip to slide his fingers down to help.

He starts by grazing them from clit to entrance, teasing me so deliciously I actively work not to come on the spot.

I'm not ready for this to be over.

Holding back gets a lot harder when he enters me, his deft fingers finding my spot and rubbing me from the inside as his tongue flicks back and forth on my clit.

"Sam, I'm going to come," I moan.

Sam groans in pleasure as another boom of thunder shakes the ground underneath us. I let out a tiny shriek, but the excitement of the storm does nothing to douse the flames he's creating between my legs. If anything, it pushes me closer to the edge.

He holds me there a torturously long time, as if he can feel just the right way to string me along. Until he finally pushes me off. I careen into my orgasm, buckling at the core as pleasure spasms through my entire body. I know I'm crying out, but I can't hear myself over the sound of a fresh downpour on the tin roof above us.

Sam's tongue and fingers don't let up until I come through to the other side, laughing and shaking him off as my flesh turns ultra-sensitive.

As soon as my vision returns to normal, I look down at him, sitting on his heels in an increasingly large puddle of muddy water, watching me like I hung the damn moon.

"Are you cold?" I ask.

Sam shakes his head. "Are you?"

I'm freezing, but I don't want to admit it. I still have a rainstorm blowjob ahead of me, so I woman up and shake my head, even as my teeth start chattering.

Sam runs his hands up my legs, and I can feel my goose bumps grow under his palms. "Let's get you into the shower."

I almost moan at the pleasure his words bring, but I hold my ground. "I want to…you know. Do you now."

Another shake of his head, this time with a sly smile. "I'm fine, princess."

The front of his shorts is telling another story, practically screaming it, considering how wet they are. He sees me looking and presses himself to his feet, bringing one hand to either side of my shoulders once more, pinning me back to the wall.

"Why don't you let me put you in a hot shower, and I'll let you watch me take care of this myself."

I whimper, unable to help myself. I'm so beyond shame right now.

Sam just smiles. "I'll take that as a yes."

Rule #27

BLAME IT ON THE RAIN

NAOMI

He scoops me up like I weigh nothing at all, my soaked shorts sliding the rest of the way off as my feet leave the ground. I glance back at my now abandoned rake, still leaning against the door to the shed. I don't wave goodbye to it, but I almost do.

The shower turns out to be an outdoor whitewashed wood stall, completely open to the sky above. I stand, naked and shivering, as Sam gets the hot water running.

I wish I knew a language beautiful enough to describe the feeling of being freezing and standing under the heavy spray of hot water while cold water also rains down on me from the sky above. The brunt of the storm has passed, taking with it the lightning, but a few dark gray clouds drift overhead, keeping the sky dim and the rain falling.

I don't know how long I stand under the hot water, slowly rotating with my eyes closed, before I feel Sam step in behind me. My brain might be slow for a number of reasons right now, but it's lightning quick to realize that if he's now in the shower with me, it means he's just as naked as I am.

I start to spin to face him, but his strong arms wrap around me, pinning my back to his chest as he holds me tightly to his body. I can feel a hard part of him press against my backside, and I wiggle my hips a bit to tease him.

"Careful, princess."

I scoff. "I was promised a show."

I hear Sam growl in response, and I'm suddenly very excited again. I've seen Sam lose control once before in my bedroom in Austin. But now that so many things have been said between us, so much familiarity and trust has been built. Am I about to witness what he's really capable of?

Still holding me tightly with one arm around my chest, Sam uses his other hand to help his huge erection slide between my thighs. I step my feet apart to allow him space to nestle in and then clamp my thighs closed around him. I smile in satisfaction at his hiss of pleasure as I squeeze him tightly.

I pulse my thigh muscles a few more times, and Sam seems to relax into me, pumping his hips softly against my backside to add friction to the tightness. He's holding me so close, and almost inside me. This is the closest I've felt to him since the first time we really met as adults, and I can't get enough of how he feels wrapped around me like this. I'm wanted. I'm protected. I'm safe.

I glance down to see his tip jutting out from between my thighs. I slide my wet fingers around it as it escapes back into my legs. He pushes it forward again, and I capture it like a sexy game of whack-a-mole.

"God, I love it when you touch me," Sam murmurs, lips pressed against my shoulder.

I can't see his face from here, but I try, turning my head, my cheek pressing against his forehead where he rests on my shoulder. "I'd love to touch you more, if you let me."

Instead of an answer, I get spun around and pressed against the far wall of the shower, my back meeting the wood with a thud. The force of his action both surprises me and turns me the hell on. I could take more of this dominant, in-charge Sam. I met him at my apartment, and I want him to come out to play.

He presses his lips to mine in a claiming, punishing kiss that I return with gusto. I can't see his cock, but I know just where to find it, my hands grazing it softly a couple of times before getting a firm grip.

But then I remember.

He wants to give me a show…and I want it.

If all he needs is a little encouragement, I'm happy to oblige.

I reach up and take one of his wrists from where it rests on the shower wall beside my head, bringing it back down between our bodies and using my other hand to close it around his cock. Then I close both of my hands around his and start to pump him.

Sam lets out a moan that may contain a few words, but I can't make them out. After a few long, hard pumps where I hold my breath and wait to see what comes next, Sam seems to snap, tossing my hands to the side and taking a step back, then another, until his back presses against the other wall.

There is only a few feet between us, so I can still feel the magnetic pull of him. I'm dying to close the gap once more, to cross through the hot shower spray and press my body against his.

But I also can't take my eyes off where he's now gripping his dick, jerking it with short, firm pulls. As I watch, the movement transforms to long strokes that include his tip. I'm finally able to look up into his eyes, and once I get a look at his face, I'm grateful I did.

As fucking hot as it is to watch the guy manhandle his cock, the savage look on Sam's face is nearly enough to send me over the edge right here and now. His eyes are dark and burning with lust, lip clenched tightly between his teeth, forehead creased in concentration. But it's more than the sum of parts. Looking at him like this, watching him watch me watching him…it's the hottest thing I've ever done in my life.

"I like seeing how you do it," I say, trying to include myself in the erotic tableau playing out before me. I want to be more than a spectator here, even if that's my role.

Sam moans at my words, his head dropping back. I can see his eyes close as he grips himself even harder.

"You do it so hard. I would be scared to be so rough. I wouldn't want to break it," I tease softly, needing his eyes back on me.

It works. His chin drops until I'm once again pinned in that icy hot stare. "You're not going to break it."

His voice is rough and strained. I calm my breathing to keep from touching myself as I imagine him talking to me in that tone with his magnificent cock buried deep in my body. My hand slides closer to my core anyway, fingertips grazing gently over my thigh.

Sam watches my hand move and lets out another moan.

"Are you thinking about fucking me right now?" I ask, holding his gaze.

He nods.

"Me, too."

Sam's eyes drop closed, and I smile a little to myself. This might be the Sam show, but I'm officially a co-star. And I love it.

"I'm going to have to touch myself soon, Sammy. I don't know how much longer I can watch."

"No," he says quickly, sharp eyes back on mine as his hand moves up and down his shaft. "I'll do it when I'm done. You just watch."

"You look like you're getting close."

His head drops back once more as his hand moves to his tip. "God, I am. I'm so close."

"You like when I watch, don't you? You're excited for me to watch you come?"

"Get on your knees."

The command is both surprising and not. I'm honestly a little disappointed I didn't think of it myself. I lower myself to my knees. The new position leaves me face-to-face with his bobbing tip, and with my head right in the stream of the now only lukewarm water.

I close my eyes against the water and take my breasts in hand, twisting my nipples softly between my fingers.

Damn, I could come right now just from this. My thighs shift against each other, and I nearly moan.

That's all it takes for Sam. I can't see very well through the water beating down on my head, but I can hear him roar as he comes. Wherever it lands, it gets washed right away, but I imagine him watching it hit me, his hot load landing just where he aimed it. I do moan then, unable to keep it together a second longer.

The water stops abruptly, leaving me kneeling on the wet shower floor, holding my tits and wriggling my butt to try to quench the desire building between my legs.

Sam's still standing, and I look up at him, glorious and ravaged, cock jutting straight out from his body. There's a small drip of cum waiting for me on his tip, and I reach up to slide my finger through it, sucking that finger straight into my mouth.

Sam drops to his knees and kisses me, diving deep between my lips, tongue seeming to search for the taste of himself on me.

I'm so lost in the passionate kiss that it's a moment before I realize he's pushing my thighs to the side, working his hand between my legs. His thumb hits my clit as two of his fingers slide easily into my drenched pussy. I lift up a bit on my knees to allow a bit more space, thanking every god that's ever existed for this man's touch.

"Are you going to be ready for me when I fuck you?" His low, gravelly words, spoken directly into the side of my neck as he fingers me, take me by surprise.

But not enough to throw me off my game. "Yes."

"How ready?" he asks, pumping me harder.

I respond by moving my own hips against his hand, riding him so his thumb presses deeply against my clit. I shift a bit back and forth, and oh my god, I'm going to come so fast like this. "I'll be so fucking ready, Sammy. You feel how wet I am?"

"Sure do, princess."

"I'm going to be wetter. I'm going to take your cock—" I can't finish my thought as I slide into the deep, dark pool of pleasure that Sam opens up for me.

It's all I can do to not collapse on his hand, but I keep grinding, holding my breath and helping him work me through an orgasm so strong it could be considered core work.

Still panting, I lift myself off his hand and collapse back against the shower wall. It's a long few moments before I'm able to open my eyes again. Glancing up, I see that the clouds have all moved on, and the sky is once again perfectly blue. I'm warm from the inside out, from Sam's touch and the hot water. The soft rays of early evening sun hit me, and life is absolutely perfect.

"I love yard work," I say, letting my head rest back against the wooden wall.

Sam laughs and slides his feet across the tile floor until our legs intertwine. "It always works wonders for my mood."

I let my eyes open slowly and smile back at him. "Oh really? When you're feeling down you just rake up some vines, take an hour-long shower, and you're right as rain?"

Sam grimaces softly, glancing up at the still dripping showerhead. "Speaking of which, I think I used my water ration for the next month this afternoon."

His tone is light, and I know it's a joke, but I can't help feeling bad. "Sorry."

He's on his knees in a flash, pulling my naked body up to meet his. "There's no need for apologies, princess. I'll go the next year without a shower if it means I get to have moments like this with you. Every second I spend with you is worth it. It's worth any cost."

Sam whips up sautéed veggies from the garden to top spicy packaged ramen noodles, which is impressive considering he had no time to prepare, and I have a feeling he eats most meals at the resort.

It's deliciously simple. This whole day has been. After so many years of always needing more, more, more...I'm getting a glimpse of a simpler kind of life. One where I go hours without even thinking about checking my phone, scrolling, or photographing something to prove to a bunch of strangers that it happened.

"Your clothes are dry," Sam says, bringing in my wrinkled, but indeed dry, outfit from earlier. I've been sporting one of his oversized tees for the evening.

"You just want me to get naked again," I tease as I take the clothes.

He flops down on the couch. "I'm here for the show."

I give him a small one, a bit of silly wiggling and turning as I change back into my shorts and tank, but not enough to take this anywhere. As much as I'd like to start something, I think I need to go back to Dom's.

I tell myself that leaving Sam's warm, welcoming house and driving back to Dom and Reina's has nothing to do with being reunited with my phone, but I know that's only partially true.

Baby steps, right? I mean, I did just go the whole day without checking it.

I arrive at Dom's just as the sun is setting though the panoramic windows. The house is empty, and I stand for what must be half an hour, watching mother nature's show. The absolute, undiluted beauty of it all takes my breath away.

I don't even try to capture the moment in a picture.

Something in me has shifted. All of a sudden, just being here is enough.

Still feeling a tad guilty after our frivolous shower session, I decide I'm clean enough to head straight to bed, setting my timer for only ten minutes of scrolling while I lay against the headboard, two soft, fluffy pillows propping me up. The internet is exactly the same as it was when I left it last night. People did stuff, people complained about stuff, and I almost click on way too many very well-targeted ads for things that would fit in perfectly with my new island lifestyle.

Instead, I shut the screen off when my time is up and plug it in across the room, sinking into my sheets and letting my memories of Sam's hands on my body lull me to sleep.

Rule #28

GO TO YOUR HAPPY PLACE

SAM

We do a couple weddings a season here at The Sands, or we have for the last few years, since Fran and Avery teamed up. I also ran high-end resorts in the States and abroad before we took this dive into resort ownership, and those properties were popular destinations for weddings. And even after all that, I have never before seen anything like this wedding.

I narrow my eyes at the security guard positioned at the front door to my lobby as he asks me for my ID. "I'm the owner and GM of this property. Why are you checking IDs at my door?"

The man's face remains stoic, taking his job seriously. "I'm just monitoring the entrances while my team transfers the wine from the secure transport to the resort refrigeration."

My eyebrows raise a bit. "And then you'll be standing guard outside the cooler door as well?"

"Yes, sir."

I nod, letting the reality of the day ahead sink in. "I'll be sure to let the restaurant staff know to get you a meal. If you can't move from your post, don't hesitate to ask my staff for food or water if you need it, okay? Dehydration can sneak up on you if you're not used to the heat."

I see a slight crack in his stern facade. "Yes, sir. Thank you, sir."

I take a long, deep breath as I step through the doorway into the lobby, trying to prepare myself for whatever could be waiting for me inside.

The first person I see, however, is exactly who I was hoping for.

Naomi's long waves bounce on her bare shoulders as she comes around the corner. Her whole face lights up when she sees me. It's been a busy few days for both of us, and we haven't managed to see each other.

I wonder briefly if that guard would stand watch outside my office for a half hour, but I shove the thought away.

"Morning, stranger," I say with a smile.

She returns my smile conspiratorially, giving me as much of an embrace with her eyes and body language as I'm going to get today. I allow memories of her skin under my hands to creep into my mind for just a moment before shaking them off.

The last thing I need right now is a boner.

"This is crazy, Sam. I knew it was going to be, especially after watching them all arrive yesterday and seeing their stuff. And their clothes! You are not going to believe the clothes on these people. I want everything." Her eyes go starry for a minute before she snaps back down to earth. "But also, I don't."

I watch as she glances down at her simple tank top dress, sage green and falling loosely to just above her knees. The straps are wide enough to cover the straps of the bra I know she's wearing from sneaking glances, and the neckline falls low enough for comfort in this heat, but not too low as to be inappropriate at work. She's the picture of island business casual.

She looks back up at me, and I can't quite read the expression there—and not for lack of trying. I want to know everything about this woman, starting with each and every thing that goes on inside her head.

"I didn't even have to steam this dress, let alone iron it. I passed a woman earlier when I was getting coffee down at Raft who was wearing these super high-waisted red pants, and I almost sat down right there in the hallway to search the internet for them, but then I thought about how long it must have taken her to get them to look like that before she put them on." The expression on her face now is obvious amazement. "It was like seven-forty-five in the morning. Can you imagine steaming pants before eight a.m.?"

I lean in just a bit closer, until my lips are inches from her ear. "I saw the red pants woman, princess. And she's got nothing on you."

Naomi's surprised little gasp and matching blush make me grind my teeth a bit as I step back to put the appropriate amount of distance back between us. The last thing I want to do is be further away from her perfect skin and the scent of her hair, but we've got a long, crazy day ahead of us, and I need to keep my head in the game.

"Anyway," she says, smoothing her dress and shaking off the same fluster that I'm feeling. "That's not why I came up here."

"Oh, something more pressing than the perfect pair of red pants?"

She narrows her eyes good naturedly at my teasing. "Yes. Fran sent me up to see if you could help with getting the long tables out of storage. She said some of them were better than others and you would be the one to ask."

I am, indeed, the one to ask about which of the identical folding tables in storage are the best.

I nod. "Let me just drop my stuff off in my office."

The day careens down the track from there. I help with the tables, then get pulled away to assign tasks at the wedding team meeting, and then I'm back up in my office, on the phone with the local transport company, trying to get our trucks to roll into the resort driveway on time.

The wedding starts at two p.m., the hottest part of the day, but also the exact time that coordinates with some kind of astrological event that's very important to the bride and groom, so we've constructed large shade sails over the rows of chairs set up on the beach. I walk the whole wedding setup with my clipboard, noting places where I think Fran could take a moment and double-check some of the crew's work.

It's nearly eleven before I finally run into Avery, who's looking a bit more flustered than usual. I brace myself for whatever could have finally gotten under the skin of my notoriously even-keeled friend.

"Sam, these people are nuts. I've been running up and down stairs all morning trying to help housekeeping and Reef answer all the calls. Everyone needs lattes in their rooms and their beds made by the staff first thing in the morning. I'm not going to be sad when this one's over."

I grimace in solidarity with him. I guess having an easy-to-work-with wedding couple did not translate to their friends and family being equally easygoing. Poor Ave is always on guest relations at these big events, while his partner in business and in life, Fran, runs the whole rest of the show.

"Let me know if it gets out of hand, and I'll see if there is any staff I can free up elsewhere to help run stairs."

"Nah, now that they've all had their beds made while they drank coffee and watched, they're starting to head downstairs. You're going to need all the staff down there you can get."

"Thanks for the heads up."

I turn to hurry back down to the pool deck adjacent to Reef, our casual fare café, to make sure they're ready for the guests but Avery stops me.

"We're all flying to Honduras, to Pristine Bay, after this shindig wraps up, if you want to join."

He tosses the invite out casually enough, but I can almost

picture him and Dom rochambeau-ing to decide who would talk to me about the vacation. It's not like I get upset about the guys taking these little trips, but I never join them. For whatever reason, they have made it a priority to always invite me, no matter how often I beg off.

"It's going to be fun. Fran and Reina are coming, and I'm sure we'll talk Naomi into it."

I search his tone for any kind of implication but come up empty. He's just reporting information.

My mind, however, is reeling.

If Naomi's going on the trip, I want to go.

On the other hand, it would be really, really difficult to get any time alone with her if all my nosy friends have nothing to do but lay around all day and watch us. Right now, the only thing our secret relationship is hinging on is the fact that my best friends are complete workaholics. Oh, and this insane wedding.

How's it going to be when the craziness passes and it's back to smooth sailing at The White Sands? Back to intimate dinner parties, bonfires, and trips to town for lunch and football games?

This might be the last real weekend of privacy we have together. I want it. Even if we have to give up this thing between us soon, I want this.

"I'll probably just stick around here, make sure things get back to normal smoothly. You know, the resort doesn't stop running when these weddings end, Ave."

Avery just smiles his knowing smile, not buying a second of my bullshit. "Whatever, man. Just think about it, okay? We booked you a room just in case."

I turn and head toward the stairs without answering. I don't know how often they book a room for me and let it sit empty when I don't join them on a spontaneous trip around the globe, but I have a feeling it's most of the time. It would be pretty bad if I finally agreed to hop on the helicopter one of these times and found myself sleeping on someone's pullout sofa when the exclusive, high-end resort was booked when we arrived.

And it's not that I don't appreciate the gesture. The guys have always worked to include me in everything from holidays to vacations to meals in five-star restaurants. They've been doing it since I lucked my way into the exclusive private school they all attended.

My mother and I lived in the next town over, sharing a one-bedroom apartment she could only afford by working two jobs. Avery, Dominic, and Ben adopted me on my first day of school, swooping in as I sat alone in the cafeteria, trying to eat my bagged lunch in peace, bringing with them a loud, rambunctious, whirlwind of arguing, teasing, scheming, and money. So, so much money.

That first month of fourth grade at Simonson Prep was my introduction to the fact that I was poor. Prior to boarding the half hour long bus ride to the academy and being adopted by the guys, I'd been surrounded by kids and families in similar situations to my own. I played with the children of the people my mom found to watch me while she worked, and every one of them lived in an apartment.

I can distinctly remember the first time I went to Ben's house, where we spent a lot of our time because his parents' estate was bordered by acres and acres of wild woods, the dream of any nine-year-old boy. We were picked up at school by a man I assumed was Ben's dad, even though it was strange how he called the guy Fred, and Fred didn't talk to us at all, not even to ask about our day.

We rolled up the long driveway to a house that looked a lot like the school we just left, and I almost asked if it was his apartment building. Luckily for my little boy pride, I kept my mouth shut.

Fred opened the doors to the town car, and I ran after the guys through the massive front doors into what turned out to be one house. For one family. We went straight to the kitchen where we were greeted not by Ben's mom, but the housekeeper, who was waiting for us with an entire meal of snacks and drinks.

It was months before I met any of their parents. Their lives were run entirely by staff members, and they all treated these adults like family and acted like it was normal. I tried to play along, but I was just pretending to understand.

That was just the beginning of nearly a decade of pretending to understand. To understand that people existed with so much excess when others had nothing. To understand that some families got to have their own pools and planes and yards bigger than parks all to themselves and didn't have to share with anyone. To understand that some kids didn't worry about anything.

This is not to say that I wasn't grateful. Hell, I'm still grateful. The opportunities I had in life were directly tied to the relationships I made during those years are plentiful.

Avery's father recommended me to Cornell, where I was guided into the Hotel Administration program, a decision that set me on the course to resort ownership.

Ben's mother got my own mother a position at the local hospital in our town that had a day shift schedule and paid enough for her to let go of her second job.

Dom's family was always going on vacation, and all of us boys were invited. I got to see parts of the world that the other people in my apartment building could only dream of visiting.

I laugh to myself now, remembering how often I hopped on a private jet and headed off to some fantastic destination, probably not more than five feet away from Naomi, the very person I'm now about to try to convince to stay home with me. I never paid her much attention. She was young enough that she occupied a different universe as me and the guys.

But I can't help but wonder. Was she okay?

I shake it off as I reach the bottom of the wide, concrete staircase that runs between the two resort towers, leading down to the massive, central pool area and deck. The last thing I need right now is to let my mind wander. There will be plenty of time to stew over all the wasted years I could have spent with Naomi after this event goes off without a hitch.

I needn't have worried. I'm sucked right into the whirlwind of troubleshooting, decision-making, and mediation that comes with the territory of being GM here at The Sands. It's the perfect combination of my unique skill sets. My flow state. My favorite place to be.

Or it was my favorite place. Now when I think of my happy place, all that comes to mind is that moment locked in the shower stall with Naomi. My arms around her body as the hot water mixed with cool rain, perfectly encapsulating us in a moment in time.

It's not that I would ever give up my position at The Sands. Not willingly anyway. But I'm starting to wonder if there might be more to life. I've always assumed I could have both. The Sands and my own little family.

But what if I had to choose?

I suck in a long, slow breath as a moment of complete clarity washes over me. I know what my decision would be, and I can hardly believe it.

Rule #29

LIFE HAPPENS IN THE MOMENT

NAOMI

This is absolutely unreal.

I say a quick thank you to the gods of endless cloud storage as I snap photo after photo of massive centerpieces made entirely of woven grass and orchids. My attention is caught by glimmering copper, and I make my way over to where an orchestra of gongs and crystal singing bowls has been set up, ready to bathe the ceremony in sacred sound.

This is the kind of rich my father scorned. The flashy, wasteful, indulgent rich. He never so much as purchased a car that wasn't black or a wristwatch that would have given himself away. And he wouldn't let us kids behave that way either.

Or he wouldn't let Dom anyway.

I was given a bit of a pass, allowed to buy myself the wardrobe of my wildest dreams. I guess he supposed subtlety was wasted on me anyway.

And look at me now. Living a life that's completely visible, sprayed over the internet like hot pink silly string. No wonder the guy won't talk to me.

I hop up and make my way back to the kitchen, where the crew is busy getting all the little snacks and appetizers ready for after the ceremony. I lean against a wall, trying to stay out of the way, and scroll through the shots I've taken. It's hard to see the screen in bright sunlight, so some of the pics are a surprise even to me. It's all epic though. The wedding practically screams *Post Me*.

I bite my lip, wondering if that's what this is all for. If these people wanted the most internet-friendly party ever, or if it's just a coincidence. Or if my jaded mind is just so used to looking for content in every situation I'm in, that it's all I can see now.

"Hey."

I jump at Sam's voice and pocket my phone, shaking off my gloomy thoughts and forcing a smile. "Hey."

"I looked everywhere for you."

"I've been doing content for Fran. This wedding is going to make the most incredible posts."

Sam looks distracted, like he's not hearing my words. I brace myself for whatever he's about to say next.

"I have to get back upstairs. I just wanted to find you."

"Sam," I say quickly, wanting to let him off the hook. "I'm totally fine. You can go do your work. I'll just be—"

"Don't go to Honduras." His words come out all in a rush, too loud, like they burst through a blockage in his throat.

I try to think quickly if I have any idea what this is about, but I'm coming up blank. "I…"

Movement over his shoulder catches my gaze, and I glance to the left. Sam turns his head quickly to follow my gaze.

Right to Fran, who's standing behind him.

His head whips back to face me, and I can see the panicked question in his eyes.

Did she hear?

I offer a shrug because I really don't know what's going on here.

"Am I interrupting something?" Fran asks, her tone lightly teasing, like she knows exactly what she just stumbled upon.

Unlike me.

"No," Sam says, taking a step back and turning so Fran is now included in our little circle. "I was just—"

"Telling Naomi not to join us in Honduras?"

He glances down at his shoes, clearly caught.

"Sam?" I ask, starting to get concerned.

"I need to get back upstairs," he says, tossing me a tight-lipped smile and escaping through the wide double doors.

Fran turns to me, grinning. "I love this."

I shake my head, still watching the doors swing. "I don't know what that was about."

"I do."

I turn my head to her, eyebrows raised.

"We're all going on a trip off the island when this wedding wraps up. Ave invited Sam earlier, but he isn't coming. He never comes. And it sounds like he was trying to get you to stay here on Faraday with him instead of joining us." She offers a satisfied smile. "I can't say it's a bad plan actually. You two would have the whole island to yourselves for once."

"Oh," I say, totally taken aback by the situation. I have a lot to process, but for now, I need to say something intelligent. "Yeah, that does sound good. I'll stay here."

"God, as much as I want to pull you into that walk-in and interrogate you, I don't have a single second to spare right now."

"Anything I can do to help?"

Fran spins, glancing around, distracted by what she's going to do next. "You just keep doing what you do best." She looks back my way and meets my eyes with a smile. "I'll see you on the other side, okay?"

I nod, and she's gone.

The ceremony proceeds like a scripted, made-for-film video shoot. I snap away, getting all the angles, running video on my phone when there's movement or high emotions. After the couple heads back down the aisle to start the all-night reception party, I take a moment to relax in the shade against a palm, flipping back through pictures to see what I captured.

I don't get to rest long, however, because I spot the green polo shirts I marked earlier as the people from the tiger conservatory. And that can only mean one thing.

I reach the low, ornately molded fence surrounding the baby tiger enclosure just as they're coaxing the tiny animals from cozy looking crates.

"Now this is something I never imagined seeing at The Sands."

I turn to smile up at Sam, who's standing a respectful eight inches behind my left shoulder. I want to lean back into him, but of course, I don't.

Good thing, too, because Fran appears on my other side a moment later and the last thing we need is to be caught canoodling by her a second time in one day.

"Isn't this amazing? I can't wait to see the website banner the graphic designer can make with these tiger cub shots."

"No!" The word flies out of my mouth, drawing attention from everyone in the vicinity. I look down, embarrassed by my outburst.

But I'm not standing down. "No, Fran. These crazy wedding people can splash baby tigers all over their own socials, but these pariahs aren't going anywhere near yours. This is an absolute scandal waiting to happen. Do you know what animal rights groups think about the practice of flying baby tigers around the world just so people can pet them? It's created a whole black market for cubs and the enormous problem that is fully grown tigers in the suburbs once they're not cute and cuddly anymore."

Fran huffs. "It's okay, the couple didn't buy the cubs. It's a tiger sanctuary, and they paid for the whole decade of—"

"I know," I interrupt, waving off her excuses. "You told me. But no one on the internet is going to stop to ask. They're going to see the opportunity to get a leg up on your rotting corpse and take you down." I let out a huff of my own. "Ask me how I know."

Fran sighs. "Dang. I never really thought about it like that. I guess that's why we need tiger sanctuaries in the first place, huh? To adopt all the unwanted tigers after they grow up?" She looks disappointed, and I can tell she's going to heed my warning. "But we can still, you know, snuggle them? If no one takes pictures?"

My face breaks into a huge grin. "Oh, yeah. You couldn't keep me away."

Fran gets permission to step over the low fence, and after making sure every camera is still busy taking pictures of the newlyweds and their adorable grandchildren, I follow. Glancing back for Sam, I find him smiling at me. I gesture with my head, and he follows me into the pen.

"I'll keep an eye out for the paparazzi," he says in a low voice once Fran is fully occupied with a cub on the other side of the enclosure.

Propriety be damned, once I'm in a pen with six baby tigers, I fall straight to my knees. One of the cuddly cubs crawls right into my lap, looking sleepy and absolutely freaking adorable. I hold the little guy to my chest and coo.

When I look up, Sam's kneeling beside me.

"Aren't they the cutest?" I ask.

He nods but only looks at me.

I almost can't stand the adorableness when a cub crawls up Sam's leg, and he scoops it into his arms. I give mine another little snuggle and look down to see that it's fallen asleep in my arms.

"This is the most internet perfect moment that I've ever had, and I can never, ever let anyone see me doing it. Isn't that ironic?"

Sam's watching his cub with much less adoration than I feel. "So, you get to enjoy it in the moment. Make a memory that you'll never forget."

"I guess so. I guess this is how I need to learn to live. Like moments are enough even if I'm the only one witnessing them."

"What if I'm there witnessing them as well?" Sam asks, and I look up. He's not watching his sleeping cub at all. All of the adoration in his gaze is directed at me.

I have to look down again as I feel myself blush. "That'd be pretty good too."

When I look back up, he's smiling.

"I'm not going on the trip with the others. I'm staying here on Faraday. I'm going to have the whole house to myself," I say in a low voice.

I watch his eyebrows raise, and his smile morph into more of a smirk. "You know, I always have my whole house to myself."

My breath catches as memories of our yard work party flash through my mind. When I meet Sam's gaze again, I can tell he's thinking about the same thing.

"Well, now we have options."

Sam lets his now squirming cub escape, and we both watch it crawl over to a young wedding guest who squeals in delight.

When I look back at him, he's already watching me.

"I'm not ready to let go yet." I mean the tiger cub, but the words fall heavy between us.

"Me neither."

My eyes fall closed at his whispered words.

"I'll see you after the wedding, okay?" he says and disappears up the stairs.

Rule #30

WHEN THE CAT'S AWAY...

NAOMI

But I don't get to see Sam after the party, or even the following day, as we're both caught up in the aftermath of the wedding. I'm helping to pack up and distribute decorations and lost belongings to their rightful owners, and Sam's days are filled to the brim with every single other thing that goes into running a resort of this size.

Luckily, he's gotten really good at keeping his phone on him, so we keep up a near constant chat under our aliases. After he told me that he named my contact Natalie, I changed his to Smith, making our inability to be in the same room at the same time more like a little game.

Naomi
That was quite a day yesterday, how are you holding up?

Sam
I got out of here at eleven, luckily, and got some sleep. Good thing, too, because I had to swing over and pick up the morning front desk person when their cart wouldn't start this morning at five.

Naomi
Daaaang. I was barely getting home at five. I stayed to help with wrapping up the party after these crazy kids danced until three and then had drinks with the staff.

Sam
Ah, I remember those days.

Naomi
The good old days?

Sam
Nah. I prefer to be the boss. Make my own schedule. Make other people stay until three and clean up after drunk wedding guests.

Naomi
What else do you like making people do, Mr. Boss?

Sam
If only you could make it up here before my next meeting, I'd show you.

Naomi
I can run stairs pretty quickly…what's your timeframe?

Sam
They just arrived. Sorry, princess.

While I'm dying to sink into Sam's arms in a private corner somewhere, it also feels really good to be an important part of this project. After my photographer duties were a wrap last night, I stayed to help wherever was needed, and it turned out that was everywhere. I can't even describe the feeling of finally watching the last guest hit the elevator call button and getting to collapse into a chair and drink wine out of a coffee cup with the rest of the crew.

I was needed. I was wanted. I was part of a team.

This morning, I got up as early as I could manage, arriving to find grateful, welcoming faces downstairs on wedding clean up. They put me to work right away, and I stay and help until the last task is marked off the list.

"Thank you so much for all you did," Fran says as she hugs me tight, preparing to hop into her golf cart and leave the resort for the first time in nearly forty-eight hours.

"You haven't even seen the pictures yet," I protest, but I'm overjoyed by her praise.

She pulls back and holds me at arm's length, grinning. "Even if there weren't fabulous pictures to look forward to, I would still appreciate you. I don't know how I'm going to pull off next month's wedding without you. They want a champagne fountain. Like it's the nineties or something."

I laugh, but her words also sting a bit. I try not to let my disappointment show.

She's so quick to assume that I'll be gone by then, and maybe she's right. I do have my own life to get back to, don't I? Fran's just trying to be supportive, to let me know that she believes in my ability to recover from the setback of my cancellation.

"That's going to be a sight to see," I say, taking a step back.

"See you in a couple days," she says, tossing me a wave as she slips into the passenger seat beside Avery. "Have fun with the island all to yourself!" A wink and they're gone.

I smile and turn back to head into the lobby, but I realize there's nothing left for me to do there.

The wedding is totally wrapped up.

I have my bag on my arm already.

I shrug and try to shake off the sudden wave of uselessness that's descending over me. It's not until I'm starting the stair climb at Reina and Dom's house that it hits me—I'm about to have Sam all to myself.

Naomi
I'm arriving home now. Will you be off sometime tonight?

Sam
I'll be here until at least seven. What time are your housemates heading out of town?

Naomi
Boat picks them up at six-thirty.

Sam
Well, I guess I know what I'm doing when I get off work.

Naomi
OMG is it me??

Sam
😉

I run the rest of the way up the steps and throw myself into the shower.

I have an epic vacation of my own to prepare for.

"Don't worry about the AC, the house is set to temperature control so it will take care of it," Reina is telling me for the third time as she follows Dom toward the front door. "Oh, and the house is smart, but only kind of smart, so if you get locked out of anything, you can override with the keypad using the code 425."

I smile at her. "Got it."

"Reina! Get out the door!" Dom yells from the front porch.

Reina grimaces happily, turning to run out the open door and past Dom down the steps. He stands in the doorway, still holding all the bags as I approach.

"Enjoy having the house to yourself," he says, and his mouth could almost be called a smile. A tiny one.

We've been mostly avoiding each other over the last couple of days, and it's worked fine for me. Hell, it's been our relationship for my entire life, so I'm used to it. Anything's better than fighting. It almost feels like a truce.

I nod. "Thanks. I'm going to enjoy the peace and quiet."

The look he gives me then is most definitely an exasperated smirk that might even be accompanied by an eye roll that he saves for after he turns away from me.

My mouth drops open as I prepare to ask what on earth that look was for, but it's too late.

"See you Wednesday," he calls back to me without turning.

I smile and wave until he's halfway down the steps and then hurry through the quiet house to find my phone.

Naomi

Parents are officially out of town.

I'm about to raid their wine cellar.

Rule #31

THE BEST KIND OF TREASON

SAM

I take my time on the steps leading up to Dom's house amazed at the boldness I feel showing up here, planning to set fire to my best friend's wishes in his own home.

When Naomi doesn't answer my knock, I let myself in. I find her in the kitchen, pulling a bottle of pink wine out of the chiller. "I see you found the wine stash."

She jumps and turns at the sound of my voice. Caught in the act, laughing, she sets the bottle on the counter. "It wasn't hard. There's wine in just about every cupboard in this house. And a fancy temperature-controlled cooler for it."

There's a pop as the vinyl cork slides out of the glistening bottle.

"This is a wine snob's house."

"Well, I hope he doesn't mind me drinking all his rosé." Naomi pours a splash into the stemless glass waiting on the counter and takes a sip. "Perfectly chilled," she jokes, grinning at me. "You want some?"

"I want you."

Naomi's eyes narrow seductively as she sets her glass down and closes the distance between us, pressing her chest right up against mine. I can smell her shampoo and feel the warmth of her skin through her thin tank top. I wrap my arms around her like I've been wanting to do for days and close my eyes, sinking into the essence of Naomi.

"I feel like it's been forever," she says, cheek still pressed against my collarbone.

"Absence makes the heart grow fonder," I tease, holding her as tightly as I can without seeming like a madman.

"Honestly, those two days went so fast. In my mind, it's like one long, amazing day."

I smile, chin pressed into the top of her head. "I'm glad you had a good time."

I didn't get to see Naomi much over the course of the event, but I know she was at the resort working the whole time. I see the appeal for her, the lavish party and the thrill of getting to be part of it all. I know she needs some distraction right now from her own job drama, so I'm happy she was able to be included.

But now that it's over, I'm even happier to be going back to Sam and Naomi, secret lovers. Sam and Naomi, kind of coworkers, gave me a bit of anxiety.

I let my arms drop and make my way over to a seat at the kitchen bar, where Naomi sets a small glass of wine in front of me. I take a sip gratefully, letting the cool, crisp liquid wash some of the stress of the day away. Unfortunately, the stress of being in this house won't budge.

"I'm not going to lie, I do wish we were safe at my house."

"Oh?" Naomi sets down her own glass and places both hands on her hips. "You want to wait until we're all the way at your house?"

She already knows the answer, but I offer it anyway. "I don't plan to make you wait."

Naomi leans on the counter, mischievous smile on her lips.

"Besides, it's perfect. Don't you feel it? Completely forbidden. We're going to be so bad."

I'm still a bit uneasy about the idea, but the last thing I want is to deny her anything.

And I have to admit. She's right.

Just being in this house, knowing all my friends are boarding a helicopter right now, being taken far away, does inspire some bad behavior in me.

I say nothing, watching as Naomi turns and walks out of the kitchen, toward the hallway where I know her room waits. I raise myself off the stool and follow her, my fate signed and sealed.

She's sitting against the low, wide window ledge on the far side of the room when I enter, clothes miraculously gone already.

"How did you manage that?" I ask, eyes narrowed as I take in her body.

"I've been practicing this whole thing in my mind for days."

"Oh, really?"

She nods, lip held tightly between her teeth.

"What happens next?"

"You come over here and pull me to my feet."

I obey, crossing the room slowly and taking one of her hands in mine, pulling her body into my arms. Her fingers are cold and a bit shaky. I wonder if she's as nervous as I am, doing her best to pretend—just like me.

"What happens now?" I whisper, grazing my lips down her neck to her shoulder.

"Now you run your hands over my body." Her whisper is just as low, nearly masking the desire in her voice.

Luckily, I'm paying close attention.

I let my hands graze down her arms and slide onto her torso, breathing in her soft sighs as she lets them escape.

"Do you know how long I've been thinking about this?" My nearly whispered words cut through the silence.

Naomi just shakes her head, keeping her gaze angled downward toward where my fingers curl into the flesh of her hip.

"Since the moment I looked up at that bar in Austin and found you looking back at me from across the table. I was expecting just another stranger I would have to introduce myself to, but instead I found you." I never expected to be telling her the truth about that moment, but now that I've started, I can't seem to stop. "And you know what I felt right then?"

She shakes her head again.

"Relief."

I slide my other hand up her back until I reach her neck, pulling her long hair to the side to expose the creamy curve of it. I trail my lips across her shoulder and up, allowing my nose to graze the shell of her ear. Naomi responds by melting more of her weight into my arms.

"I thought to myself, this woman already knows me. I can just be myself. Which is crazy, because I'm not sure that's even how I feel about people who know me. Sometimes when I'm around people who know me, all I want to do is hide my true self."

"But you didn't hide from me?" Her question is barely audible.

"I didn't hide. You never made me feel like I needed to. I felt safe with you from the first second. You took me home, and I still felt safe, even if I was a little nervous."

I can feel her cheek shift as she smiles.

"I don't know what to do with these feelings, Naomi."

"What do you want to do?"

I shrug, even though she can't see me.

Even though I know damn well what the answer is.

"I didn't come to this island for Dom, you know," she says.

I let the meaning of her statement hit me. I'm just about to say something, anything, to keep her from saying what I know she's about to, but I don't get the words out in time.

"Dom isn't exactly the person I would choose to run to when

I'm in trouble. There were money issues when I pissed my dad off, but I could have managed for a while. I just felt like I needed to be near you. I came here for you. When my life was crumbling down around me, the only thing I could think about was how safe I would be with you."

"Naomi..." My heart is breaking with all the ways I can't give her what she needs.

What I need.

"I know. I know that's a lot. I shouldn't have said it. But it's true."

"I want this to be different. You know that."

She takes a step back, forcing my hands to drop. They hit the sides of my body as she stares up at me, eyes glassy but still fierce. "I know."

I wait for her to call me out as the coward that I am. To tell me that I'm failing her and that she knows I'm living a lie. But she doesn't.

When my lips touch down on hers, it ignites a fire in me I've felt before.

The last time I had this woman in my arms.

I press into her as she opens easily, taking me in and giving just as eagerly. My hands are everywhere now, no longer moving softly or slowly, but greedily trying to touch every inch of her naked body at once.

I'm lost in the taste of her, the feel of her, spinning in my own internal universe, when she pulls me back to the present moment with a lift of my shirt. I reach down and take the hem from her hand, pulling it off and tossing it to the side.

Naomi's warm palms run down my chest and across my stomach, curling around my hip bones and under the waistband of my jeans.

I'm not ready to take them off.

Not ready for what any of this could mean.

But when has not being ready ever stopped life from unfolding?

Rule #32

FIND THE RIGHT ANGLE

NAOMI

Sam pulls his belt buckle open with his lips still pressed to mine.

I thought I felt a hint of hesitation before he gave in to taking his pants off.

And when he took his shirt off.

And at every step of the way since the first moment we met.

But he keeps going. So, I allow him to lead me.

I know this is a lot for him. He's got a lot on the line. But so do I.

It's not the same, I tell myself.

Mine might be worse.

Because while he's falling into the arms of his best friend's little sister, something that seems to scare him enough to make him hide, I'm taking the heart of a good, kind man and using it for what could be some sort of rebound as I crawl from the ashes of my ruined life.

He's a lifeline.

One that feels really, really good.

I feel safe with Sam.

But I know damn well he's not safe with me.

This man needs a trustworthy, dependable woman to settle down with and start a life together.

A family.

And the only thing I've ever succeeded in settling was the tab at the end of taco night with the girls.

Panic rises in my chest as I allow my brain to drag me down a dark path to a future where I've let this guy fall for me, let him ruin his working relationship with his best friend, and then I've just bailed. Because that's what I do. Because online I'm fun and pretty and perfect, but in real life, I'm nothing. My own father never wanted me.

"Sam." I start to pull away, but he holds me close. "Sam, maybe this..."

"Tell me to leave," Sam says into my collarbone as he holds me against his body.

I shake my head. I'm never going to do that.

"Naomi, I'm standing here in my underwear with a hard-on that's been screaming your name for months now. If I'm leaving, I need to do it now."

I shake my head again.

Fuck it.

"Don't leave."

"Oh? And what should I do instead?"

I can barely hear myself think over the blood pounding in my ears. This Sam, this unleashed, wild Sam, the one who only seems to come out at times like these, I'm addicted to this guy. Nice guy Sam is great, but this guy? He's the stuff my dreams are made of.

"Take them off," I hear myself say, trying not to yell over the noise in my head.

He obeys, and it's all I can do not to fall to my knees and admire him. Taste him.

His arms keep me upright, though, and I feel him backing us

toward the wall. I nearly trip over a pile of unpacked shoes as I stumble backward.

When my back hits the firmness of the wall, Sam pins me there with his hands pressing my shoulders. His hard cock juts into my stomach, and it's all I can do not to look down.

Instead, I hold his gaze. Ready for whatever he's about to offer me.

But nothing could prepare me for his next words.

"Are you filming us right now?"

It takes a full breath for me to process. When I do, I stammer, "What?" even though we both know damn well I heard him.

"Are. You. Filming. Us?" Sam's voice is a growl as he presses his forehead to mine. "Is that why you wanted to be in your room so badly?"

It hadn't even crossed my mind, but I understand why he's asking.

"What if I was?" I conjure up all the bravery I can find and inject the words with confidence.

Sam doesn't even flinch. "You told me before that you watch the video of us fooling around, and when it's over, you close your eyes and imagine me fucking you."

My heart is racing, and I'm pretty sure I'm dripping down my inner thighs right now. I take a breath and pray my voice doesn't come out as a squeak. "That's right."

He pulls his head away from mine just enough to look down at me, his eyes dark and those suckable lips twisted into a sly smirk. "I just thought that if you happened to be filming us again,"—he takes a step forward, his cock sinking deeper into the flesh of my stomach—"we better give you what you need this time."

Oh, sweet baby Jesus.

His words light a fire in me that starts between my soaked thighs and shoots straight out of my mouth. Consequences be damned. "You want to watch us fuck just as badly as I do."

His smirk deepens. "I want to fuck you."

"And then you want to watch."

He pauses for a moment, pupils dilated, tongue grazing the back of his lower teeth.

"I'd watch."

All I want in this moment is to match his confidence and respond as the sassy, fearless woman that I was back in my apartment the first time we were together, but my voice cracks. "Well, I'll just hit record, then."

My words break the spell. Sam takes a step back and then another.

It's warm in here, but I feel a chill at the loss of his heat.

He glances around the room, and I panic, thinking he's going to bail.

Instead, he pins me with his gaze. "Where are you filming from?"

With all the confidence I can muster, I cross the room and grab my phone from where I tossed it on the chair. "I've never filmed in this room, but…" I glance around until my eyes fall on a low dresser across from the bed. "Here should work."

I lean my phone up against a large conch shell on top of the dresser with the screen facing forward so I can properly frame the shot.

"Will you sit on the bed so I can see if you're in frame?"

Looking as if he can't believe he's agreeing to this, Sam walks over and sits naked on the edge of the bed.

I consider the image on the screen. "Too far."

The dresser makes the world's loudest screech as I start to pull it away from the wall and Sam jumps up to help me lift it. I can't meet his eyes as we carry the dresser across the room, both buck naked, and situate it next to the bed.

He climbs back on and reclines in the center.

It's perfect.

I flip the phone around so I can film with the powerful back camera and hit record.

And then I freeze.

This is not the first time I've gotten freaky for the camera, obviously, but it's the first time I've performed with a partner when both of us know what's going on.

I never expected to be feeling stage fright.

"Come here," Sam says, reading my mind.

"I just—"

"Come here," he says again, more firmly this time.

I obey, crawling over to meet him.

"You're not camera shy," he murmurs as he pulls my body close and drops his mouth into the crook of my neck.

I shake my head.

"So, what's going on?"

I shake my head again, unable to find the right words. "It's just never been like this before."

"Consensual?" Sam asks with a soft laugh.

I smile at his joke, even though it's not really a joke at all. "I guess. I don't know. This just feels important. It never felt like that with anyone else."

"I don't want you thinking about anyone else right now."

"Oh, I'm not. I'm definitely not." Gun to my head, I couldn't conjure up the name of any former partners right now, let alone their faces. Not with this man wrapped around me.

"Then what's going on?"

"When I make videos like this for myself," I start, face flushing bright red in anticipation of the deep, dark secret I'm about to reveal. "I like to be surprised by what happens. But now that I feel like I'm making this video for you, I'm worried I won't be good enough."

Sam lifts his face from my neck and presses me onto my back on the bed with one strong hand on my ribcage, palm right between my breasts. "You could never be anything but perfect."

I have to close my eyes briefly as the genuine care of his statement radiates out of his gaze and leaves me breathless.

"But you said you like to be surprised by what happens," he goes on, "I think that's something I can manage."

I have zero doubt that's true. Everything he's done since he stepped into my room this afternoon has been a complete surprise.

I'm still woefully unprepared for his next move.

Sam pulls me up to my knees, my body following willingly, a puppet in his arms. He situates himself kneeling behind me with his knees together and pulls me right against his body, thighs splayed over his, my back pressed to his chest. He holds me there with one strong arm around my torso.

I'm barely breathing as I wait for him to touch me. I know it's coming. I can feel his other hand curling around my body, tracing a slow trail across my skin.

My eyes drop closed, and somehow, he knows.

"Eyes open. Look at the camera."

My eyes pop open and find my pink phone directly in front of where I lean against Sam's body, knees splayed.

This is going to be one hell of a shot.

I get wetter just thinking about Sam watching it later.

As soon as that thought crosses my mind, my hesitation melts away.

I'm performing for him now.

Rule #33

SOME MOMENTS ARE WORTH THE WAIT

NAOMI

Sam's hand curves around my thigh and meets my center and not a second too soon. I gasp and moan as he circles my raging nerves, bucking my hips forward against his palm.

"Eager are we, princess?"

"Yes," I moan out shamelessly, still chasing contact by driving my hips forward.

"Well, I suppose there's not really any time to waste, huh?"

I bite my lip and refuse to follow his words into dark thoughts about what comes next. About how everyone will come home, and our little paradise will no longer be ours.

"That feels so good," I say, spurring him forward instead.

I get what I'm asking for.

His fingers splay, spreading my sex wide open. I gasp as the air touches nerves that are usually so protected. Sam slides one finger down and teases around my entrance, slipping inside just enough to give me a taste of what's coming. Then up and around again, tortuously slow

When he enters me again, he does it with at least two fingers, stretching me open and grinding his palm into my clit as he slides in and out. His other hand drifts to my breast and he manages to get my nipple between thumb and forefinger as he uses his grip to keep me pressed close to his body.

I let my eyes drift down to watch his hand fucking me, mesmerized by the view. I'm so wet he slides in and out easily, the only sound in the room the soft squelch of his fingers penetrating my soaked pussy.

I'm going to come. There's no stopping it now.

"Sammy…" I get out through clenched teeth.

"Look straight at the camera when you come, princess."

Well, hell. If I wasn't already on the edge, those words alone might have put me there.

I suck in a deep breath and blink rapidly a few times to clear away the wetness that's gathered on my lashes while watching Sam finger fuck me. My focus lasers in on my phone's camera, and I hold my gaze.

Right over the edge.

It's all I can do not to buckle at my core as my orgasm overtakes me, but Sam's strong arm keeps me upright. I moan and spasm on his hand, still grinding my hips downward, chasing the wave of pleasure that threatens to drown me.

All the while, I keep both eyes open and focused on the tiny lens.

The moment I still, Sam releases me, pussy first and then chest. I fall forward onto my hands, still panting, my eyes dropping closed for the first time in what feels like ages.

He doesn't give me more than a split second to recover before he's forcing my body to rotate, moving me around ninety degrees so our bodies are now perpendicular with the dresser and the camera.

I brace myself for impact, but he just sits my butt back and down so it rests on the tops of his thighs. I can feel his stiff cock resting heavily on my lower back.

Sam reaches forward and gathers my long hair in one hand,

twisting it into a sloppy ponytail and winding his fist in it once, twice.

He uses his new leash to pull my head back far enough that I spot the ceiling.

"Tell me to fuck you," he says. His voice comes from outside my field of vision.

"Fuck me," I manage to get out through my angled throat.

"I meant beg," he says, unimpressed.

I'm dying to see the look that accompanies that kind of statement, but he's holding me too tightly for me to move my head toward him.

"Please, Sammy. Please fuck me."

"More."

"I'm dying to have your cock inside me. I'm so wet for you. You did this to me. Now you have to fuck me. Please don't make me wait."

I hear a huffed laugh behind me. "You're awfully good at begging, princess."

With his free hand, Sam pushes my hips back up so I'm spread before him on all fours. He lifts up as well, keeping my hair in his tight fist as he lines his tip up with my entrance.

"Yes," I moan as I feel him start to press into me.

Have I ever wanted anything as much as I want his cock right now?

After the build up of not getting him inside me the last two times, I worried he might draw this out, make me wait, or, god forbid, decide not to go all the way again.

That doesn't seem to be a problem.

No waiting, no discussion, no condom wrappers or discussion of testing, just his fat tip stretching my body open.

I think I moan the entire time he slides slowly into me. I'm a lucky girl to be able to verify that later. Maybe even with Sam by my side.

I moan louder at the thought of watching this whole scene on video, just as he bottoms out.

"How does it feel to have me inside you, princess?"

"So good," I manage.

"I shouldn't be doing this."

I clench my lip between my teeth as he slides out an inch and then pounds back in.

"It's so wrong," I agree, happy to dive into his game.

"So fucking wrong."

He lets my hair go, and my head drops forward as he slides himself all the way out. I can feel his tip teasing a circle around my entrance. I drop down to my elbows, allowing my body to splay further, praying it's not over.

My prayers are answered by his cock sliding back inside.

"You are so off-limits, princess."

I smile to myself at this forbidden love game. "Completely."

"I shouldn't even be here. I shouldn't be sticking my dick in you. My bare fucking dick."

He's got my hips in both hands now, giving my body a few quick pumps. I can feel the energy rising as he gets himself worked up.

"I wanted your bare cock inside me. I wanted you to fill me up."

"You begged for it," he agrees in a growl, slapping my ass with a sharp crack as he bottoms out once more.

"Please, Sammy, fuck me harder."

He obeys, gripping my hips as he fucks mercilessly into my body, pressing my face hard into the mattress.

"I'm going to fill you up, princess. Just like you wanted."

I smile to myself as I brush enough hair off my face to see the camera. When this man said he was going to surprise me, I really had no idea what I was in for.

Color me shocked. In the best possible way.

"I've been thinking about doing this for so long," Sam says behind me, hips driving him deep into my body over and over. "But I never imagined it could feel so good. I've never felt so good in my entire life."

I offer a clench of my internal muscles in response and smile to myself as he grunts.

Sam draws his tip to my shallow front wall and starts a slow, short massage. "This is where I touched you before. You like it there?"

I like it so, so much.

"Yes," I whimper out, forcing myself to take a breath. I'm not ready to hold it yet. I'm not ready for this to be over.

Especially since I have no idea if it will ever happen again.

His hand reaches around to my clit, and my eyes shut, knowing I'll never survive this.

"I've been waiting so long to feel you come around my cock, princess. Don't make me wait."

"Sam, I…" I want to beg him to go slower, but I can't. I want to come so badly the words won't form.

"You're going to come for me like a good girl." His fingers press into either side of my clit as he rocks my hips forward and back with the motion of his cock against my G-spot.

I couldn't hold on now if my life depended on it.

"Sammy…" is all I can get out as I succumb to my orgasm.

There really is something different about coming when you're filled up with cock. My body grabs the soft, rock-hard flesh of him and holds on for dear life as I roll through spasms of pleasure.

I can hear him barely holding on himself as I hold him tightly. He moans and curses in the most deliciously uncensored way.

I know for a fact that in this moment, this is the real Sam. There's no hiding your true self at a moment like this.

I release him from my pussy death grip and suck in a breath as the moment passes. I feel his hand, wet from my orgasm, slide back up my hip and grip me once more.

Never in my life have I been more excited to feel someone finish. The thought of him preparing to fuck me till he comes, spilling his pleasure and his seed into my waiting body is doing things to me.

Things I wasn't exactly prepared to feel.

I'll be damned if Sam's wild side hasn't rubbed off on me a bit. I was just acting before, but the craving I'm feeling in every cell is no act.

"Fuck, you feel so good, princess. Are you ready for me to come inside you?"

"Yes," I cry out, feeding my hips back against his thrusts with a gusto that I know is appreciated by his increased pace.

"I'm going to fill your sweet pussy."

"Yes, Sammy," I moan.

"I love it when you call me that. No one else calls me that. Only you."

And with those words, he's buckling above me, driving his cock as far as it will go and pulsing there, emptying himself into the vessel of my body.

I hold my breath as I savor the feeling of being merged with him. I want to hold on tight, but I know it won't do any good. My eyes close to further narrow down my senses, allowing my skin to ramp up the sensations of his hands on my hips, allowing my nose to dance in the sweet, musky scent of the man moaning and panting above me.

Allowing my heart to expand with a rush of completely inappropriate feelings.

Feelings I'll just have to dispose of later, but for now, I let them have their fun.

He pulls out only to shove back in a second later, drawing a gasp from my lungs as his tip slides through my sensitive flesh.

"You feel so good," he murmurs as he slides himself centimeters in and out, refusing to give up the territory he so mercilessly conquered.

I wait, chest flat on the bed, arms splayed over my head, eyes still softly closed, and allow myself to enjoy the last of the pleasure chemicals rushing through my brain.

This is the best kind of high, and Sam is the absolute best drug.

I'll never be able to go back to the person I was before this happened.

He slides out and comes to a seat on his heels behind me, hands still holding my hips. One hand slides down through my spread cheeks and over my rosebud, down to where my entrance must be gushing with the combination of our orgasms.

His fingers press shallowly into my body, and I hear his breathing catch. I'm dying to see what he's doing, what his face looks like, but I relax knowing I'll have the chance later.

"This is so fucking hot," he murmurs, fingers still moving in and out of me. "I've never done anything like this."

"I've never let anyone do that," I respond honestly. It's never even been on the table before.

"Good," he says. "I want it to be just me."

I don't know how to respond to that, so I say nothing.

"I know I shouldn't have done it. I should have asked. But I don't know if you could have stopped me. I don't know if I could have stopped myself."

"That's not true, Sam."

His wet fingers finally give up their task and slide over the round of my ass, up to my lower back. "What do you mean?"

He's leaning over me, brushing the hair out of my face. I get my first glimpse of his smiling face since this all started. I smile back. "If I had told you to put on a condom, you would have."

His smile widens, turning sheepish. "That's true. I would've. You didn't, though. I hope that's okay."

It's a little late to be asking now, but I really don't mind. "It's okay. It's better than okay. It was amazing."

His eyes drift back down my body. "Yeah."

"I need to roll over. Or straighten my legs. Or something."

Sam jumps to the side, and I press my legs out straight, moaning in pleasure as my circulation returns. I roll a bit side to side, eyes closed, enjoying the delicious stretch. My body stills when I feel his hand on my belly, tracing around my navel and up to the lower tips of my ribs. Glancing down, I watch his tanned finger outline my rib bones with slow, intentional movements.

Shifting my gaze to his face, my breath is taken away by what I find there. Gone is my dirty talking, bossy bedmate, replaced once more by the sweetest man who's ever lived. And the look that he's giving my body right now could only be described as reverence.

How come every time we're together, it feels like he's about to say this thing between us is real? Maybe that's just wishful thinking on my part.

"What are you thinking about?" I ask, just to break the silence, the spell of this heavy moment.

Sam's eyes drift up to mine, and when our gazes meet, I know I made the wrong choice. Nothing he's about to say is going to lighten the moment one bit.

"I was thinking about when we were out raking in my yard. I was watching you, you know. Whenever you weren't looking in my direction." His gaze drops back down to my stomach as his hand resumes tracing circles around my navel, one side and then the other.

"I've been working alone in that yard for a lot of years. It felt good to have someone out there with me. Someone to shower with and curl up on the couch with afterward." He bites his lip as he watches his finger travel across my skin. "I've just been alone for a long time."

I shift so I can see his face better, see where his hand is resting on my stomach. My heart aches with longing for this man, but there's no denying the wall that seems to be standing strong between us. If it wasn't there, if it wasn't so goddamn solid, his voice wouldn't be so sad.

I close my eyes and sigh, unsure of how to respond. I can't shake the feeling that this whole thing is out of my control. Like he's a puppy I found lost in the woods, and now I have to convince my parents to let me keep him. I somehow have to convince him it's safe. Even when I don't know that for sure.

I'm not used to letting such big, important decisions about my life be at the whim of other people. I've been independent for a long time. Too long. Much longer than I should have been at only thirty-two. It's always been me looking out for myself.

Maybe this crazy, indecisive anxiety is just what it feels like to finally care about another person as much as I care about myself. I want Sam. I want him so badly it's burning me alive.

But I also want him to be safe and happy and not crushed under the weight of my baggage.

I focus on the slow, steady movement of Sam's finger on my belly to ground myself. As I watch, however, I start to see that he's not drawing circles at all.

He's tracing hearts.

I shift my hips suddenly, so that I'm lying on my side, effectively tossing his hand from my stomach. He stretches out on his own side, gaze finally making it up to meet mine.

And it's time to be brave.

"I've been alone for a long time, too. Most of my life. My mother...well, you know what happened to her. And my father never looked at me. I assumed it was because I look so much like her, but I'm not her. Dom was whatever, gone, busy. It was just me. I made it work. I made myself a life. I finally had something going. I trusted people." I pause as my voice breaks, rolling back to my back, using both hands to wipe my face. Sam just waits for me to calm down. I can feel his gaze on me. "I don't know what to do now. But I do know this. It feels good here. It feels safe." I finally drop my eyes to meet his. "You feel safe. But I need that to be true for both of us."

For a minute, I think Sam might cry as well, but then his deep look turns pensive. "I don't know what happened to your mother."

I feel the surprise hit my expression at his words, and I struggle to find a response.

"Do you?" Sam asks, seeing my hesitation.

This is not something I talk about often. Actually I've never talked about it before.

No one has ever asked.

After a long moment and a few deep breaths, I nod. "She died of…me, I guess."

Sam visibly flinches, and I leap in to save him. "It was a long time ago."

"My mom told me something vague about complications with childbirth, and I always just imagined a wound that never healed."

"I suppose that's correct."

Sam shifts closer and pulls me into his body, curling around me until I'm wrapped in his warmth. "I always knew that your house wasn't a safe place for anyone to talk about their feelings."

"What did Dom say about it?" I ask, suddenly curious. In addition to my father never mentioning my mother's name after her death, my brother also seemed to just forget about her.

Sam is quiet for a moment, considering. "It wasn't exactly something he brought up often. But before you were born, when your mom was pregnant with you, he talked about you a lot. He was really excited to have a little sister."

"Until that sister stole his mother away." I don't mean to sound so bitter. None of this is Sam's fault, and it really was a long time ago. I'm over it.

I feel Sam shake his head against my body. "It wasn't like that. It was almost like he was scared of you. Or scared you would get hurt. He never wanted you to come with us because what we were doing was too dangerous, even if it was something simple like riding our bikes to town. He would yell at you to go back home, and when one of the other guys would ask him why he was so mean, he would just say that you were too little to come. What if you got hurt, he would ask?"

"Protective since day one, I guess." I huff. "I guess that explains our current predicament."

"We protect the things we love the most, Naomi. Not the things we don't care about."

Sam's words hold so much truth, I can't bear to have them land on me. I'm not ready to forgive. I'm not ready to admit that the two men who caused me the most pain in life were just in pain themselves. Instead, I just snuggle deeper into Sam's arms and close my eyes.

I have no idea when he gets up and stops the recording, but when I wake the next morning, my phone is plugged in beside the bed.

Rule #34

ARE YOU STILL PRETENDING?

NAOMI

I'm lounging in the passenger seat of Sam's golf cart, feet kicked up on the dash, hair blowing in the warm, tropical breeze, pretending this is my goddamn life.

What was it he said the other day? The words came out as if by accident.

I was pretending it was my life.

Well, I know the feeling.

I look over at Sam, and he grins back, his eyes already on me. I sigh and turn back to the view out the passenger door, heart aching.

We're heading to the island village, Saubry, for breakfast after sleeping late and having coffee on Dom's magnificent patio. I was nervous to suggest the trip to town. After all, secretly sleeping together is very different than parading around in public, but Sam was quick to agree.

He pulls up in front of a low, gray, cinder block building, the same place Reina parked when we came to town together last week.

He doesn't help me out of the car or hold my hand as he leads me down the sandy path through the open fence of a restaurant and bar. There's an outdoor seating area with tables made of plywood and colorfully painted golf cart tires, and a fire pit surrounded by low stools made of the same.

I smile at the clever recycling idea and pause to take a few pictures. They would be better if I was in them, as pictures of people always perform better, but I don't want to bother Sam to take my picture sitting here like some kind of tourist.

Instead, I quickly pocket my phone when he pauses in the doorway and looks back for me, rushing up to his side—too close—before remembering myself and taking a step back.

He just leads the way in as if I wasn't having a complete social anxiety meltdown over how I should be acting right now.

"Do you want to grab a table?" he suggests. "I'll get you a menu."

I choose a seat on a bench at the end of a long, empty table, figuring it will look less like a date that way. Sam slides in across from me and lays a laminated menu down in front of me.

I smile up at him. "You don't need a menu?"

"Nope," he says, grinning. "I always get the same thing. I think the cook might have a heart attack if I tried to order something different. She's probably already getting it ready for me."

I get stabbed by a pang of longing, something that's been happening more and more. This time it's for the simple familiarity of his words. To be known by someone—in real life. To show up at the same place and order the same thing enough times that it's some kind of tradition.

It's never that way in my life. Once I've been somewhere and been photographed eating the food or posing in front of the stylized fireplace, there's not much point in going back. I always need something new.

"Well, maybe I should just get the same thing you always get," I say, glancing over the menu but not being able to process the words over the chattering in my mind.

"It's not a bad choice," Sam responds.

I push the menu toward him and drag a happy smile back onto my face. "Perfect."

He places my order at the bar and comes back to the table with two waters in plastic cups and sits down on my bench instead of across from me.

"Slide over." He laughs when I stay frozen to the spot.

I obey, and he keeps sliding until he's right next to me.

"You sure you want to be seen so close to me?" I ask, even though I tell myself not to.

"I'm not afraid to be seen with you, Naomi."

"Because your friends are all in a different country?" I don't know what's come over me, but I'm having a lot of feelings right now, and most of them aren't good.

I'm just jealous, I guess.

Jealous of this life Sam gets. A life of real friends and community and self-assurance.

Jealous of the girl I was pretending to be in the golf cart. The girl who got to live this life with him.

Because I sure as fuck am not that girl.

"I'm going to go to the bathroom," I blurt out, practically jumping to my feet.

I'm sure Sam noticed something was wrong, but the last thing I want to do is make a scene in his favorite bar and embarrass him in front of all the people who clearly know who he is.

I cross the sandy floor and lock myself in the tiny, hot bathroom stall, leaning back against the wooden door. I hate that this is the reaction I'm having. We just did it for the first time, and it was so amazing and fun.

I want to be that amazing, fun girl.

I want to be cool.

I want to just take this as it comes and not be so desperately, clingingly attached to something I cannot ever have.

But I'm not that girl.

Rule #35

YOU KNOW NOTHING

SAM

Naomi's not gone two minutes before someone slides onto the bench across from me. I look up from my phone into the smiling face of Max, the caretaker of the guys' property on Merit Island, the close island neighbor to Faraday.

Max is an old sage and has been known to swoop in to help many people solve problems with his surprisingly astute insights. I know Avery, for one, makes special trips over to Merit just to seek out his counsel.

I haven't had as much of a personal relationship with Max as the other guys. I don't spend much time at the Merit mansion, but he and I have a comfortable friendship built over years of seeing each other at events and around town.

"Hey, Max. How are you?"

His big Buddha smile beams on his round, happy face. "Enjoying the only day I was given."

I laugh at the perfectly Max response and nod. "That sounds about right. What brings you to Faraday?"

"I just had a feeling I should come to this place."

I stifle another grin. It's hard to keep a straight face in the presence of this peacefully joyful soul. "Well, can I buy you a drink?"

"It appears you already have two," Max observes.

"I do. I have a…a date, I guess."

"A date he guesses. I see I chose the right table to sit down at."

I narrow my eyes at his still smiling face. "What's that supposed to mean?"

"You tell me."

I take a long sip of my water through a straw as the bartender sets a glass down in front of Max. The old man pulls his drink toward himself without taking his eyes off me. He takes a sip and continues to watch me.

Finally, I lose the battle. "I'm sleeping with Dom's little sister, and I think I might be in love with her."

Max's grin grows impossibly wider. "Fantastic."

I shake my head. "It might be fantastic, but I know Dom's going to freak if he ever finds out."

"You know nothing."

A deep sigh escapes my lungs at his answer. I was hoping for some advice, not a cryptic fortune cookie message, no matter how well meaning. "I guess."

"Tell me about the woman."

I feel myself smile involuntarily. "She's amazing. She just has this essence about her, like the warm bath I've been searching for my whole life. Like I can relax for the first time. Honestly, I hadn't even realized how hard I was searching for my person. How much mental energy went into worrying that I would never find her. But now that she's here, I feel like a weight has been lifted. Like I stepped out of a fog."

"But you would consider walking away from this to not risk upsetting your friend."

"I don't see what choice I have, really. If Dom isn't on my

side…" I stop, not ready to admit my greatest shame. Not even to this seemingly safe third party.

"You worry about upsetting Dominic because you've come to believe that you are the lesser of your friends due to your family's financial situation. And having Dominic as a close friend and business partner offers you the financial security you feel is necessary for your continued belonging in the group."

My mouth falls open. "How do you know any of that?"

Max just sips his drink, calm smile still plastered on his face. "It's written right across your face."

I rub my hand over my face absentmindedly, as if I could feel my darkest secrets written there in braille.

Max's smile widens. "This is a wound from your childhood that you need to heal in order to move on. If you want to move on, that is. You don't have to."

"What do you mean I don't have to?"

He looks at me pointedly. "You don't have to do anything. That's the beauty, and the curse I suppose, of free will. You have made a nice place for yourself here in this life. You have the resort, and you have your friends. You have comfort and financial security. Many people would be very happy to live out the rest of this lifetime in your position, not rocking the boat."

I can feel the but coming. I don't even bother to ask for it.

"But if you're not content with what you have, then boat rocking is your only option."

The truth of his words strikes through me with actual, physical pain. I feel myself grimace as I look down at the straw between my fingers.

I already knew this.

I already took inventory of my life. Found it overflowing with opportunity and happiness and blessings.

And found it lacking.

"But…" I start, not having any idea what question to ask to get the answer I need.

"But what if you get wet?" Max offers.

I nod.

He shrugs. "A special design feature of human beings." He taps the skin on his arm with two fingers. "We're waterproof. And we dry quickly."

"Hi," Naomi says, climbing back onto the bench beside me.

"Hello, my dear," Max coos at her, rising a bit to extend both hands across the table toward her.

Naomi's face cracks into a smile as she takes them both and lets him hold them.

"It's an absolute pleasure to meet you."

I grin at the look on Naomi's face. It's not uncommon for people to fall so quickly under Max's spell. She's smiling at him wide-eyed, still holding both of his hands.

When he releases her and stands, she turns her head up, forehead creasing. "Do you want to join us?" she asks.

Max shakes his head. "Alas, my own boat is waiting."

We watch him walk away in silence.

After a long moment, Naomi turns to me. "Who was that guy?"

I smile up at the bartender as he sets two plates of blueberry pancakes, scrambled eggs, and crispy bacon in front of us. "Max. He and his wife live on Merit Island where the guys have another house. He's a bit of a local counselor."

"Ooh," Naomi says, mostly to her steaming plate. "Did he offer you any advice?"

I shove my loaded fork into my mouth to buy myself some time. I'm not sure how much of what Max said is worth sharing or how much I'm brave enough to share.

What would it mean to admit all this to her? All my feelings and fears? How deep I am in the pit of worry about what's going to happen between us?

And what will happen to me if I end up making the wrong choice?

"He told me that if I rock the boat, I'm going to get wet."

She raises her eyebrows, pausing midchew to gape at me. "And?"

I shrug, eyes on my plate as I load my fork once more. "And he reminded me that I'm waterproof."

Rule #36

NOW'S THE TIME TO RUN...OR NOT

NAOMI

We stop in front of Dom's house just long enough for me to decide there isn't anything in there worth going up the stairs for, then Sam drives us back to his place.

I brace myself for the feeling of homecoming, but I'm still not prepared for how hard it hits me. I don't fall out of the golf cart, but only because I'm holding on.

"Why don't you snuggle up on the couch? I'm just going to check in with The Sands, and I'll join you."

"For a nap?" I tease, but Sam nods.

I laugh in spite of myself. "I expected you to say no."

He pretends to look offended as he snatches his phone from the counter. "Come on. Sleeping in, pancakes, nap. I may be a workaholic, but I know how to have a day off."

"Is this how you spend all your days off?" It's supposed to be another bit of light teasing, but I can hear the edge in my voice.

Sam crosses the living room to where I'm standing, holding his ringing cell in one hand. He presses a light kiss to my forehead. "I never had a day off before I met you."

A voice sounds through his small phone speaker as someone answers at the resort. He winks at me and then strolls away, bringing the phone to his ear and greeting the person on the other end.

I flop straight back onto the couch, lips vibrating with a forced exhale.

What the fuck!

This is all so perfect and sweet and incredible.

But is there really a future here?

I don't even know how to ask. All I know is that I'm completely lost in it. When Sam bails, which is the most likely outcome, I'm going to be wrecked.

Unless I bail first.

I bite my lip and consider my options.

I've been ignoring messages from my PR company for the last two days. They think it's time for me to try posting again. To offer up some new little tidbit from my life to test the waters.

I'm petrified to do it. And I have no idea how to feel about that. Posting is what I've always done. It's my happy place. I've said in a joking, not so joking, manner that if I don't post it, it didn't happen. And I really, truly believed that.

But my life is different now. In the short span of my time here on Faraday, I'm living a different truth. Because I haven't posted a thing, and yet my life feels more real than it ever has before.

"Resort's still standing. We're free for the rest of the day." He tosses his phone into a basket on the counter and flops down beside me. "Theoretically."

I smile, understanding perfectly. He's always on call.

"You okay?" he asks, forehead crinkling as he watches me.

Damn. I thought I was doing a good job of masking my worries, but I guess not. This hound dog can sniff out my mood, even when I try to distract him by pulling my top a bit lower.

"Yeah, I'm just really ready for this nap, I guess."

And ready to have a few moments to myself to freak the hell out without someone watching.

Sam curls his warm body around mine where I sit, and I laugh in spite of my gloomy thoughts, wiggling and sliding down until I'm lying face to face with him on the narrow couch. We're both on our sides, slotted together like little sardines.

"Do you have enough room?" he asks.

I'm on the inside, pressed against the soft back of the sofa. I wriggle myself into the back a few more inches, because I'm sure Sam's back is hanging off the edge. "Yeah. Do you?"

He smiles. "You might have to hold on to me."

I lock my arms behind his back, taking my job very seriously.

Sam closes his eyes and slips right into his nap. I watch him for a few minutes, matching my breathing to his. Is he really so carefree about this whole thing? The peaceful look on his face as he sleeps sure looks like it.

And here I am, totally and completely wrecked. I don't know what to do. I can almost feel myself preparing to run, even though I don't want to. I want this.

Tears bubble up in my eyes, and I hold them closed to hide it, just in case Sam opens his.

I wake with a start when Sam performs the masterful acrobatic move of rolling over in my arms, balanced on his six inches of couch.

I wait for him to settle his back into me like the little spoon, and then I curl around him, holding him tighter than ever. I drift back off to nap-land convinced I can hold him forever.

Rule #37

IT'S A BIT LIKE QUICKSAND

SAM

"You escaped."

I smile up at Naomi from my seat on the front porch. "I didn't want to wake you. I made coffee if you want a cup."

"Can I just have a sip of yours?"

I hand over my favorite yellow mug, a gift from an employee at the end of last season, and watch Naomi drink from it and smile. "Gotta love a man who knows how to make a cup of coffee."

I keep my smile in place but say nothing. I have no idea how to respond to that.

She grimaces slightly and looks up at me apologetically. "I just meant..." Her eyes fall back to the cup. "Good coffee."

I'll make it for you every day for the rest of your life, princess.

"Thanks."

"So, what's on the agenda for today? More raking?" She goes for a subject change, and I allow it.

"You did seem to take to that rake like a natural."

Naomi smirks. "Yeah, well. I'm multi-talented."

"Honestly, I thought we could work in the bedroom today," I break off and join her in a laugh as the words leave my mouth. "That's not exactly what I meant." I shake my head and try again. "It's supposed to be a hot one, so I thought I'd kick on the AC in the new bunk room, and we could work on getting it finished. I think all it needs is a good sweep, some white paint on the windowsills, and then the mattress dragged down."

"And sheets and blankets and pillows," she says, handing my cup back.

I nod. "Yup. I have all that. Fresh sheets are on the line right now, in fact."

Naomi takes to painting in the same adorable way she took to raking—with the solemn concentration and determination of someone who has definitely never done this before. She's just finishing up the third of eight windowsills when the questions start.

"Why don't you ever go on vacation?"

I smile over at her from where I'm reattaching a light switch cover. "I do."

I know exactly what she's asking, but for some reason, I'm nervous to get into my personal stuff. I should be offering it right up on a silver platter after her intimate confessions from the night before, but I'm not used to sharing deeply personal information with people who don't already know the answers.

"Fran told me that they always invite you to come on their little trips and you always say no."

I open my mouth to answer, but she cuts in. "And don't say it's because you have to work or the resort needs you. I know firsthand that you can take a day off if you want. And it's not a money thing, unless you're hiding a secret gambling problem or something. You have a damn good job."

I laugh softly, turning my gaze back to the screwdriver. "I just like doing fewer things."

"That's not the impression I got last night," Naomi teases me.

Her little joke does a lot to set me at ease. "I grew up in a different world than those guys, but I spent most of my time with them. Something I noticed pretty quickly was that nothing was special. In the life I had with my mom, things were really special. We went to Frank's Waffle Castle for my birthday every year, for instance. She has an album with a picture of us together there each and every year. She's holding up fingers for how old I am in every shot, until I got too old and had to hold up mine as well."

I smile to myself at the memory. "It was special because it was the birthday place. She made it special by never going there any other time, even though we loved it. Even though I begged."

"So, you never go on vacation because you want the one vacation you take to be special."

I nod my head side to side, finishing with the light switch cover and standing up, stretching my legs. "I go on vacation twice every year. Once, for around a month, when the resort closes for the season. It's the hottest time of the year here, and I chose somewhere I've never been before. Somewhere that's at its best in July."

"Where are you going this year?"

"Florence."

"Okay. What's your other vacation?"

"Every year, I rent a house in Sag Harbor for the week after Christmas. Me and my mom go up together and do puzzles."

Naomi laughs out loud but recovers quickly at my raised eyebrows. "That is so perfectly, amazingly, Sam."

She's grinning at me, and I can't help but drop my eyes to the floor, feeling very exposed. "My mom went there on a weekend trip in college, and I grew up hearing stories about Sag Harbor. It became this place of legend. The most perfect, storybook town, where everyone is solving mysteries and waiting for their fisherman husbands to come home. We never had the money to go when I was a kid, but as soon as I could afford it, I surprised her with a holiday trip. Now we go every year."

"Let me guess. You go to the same little cottage you did the first time, even though you're now a baller resort owner and could afford something much nicer?"

I grin at the utility cover in front of me, securing the little screw in the threads. "That was true for about a decade, but then the owner sold it and the property got developed. We walked the beach that last year and chose the perfect house to keep up the tradition, so now we rent that one."

Naomi is practically glowing. She grins down at me, white paintbrush in hand. "That is the most adorably amazing story I've ever heard. I want to spend the rest of my life inside that story."

I smile, but I'm not sure she gets it. "And yet, hopping in a helicopter and flying off to some fabulous resort every weekend is the ideal lifestyle. Even you were questioning why I don't go."

"I was questioning. I'm not questioning anymore. I'm fully converted. I'm going to spend my time doing yard work, eating ramen, and enjoying the hell out of my week at the seaside each December. It's my new ten-year plan."

"She would adore you." The words just slip out. Luckily, they're quiet enough that I'm not sure Naomi hears.

"Who?"

No such luck.

"My mom."

"Oh."

There's a heavy pause where we both focus on our projects. I know I should say something to break the tension, but my brain isn't coming up with any rational thoughts.

The woman just proclaimed my quiet, simple life as her ten-year plan. The idea of her living here, working on the house with me, hanging the sheets, driving to the beach to watch the sunset after dinner, sharing a mug of cocoa or tea as we pray for a green flash.

Hanging out with my mom in Sag Harbor every December.

"I didn't mean..." Naomi apparently decides to try to take it back, to tell me I misunderstood, and I brace myself for it. "I just meant..."

"I know."

"Sam."

I push myself up to standing and turn in a circle, admiring how much work we've gotten done. "The windowsills look great."

Naomi looks apologetic and nervous and sad all at once, but she offers me a smile. "Thanks."

"You got some paint on your face, though."

Her mouth drops open, and she spins, searching the walls for a mirror that isn't there. "Where?"

With a grin, I close the distance between us, dragging my finger lightly over the brush that's still in her hand before touching her nose. "Right there."

She laughs and squeals, trying to get away but I catch her and pull her to me, making sure her brush hand doesn't end up between us.

When I kiss her, she closes her eyes and presses into me, lifting up on her toes to deepen our connection.

And to push her nose into mine.

She breaks away and cackles with glee. "Now you have some paint on your face, Sam."

And the thought that hits my brain, sent there by my exploding heart...

This is the happiest moment of my life.

Rule #38

KISS IT BETTER

NAOMI

We get take-out from a self-pronounced "chicken shack" and eat it on the porch, followed by the first episode of Firefly, watched on his tiny TV from an actual DVD.

"So great, right?" he asks with complete sincerity once the credits roll.

"Yeah. So great."

Sam narrows his eyes at me. "Are you just saying that?"

"No. It was really fun."

"It seemed like you were making fun of it, and that kind of thing isn't allowed in this house."

I grin at him. "I wasn't making fun of the show. I was making fun of your DVD collection. What are you going to do when season two comes out? Buy it on DVD also?"

"There was no season two. It got canceled after season one."

"That cinematic masterpiece? What for?"

He shakes his head solemnly. "No one knows."

When he leads me out to the newly finished bedroom, we christen the bed with orgasm after orgasm—most of them mine.

"I feel like a teenager when I'm around you, princess. It's like I can't get enough."

I laugh up at him from where I lay naked on the white sheets. "Your dick never gets, you know, sore?"

His forehead creases as he cocks his head. "Are you sore?"

"A little."

"Why didn't you tell me?"

"It's not a bad thing. I kind of like it. I can feel you even when you're not inside me."

His gaze drops to the tip of his cock, still bouncing at half-mast inches from my spread legs. Then his gaze shifts to me. Sliding back a few inches, Sam settles himself on his elbows, stretched out long with his legs hanging off the bed, and proceeds to kiss every inch of me, from clit to rosebud. He kisses around my entrance especially slowly, making sure every inch of my skin is graced with his healing touch.

"Okay, you kissed it all better. I'm ready to go again," I say, only half joking.

His head pops up from between my legs, and he's grinning. "That's not why I did it."

I shrug. "Happy side effect, I guess."

When he shifts back to his knees, I can see his stiff erection. "Looks like it worked its magic on you as well."

"I've never seen this guy so eager."

I push up to my knees and meet his lips with mine, tasting myself. Sam sits back as I press lightly on his chest until I'm on top, straddling his hips. I stroke my wet, still slightly sore, pussy up and down his length.

I'm about to angle my hips and let his tip slip inside me, but I change my mind. Gripping his base firmly in my fist, I slide down until I can trace the head of his cock with my tongue. Sam must have seen it coming, but he still hisses as I make contact. The sound brings a smile to my lips as I open and slide him in.

"I dream about this, princess," Sam moans as I take him deep, sucking and swirling.

His tip makes a little pop as I slide him out, working his shaft with my hand. "Not my other parts, huh?"

"Oh, I dream about those too."

"Sounds like you're being kept up at night with all these wet dreams."

"I've never slept better in my life than I do when you're next to me."

I could respond that the same is true for me, because it is, but we've already gone deeper into this territory today than I ever thought I'd tread. Instead, I take him deep fast, shutting us both up.

Sam squirms under me as I pump him through my lips. I can feel him holding back moving his own hips.

"You can help, you know. If you want to," I say, sliding him out.

"I don't want to hurt you."

I grin and trace the tip of his cock with my tongue. "You're not going to hurt me, Sammy. Especially not with me on top like this. Why don't you try?"

I don't give him time to answer before sucking him back into my mouth. He slowly relaxes his grip on the bed, and I stifle a grin as I feel one of those hands snake into my hair. Holding me as gently as he can while fisting my long curls, he starts to move his hips.

Cheeks hollowed, I brace for his thrusts.

They start off slow and easy, and I move against them, creating the perfect push and pull. Sam alternates between gasps and holding his breath. When I look up, eyes starting to water from the force of him, I find his gaze locked on my face.

I grin, and his eyes roll back for a brief moment before he locks gazes with me once more.

"You are the sexiest thing I've ever seen."

I murmur my agreement, because I am feeling awfully sexy right now, and the vibration must set something off in Sam because his thrusts get deeper, harder. I firm up my tongue on the underside of his shaft and just brace, letting him explore his own pleasure.

Just when his ever-growing moans have me thinking I'm about to swallow, he pulls up sharply on my hair and pops out of my mouth.

I pant for a short, surprised moment, mouth hanging open, before I gather myself enough to speak. "I thought you were going to come."

Sam releases my hair and throws both of his arms overhead on the bed. "I was. But I don't want to do it like that." He reaches down and grips my upper arms, pulling my body forward until my core is hovering above his cock.

When he takes me by the hips and pulls down, driving himself into me, we both gasp.

"I only want to come in here. Ever."

I can't argue with that, rocking my hips against his increasingly frantic upward thrusts. Reaching down, I press one finger over my clit as I ride him, and it's not long before my breathing matches his erratic pace.

We come together in a rush of breath and light and holding on just long enough to get the other person through. It's chaotic and messy, and for a moment, I can't tell which of us is making which noises.

Sam stills before I do, holding my hips as I grind myself against his pelvic bone, chasing the last of the feeling. When I finally come out the other side, I hang my head and bow my shoulders, drooping over him. He pushes my hair out of my face and pulls my lips down to meet his. I collapse beside him, inside the embrace of his strong arms, and open for his tongue as it traces mine.

"We got the clean sheets all dirty," I say when he pulls away.

"That's what they're for," he responds softly with a sleepy smile.

I don't answer, but he hears me, climbing up and fetching a pair of small towels from the main house and handing me one. We clean ourselves up as much as we can before wordlessly tangling our limbs once more, creating a braid of our bodies in the tousled sheets.

Rule #39

YOU'D SETTLE FOR SAFE. YOU GOT EVERYTHING

NAOMI

I wake when it's still dark outside, moonlight through the sheer curtains casting the room in an eerie glow. With Sam curled around me like a cat, I have to stretch very carefully to keep from waking him. It takes several long, slow tries for me to get my outstretched hand on my phone. I bring it back with me and wait for a long moment to let him settle back to sleep before lighting the screen up.

Usually, I would go through the motions of checking each of my favorite apps for notifications one after the other, and then go back through each one, letting the algorithms serve up the exact stream of posts my dopamine-starved brain was searching for. After nearly a whole day away from my screen, there are so many things to check.

Right now, however, I can't even hear the call of the apps. And I know it's not because there are no notifications waiting for me due to my complete lack of posting. That's never stopped me before.

No, this time, it just feels different. The phone feels the same, the same heavy plastic, the same glass screen that seems to breathe like a living thing under my fingers. But there's only one thing I want to see on this device, and it's not contained within any app.

I find the video tucked into my password-protected folder and key in the code. Making sure the volume is down all the way, I hit play.

I smile at the scene that jumps out of the glowing screen at me. I'm setting the camera up on the dresser in my room at Dom's, trying to get it pointed at the right angle to capture the whole bed. I look backward and call out to Sam, and he struts over and sits on the edge of the bed, grinning at me. I say something else, and he's beside me, pulling the dresser closer to the bed while I try to keep the phone from falling off.

I scrub through the video a bit until I get to the frame where he has me spread over his body, my knees on either side of his, my back arched over his chest. One of his strong arms holds me around my ribcage, just under my breasts. The other snakes between my legs.

I have my eyes closed and my lip bit between my teeth. I was posing. I knew that at the time. I loved the feeling of being displayed for the video this way. My eyes linger on my own body for a second more before finding what I really came here for.

Sam's expression.

The first time I used my phone to record an intimate moment, it wasn't even my idea. The closest thing I had to a high school boyfriend, this guy who used to come over to the house and swim in the pool, watch movies with me in our home theater, and later started sleeping in my bed, suggested it.

I wasn't stupid enough to let him record it on his own phone, but I was curious about how it all looked. How we looked.

How he looked at me.

So, I videoed the whole thing on my Nokia N95 slider, the absolute top of the line phone at the time. I smile thinking back on that crappy, pixelated video now, but it was the start of something big for me.

The guy wanted to watch the video after, and we did, but I never got pulled into the action like I know he did. For me, it was all about the faces. What we looked like, where we were looking, what expressions were captured on our faces when we were lost to the heat of the moment.

iPhones upped the video game a few years later, and my little hobby took on a life of its own.

I wanted to see.

Talk about distracting, it was all I could do not to perform for the camera. Not to look over at where I often had it hidden during my various one-night stands or one-week relationships over the years.

Soon enough, however, I realized that the real prize wasn't my own face, it was the face of my partner. What expression he had. Which things I did made that expression turn favorable. Whether or not he was actually into me, or if he was just sticking his dick somewhere.

Whether I was good enough.

Looking at Sam's face now, in the paused image of my own body spread open for the camera, I can barely breathe.

He's looking down over my shoulder, his gaze cast over my body to where his fingers are trailing closer and closer to my core. His eyes are a little wider than usual, his cheeks flushed. The expression on his mouth could almost be reaching for a smile, but caught before it got there, slightly tipped, eager, like he's dying to get his lips on my skin. It's not hard to see that his entire being, every ounce of his focus, is trained on me.

I slowly move the video forward a bit, watching Sam's face the whole time. He slips his fingers inside me, and his eyes roll back before dropping closed and then shooting open once more to watch with reverence as he sinks knuckle deep into my wetness. When I come, his whole face lights up with pleasure and desire, as if he's having an orgasm right alongside me.

I move forward until I'm on my hands and knees, and Sam reaches forward to wrap my long hair in his fist. His forehead is creased with concentration as he gets a better grip on me, pulling me up by my hair until my head lifts toward him.

"Tell me to fuck you." I remember him saying. I can see the intensity of his body language as he says it.

His face snarls at my answer, and I can feel a pulse between my legs even now, remembering how it felt when he turned feral.

"I meant beg."

I almost slide my hand down between our bodies, underneath the soft, light blanket Sam draped over us against the slight chill of the tropical night, but then I remember why I got my phone in the first place.

It wasn't to get riled up by the action scenes, or even to scroll through the library of Sam's facial expressions, cataloging each one in my memory bank.

No, I took this risk, gave up these moments snuggled up asleep in Sam's arms, for a reason. And that reason is at the end of the video.

I scrub all the way to the end, smiling as we move through sexual motions at lightning speed, until I get to the part where we're lying still on the bed, side by side. Sam's propped on one elbow, facing the camera. I'm on my back with my side tucked in close to the curve of his ribs and hips.

I can see myself talking, but I don't dare to turn the volume up, not with the man in question sleeping so peacefully beside me now.

I know what I said. *"Tell me what you're thinking."*

I watch as Sam's face spreads into one of his heart-melting smiles, and he starts to tell me about how much he loved having me there to do yard work with him.

I watch as I get into the stuff about my mother's death and how it changed our family, words I've never spoken aloud to anyone.

He watches me speak, his face calm and sad and empathetic. He smiles, closes his eyes, and raises his eyebrows before he scoffs and turns serious. All the while, never taking his attention off me for a second.

He loves me.

The thought shakes me so much that I startle a bit, nearly dropping the phone onto the head of the sleeping man in my arms.

He stirs, and I quickly close the screen, sending the phone into darkness. I drop it over my shoulder onto the bed behind me as Sam cracks one eye open, peering up at me in his half-asleep state.

"You awake?" he asks.

I shake my head, even though it's obvious that I am. "I was just…something woke me, but I'm going back to sleep."

He curls himself a bit lower, leaning his face forward to place a line of kisses on my naked torso, starting at my navel and continuing up between my breasts. He kisses the nape of my neck last and then curls into his sleeping fetal position once more, arms draped over my body.

I lay my hand on his head, stroking his short hair gently as his breathing evens out once more, falling into a long, slow rhythm.

He loves me.

He's never said it, but I know it's true.

Honestly, I can't believe I didn't see it before. In the way he takes care of me, the way I catch him smiling every time he looks my way.

The way he offered to do the one thing he's so scared of and tell Dom about us, just so I wouldn't feel like he was ashamed of me.

I said no, and I don't regret my choice. These days we've spent together, alone in our little cocoon of secret looks and touches and smiles, have been the most transformative of my life.

I love Sam.

That thought shakes me even more.

Is it true?

Yes.

Is it convenient to have fallen so utterly and hopelessly in love with a man who lives a million miles away from my entire life and who is so inextricably connected to my brother—the last person in the world I would want in my personal life? Hardly.

But I guess that's how it goes.

For so many years, I've waited to find my person. Hoped and even prayed. Searched and been patient. Did all the things you're supposed to do. I wanted to find a person who would slot into my life seamlessly. Probably move into my apartment, settle into the routine of my job and hobbies. Someone who wouldn't rock the boat of what I thought was the perfect life I'd built for myself.

I guess it's lucky I never found that person. Not when the life I was so proud of turned out to be one giant lie. All my connections and friends turning on me just when I needed them most.

What would have happened if this perfect partner had a channel of his own? A personal brand he needed to protect. Would he have turned on me just as quickly to save himself?

For a moment, I'm completely and utterly blown away by the mysterious ways of the universe. How it saved me from the dumb shit I thought I wanted and delivered me straight into the arms of this perfect man.

Ask and you shall receive. Isn't that what all the Instagram manifestation coaches drill into us with their ten second reels and heavily stylized lifestyle photos?

I'll admit, I got impatient. But I also asked for the wrong thing.

At least my brain did.

Turns out, my heart and soul were asking for just what I needed all along.

And here he is.

Rule #40

YOU WERE NEVER MEANT TO GO IT ALONE

NAOMI

Sam's up early the next morning getting ready for work. He waits until the last second to come wake me to say goodbye. I've been awake for a while, listening to him shuffle around in the bedroom, moving back and forth between this room and the main room.

When he finally sits on the edge of the bed, he's got a cup of coffee in his hand.

"Morning, sunshine," I say.

His eyes widen in surprise, smile growing ever wider. "That's what I was going to say."

I can't help but smile back. "I know."

He leans down to kiss me, and I can taste the mint of his toothpaste. Smell the scent of shampoo on his still wet hair. "I have to head into work. I'll probably be there most of the day. Feel free to hang out as long as you like."

Stay forever.

He doesn't say the words, but they hang in the air like fireflies, waiting to be captured.

"Okay. I've got a bit of work to do on the pictures and videos I shot for the wedding, but I can probably do that here."

Sam's face twists to the side in a slight grimace. "I don't have the fastest internet out here. Feel free to come down to The Sands. You can sit by the pool or work in one of the conference rooms."

He doesn't suggest the obvious place, my room at Dom's house where the internet is lightning fast. Sam wants me to come to him.

I smile and nod, finally sitting up to take the steaming mug from his hands. "Okay. I'll probably need to do that a little later. For now, I'm going to work naked in bed for as long as I can."

He groans and drapes his body over my outstretched legs. "If only I could call in sick."

"You can't?" I know the answer, but I want to keep him talking. Keep him here longer.

He makes a sad face, peering up at me from where his ear rests on my knees. "Too many other people did. I have to go figure out how to get their jobs done along with my own."

"Big boss man."

He sits up and adjusts his button-up work shirt. "That's why they pay me the big bucks."

I smile at his joke but can't think of anything to say.

"See you this afternoon, maybe?"

I nod. "I'll be there."

It's nearly an hour before my bladder drags me out of bed and into the main house. My coffee cup has long since gone cold, and I search for the kettle after freshening myself up a bit.

It's kind of odd, having all the things I need in different little houses and having to go outside to reach each one, but not in a bad way. I'm starting to like the feeling of having the outdoors be my hallway. I like the uneven, unfinished doorway ledges that I have to remember not to stub my toes on. I like waiting next to the gas burner for the water to boil, watching geckos hunt for gnats on the window screens.

But, as excited as I am about this house and the tsunami of feelings I'm having for Sam, right now all I want is to dive into my content from the wedding. From the gold-plated silverware to the full violin orchestra dressed all in ombre sunset colors, to the rare, black orchid-lined aisle. That wedding was a spectacle in the best possible way.

I start by sorting the pictures into ones to keep and ones to delete. From there, I sort the keepers into ones I'm going to edit first and ones I might get to later.

Once I have the absolute best of the best ready to go, I fire up my laptop to start editing.

It becomes clear almost immediately that this isn't going to work. The photos I deleted or moved to their own folders are all still in the giant dump of my recent photos, the internet out here failing to update my cloud at any workable pace.

I settle for texting a dozen or so of the very best shots to Fran, who I know is going to be just as excited as I am.

Fran
Girl! These are the best pictures I've ever seen! How did you do this with your phone? I've seen some of the shots from the photographers already, and they are nothing like this.

I smile at her gushing praise. It feels really good to be able to participate on such a meaningful level. The feelings I was having during the wedding wrap-up, of being part of a team, come rushing back in, warming me from the inside out.

Naomi
Thanks! There are a ton more. I can't do any editing here because the internet is too slow, but I'm going to head to The Sands in a few. Want to meet me there for lunch?

Fran
What's wrong with the internet? Does Dom know? I know for sure he'll have techs out there within the hour if his prize router is having issues.

Oops. Of course she would assume I was at Dom's house, not curled up on Sam's couch.

Naomi
Oh. Right. Well, I'm not exactly at Dom's...

Fran
😂 😍 Say no more. I love it. I love this so much.

Naomi
It's...it's a whole thing.

Fran
What time's lunch?

Rule #41

ALWAYS WATCH YOUR BACK

SAM

It's not unusual for me to walk the halls of The Sands, smile on my face, greeting each person I meet. Today, however, I know there's a little something extra in that smile, in my demeanor, and I know everyone can see it.

I couldn't hide it if I tried.

This is, hands down, the happiest I've ever been in my life. Joy and excitement and hope for the future are pumping through my veins like the fountain of youth, energizing my every step. By the time I make it down to Reef for coffee and a cinnamon roll and back up to my office, I've already chatted with a dozen people, all of whom were smiling by the time they walked away, no matter how heavy their morning was before they found me.

I'm a walking ray of sunshine.

I settle into my desk and spend a few moments just enjoying the perfect contrast of the sweet pastry with the rich, strong black coffee. This might be the best breakfast I've ever had.

I smile at my ridiculously good mood.

I know exactly where the credit lies.

Hopefully, she's still lying in my bed.

Yesterday was so incredible. Waking up together and having a little breakfast date in town like a real couple. Napping on my couch like it was something we did all the time. She's always just as excited as I am to head out and tackle yard projects, and watching her experience the joy of transforming the bedroom with just a paintbrush and a little elbow grease was one of the highlights of my life thus far.

Suddenly, everything that's ever happened to me, all the wonderful, memorable moments, seem to pale in comparison to yesterday.

The day I officially fell in love.

It's been coming for a while. I could see it like a boat offshore, careening toward the beach as if it had lost control entirely.

That's a pretty good summation of how I feel. Moving too fast for the environment I find myself in. Speeding headlong toward an inevitable end. Blissfully unbothered by the coming impact.

I've passed the point of turning back. Of letting her go.

Now that I've experienced how it can feel to have it all—my dream job working at the resort I own and my dream home life with a woman I love waiting there for me—giving it up is no longer in the cards. It's exactly what I've imagined all these years. A work life and a home life. Both equally satisfying. And gloriously separate. A home that's still my refuge from the resort, as much as I love it here. I know that's what I need.

I inhale deeply and breathe the air out, not wanting to sink into worry about what's going to happen when we decide it's time to go public. Not ready to ruin the high of this morning.

Unfortunately, my high is short-lived.

My office door gets pushed hard from the outside and swings open quickly, hitting the wall and bouncing off again, only to be caught in the hand of Dom himself.

Speak of the devil.

It's not that I want to think of one of my best friends that way. It's just that, since this whole thing started, he's officially the only thing standing in the way of having everything I've ever wanted.

No, it's not him. It's a conversation. A difficult conversation, sure, but a simple one. That's what's standing between me and my new relationship being more than a special little secret.

And I am nothing if not good at handling difficult conversations.

"Morning, Dom."

He folds his arms across his chest and narrows his eyes at me.

Wait, does he already know?

My mind starts to reel, even as I keep my face calm and neutral.

Fran knows, but Naomi said she was going to keep it to herself. But that was before the little trip they just took to blow off steam after the wedding. Who knows what kind of drunken conversations went on.

I brace myself.

"We're all meeting at the big table down at Reef."

I blink at him and then glance down at my desk calendar to see if there's a meeting scheduled for this morning that I somehow forgot about. Nothing.

"We?" I ask.

"Yeah. Me and the guys and Fran and Reina. You planning on joining us?"

I'm already getting to my feet, replacing the plastic lid on my coffee cup. "This is the first I'm hearing about it, but of course I'll join you. Ben's here?"

"He came to Honduras with us. Now he and Victoria are here for the day."

"For this meeting. What's this all about?" I'm starting to get nervous. I know I'm not going to get much out of Dom, but it's worth a try. Better to be as prepared as I can be for whatever I'm walking into.

"Resort stuff."

I almost smile at his gruff, predictably short answer.

"Resort stuff," I reply, tucking my phone into my pocket. When I glance up, however, he's already gone.

I hurry to catch up as he storms through the hallways toward the stairs leading down to the pool patio. When we blow through the café doors, I find everyone already seated at a long table against the back wall. Ben, Avery, Fran, and Reina. They're all lounging casually, drinking coffee and laughing. This looks nothing like the grim dressing down I was expecting after Dom's gruff invitation.

"Morning, Sam," Reina calls, climbing to her feet. I offer her the embrace she's expecting and find my seat.

"We missed you in Pristine Bay," Ben calls out in greeting, a kind, knowing expression on his face.

I offer my usual smile and eyebrow raise. "You guys have a good time?"

The next ten minutes are filled with lively stories of sun, pool time, and late nights at the famous beach club restaurant and bar on the property. I take in the words, nodding and smiling, feeling genuinely happy that they had a good time.

Even as I grow more and more antsy to learn why we're all here.

"Enough. Let's get this over with so I can go back to work." For once, I agree with Dom's harsh pronouncement.

Reina just laughs. "You are such a beast."

Dom smiles over at her, softening.

That's the look that's going to save me. The fact that this man now knows what love can do. He's not going to deny me that, is he?

Avery clears his throat, and we all look to him. "We did some talking on our trip, and we have a great idea for how to make the resort and all of our future events even better."

I feel my eyebrows lift as I try not to laugh in surprise. "Okay. Fantastic. Let's hear it."

A hush falls over the room, and I look from face to face, trying to determine the source of it.

Finally, Fran speaks. "After a fabulous lunch meeting, where we pored over the content from the last wedding and were so inspired by her enthusiasm and positive attitude, Ave and I, and now the rest of the team, came to the only possible conclusion. We want to offer Naomi the position of social media manager for Paradise Events and The Sands."

The hush returns to the table, the group waiting with bated breath for my answer as if they know what kind of bomb this is.

Unfortunately for everyone involved, no one has any idea. Not even me.

"No." The word is out of my mouth before I even think.

"Sam, it's—"

"No!" I hear myself shout but can't seem to stop it.

My heart races, and I'm starting to sweat. My brain is descending into madness, and I can't bring a rational thought forward through the muck of internal screaming.

No.

This can't be.

She's my home, not work.

They can't have her.

She's mine.

I'm on my feet, even though I don't remember standing up. All my friends gape at me, a couple of mouths actually hanging open.

Of course, it's Ben who also stands. The voice of reason. "Sam, we were just thinking that since she did such a good job on the wedding and The Sands already lost their on-site social media manager—"

"No." I shake my head like a crazy person. "It's a terrible idea. She's completely inexperienced in high-end resort social media management. We haven't even interviewed for the position yet. To just choose her without holding interviews would be inappropriate. Nepotism."

I'm grasping at straws here, my defenses sounding ridiculous even to me. They're going to override me. I can already tell. This isn't a meeting to ask my opinion. It's a meeting where they tell me something they've already decided.

They decided to take Naomi from me, turn her into just another thing to handle at work. Just another coworker who I smile at in the hallway. Someone who will want to talk about the resort at home, the last thing I ever want to do.

I need my work and home life separate. A thick, black line drawn between the two. Work is where I have to be who the guys need me to be. Their lesser, the one who was never good enough.

Home is where I just get to be me.

I can see it in their faces. They're surprised by my reaction, but not a bit worried.

They don't need to be.

They clearly have the votes.

I pull my trump card out and consider the damage it might cause.

I don't have a choice.

I throw the damn thing on the table.

"She's already caused one terrible scandal that got her canceled from the internet. How can we trust her to manage the resort's reputation after what she did to her own?"

A different kind of hush falls over the table now. I finally get the nerve to look up from where my hands rest on the smooth, cool wood, bracing myself for the shocked faces.

But no one is looking at me.

With cold dread pumping through my veins, I follow their gazes behind me.

Where I find Naomi, looking just as shocked and hurt as she should.

Our eyes lock for a split second, in which time I try to convey to her how sorry I am and all my many reasons for saying the terrible things I just said.

But it doesn't work.

She turns and runs from the room.

I follow after her immediately, ignoring the surprised shouts behind me.

Down the hallway I run. Up the stairs to the lobby level and then up a few more flights. She's running aimlessly it seems, just trying to lose me.

It's not going to work. She may have a head start, but I'm bigger. I know my way around these hallways better.

I catch sight of her golden-brown hair glinting in the sunlight from a high window as she disappears down the third-floor hallway, around the corner, and through the door into the emergency stairwell.

With a deep sigh, knowing that I have little recourse here, I pull open the door and follow her in.

Once the heavy fire door closes behind me, the world goes cool, dim, and quiet. The only sound is her flip-flops hurrying down the concrete steps.

"Naomi, stop." My voice echoes through the stairwell.

She does not stop.

"Naomi, let me explain."

"Are you fucking kidding me?" Her words bounce off the walls, breathless and angry.

She still doesn't stop.

I start to jog down the steps, but I'm too far behind. I hear the ground floor exit door slam when I'm making the turn to the second floor. By the time I emerge into the hot morning sun, she's nowhere to be found.

Rule #42

THE TRUTH DIDN'T BREAK YOU—BELIEVING DID

NAOMI

My mind is a blur of rage and sadness and shame. It's screaming at me to run and fight and hide and attack, attack, attack. I can't even force the spinning wheel of thoughts to slow, let alone stop.

This is it. This is the moment I was somehow, in the dark depths of my mind, waiting for.

I know better than to trust people.

I trusted my influencer community, and I got burned alive.

My own family never wanted me.

What a damn fool I was to think it would ever be different. That I could ever be a person who was important enough to someone to keep around. To make real sacrifices for.

That I was, all of a sudden, after never once in my life being good enough for anyone, good enough for Sam.

Well, he sure showed me.

After my big blowout on the internet back in Austin, I was convinced that nothing could ever surprise me again. That whole thing came so far out of left field, blindsided me to the point where I thought it was a joke for hours after it all started to go up in flames.

It's only all these weeks later that I was finally starting to process what happened. Starting to see the signs I chose to ignore from the beginning. Starting to reevaluate the relationships I thought were so solid.

It was the safety of Sam's arms that gave me the space to be able to do that.

Maybe that's where I went wrong. I felt secure and cared for and allowed myself to get distracted. To let my mind wander.

When I should have been paying more attention to the current snake in the room.

My heart aches for the simplicity of yesterday. Of this morning, even.

When I woke in that bed, Sam bringing me coffee and kissing me goodbye before work. He really did all that thinking I was a loser. Someone who couldn't be trusted.

A fresh wave of shame washes over me as I allow myself to see the truth.

He never had any intention of making things real between us. He's a responsible adult with a real job and a community. Friends and a resort he needs to watch out for.

And what am I?

I'm nothing. I'm a loser with no plan for life. Nowhere to go. No one to turn to.

"Naomi!"

I turn my head out of instinct but immediately turn it back forward when I see Sam jogging up the path behind me.

"God you're fast." He's huffing like he just ran the whole way up the sandy trail from the resort.

I continue to ignore him, arms folded, eyes focused on the ground in front of me as I put one foot in front of the other. I only have to make it to the employee parking lot where I left my loaner golf cart, and then I'm free. I have no idea where I'll go, but wherever it is, I'm going there fast.

"If you don't stop walking in one second, I'm going to make you stop," he says, still keeping pace with me as I refuse to look over.

I huff out a laugh and pick up my pace.

A strong hand clamps down on my upper arm and pulls sharply, forcing me to stop and turn to face him. I hang my head and try to look away.

Thank god for mirrored sunglasses. He can't see how much I've been crying.

"That was…it wasn't what it sounded like," he starts, and I consider kicking him, so he'll let me go.

Actually that's not a bad plan.

I land a sharp kick on his shin with the sole of my flip-flop.

Sam barks in pain and drops my arm. I continue up the hill.

"Okay, I deserved that. I get it. You're pissed, and you have every right to be. You weren't supposed to be there."

Red rage renders me blind and sucks all the rational thought from my mind. I stop and whirl to face him. "I wasn't supposed to be there? That's your excuse? You have got to be kidding me!"

I start to walk once more, and Sam chases after me. "It wasn't an excuse. You weren't supposed to be there, though. That was a meeting of the owners of the resort, and we were talking about business."

"The owners of the resort and their girlfriends."

Something I will never be.

Fresh tears spark in the corners of my eyes. I've got to get to my golf cart.

"Yeah, the owners and their partners, who are also on the resort management team. And what you heard…I can explain."

I whirl to face him once more. "You can explain why you blocked a plan to have me work at The Sands because I'm too much of a risk to the resort's reputation after ruining my own?

Maybe you can also explain why you've been telling me that you want this, whatever it is, between us to be real, when you just straight up told the people closest to you that you didn't want me around. That was an opportunity for me to join that table, Sam. For us to be together like they are. I thought that's what you wanted. But you looked at those couples and knew I wasn't good enough for that. Knew I wasn't good enough for any of it."

Sam's listening to me speak with wide eyes and a slack jaw.

I surprised him with my expert deduction skills. He clearly wasn't expecting to be called out for what he really feels.

Well, take that, asshole.

When he finally speaks, his words are soft, cautious. "Naomi, you can't actually think those things."

I'm still on the attack. "Me? Are you kidding me right now? This discussion isn't about what I think. I'm not the one who just stood up in front of everyone and announced that I was too big of a risk to the resort's reputation—" I spit the last word out before Sam interrupts me.

"You don't understand."

"I understand perfectly." I turn on my heel and start to walk away, but Sam's voice stops me.

"Those guys get everything."

It's not so much the words as it is his tone. It's broken, jagged, laced with years of pent-up emotions.

I pause my march and stand looking at the ground in front of me, not turning back.

"My whole goddamn life." His voice cracks, and I can hear his labored breathing, but I still don't turn around. "My whole life those guys have had everything. They had everything, and they took anything else they wanted. Anything of mine, anything of anyone's. I gave it all up because how could I not? They were generous to me, and their families were generous. I wouldn't be anywhere near where I am today if not for those guys and their money and their power and privilege. But even though I stand next to them, I'm not one of them. I don't have a drop of what they have."

I finally turn to face him. "You have got to be fucking kidding me with that line. You really expect me to believe that? You own the damn resort, Sam. That's not nothing."

He just stares at me, and I have to look away from the sadness I see in his eyes. I'm not here to forgive him or feel sorry for him. He can have all the feelings he wants. They have nothing to do with me.

"You think I somehow pulled almost thirty million dollars out of my pocket to buy into this resort? How the hell would I have done that? I signed away my life, my sweat and blood, to this resort, but it's all just paper. Dom paid my share. The Fuentes family fortune paid my share, just like they always did. Hell, you're more of an owner of the damn resort than I am."

I suck in a breath so sharply that it's audible in the silence that falls after his words.

I'm fully prepared to continue my journey up the hill, get in my golf cart, and drive away from this man. From this life. The one I thought I wanted. The one I thought I somehow deserved.

But Sam's words...Sam's truth keeps me still.

"I just wanted this one thing, all to myself. Mine. I've never stood up to those guys, not on anything that mattered. I just let them have their way and try to be grateful they let me stick around. You think I'm scared to lose a friend when we talk about telling Dom about us? I'm scared to lose everything. And this is why. I don't actually have anything. But I had you. And I'll be goddamned if those guys are going to take you from me."

"They don't have to, Sam." I shake my head. "You really don't get it, do you? What you thought you had with me ended the second you spoke those words. If that's the kind of thing that you're thinking, this thing between us was never real. So, good luck with this mess." I wave my hand in a dismissive gesture to the trees and the paths and the resort below, taking one last look at the gorgeous view that I thought would be mine. "Maybe I'll see you around."

I turn and start back up the path without waiting for his response.

Sam doesn't follow me to my cart, but I catch sight of him at the edge of the lot as I pull out, watching me go.

Rule #43

IT'S TIME FOR A NEW STORY

NAOMI

Most of my stuff is at Dom's house, so that's where I should go, but I just can't. The thought of Sam following me and watching me climb the stairs of humiliation is just too much.

I steer my cart onto the main road and head for town instead. My suitcase will still be waiting for me later.

I park next to the shipping building like everyone else and walk down the narrow lane that runs through the village down to the beach. It's quiet at this time of day, all the sane people sheltering from the hot afternoon sun, rather than parading down the street with no hat or sunscreen. I'm lucky to have my wallet with me, as I was coming in to get another coffee when fate ambushed me.

I don't even have my purse.

Wait, I don't have my phone.

I pat my whole self down to make sure, a futile exercise as I'm wearing tropical clothes with very few places to hide anything.

I must have left it at my table at The Sands, along with my

laptop, bag, and everything else I'd brought to the resort with me that morning for a full day of work.

I keep walking until I reach the beach, flopping down in the sand and shielding my eyes from the overhead sun. I'm just settling into my warm sand bed, content to spend the rest of my life laying here, listening to the waves crash, when someone calls my name.

Or my last name anyway.

"Ms. Fuentes!"

I sit up enough to prop my upper body on my elbows and glance around, finding no one in my line of sight.

"Over here." The voice comes again.

I turn all the way around to find a man smiling at me from a table in the closest café. I recognize him from breakfast with Sam so I smile and wave, hoping that will be enough to satisfy him.

It's not.

"Come join us for a drink. It must be hot out there in the sun."

Because it is very hot, and because I don't have my phone to distract me from all my thoughts and feelings, I drag myself out of the sand and walk over.

The slight, black-haired man is sitting at a square table with a round, cheerful looking woman his same age, both of them smiling up at me. I settle into the third chair and immediately feel relief as the shade from the umbrella takes away the heat of the direct sun.

"Thank you. I didn't realize how hot I was."

"You young ladies never do," the woman at the table states, laughing at her own joke.

I watch her, wide-eyed, and the first smile in what feels like hours spreads over my face. "I guess that's true."

"The plight of the young. To not know how good you have it," the man says, his grin as wide as his companion's. "I'm Max. We met at breakfast the other day. This is my wife, Petunia." He gestures to the woman, who bows slightly.

"Nice to see you again," I say to Max. "I'm Naomi."

"Oh, we know who you are," Petunia says slyly before sharing a glance with her husband.

"Okay…"

What do they think they know about me?

"You're Dominic's little sister."

I relax. "You got me."

"Here on a mission to figure out your purpose in life."

Wait, what?

"I…I'm sorry?"

The waiter chooses that moment to swoop in and take my drink order. I hastily ask for an iced tea to get him to go away.

The two of them are still smiling at me like they don't have a care in the world when I turn my glare on them. "How do you know that about me?"

Max shrugs. "It's what you all say when I ask. Seems to be the plight of most of your generation."

I smile in relief. He wasn't reading my mind. He was just making a general observation. "Gotcha."

"But you, my dear, seem to have something deeper going on. It's just a guess, based on how you threw yourself into the sand, but I would be willing to bet that whatever it was you thought you found isn't working out the way you planned."

I accept my iced tea with a smile and try to decide how much of this I want to get into with these complete strangers. I don't have my phone, and I don't have anyone I could call even if I did, so what the hell.

"Yeah. I just hit a bit of a bump in the road."

Neither of them makes any signs of speaking as they give me their full attention, so I go on. "I lost my business back in the States by doing something incredibly stupid that I didn't know was stupid at the time. And then I ran here to hide, but ended up falling for the last guy on the planet I should have fallen for. And it seemed to be going pretty well until I just overheard him telling all his friends what a loser I am, simultaneously breaking my heart and stealing away the fantastic new job opportunity that was about to come my way."

I almost laugh at my ridiculous summation of the last month of my life, but I'm worried it will come out as a sob, so I just sip my iced tea and wait for one of them to speak.

"I wonder if you could tell your story again, but this time, tell the truth," Max says finally.

My mouth falls open. This day is just full of surprises. "That was the truth."

"Was it?"

There's no malice in his tone. Nothing to make me defensive, so I take a moment and consider. "No, I guess not."

I glance out at the ocean and try to formulate my true story.

"Okay. I've been working for my whole adult life to build a personal brand and channel that represents me. Or at least the me that I want the world to see. I'm good at it, and I've been really successful. But I knew that it wasn't real life, even as much as I wanted it to be. I've always struggled with personal relationships. Online relationships are so much easier. Simpler. I almost never have to meet anyone in person, and I can curate how I come across in photos and texts. It was all so perfectly contained. Under my control. Until it wasn't. I was just working to promote brands, like we all do on the internet, but some people I'd built online friendships with decided to go behind my back and take me down to grow their own channels. It's something I've done before. We all do it. I didn't even think it was that wrong until it happened to me. Suddenly I was left with nothing and no one. I've never had close relationships with my family and never made many in-person friends since I had my online community."

I'm hesitant to get into so much detail about a person I know they know well, but I can't bring myself to stop now that I've started. "But there was one person. One person who I thought would be a safe place to turn. I can't even say why I thought that. I barely knew the guy. But it was enough. So, I flew out here and found him. It was hard at first, but he was exactly as wonderful as I imagined, and I started to see a new life for myself. A life where I belonged and where people saw me as who I really was. In person. I thought he felt the same way."

I pause to glance down at my hands where they rest on the colorful floral tablecloth.

"Then this afternoon I overheard him telling his friends that he didn't want me to come work with them because it would put the resort at risk. That I was untested and possibly untrustworthy. It sucked because I didn't even want the job they were discussing offering me. I would have turned it down, the main part of it anyway. But to hear him say those terrible things about me, like he had just been pretending to care about me all this time."

"That sounds bad. What did this mystery man have to say for himself?" Petunia asks.

I smile up at her, even though I feel like I might cry as I try to tell the next part. "He said that he was just trying to keep me all for himself. That the other guys take everything, and he's always let them, but this time he wanted to keep me for himself. And that he was sorry, and he didn't mean any of it."

They let me cry in silence for a long moment, not offering me comfort or a napkin or anything. The wave of sadness passes on its own, and I look back up into their kind faces, already feeling better.

Already knowing what Max is about to say.

"Now that you've said that aloud, does it seem like the truth?"

I nod.

He and Petunia nod as well.

"But what can I do? Tell Dom or let him tell Dom about us? It will ruin that lifelong friendship and put his whole job, his whole life in jeopardy. I can't ask him to do that for me."

"Is that the truth?" Max asks.

I narrow my eyes accusingly at him as I prepare to take him to task.

But my anger quickly sees reason. I flop back in my chair and sigh. "No. Probably not."

"It's a fun story, though. Very dramatic."

I can't help but smile and shake my head. "Yeah, yeah. I get it."

"Being afraid is sometimes easier than doing hard things. Especially if those hard things go against what we've always done. Sam has never stood up to his friends because he sees himself as less. You refuse to fight for what you want for the same reason."

Petunia claps her hands together, excitement lighting up her face. "I can't wait to see what happens."

"I agree," Max concurs, smiling at his wife.

I want to be mad. I want to be annoyed as hell at the way they're making light of the crushing reality of my situation. But even in the lowest place of my life, I can see the futility of it. "Yeah, I guess I'm looking forward to it as well. At least, I am now."

They beam at me.

It's impossible not to smile back.

Rule #44

WHEN IN DOUBT, STAKEOUT

SAM

I walk back down the sandy trail to the resort with heavy feet. And a heavy heart.

I lost my mind during that meeting.

I wasn't thinking. I wasn't myself.

I can't believe I said those things. Things that I have never, not one single time, thought before. I just needed them to change their minds, and I was willing to say anything.

I'm not just sorry because Naomi was there to overhear. I would be sorry for my words either way.

But the fact that she just drove away thinking that's how I see her? It breaks my heart.

I've watched her come so far over the last couple of weeks. Coming out of her shell. Finding joy in little things. She was starting to trust herself again.

And I just ruined all of that.

The rush of air conditioning hits me as I push through the lobby doors, and I breathe a sigh of relief that I don't deserve.

I caused this whole mess by choosing not to be truthful from the very beginning.

Never in my life have I created anything close to the web of lies I now find myself living in and look where it got me. My reputation is built on my integrity. If anything was going to put my standing at the resort and my friendships at risk, it was breaking that trust.

Not falling in love.

I want to hate myself for my stupidity, but it won't change anything. And it certainly won't help solve this mess I've made.

Only one thing will help with that.

I bypass my office and head straight to the Raft kitchen.

"Hey," I say when I spot Dom. "We need to talk."

He turns from where he's helping a cook outline a prep list and glares at me. "So you can explain why you busted out of that meeting like a crazy person? Yeah, I'd say we need to talk."

I fold my arms, not standing down. "My office or yours?"

He glances over his shoulder at the closed door of his shared restaurant office. "Yours."

"Fine."

I turn and walk back toward the lobby without waiting. I'm sitting at my desk when he finally pushes my office door open.

We just stare at each other for a moment, both of us with our arms crossed on our chests. I want to see the humor in this situation, this standoff, but I'm too anxious. I just blurt out my next words.

"I'm in love with your sister. I know I said some crazy shit at that meeting, but it's complicated, and we're going to work it out. If you need me to resign, I accept that."

There. He has the information now. He can do with it what he will.

Dom's quiet for a long moment, his gaze locked on mine. When he finally starts to narrow his eyes, I brace myself.

He takes two steps forward until he's standing right up

against my desk. He leans over to place both hands flat on the surface, his face now a mere foot from mine. "What the fuck are you talking about?"

The emotion that flares in me is some mixture of annoyance and impatience. He couldn't just make this easy, huh?

"I understand that my having a relationship with Naomi is unacceptable to you, and I'll resign my position if needed. I'm not giving her up."

I can almost see the tremor go through Dom's body. I wonder briefly if he's going to headbutt me, but I continue to stand my ground.

"Why the hell would you think I'd want you to resign?"

I shake my head at his arrogant pigheadedness. "I was there at the meeting when you told all the guys that you'd murder them if they touched your sister. I know how you feel about protecting her."

"Oh, the meeting that you weren't invited to?" He stands back up, face starting to color as he huffs out his next words. "I was telling all those fuckboy pool cleaners and bartenders that, Sam." He gestures wildly in what he must think is the direction of the bar or pool. "I wasn't telling that to you. Are you kidding me? There isn't a guy on this planet who wouldn't want you for his little sister."

He spins to face the door and drags both hands down his face before turning back to me, all composure lost. "You've just been sneaking around thinking I was going to run you off the island if you told me?"

My mistake is now glaringly obvious, and I feel more stupid than I ever have in my life. I got so caught up in my people-pleasing that I apparently never stopped for a second to consider if the story I was telling myself was true.

"Well, it sounds ridiculous when you put it like that, but yeah. That's pretty much what's been going on."

"How long?" he asks, his voice softer now.

"I ran into her when I was up in Austin. We hung out then, and she's been all I can think about since."

He folds his arms and sighs, collapsing into one of the chairs across from my desk. "I've been so worried about her. All this shit she's going through, and she seemed to be going through it all alone, because fuck knows she never wants to spend a second at the house with Reina and me. And she flat out told me that she doesn't think she's the kind of person people want to date, not that I gave her much of a chance when I told everyone to stay the hell away from her. When we got home last night, I waited up for her to come back, and when she never did, I just about called the police."

He levels me with an accusatory glare. "I pictured her off on some deserted beach, alone, crying into a bottle of wine or something. Jesus, Sam. You could have saved me a lot of worry."

"I'm sorry."

He scoffs. "Don't fucking be sorry. It's fine. You don't need to be sorry. I'm fucking sorry, as a matter of fact. You think I don't know why people are scared to tell me shit?" He lets out a dark laugh. "I'm working on my 'demeanor' as Reina calls it, but I know I'm still an asshole."

I nod, and he laughs again.

"Jesus fucking Christ, man. That's great. Or, it was great, anyway?" His expression turns questioning. "That can't have been an easy conversation for her to overhear."

"No, it wasn't."

"Where is she?"

"I don't know."

He pushes up to his feet. "Well, her phone and MacBook are on a table down by the pool, so chances are, she's coming back."

I'm on my feet and heading for the door when Dom pulls me in for a hug. "Let me know if I can help, okay?" he asks.

"Sure, man." I start to slip through my office door into the hallway when I pause and turn back. "There is one more thing,

Dom. If I ever hear you speaking to Naomi like she's beneath you again, we're going to have a serious problem. Is that clear?"

His eyes drop to the ground as his head bows.

For a long moment, I think he's not going to respond at all, but then his gaze lifts and meets mine. "I'm sorry, man. Old habits die hard. I'll tell Naomi I'm sorry, too. It won't happen again."

I clap a hand on his shoulder and give him a squeeze to let him know I appreciate his honesty. He nods back, letting me know he appreciates mine.

I'm sure there's plenty more to be said here, but my priority is getting to that table, so I don't miss Naomi when she comes, so I take him at his word.

I jog down to the pool where indeed, Naomi's phone, computer, sunglasses, and colorful bag are all parked on a table next to a towel-covered chaise lounge.

I collapse into the chair, too exhausted by my mental gymnastics to come up with any sort of plan. I'll just rest here a minute and process everything that just happened, from the ill-fated meeting to my talk with Naomi on the trail to my confessional with Dom.

I'm startled awake by a loud scraping noise. Glancing around, I find one of the pool bartenders dragging a heavy umbrella over and positioning it next to my chair.

"You've been in the sun for a while, Sam. I'm just getting you some shade."

I pull out my phone and gape at the clock on screen. It's been over an hour. "Thank you. Sorry, I didn't mean to fall asleep."

The bartender just smiles. "Everyone needs a break. Can I grab you a drink?"

"A bottle of water would be great."

He walks off, and I look around. All of Naomi's things are still here, which means she hasn't come yet. And it means she still has to.

I settle in for the long haul.

Waiting and ruminating.

I can't say that my meeting with Dom gave me the relief it would have yesterday. If only I'd found out that my whole plan for hiding my love away was so stupid before I went and shot off my mouth, ruining my chances with Naomi.

Even so, it does feel like a weight was lifted. I'm free to chase her down and get her back—without having to lie about it to everyone around me. I'm not very excited about my friends watching as I grovel, but it's what I deserve. They all watched me screw up, saying those terrible things in a flailing attempt to keep the cozy little nest she and I created intact. I suppose it's only fitting that some, or all of them, should get to watch me beg for forgiveness.

I'm halfway through my second cold, refreshing bottle of water when I start regretting my choice. I can hardly leave to go to the bathroom now. With my luck, she'll swoop in, grab her stuff, and be gone before I return.

I'm just considering which of the pool workers I know well enough to ask to keep her here until I get back, when a long, feminine shadow falls over me. I suck in my breath and turn to look up, prepared to dive off a cliff to make it up to this woman.

"Oh, Sam," Fran says, her voice filled with soft, kind, sympathy.

I let out my breath and look down at my hands, trying not to let my disappointment show.

"What's the plan here? Stake out her stuff?"

I shrug, still not looking up. "She has to come get it eventually, and when she does, I'm going to be here to explain, apologize again, and make things right."

"Well, she sent me instead."

My head lifts quickly, and I pin Fran with my gaze. "You know where she is?"

"She's at my house, having drinks with Avery."

I turn and start carefully sliding all of Naomi's electronics and accessories into her bag.

"You think I'm going to let you bring that to her, huh?" Fran asks, but there's no malice in her voice.

I stand and shoulder the bag. "I think you couldn't stop me if you tried."

She smiles. "My cart or yours?"

"I'll follow you."

Rule #45

LOVE IS THE EASY PART

NAOMI

"Of course, it was the Coast Guard coming to investigate because of the black and orange T-shirt I'd decided to run up the mast. They thought we were hostages or something. The rest of us guys were too far gone to explain, but good old Sam rescued our drunk asses by explaining that we weren't captives, just idiots."

I smile at the story, wishing I could enjoy it a bit more. Something about the hero of the tale being the love of my life now in limbo detracts from the punchline a bit.

"Tell me a story that doesn't involve you know who," I beg, pouring myself another glass of sangria.

Avery huffs out a laugh. "I was told to butter you up, so you'll forgive him. I'm going to be in trouble if Fran gets back and I haven't done my job."

I flop back in my chaise, shielding my eyes from the sun glinting off the pool in Fran and Avery's backyard. This place never fails to amaze me. A villa tucked into the jungle, so opulent and over the top that it was probably built by the mob.

I'm hiding out here after coming back from town with no real plan. It wasn't my intention to spill my secrets to Avery, but after the straightening out I got from the village elders, I decided it didn't matter anymore. I need honesty and friendship, and the shoulder I found to lean on is attached to this unbelievably handsome, perfectly sculpted billionaire.

I don't know how Fran sleeps at night with this man as her partner, but it probably has something to do with her being twenty-something and equally as hot. Even though I had a crush on him as a girl, same as every other kid in my school, he certainly wouldn't be my choice anymore.

I know who I'd pick. Who I did pick.

And who I now don't know if I'll get to have.

Sam's apology and his explanation were sincere. I'm sure he didn't mean the things he said. But he said them.

Can I ever unhear him telling those people I didn't deserve a chance because of one mistake I'd made?

I cringe as I hear the answer in my question.

"I see those doomsday eyes over there, Nay. Spill it."

"I guess I just realized that I'm canceling Sam for what he said even though it was a mistake, and he apologized."

"Ooh, dang. Just like those mean girls did to you on the internet. Man, I don't know what Fran was so worried about. Maybe if you were a dude, someone would need to talk some sense into you, but you ladies are too good at coming to these conclusions on your own."

I offer him a sad smile. "I still don't know what to do about it. This whole thing with Sam has been great. The best thing that's ever happened to me, as a matter of fact. But it doesn't change the fact that it's still a secret relationship that doesn't really have a future."

"Well, good luck with that whole no-future thing," Avery responds with a smile.

"What do you mean?"

He gestures to the house with his chin, and I spin, squinting against the bright sun.

"Sam," I whisper as he walks toward me with my computer bag slung over one shoulder.

"That's my cue," Avery says, sliding off his chaise and diving straight into the pool, emerging on the other side and disappearing into the house.

Sam flops down in the now-empty chair and cringes. "This cushion is sweaty."

I laugh in spite of myself. In spite of the situation. "We've been out here for a while."

"Any life-changing pearls of wisdom come out of Ave's mouth?"

"He was just telling me stories about times when you saved his life."

"There should not be so many of those stories."

Silence falls, and I'm not sure how to break it. Or if I even want to.

I have no idea where to go from here. I want to forgive him, to move past this, but I'm stuck on the other side, knee deep in fear.

"I talked to Dom," Sam says finally.

I gape at him over the top of my mirrored sunglasses. "Really? How'd that go?"

He shrugs. "Fine. I told him I'd resign, and he pretty much blew that off. Told me there wasn't a man on the planet who wouldn't want me to be with their little sister."

I cough out a surprised laugh and gape at him. "You were going to resign? For what? I told you it was over."

"It's not over for me."

It's not over for me, either, but I'm not ready to admit it.

"I fucked up in there, but I'm going to make it up to you."

"You can't do that if I leave the island."

"Of course I can. I already submitted my resignation to the

resort, even if it was denied. I'll give it all up. I'll do whatever it takes. You are the most important thing in the world to me. I know my actions over the last few weeks may not have made that clear. And my words in that meeting made it all so much worse. But I will prove myself to you. I don't care how long it takes."

I flip my sunglasses back down and flop into the chair.

I've already forgiven him. I've almost already moved past this whole thing.

It's just...I thought when I got to the other side, what I'd find there was certainty. Certainty about Sam and our life together. Certainty about where I belonged.

Instead, my future—with Sam or alone—is nothing but a giant black hole, sucking the life out of me.

I let out a heavy sigh. "I'm exhausted."

Sam doesn't answer, swinging his feet onto his chair and lying back.

"I forgive you," I say finally. "And I want so badly for that to be enough. Back when we were at your house, and this whole thing was secret and exciting, it seemed like an easy choice to keep doing it forever. But now? Now that I get to choose you and this island and this life, I'm so scared. I've never done anything like this. I make all my decisions based on my own needs. I'm not sure I've ever compromised a single time in my life. What if I give up on Austin, and you decide I'm not good enough for you? It won't be like the internet where I can just disappear and people forget about me. Everyone will see."

And there it is. The real mystery of me. How do I allow myself to be visible and vulnerable in front of real people?

"You have to let people love you."

Sam's words hit straight to my heart, and I close my eyes against the tears.

"You let me see you, Naomi. The real you. And I love you. It's okay to be scared. I'm scared too. But we can do this together."

I roll to my side, and Sam leans over to take my sunglasses

off, revealing my red, wet eyes. His eyes go soft as he takes me in.

I feel so laid bare. Like my entire insides are on display.

But Sam doesn't laugh or make fun of me or shy away.

He gets up and crosses over the space between us, slotting himself onto the narrow wedge of cushion on the edge of my chaise lounge. I scoot back a few inches, and he pulls me into his warmth, his safety.

And maybe this can be enough.

Maybe I can finally be a person who is good enough.

"I didn't know about that job at the resort," I finally say into the silence. It's the one thing I still feel like is hanging over us. "They didn't ask me if I wanted it or even mention it to me."

Sam shakes his head, still curled tightly around me. "That doesn't surprise me. They're used to getting what they want."

I'm also used to getting what I want, so I know what they must have been thinking.

And it wasn't the worst idea. After my lunch with Fran where we went over the wedding pictures and my ideas for content using them, I knew she was impressed. Hell, I was impressed with myself.

I've spent a lot of years making myself and others look good enough to buy, and I've always done it following the guidelines of the very specific aesthetic I'd built for my channel. This wedding was a total leap outside that box. An opportunity to present content in whatever colorful, over-the-top way it actually was, rather than in my own specific color and font set.

It sparked so many new ideas in my mind to let my creativity be free. I know it's where my future lies, Faraday or not. I won't be selling myself anymore. I'm going to help other people sell themselves. Not at the resort, but possibly for Paradise Events.

"You'd be great for the job," Sam says matter-of-factly, in his GM voice.

"Yeah, I would, but I'm more of a freelancer. And it doesn't seem like the best fit for you, having me there."

He's quiet for a moment. "I felt like that at first. You saw the way I reacted when put on the spot about it. I lashed out, and I know it's because the thought of sharing you with them, with the world, scares me. I love having you all to myself, alone in my house, where I can be the man I want to be. The man I want to show you. I worry about having you at the resort every day where you'll see the hard parts. And you'll meet all the rich vacationers, and maybe you'll see that I'm not so special. That you can do better."

"You can't keep me locked in your house for the rest of my life, job at The Sands or not."

He holds me tighter. "I know. But a guy can dream."

I smile and place a kiss on the top of his head. If there's one thing in the world I can relate to, it's insecurities. "Why is it so hard for us to feel like we're enough? Why is it always such a struggle, such a dance, to just see ourselves as worthy of love, of fitting in?"

Sam shrugs. "I'm not sure. I thought it was just me, to be honest, growing up. Once I started managing hotels and offering counsel to employees, it became clear that most conflicts and drama stemmed from fears of not fitting in with the group. And most people are convinced that everyone fits in but them."

"And somehow you never used that little insight to convince yourself that being an outsider was all in your head?"

"I wish. I went the other direction. Doubled down on being the poor kid of the group, the one always having to accept handouts. I just got more defensive as I got older, fiercely protecting my way of life as somehow morally superior, because that's the only option I had for being better than other people. Because that's just it, isn't it? It's not enough to belong, we have to be better."

Naomi nods sadly. "I'm sure I wanted to fit in with my family when I was young, but by the time I was old enough to understand what was going on, that the way my household functioned wasn't normal, all I wanted to do was be different from them.

They had clearly chosen their outlooks on the world, and I was determined to see it all differently. To live a different kind of life. I get what you mean about just wanting to feel better than everyone around you. It's not enough to fit in. It's like there's always something to prove. That's definitely how it is on the internet. It's a constant game of one-upmanship. I guess that's why people take each other down like they do. It's not really about community at all, even as much as everyone claims it is. Every person you can cancel is one less competitor for the ultimate prize. Which doesn't even exist, as far as I can tell."

"We are an interesting species, aren't we?"

"It's a miracle we've survived this long."

"Speaking of which, I don't know if I'm going to survive much longer in this sun. I already had an hour-long nap waiting next to your computer, and I'm fried."

I look down at his sweat-misted forehead and brush a lock of his short hair to the side, placing a kiss there. "Home?"

He twists enough to look up at me. "Let's go home."

I let him pull me to my feet and follow him around the massive pool toward the back doors of the house. "I was starting to feel like a mob wife out there and not in a good way. In a 'feds about to seize all my possessions' kind of way."

Sam laughs and pulls me closer as we pass through the wide double doors into the equally luxurious house. Fran and Avery are nowhere to be seen. "So, what you're saying is that you're happy living in a three-shack homestead for the rest of your life?"

His tone is light, but I can hear the real question there. I consider my answer as he tucks me into the passenger seat of his golf cart. Mine will have to get picked up another day. "Is that what you want? To stay in that house?"

Sam's eyes are on the road as he pulls us out of the circular driveway and onto the bumpy sand road. "That's certainly what I would have told anyone who asked."

Interesting. "But?"

He shrugs, tossing me a glance before turning back to the road. "But I guess once I start questioning things, I have to look at that as well. There's a big difference between choosing to live in a three-shack homestead, spending ten years making it into a passable house because it's your dream and you love it. And having to live in a three-shack homestead because it's all you can afford."

"I can see that."

He shrugs. "I've spent so long selling that place as my dream that I'm not entirely certain I know the truth anymore. It was the first house I ever bought, so there was some romanticism about it, but whether or not it's what I'd still choose, I'm not sure. I told you earlier about my tendency to double down on my bad choices so that they can't be called out as mistakes. I'm not saying my house is a mistake, but it's not the hill I'm going to die on. Especially not if you need something more. You may be slumming it in guest rooms right now, but it's not going to be long before you're a very rich woman."

I'm quiet for the long stretch of bumpy road leading to Sam's driveway. There has been a lot of change, a lot of self-reflection over the last few weeks. My impending inheritance is something I've pushed to the back burner for so long that it almost doesn't feel real how close I am to it.

But it's very real, and I'm not surprised Sam wants to bring it up after all this talk about his childhood, growing up as the poor kid.

Sam turns down the driveway to the homestead, and my heart swells, giving me the words I've been desperately trying to find. "I spent eighteen years in a massive estate with a staff and fancy cars and the whole lot. I never once felt happy there. No one in that house was ever happy. I know I've got a lot of money coming, but the truth is that I've always had a lot of money. I could have lived anywhere and done anything, but the only place I wanted to be was my apartment in Austin, making my own way in the world. Once I came here, to the island and to your house, I felt that way again. Safe. Happy. Calm. Like I could be myself and live the life I want to live. I know it's not the house that's giving me those feelings. It's you. But for now, this is where I want to be."

Sam is smiling as he parks in his usual spot and hurries around to help me out of the cart. "And wherever you are is where I want to be," he answers, placing a kiss to the top of my head.

And what if that's enough? What if there isn't anything left to prove? For so long I've been striving to be enough, to have a career of my own, to prove that I'm worth something.

But right now, in this little jungle home, in the arms of a man who I know loves me for me, it is enough. I am enough.

"I feel like I should carry you over the threshold or something," Sam says bashfully as we climb the few steps hand in hand.

"I'll allow it," I reply.

Rule #46

IT'S NEVER TOO LATE

NAOMI

The last thing I ever want to do is leave this man sleeping in bed, but I have to. He needs to rest for his shift in a few hours, and I have an important conversation looming over my head.

I creep out to Sam's golf cart and click the key, navigating out to the main road and toward the resort. Toward my brother's house.

I find him making coffee alone in the kitchen. "Morning."

He raises his eyebrows but pulls another cup from the cupboard and fills them both. I watch with a smile as he adds two spoonfuls of brown sugar and a half inch of cream to mine. When he finally speaks, the tone of his voice takes me by surprise.

"I almost came looking for you, but Reina convinced me to wait for you to be ready and come to me." The tenderness in his words is reflected in his eyes.

If I didn't know better, I'd say this man had been crying.

My guard is so confused, all I can do is fall back on old habits and apologize for having done nothing wrong. "Sorry. I could have called. I was just busy with other things."

His face twists into a wry smile. "Busy with other things could be the title of our entire relationship."

I take the cup from him in silence, no idea what to say to that.

"Want to sit out on the patio?"

I nod and follow him out to the expansive deck overlooking the resort and the teal blue ocean, glittering in the early morning sun.

"You really are the king up here, huh?"

I mean it as a joke to lighten up the mood, but when Dom doesn't answer, I feel the need to apologize once more. "Sorry, I—"

"No. I know what you mean. You're not the first person to have made that observation."

His tone is unreadable, and I shift uncomfortably, like a child about to get in trouble. What is it about this man that does this to me? Probably a lifetime of history. And his resemblance to my father, who only spoke to me when I was in trouble.

"Sit," he says, motioning to the chair next to his on the deck, facing out over the unobstructed view.

I obey, crossing my legs and taking a sip of the delicious coffee. "Dang, this is really good."

"I can order you a machine like I have, if you want."

I smile over at him, hearing his words for what they are. An attempt at a truce.

I open my mouth to let him off the hook, but he stops me.

"Let me start, okay?" He doesn't wait for my permission before going on, looking out over the ocean instead of at me. "I talked with Sam, but I'm sure you know that already. He…I…"

He breaks off in uncharacteristic hesitation, shifting in his seat to face me. "I'm sorry for how all of this went down. I'm sorry that I haven't been there for you all these years. I had so many reasons and excuses planned for when we finally talked, but they all sound so stupid now. I just…I just lost a lot when she died. I was a kid, and Mom was my entire world. You didn't get to know her, which sucks, but I did. Twelve years is almost an entire childhood. She was the center of my universe and to have her sucked away so suddenly, it really affected me. I know it wasn't your fault, but she was gone, and you were there instead, and I wasn't able to ever separate the two things. It was all made worse by the fact that without her there, Dad turned all his focus on me. When she was alive, she shielded me from the brunt of it, mostly, or maybe I was too young for him to bother with. But once he lost her, turning me into the man he wanted became his only goal in life."

He pauses for so long that it feels right to say something, so I do. "I'm not sure if that was worse than being ignored completely."

Dom meets my gaze. "I don't know either. I know that back then, I would have given anything to be left alone completely. I was jealous of the freedom you had. But the loneliness must have been hard as well. It's not like there were many other options out there."

I shrug. "I didn't really know any different."

We fall into silence for a few moments. When he finally speaks, it's to offer something I dreamed of hearing my whole life—a glimpse into the family I never had. I should have known it wouldn't be a fairy tale, considering how it all ended.

"They never really got along. No, I guess that's not right. It was more like we hid from him. Mom and I would spend whole evenings tucked away in giant closets upstairs when he would get into his moods, which I understand now meant he was drunk. She spent her life avoiding him as much as possible. I don't know why she never left. Maybe it was impossible. I'm sure it would have been very difficult, considering he was the one with the fortune. She came from a local family, and her parents had been killed in her late teens. Car accident. If I could go back, I'd ask her why she married him. I would give anything to know the story of how it all started."

He looks out at the view. "I was too young to know to ask those kinds of things. When she got pregnant again, things got better. Dad was the happiest I ever remember seeing him. We went on family outings and had meals together. He was a changed person. I remember him smiling, kissing her belly. They would laugh and talk. It was the first time in my life I felt like I had parents, rather than just me and Mom hiding from the scary monster. When it was time for you to come, I was sent away to stay with Ben's family. And I never saw her again."

The casket had been closed. I know that from pictures in the local paper I'd found at the library years later.

"What happened?"

He sighs. "I'm not sure. I doubt we'll ever know. They had private doctors. The birth was at the estate. There's no record of what went wrong or how long she was alive after you were born. I suppose it could have been complications, like we were all told. But I just don't know. She was young, healthy."

I'm crying now, wiping tears with the crook of my arm. Dom glances over at me and nods. He's not shedding tears, but I can see the emotion raging in his eyes.

"When I was finally allowed to come home, he told me she was gone and that we had another girl to deal with. Those were his words. The anger was back. The monster was back. He was drunk all the time, and she wasn't there to help me hide. I couldn't have hidden you anyway. You had nurses and nannies. A whole team of women who kept you tucked away in your own wing of the house. They must have known about him. But I didn't know that. I only knew what he told me, which was that you had taken her from us. That she was the only person he'd ever loved, and now she was gone. I wasn't too young to understand what that would mean for you. So, I took him on. I made a decision right then, two weeks before my thirteenth birthday. I became a man and stepped into his world. Let him have me.

And it worked. I saved you from him, but I lost you in the process. And I wanted you to be born. I wanted a sister. And I want you here now. I'm glad you were born even though I fucked it all up."

Anger and sadness burn through me as I try to process his words. The longing for the life we could have had is almost too much to bear.

I know the next part, but I let him tell it anyway.

"I graduated with my MBA, fulfilling my part of the contract for the trust. I was free. With that money, I never had to kneel to him again. I asked you to come with me."

"I hated you."

His shoulders slump. "I know. Somehow, I thought that, even after all those years of ignoring you, you'd understand that I was doing it to protect you and run to my car with your suitcase, and we would escape together. I had these dreams of hopping on a plane and flying somewhere he could never find us."

"Why didn't you tell me?"

"Young and stupid, I guess. But you weren't a kid anymore. You were going on fifteen, with a life you made all by yourself and opinions and ideas. In my escape fantasies, you were always a little thing, looking up to me like I was your savior."

"You could have been."

"I know. And I live with that regret every day. But there's no way to know if it really would have been better for you. It's not like I turned out to be the nicest guy on the planet. Who's to say if living with me while I traveled the world and worked eighty hours a week would have been much different. The only thing that definitely would have changed is that you'd have left everything you knew behind. So, when you refused to even consider coming with me, I left you there. And you did the same thing you'd done your whole life. Survived on your own."

He turns back to me, sad eyes and sad smile. "And you did a pretty good job, all things considered."

"I'm not looking for your approval."

"Yeah, I get that. And you don't need it, either. But just know that I've thought about you a lot over the years, even after I left town. Especially after I left. And it may have seemed like I didn't care, but it's the opposite. I cared so much, but the only way I'd been taught to keep people safe was to hide when things got bad."

"Well, I learned to take care of myself and not take any shit from anyone."

Dom laughs and shakes his head. "See? You were better off without me. You are one of the strongest women I know. I'm proud of who you became even if I have no right to be."

It's my turn to shake my head, salty cheeks finally drying in the sun. "Why are you telling me all this?"

"When Sam told me that you guys had been sneaking around because you were afraid I'd be pissed, I kind of lost it. It was my whole childhood thrown back in my face. Something great was happening between two people who I love, and they were afraid to tell me because I'm such an asshole. Sam was afraid of retaliation. From me. His best friend."

Dom's voice cracks a bit, and I peek over to see if I can spot my first ever big brother tear. No luck.

"I turned into Dad after all."

"No. That's not it. You aren't him. Or, at least, you aren't him yet. You still have a functioning heart. I see it when Reina is around. You can still pull yourself back from turning into him."

"And I'm going to. I guess I needed to see myself reflected like this to really get it. But I get it now. It's a slippery slope to decide that you know best, and everyone needs to follow your rules. I guess that's how I did so well in restaurants. It's like the military in there, a strong leader is essential. But I learned a few years back that I still need to let people in. Let them share in my life and what's going on with me. I almost lost Reina because I was so slow to come around. And the same goes here. I'm stubborn and pigheaded, but I'm learning. I'm not going to lose you or Sam over this. I'm going to do whatever it takes to be the person you both need me to be. Always."

"Thanks, Dom. I appreciate knowing all this. It's a side of you I didn't know existed."

"Well, I'm new to showing it off. I thought for a long time that it made me weak. I was told growing up that it made me weak. But I know now that vulnerability is the true strength. Even if I still forget sometimes."

"Dad's going to freak when he realizes we're a team. Pitting us against each other has always been his best control strategy."

Dom's head turns sharply in my direction. "Team, huh?"

His words are simple, but his tone is telling. If I didn't know him so well, I might have missed the underlying emotion in the question, but it's there.

I smile over at him, happy to have finally broken through his gruff exterior. "If you'll have me."

He huffs and smiles. "We would be a force to be reckoned with."

"Unstoppable."

He folds his arms and cocks his head at me. "Speaking of which, you're getting awfully close to accessing your trust. Any big plans?"

I shake my head. "My big plans are here on Faraday. In a little room in the jungle. Maybe a small Wi-Fi upgrade, but that's about it for now."

Dom actually laughs at that. "That damn property. He won't give it up, even with all the trouble it's caused him."

"It's a point of contention."

"Yeah, I know."

"You know? You know that he feels like he's less than you guys and is always trying to find ways to prove he's good enough? Why don't you do something about it?"

Dom shrugs. "What can I do? He feels that way despite all of us reassuring him that he's an important part of the team, the most important part if we're being serious. That's his own demon to battle. Nothing I can do is going to change any of it."

"You could sign over his part of the resort to him."

He looks over at me sharply. "What do you mean?"

"Sam told me that you paid his share. That he isn't a partner at all, that I'm more of an owner than he is because all the money came from the Fuentes fortune."

"Shit."

"Yeah."

"That's not true. Or, at least, it's not entirely true." He lets out a heavy sigh. "I'll look into it. I never paid that much attention to the paperwork. Ben handled it all. But if Sam thinks that, he must have seen something in those contracts that I didn't."

I watch as his forehead crinkles, and his eyes fall closed. "I wish he would have said something sooner."

"It seems you're not the only one with communication skills to work on." I get a bit of side-eye from Dom and smile. "I guess we all have something."

"So, you're staying on the island."

I nod.

"Well, if you need a place to stay, your room is always open. Or we could get you an apartment or a house or something. You know, if it's too soon for you to live in shanty town with Sam."

"You can't call it that," I say with a laugh.

Dom laughs, too. "I know. Bad habit. But seriously, let me know. And if you want a job…"

I smile and shake my head. "The job at The Sands isn't what I'm looking for, but I am going to start working with Fran on weddings."

He smiles. "She'll be happy to hear that."

We fall into a comfortable silence, both looking out over the gorgeous view, sipping our now cold coffee.

I start to hear noises from inside the house and feel our sibling time coming to an end. "Dom?"

He looks over at me. "Hmm?"

"I'm glad to have you now. Even though we missed a lot of years. I'm happy we made it here."

"It's not too late?"

The sadness in his voice hits me right in the gut. I know we still have a lot to work through after this conversation, but I know I have my brother now, and it feels good.

"No, it's not too late."

Rule #47

BOYS CRY TOO

SAM

"Sam, can I get a minute?"

My head turns at the sound of Ben's voice from the doorway of my office. I'm just packing my stuff up and getting ready to head out after putting in a solid half-day. Now that I know the resort can run just fine without me, I may be taking a few more of these now and then.

It doesn't hurt that there's now going to be someone waiting at home for me either.

"Sure, man. Of course. I didn't realize you were still on the island. What's up?"

He remains leaning on the doorframe, tall and dark, looking more business casual than usual in black shorts and a short sleeve button-up. Ben recently found love himself, and it looks good on him. We don't see him down here as much as we'd like, as his world mostly revolves around his New York office, his son who's in college up there, and now his lovely Pilates instructor fiancée. Still, once every other month or so is more often than most people get to escape to the tropics, even if he is working quite a bit when he's on island.

"Upstairs. In the conference room," he replies.

My eyebrows go up, but I remain firmly seated in my chair.

It's not that I don't love a good meeting, but the last time I got pulled away for one of these mysterious meetups by one of the owners, it didn't go so well for me.

Ben sees my hesitation and softens. "Nothing painful, I promise. Just got some paperwork laid out up there."

Leave it to one of your best friends to know your weaknesses.

I'll never say no to some good, old-fashioned paperwork.

He holds the door to the third-floor conference room open to let me enter ahead of him.

I have to hold back my surprise at the crowd gathered in the medium-sized room.

Avery, of course, with Fran tucked under one arm. Reina and Victoria, Ben's fiancée, share the love seat along one wall. Our HR manager and her staff are standing beside them, as well as most of the department managers from the resort. I see Daniel from the spa and Marcus from Reef. I nod in greeting to our real estate agent, Karen, and Mackenzie, the local import/export boss.

After glancing around the full room, my eyes fall to the table where, indeed, there is quite a bit of paperwork laid out. As curious as I am about the cohort of people assembled here, I'm even more interested in the papers. I can see copies of the original purchase agreements for the resort. I see the legal documents Ben drew up for our new corporation, one where we would all be partners in this crazy venture.

I'm just taking a step forward to examine them closer when the door flies open once more, hitting the wall behind it and making the room jump collectively.

"Sorry I'm late," Dom says, "Naomi was up at the house, and we got talking."

I watch as his face transforms. I've been getting more and more used to seeing emotion on the hard features of my most closed-off friend when he looks at his bride-to-be, but this is different.

If I didn't know better, I'd say the guy's been crying.

"It's no prob—"

I start to reassure him, although it's hardly my place to do so, considering I have no idea what he's late for, but he silences me with a massive hug.

"I've missed her so much."

I let the words and their meaning settle over me and slowly bring my arms up to hug him back. I can't think of anything to say, so I just hold him for a long moment.

When he pulls away, he's indeed wiping his eyes.

"I probably would have died not ever knowing Naomi as a person. I never would have backed down from that old shit. I would have died on my damn hill, waiting for her to be the first one to call. But you"—he pins me with the intense stare I've gotten used to holding my ground over the years—"you're going to keep her here, on my island, where I'll get to know her. Sam, I never could have asked for that. I never would have thought to suggest it. Never would have taken a step back and looked at myself long enough to know that having her in my life was even what I needed. But that's the Sam magic."

He takes another step back, and Ben comes up to stand beside him, one hand resting on his shoulder supportively. I watch as Avery takes up his other side.

"You just fix things. Things no one else even realizes need fixing. We all just slog along, putting up with whatever bullshit we've thought up for ourselves. But one look from you, and you fix it all. Take the weight off our backs without bringing it onto your own. Have any of you ever known anyone else who could do that?"

He looks around the room, and I follow his gaze, watching heads shaking one by one.

"We put out the word that we were looking for a few employees and islanders to come and tell you what an impact you've made on their lives, and I don't know what we were thinking. We actually thought all the people who wanted to share their appreciation would fit in one damn room."

I feel myself start to blush a little and glance around the room once more, nodding my own appreciation to the people they clearly gathered here for this very purpose.

"Not these people. I mean, yes, these people, but also." He takes me by the shoulders and turns me, pushing me ahead of him until we cross the conference room and stand facing the large, ocean-view windows. "But I'm talking about all of these people."

He pulls the shade to the side, and a soft, surprised laugh escapes my lips as I look out over the crowd in amazement.

The pool patio below is filled with people. They fill the steps leading down to the beach and the beach itself. Employees and locals and people I can't identify from here standing shoulder to shoulder, all looking up at the window.

Dom reaches over me once more to release the latch and swing the large window open, and everyone cheers.

I laugh once more as I lift a hand to wave at the crowd, causing them to cheer louder.

I can hear shouts of "thank you" and "we love you, Sam."

"Everyone in the whole resort wanted to come. And half the damn island."

I turn back to him and shake my head. "Shouldn't these people be working?"

Dom just laughs. A big, loud, genuine laugh that I have to pause and absorb for a moment. I can't remember the last time I saw the guy this happy. This open and present.

I feel arms snaking around me from the other side and look down to see my girl, Naomi, tucking herself into my side. I lean down and kiss her on the forehead. "Did you know about all of this?"

She shakes her head.

"There will be plenty of time to greet everyone later, Sam, but you were promised paperwork, and paperwork you will get." Ben draws our attention back to the long table in the center of the room where he and Avery are already sitting. I slip away from Naomi, giving one of her soft hands a quick squeeze. She heads over to curl onto the small sofa next to Reina, who pulls her in close.

I cross the room and take the seat to Avery's left, just like I did that day over a decade ago, when we started this whole adventure.

Dom sits down next to me and the real estate lawyer who's been with us all this time takes his seat across from us.

"It's come to my attention that we need to revisit the old contracts. I've gone ahead and printed up a new copy for all of you." Our lawyer taps each stack of papers to straighten them before sliding one set in front of each of us guys.

I drag my hands down my face before turning to look at Dom, then over at Ben and Avery. "You guys didn't have to do this."

Dom huffs beside me. "Apparently we should have done it sooner if you thought you could just walk away from this resort, and it would go on functioning without you."

"There's a lot more to this contract than money, Sam," Ben says. "And, if you remember, no one would even be here if you hadn't found this abandoned resort on Zillow and somehow convinced Ave, Dom, and me to take the leap. You started a new chapter in our lives. And not a single one of us, not a single person in this room or outside that window, will ever forget that it was you who gave this all to us."

I'm still shaking my head, trying not to get too emotional when Avery starts in on me.

"This place was the first home I ever had, Sam. And I've lived a thousand places. But you turned this little slice of paradise into a safe space for me. For all of us. A place we could work hard and be appreciated and feel supported enough to find ourselves. I know I did. I found myself, I found Fran, and I found a purpose for my life. And it didn't just start with these papers." He lifts his own stack and taps the ends before tossing them back on the table. "It started that first day in fourth grade when you took one look at me, hanging back from the rest of the guys. Do you remember what you said to me?"

I don't answer, but he goes on. "You said, 'I really liked your owl poster.' The stupid poster board project I'd done for science class. That was the first moment I realized something wasn't right about my home life. Because no one had even looked at my poster before I turned it in. No one had ever told me I did a good job at anything. But you? You never stopped telling me. You showed up at all my games and both graduations, even when I didn't invite you. You dragged these guys along, too. You showed me what it looked like to have a family, Sam. You were the first real family I ever had."

"You showed us all," Dom says from my other side.

I want to look over at him as he speaks but I'm right on the edge of too much emotion, the feelings threatening to swallow me whole. Instead, I look down at my hands as he continues.

"We all grew up in a different world than you, with different families and different values. And people think all that money is what we should be striving for. That's all bullshit. Money ruined each and every one of our families and most of our childhoods."

I'm crying now, there's no stopping it. Dom's eyes are misty as well, although he keeps wiping them with his hands to try to hide it as he goes on.

"Do you remember my Yankees jersey? The one I got signed by Donnie Baseball at that game for my tenth birthday?"

I nod, unsure of where this is going.

"Do you remember when I tore the side of that shirt crashing my bike? And my dad called up the owner of the team and ordered me another jersey with the same signature. And grounded me for a month when I threw a fit about not wanting a new jersey. About just wanting my old one. He threw it away and yelled at me for being ungrateful. Do you remember what you did?"

I huff out a soft laugh. "I'm pretty sure I snuck onto your estate and pulled it out of the trash."

"But that's not all," Dom says and takes a deep breath. "You had your mom sew it up for me."

I laugh again, remembering. "Yeah, I guess I do remember that. I'm surprised you remember, honestly. You had so many signed jerseys from all the players."

"Yeah, but what I didn't have was a mom who would help me fix what I broke. All I had was a father who threw money at me like I was a problem he wanted to silence. Who never took one second to try to understand why I was upset in the first place. You, though. You had a great mom. Still do. That's what we were all missing. Someone who cared enough to show up with time and attention, rather than just sending gifts from afar. You learned that from her, and you gave it to us. I show up now in my own life, for my fiancée, for my employees and my friends, because of you. Because you showed me how. And shit, Sam, if you ever didn't know that, I'm sorry. I'm sorry you've been thinking you don't contribute to our lives because you don't have the same-sized pockets. Without you, I would be my father."

"Same," Ben calls from down the table.

"Oh, hell yes. I would absolutely be that asshole," Avery agrees with a full body shudder.

"You guys," I start, but I get silenced by all three of them standing to pull me into a group hug. It's just as well because I have no words to describe how much this all means to me.

I've lived the better part of my life feeling like I owe them something, when the whole time they were feeling the same way about me. I make a mental note to speak up in the future when I'm having doubts about my worthiness. I have spent years building trust in my friend group and in this community. I would be a fool not to lean on that support when I need it.

When we all finally pull away, I glance around the room, where there's not a dry eye in sight. I smile at the sight of my entire management team and extended business partners all in one room together sharing a cry.

A soft throat clearing brings our attention back to the table, and we retake our seats, turning to the lawyer who is still wiping his misty eyes. I feel a hand on my shoulder and look up to find Naomi there, red eyes glittering lovingly down at me.

"We…" The lawyer pauses to cough once more to settle his voice. "We are here this afternoon to go over the original contracts and to sign and get notarized a new amendment Mr. Adams has brought to the table."

I glance over at Ben, who gives me an encouraging eyebrow raise.

"The original papers are what you remember, of course. I'll have you turn to the signature pages at the end of the corporate contract."

He pauses while we get there. Ben finds it first and shows Avery the page number. When we're all staring down at the black, photographed copies of our decade-old signatures, he goes on.

"There seems to be some misunderstanding about the structure of the corporation, so we're here today to work that out. The purchase contract was drawn up here on Faraday, making the sale a foreign transaction, owned jointly by the four of you, as we can see on the signature page of that contract. The privately held company, however, is registered in New York. Subject to New York law, the four of you each hold twenty-five percent ownership of the corporation, and you also make up the entire board. To be clear, the purchase agreement, and the investment of funds decided by that agreement, is a completely separate entity from the corporation itself. The purchase agreement can in no way be used by any of the owners to claim a majority share of the corporation nor can it be used to gain additional voting power over the other board members."

I nod to the man, understanding why we're all here. I suppose I could have looked these papers over myself and come to these same conclusions, but having it spelled out in black and white by a lawyer does make me feel all that much better.

"That being said," the lawyer goes on. "At the time of creation, you four, the board members, did not elect to assign yourselves titles. As you can see on the final signatory page, each of you was named as Partner only. And that is what we're here today to change. If you'll turn now to the new documents below the original contracts."

I flip alongside the guys until we've all reached the new documents. They carry the letterhead from Ben's firm back in the States.

"These documents have been drawn up to assign titles to the four board members. You can all turn to the last page where you will sign under your new assigned role to accept. We have a notary on hand today to finalize the paperwork."

I glance to my best friends and co-owners on either side of me, none of whom are in any hurry to get to the last page.

They already know what they're going to find there.

With a sigh, I flip to the end and find my own name, and the words underneath it, right above the blank signature line.

President.

I scan quickly to find the other assigned roles and find the titles. Dom is Vice President. Avery is Secretary. Ben is Treasurer.

"Does this mean we're going to start having board meetings?" I joke quietly to the guys beside me.

"We already have board meetings, Sam. The four of us meet to make decisions about the resort every other month. Now they just have an official title. And we all have official roles. We should have done this at the beginning, but we were young and dumb. Better late than never."

I look back at the papers in front of me. "President?"

"You've always been the damn boss, Sam, just sign the papers."

I toss Dom some side-eye as I pick up the pen. "This means a lot more knocks on my office door when there are problems, huh?"

Dom huffs. "This means we're removing your office door. As if we could ever solve a problem around here without you."

I'm smiling as I sign my name on the line.

I didn't need this title, but I'm certainly not turning it down. This resort means the world to me, and the knowledge that my place here is safe gives me a sense of freedom and security that I didn't realize I was missing until this point.

I was ready and willing to gamble everything for love, but now I know I don't have to. I can stand in my power, with my partners, friends, and my woman by my side.

I feel unstoppable. I feel calm and proud, and ready to tackle the next decade of resort ownership and life with all its ups, downs, and sideways.

Rule #48

THIS IS HOW A NEW CHAPTER BEGINS

SAM

After many hugs and congratulations from the room, we all parade down to the pool patio outside Reef to join the party. Naomi holds tightly to my hand as we get stopped every two feet to greet an employee or longtime guest who came out to join the celebration.

When we finally make it inside the café, I pull her down the short hallway to a nook just outside the kitchen so we can have a quiet moment alone.

Naomi slips something into my pants pocket, and I slide my hand in after hers, smiling as I feel my golf cart keys.

"You know, when you weren't there when I woke up this morning, I was worried you'd run off."

She steps forward until her chest presses against mine, leaning us both into the wall behind me. "You're not getting rid of me that easily."

As if I needed another reason to be happy and grateful for my life, I reach my arms around her and pull her even closer.

"I went and had coffee with Dom," she says.

"I heard. How'd that go?"

Naomi takes a step back and leans against a rack of take-out packaging. "Really good actually. He told me a lot of stuff about his childhood that I didn't know. Stuff about my mom when she was alive. He apologized for being such a dick and promised to do better."

"That's great. I'm glad you two got to talk."

Her face turns pensive. "I'm not sure how it never occurred to me that he would know stuff like that. That he would have stories about her. We never talked about her. Or anything, really. But maybe we can now."

My heart swells at her hopeful words. I know how badly she wants this, and I also know how much it means to Dom to have her in his life. My friend has been through a lot, and he carries a lot of sadness and regret from his childhood. I hope this can be the first step in healing, for both of them.

"It's a whole new chapter for the Fuentes family," I say with a smile.

Her own smile turns sly. "And a new chapter for you and me. No more sneaking around." She bites her lip as she watches for my reaction. "I mean, I get it if you aren't ready to tell—"

"Princess, let's shout it from the rooftops. I'm going to change my nametag to Sam, GM, Naomi is mine."

She laughs, and I push off the wall, crossing the hallway to pull her back into my arms.

"Ready to head out to the party?" I ask.

"We wouldn't want to keep your adoring fans waiting."

My face breaks into a bashful grin, and I shake my head, feeling my blush from earlier return.

Naomi spots it and lifts up on her toes to kiss each of my cheeks. I close my eyes and breathe in the essence of her. Breathe her presence into my soul.

She takes both of my hands in hers. "They can all have their turn telling you how wonderful you are, but they're going to have to do it with me on your arm. Everyone's going to have to get used to seeing me at the resort on the regular. As your permanent coffee date."

"I like the sound of permanent."

And when I kiss her, that's exactly how it feels. Like my life has taken a permanent shape. Like it's a real thing I can reach out and touch. I glide my hands down her back and around her hips, pulling her in close. The solidity of her body under my touch is the closest thing to a miracle I've ever experienced.

The miracle of us.

Rule #49

MAKE IT POETIC

SAM

I've made my fair share of mistakes in my time, but never have I been willing to put it all on the line for forgiveness like I am now. I wasn't lying when I told Naomi that I'd walk away from everything. I'd do it still if that's what it takes to prove to her that she's my priority.

She told me that she forgives me for what I said, and I believe her. I also know that I'm going to spend the next few years showing her every single day that I'm her biggest supporter. No matter what path her career takes. And yes, that means if she decides she wants to accept the job at The Sands that my other partners are dying to give her, I'll welcome her to the team with open arms.

Hell, it might be kind of nice to have her around me every second of every day. I'm not sure now why I ever thought that could be a bad thing. She helps me focus on my purpose in life. She shows me the beauty in every little flower and brass doorknob and crown molding. She makes me want to be a better man, a better version of myself. Having her at work might very well be an asset.

"You got some sun," Naomi observes, running her fingers over my forehead to brush my hair behind my ear as we lean against the low countertop in the main room of my house.

Our house.

We managed to sneak away after a full tour of the party, everyone smiling and offering thanks and congratulations to me, greetings and hugs to Naomi. She met so many happy faces, I'm sure she'll never remember everyone's name.

"Yeah, I spent a bit too long in a chaise lounge by the pool yesterday. Luckily, I have great employees looking out for me, or I'd be a lobster."

She narrows her eyes at me with a sly smile, questioning, but I just shake my head. "Later, okay? I'll tell you the whole story of my stakeout and nap by the pool later, but right now…" I drop to my knees before her and run my hands up her bare thighs and over the swell of her hips to hold her as I place kiss after kiss to her navel, her stomach, and her hip bones. "I have something else in mind that doesn't involve talking."

"Oh, really?"

I nod. "Do you want to get your phone set up?"

Naomi's mouth parts in surprise, but then she closes it and shakes her head. "Not this time."

"Oh, really? Just you and me, the old-fashioned way?"

She smiles and nods. I can see a twinge of sadness there, but also joy. I get that. These last couple of days have been a lot. I'm just grateful we made it out the other side.

And I'm ready to show her.

"New bedroom, loft, or sofa? Shower?" I ask as I pull her sweaty top off and toss it onto a stool.

"You choose," she whispers as she steps side to side to allow me to slide her shorts off.

I stand and take her in, naked and smiling in our living room, hands on my hips. "If it's up to me, I'm going to choose all of them."

Naomi just shrugs, and I pull her to me, wrapping her naked body in my arms.

"Starting with the kitchen."

She lets out a little shriek and laughs as I start to march her backward, still held tightly in my arms, toward the back door of this house and over the stone path to the little detached kitchen. I kick the door closed behind us and finally release her.

She takes a few steps back until she's leaning against the waist-height butcher block counter.

I bare my teeth as she leans back on her elbows, offering her breasts and pebbled nipples to me like a feast. I drop to my knees and lick each one, up and around, before capturing her nipples and nibbling until she's moaning and rubbing her thighs together.

My hand slides up her thigh and finds her core, already wet for me. "Is the thought of being bent over the kitchen counter turning you on, princess?"

She bites her lip. "The thought of you bending me over anywhere turns me on."

I raise my eyebrows at that, lifting myself to my feet and spinning her so those lovely breasts rest right on the counter as I press myself into her back. "Well, I've got a thing for kitchen sex. And I've been thinking about taking you in the kitchen since you made me breakfast that first morning. Do you remember that?"

"I remember what you told me. That you were pretending it was your life. I was pretending too."

The thought of the two of us there, so ignorant to all that was going to happen.

The thought of myself there, so lost and untethered. Grasping blindly for a way out of what I saw as a lifetime of loneliness. Little did I know my rock was standing right there, flipping bacon.

I hadn't even let myself consider the possibility that whatever little spark we both felt between us that morning could be kindled into a flame. It was too impossible, the mountain too high to summit.

But I'd let myself fantasize. And in those fantasies, she was bent over the counter, just like she is right now.

"Don't move," I say as I lower myself back down to my knees on the cool tile floor.

The round spread of her ass and pussy greet me like a smile as I spread her legs wider to reveal the treasure between them.

I hear a growl escape my lips that sounds too animalistic to have come from me. Naomi responds by opening herself wider, and I take the hint, diving in tongue first.

Her sweetness makes my mouth water as I lick from her entrance to her clit, swirling up and around, pausing when her moan deepens and working her soft flesh until she's panting. When I reach up and slide my fingers into her, the wetness that greets me there nearly makes my eyes roll back in my head. I don't want to rush her, but I'm dying to sink myself into her warm, wet body.

"Fuck, Sammy, don't stop," Naomi moans out, gyrating her hips against my mouth.

I wouldn't dream of stopping, holding firm as she shows me just where I need to lick to get her where she wants so badly to go.

It doesn't take long.

I pump her and lick as her body goes taut and her breath catches, followed quickly by the spasms and cries of pleasure that I know I'll be hearing in my dreams.

She pours into my waiting mouth, and I lick her up. A communion. A prayer.

She pulls away before I'm ready, and I sit back on my heels, eyes closed, trying to come down from the high of her taste on my tongue.

"What did I hear about bending me over the counter?"

I look up to find Naomi still leaning forward, looking seductively at me over her shoulder. The last thing I want to do is keep her waiting. "Oh, I'm going to fuck you on this counter, princess. The only question is how many more times I can get you to scream like you just did."

She bites her lip and watches as I rise to my feet and drop my pants, achingly hard erection bouncing back up and slapping my stomach.

"Is that for me?" she asks, breathless.

"It's always for you, princess. Everything is for you."

I slide one hand up to grip her hip as I drive myself into her without another word. We both moan as my tip slides deeper into her body, settling at the hilt.

"Do you know how good it feels to sink my bare cock into your pussy?" I don't know how I'm managing to get the words out with no breath left in my body.

Naomi just shakes her head where it hangs, forehead nearly touching the mahogany cutting board.

"It feels like diving off a cliff, straight into heaven."

Naomi laughs softly, her body shaking and pussy clenching tightly around my cock. "You are quite the poet, Sammy."

I shake my head, eyes glued to the place where I'm sliding out of her body right to the tip before slamming back in. "I wasn't until I met you, princess. You do something to me."

"Something poetic?" Naomi moans as I hit my stride, gripping both of her hips and working her body as she holds onto the countertop.

"Yeah," I say, leaning down to press a kiss between her shoulder blades. "Something poetic."

There are so many more things to say, so many more ways she's changed me in just the short time I've been blessed with her presence, but I can't find the words in this moment.

And I know I don't need to. I have time to tell her everything.

"I love you, princess," I say, and the words tip me over the edge. I buckle at the core as I spill inside her, eyes clenching closed against the onslaught of nearly debilitating pleasure. I somehow manage to stay on my feet and pump through it, Naomi's body tightening around my cock, sucking my orgasm from me.

I let her have it.

When my brain finally clicks back into gear, I pull her up until her back meets my chest, and she's wrapped tightly in both arms.

We're both still breathing heavily and after a moment, our breathing syncs up and we're like one set of lungs. Her heart pounds in time with mine, and it's one heart.

"I love you, too, Sammy."

Rule #50

JUST SAY YES

NAOMI

Eight Months Later

"Keeping this bag or donating it?"

I turn to where Sam's standing in the corner of the living room in my Austin apartment, holding up a white plastic bag.

I cock my head to the side, considering. I know what I shoved in there. All the beautiful wool scarves I've collected over the years.

Won't have much use for those on Faraday Island.

"Donate," I decide with a smile.

We're finishing up the last of the packing and getting ready for the real estate agent to start staging for listing photos.

We talked about keeping the place as a getaway in the city, but I finally decided I wanted to let it go. I want this chapter of my life, the lonely, searching, empty chapter, officially closed. We can always buy a new place in Austin if we end up spending time here. Goodness knows we'll be able to afford it.

The last eight months have been a whirlwind of emotions,

introductions, and new beginnings. I'm officially settled into the homestead. I even have my own set of chores. Every day feels like a labor of love. Like I'm building something with my own two hands. Sam and I are building a life together.

After deciding not to reinvest my time back into my lifestyle channel, Reina, Fran, and I had a ceremony on the beach where I got to say goodbye to an era of my life and invite in a new one.

I'm happy to say it's going really well. I already have three clients, properties on Faraday and neighboring islands, that I'm doing content creation for. And then there's Paradise Events, my main client, who keeps me busy with weddings at The Sands and all over the world.

It feels crazy being back in this apartment, where I spent so many years thinking my life could only be so big. That I only had so much room in my heart, and I needed to protect it.

Things could not be more different now. It's like my heart, my life, my soul, have blown wide open and the amount of space I have to live and love is endless.

"Why don't you pick your favorite one and keep it?" Sam says, walking over with the bag of scarves. "You never know."

I grin at him and dig into the bag, pulling out a long, jewel blue and gold one that I bought on a trip to Amsterdam my senior year of high school. I toss it around the back of Sam's shoulders, using it to pull him close. "I guess these can come in handy, huh?"

He allows me to take him in my arms, letting the bag fall to the side. "We're pretty close to being done here," he says, resting his forehead on mine as I hold him tightly with both arms.

"So, we deserve a break?" I tease back.

Sam's eyebrows go up. "What did you have in mind?"

I start walking backward, pulling him along with the scarf still draped around his back. "I thought we could revisit the room where this all started."

"Oh, really?" he answers, clearly on board for whatever I have planned.

"Do you remember the night we first met?"

"Of course," Sam says. "I remember."

"Well, I thought that since we're back at the scene of the crime, and you never got to do what you really wanted to do when we were here the first time…"

Sam's lips graze down my cheek and tuck into the crook of my neck. I can feel his warm breath as he answers. "Now's my chance?"

"Exactly."

His hands are everywhere, softly tracing my curves and teasing the edges of my shirt and shorts. Just when I think he's going to use those strong hands to strip me bare, however, he drops them to his sides and takes a step back.

"Okay," he says.

"Okay," I agree, biting my lower lip. "I'll lead the way."

I turn and start down the hall toward the bedroom that used to contain my queen-sized bed and pink love seat. The room where I first let my crush on this man blossom into something more.

"Naomi."

Sam's firm voice stops me, and I turn.

He's still standing right where I left him, arms dangling at his sides.

As I watch, he drops to one knee.

"What…" The word drifts off as I raise my hand to my mouth in surprise.

"You told me to do exactly what I wanted to that first night we were here. Well, this is what I wanted to do."

I walk back until I'm standing a foot away from where he still kneels in the soft carpeting. As I look down into his upturned gaze, I know he's telling the truth.

"I could not be happier that we get to create this life together. I've been dreaming about my soul mate for a long time, Naomi. I'm so grateful that life finally brought us together."

At his words, I drop my hands from where they're still

clasped over my mouth and allow him to take them in his. "I'm grateful, too. I never imagined this would happen for me. I thought it was too late."

Sam smiles, and heaven and earth move. "The timing could not have been more perfect."

He reaches into his pocket and pulls out a little blue velvet bag, tied at the top with sparkling gold thread. When he pours the ring into his palm, I gasp.

"Is that?" I can't bring myself to say the words.

"Your mother's ring. Sure is. Dom gave it to me months ago."

"I thought he was going to give it to Reina."

"It was always meant for you."

I haven't thought about the thin gold band, with its princess-cut solitaire, for many years. It disappeared from our house when Dom did, and I never thought I'd see it again.

"Sam," I start in a whisper, trailing off when the emotion of the moment threatens to turn my words into sobs.

Sam just takes my hands in his once more, holding me tightly, grounding me back into this moment. "Let me get through this, okay?"

Tears roll down my cheeks even as I nod, a small breathy laugh escaping my lips.

Sam's eyes well with tears of his own, but his voice is steady as he says the words I've dreamed about hearing.

"Naomi, now that I have you, I can't believe I ever lived without you in my life. This ring is a promise that I will show up every day and prove to you how grateful I am that we found each other. That somehow, in this great big world, you and I got to cross paths. That in the grand scheme of the universe and endless time and space, you and I get to exist in this same moment, together."

His tears are rolling now, but he doesn't brush them away. "I was going to do this when we got home, after all your stuff was at our house and it was official that your world and my world were combined. But I think you're right that this is the perfect place. It feels like coming full circle. So, my love, will you make me the happiest man on the planet and marry me?"

I'm nodding before he even finishes speaking. "Yes, Sam. Of course. I love you. I would love to marry you."

He slides the ring onto my finger, and for a moment, I'm transported back to my childhood bedroom, slipping this very ring onto my tiny finger, imagining a life where someone loved me enough to keep me forever.

But I don't have to imagine anymore.

Because he's right here.

My vision is a little fuzzy from my tears, but I can see clearly enough to see our bright future reflected in his eyes. It's deep and blue and black and white with hints of green. Like the cosmos and our island home and the warm feeling of everything I've ever needed in life, wrapped around me in an embrace.

Rule #51

RIGHT HERE, RIGHT NOW

NAOMI

One Year Later

"Maybe we should call off the ceremony."

I turn to Sam, aghast. "What do you mean, call off the ceremony? Are you crazy?"

He's giving me those extra calm eyes that let me know he thinks I might be the crazy one. "We planned this before…well, you know. The timing could not be worse. Krista has been pulling her hair out all week."

"It's thirty-eight steps, Sam. Fifty feet. That's closer than my bed to Reef. I think I'll be okay."

He kneels down next to the sofa in our two-bedroom suite at The White Sands, where we've been camping out for almost three weeks—to keep me within running distance of Krista, our resident resort doctor.

At first, I refused to accept that I was *high risk* just because of my age. I'm just as healthy as any of these twenty-year-olds popping out babies. I ate all the right things. I did the yoga. I practiced the breathing.

But eventually, I had to accept the fact that my body wasn't going to tolerate a stand-up paddleboard photo shoot at eight months, like Reina's. I needed to stay close to home and keep myself near the AC and, apparently, become a ward of the resort with my own private doctor.

Not that I'm complaining. I thank my lucky stars each and every day that I'm even in a position to be able to have such incredible care.

But I'll be damned if I'm going to miss my own wedding.

Fran breezes through the door, wearing the same *"I'm freaking out but don't want to let the nine-month preggo bridezilla know"* look that everyone has been wearing all week.

I hold up my hand to stop whatever she's about to tell me. "Just get the fucking dress, Fran."

And so it is. In the grand tradition of brides, going back hundreds of years, everyone bows to my demands.

My stunning empire waist gown, that was luckily able to be custom altered twice as my belly swelled, is the palest ice blue with white sequin flowers flowing around the bust and trailing down the back. It zips, thank goodness, and Fran secures my long veil in place.

We're foregoing some traditions out of pure necessity—and Sam's complete and utter refusal to leave my side. Sam is not only seeing me before the ceremony, but he's joining Dom in walking me down the aisle. The two men get me down to the pool patio doors where all of our friends and family wait just outside, facing the ocean view. Live piano plays as the palms sway in the gentle breeze.

"Ready?" he asks, patient and kind and everything in this world that I've always needed but never thought I deserved.

I nod.

But I'm wrong.

I only make it one step before it becomes clear that it's all over.

Holding my ground on that wooden stair, I try to catch my breath, but it's impossible.

The two men who anchor the orbit of my universe hold me steady by my arms on each side, both of them wanting to ask, but neither of them daring.

"Back up," I whisper, and four strong arms lift me straight up and back onto the solid ground of the concrete pool patio.

Everyone has turned in their chairs to send me sunglass gazes. I can find plenty of smiles. Plenty of concerned eyebrows. At a gesture from Sam, Max, Reina, Fran, Vicki, Ben, and Avery, the whole wedding crew, come hurrying down the aisle and quickly reform their ranks around where we stand, with the lovely White Sands as the backdrop.

Maybe it's meant to be this way anyway.

This place, that was once just an afterthought, someone else's dream come true, has quickly become the joyous, rapturous, beating heart of my entire life. I know each of the employees by name. Their children bring me plums and mangos from the trees in their yards. I didn't even ask for acceptance, I didn't need to. The glittering, vibrating aura that is The Sands just opened up and swallowed me whole.

And I'm not fighting to escape.

I am, however, fighting to remain standing on this perch, in the hot sun, in a dress that probably weights three times what my new baby will.

As if conjured, the little creature shifts inside me.

"Hurry," I whisper.

We have carefully crafted vows written on White Sands stationery tucked into Max's pocket, but they're quickly forgotten.

"Do you, Sam?"

"I do," Sam answers, eyes locked on mine.

"And do you, Naomi?"

"Yes," I whisper. "I do."

"It is the high honor and privilege of my life to pronounce these two, Naomi and Sam—"

My grip on Sam's hands between us at the makeshift altar turns to cat claws as my body seizes in agony. The wave passes quickly, and my vision clears. I blink up at Sam, not quite believing I'm still standing.

"Wife and husband!"

The crowd is on their feet, cheering.

I can't breathe. Can't loosen my grip.

"Please, please give a kiss," Max is urging us. "And then we will pronounce you two parents, I think."

A nervous laugh filters through the crowd as people start to murmur.

"You okay?" Sam whispers, leaning down to place his forehead against mine. You'd never tell by his calm, gentle presence that my perfectly manicured nails are about to draw blood from his forearms.

I nod, then shake my head.

Then tilt my face up. I have to close my eyes against the sun, but I trust Sam to understand.

I want this kiss.

And I get it.

And then the whole world goes fuzzy…and sideways.

I wake in the luxurious hospital suite at the resort. It was built slowly over the last nine months. Everyone on the island has been excited about the development because, in true White Sands nature, our new doctor and nurses, as well as our new hospital recovery room, is available to islanders in crisis as well as resort guests. Everyone has to be helicoptered off, of course, but we now have a state-of-the-art crisis center to keep people safe until transport is ready.

Not that I'd be kept waiting.

Ben's helicopter has been parked on the roof for the last six months, full time pilot paid to live at the resort and be on call twenty-four hours a day.

That's my first thought as I come to.

I turn my head to find Sam right at my side.

"I don't want the helicopter." I clear my throat. "I don't want to leave."

His calm smile tells me everything I need to know. "Krista doesn't think you'll need to. You shouldn't have been standing out in the sun in that dress—"

"Like I told you a million times," our doctor, Krista, calls from across the room, where she's preparing a cart with supplies along with her team of nurses.

"Like Dr. K told us a million times," Sam finishes with a smile. "But she says your vitals are stable—"

"And the baby?" I gasp the words out.

"And the baby is doing just fine. It's in position now."

Amazed, terrified, grateful tears swell in my eyes. "It's not going to be an it," I manage to whisper.

Sam shakes his head. "Not for much longer."

And thanks to modern science, to centuries of generational wealth, and to whatever gods or goddesses happen to be tasked with watching over me, I get my wish of welcoming our child into the world in the deep, cool bath overlooking the ocean.

He's pink and purple and confused and so utterly, unspeakably perfect.

When we're both dry and tucked back into the massive hospital room bed, Sam crawls in next to me. "How's Freddy Mercury doing?"

I smile down at our sleeping baby and shake my head.

There's been a betting pool among the staff at the resort for the name of the new White Sands baby. Sam, Ben, Dominic, and Avery have all been top contenders, as well as, puzzlingly, Freddy Mercury.

"Ezra."

Sam nods. This was in the top three of our own secret list. "Dominic?"

I nod back at him.

And we both stare down at the brand-new center of the universe.

Ezra Dominic Griffin.

Welcome to the world, little guy.

A Look At Book Five:

RED VELVET

He's passing through. I'm staying put. So why does everything about him feel like home?

I didn't come to Faraday Island looking for a distraction. I came to open a bakery, recruit a legendary pastry chef, and prove I'm exactly as capable as everyone seems to doubt. The last thing I needed was a broad-shouldered Alabama lumberjack showing up at the bar, arguing about red velvet cake, and making me forget every sensible rule I've ever lived by.

James doesn't live here. He's fixing up a house to sell and heading back to his real life. I know better than to want someone I can't keep. But he shows up everywhere, learns my coffee order, fixes things I didn't know were broken, and looks at me like I'm the most interesting thing on this island.

But he's hiding something. And the closer I get, the more I realize his secrets aren't just his to keep.

Some recipes can't be rushed. Some risks can't be taken back.

AVAILABLE MAY 2026

Acknowledgments

How're you doing with your phone?

I'm doing medium—on a good day. At this moment, I have zero social apps except TikTok for work purposes, and my screen is in gray scale. I just woke up from a dream where Chipp chose the password for my screen time restrictions, and then he forgot it, and I was never able to open socials again.

So, you know. It's a work in progress.

When I decided to quit drinking almost a decade ago, it felt like freedom. I walked away from that lifestyle and never looked back. When I finally tackled smoking, however, a year into my sobriety, what I found there was a different beast altogether. My mind freaked the fuck out about not having its normal dose of its current drug of choice. I was sad and angry and confused and so, so tired all the time from having to constantly comfort myself —while still denying my brain the one thing it wanted.

I replaced my nicotine addiction with sugar, as one does, a choice I'm still to this day trying to recover from. The whole phone thing happened slowly and, in hindsight, almost as intentionally. It's like I watched myself getting more and more attached to the thing and did nothing to stop it.

I have this one memory of a particularly hard night at juggle club (lol) where I was upset about some family stuff and ended up leaving in tears. I recognized that I was crying too hard to be safe driving, so I pulled over a few blocks away and scrolled for a few minutes.

It calmed me right down. I wasn't seeking out funny or

happy videos. I was just mindlessly scrolling a feed of people posting whatever they post. Like taking any drug, it worked its magic. I was able to get ahold of myself and drive home.

I think about that moment a lot—because it happens now more than I'd like to admit. When I'm here at my keyboard and something gets hard or I'm feeling stuck or overwhelmed, I reach for my phone. Anytime I have the smallest amount of downtime in my day—phone. If I have a stressful day ahead of me, I take some extra time in the morning to post in multiple places, so I'll have an extra boost of notifications throughout the day to keep me going.

What is that if not a drug?

And what am I if not addicted.

This book started in my head with that scene in the hotel lobby where Naomi blurts out that she videoed the two of them. Most books start from one little idea and grow into these beasts that I spend months wrangling. I had no intention of trying to tackle my own phone concerns through fiction, but that's how it always turns out. Whatever problems I'm worrying about, even subconsciously, make it onto the page.

In the end, I like to think Naomi found some kind of balance with her phone, even if all she did was move to a place where reception is so bad that you can only use it sporadically throughout the day...something I have considered for myself. I'm not there yet, but it's good to know I have options.

This book was a massive effort from my wonderful team of helpers. As always, Karen helped me flesh out a couple of difficult conversations that needed to happen to make sure everyone got the closure they needed. Morgan, my courageous assistant, who makes everything so beautiful in Lore Townsend internet land, and is always just a text message away when I'm freaking out about one thing or another. Cathryn, my sushi (and sashimi) friend, who never lets me get away with a single typo...bless her heart. The full LT ARC team, who boost my morale during the huge emotional push of publishing a new book by pouring encouragement and praise into our FB group.

Of course, Chipp, who puts up with all this smut craziness, including the early mornings, flights around the country for events, and closets filled with outdated paperbacks and cheap, novelty vibrators.

Last but certainly not least, thanks to you! This series changed my life in all sorts of ways, the most amazing of which was the community I was able to build while writing it. You read my book! And, if you read this one, you probably read the last three in this series. I'm still astounded every day that I made it here, to these acknowledgments, and that you're here with me, reading them.

I did a lot of reflecting as I prepared to publish this book, the last in the originally planned four of the series. I'm not a planner, per se. I had no idea when I started *Off the Menu* what the rest of the books would look like. I had a list of the guys' first names, that's it. Reading back through the older books, I love each of them so intensely, and I can also watch my own growth as an author. I'm so unbelievably excited for what comes next. Thanks again for sticking with me on this journey.

If you want to join us in the Romance Club, you can find that info on the next page. You can also message me anytime on IG or shoot me an email if you have thoughts or ideas or just want to chat. I'd love to hear from you.

Lore

You can learn plenty of normal things about me in my various platform bios, so here's some things you can only learn in the back of this book:

Q: What's your go-to writing snack or drink?

A: Well, I mostly always write first thing in the morning, so my first snack is a mushroom coffee Oatly latte followed immediately by another one. Then I have a banana, and then I'm either interrupted, or I force myself to sit down for cereal, or I eat whatever granola or protein bars Chipp has stashed in the cupboards as I continue to bust out words. It's always been a struggle. As a serious morning person, I'm hungry as soon as I wake up, and the more coffee I drink on an empty stomach, the worse I feel. And yet…it's hard for me to take a break long enough to walk to the kitchen and grab a banana. Once I stop writing in the morning, that's it for the day, and every time I stop—even if just for a moment to pee or eat—it feels like it could be the end for that day. And I never want it to end.

Q: Have you ever put a real fight or heartbreak into a book scene?

A: Hmm…not exactly. I mean, describing people's feelings always seems kind of familiar. Like, I can feel them in my chest as I write them, and some of those are phantom feelings of my own. I think all the things that happen to us as humans—fights, loss, heartbreak, joy, whatever—have a set of feelings that could be for a whole host of situations. So, when someone is feeling lonely or betrayed, I can reach into a memory bank of how it felt when I was betrayed in a whole different way and those feelings still translate.

Q: If you weren't a writer, what would you be doing instead?

A: I'm a social worker and mental health counselor at a crisis stabilization and detox center. I went back to work full time last fall when we moved back to the island. I also own a handmade bag company with Chipp. He's an incredible artist and craftsman and makes all the products, while I deal with customers and shipping and online sales. I am very busy lol.

Q: Do you believe in love at first sight?

A: Yes! I think I'm in a love at first sight situation right now. Once, what feels like a million years ago, I saw Chipp's bio pic on the wall of the yoga studio where he worked. I'd never met him or taken his class, but I thought to myself then and there—that's my person. It took a while (and many yoga classes) to get up the nerve to ever make a move, but in the end, I great gatsby'd him with the help of our mutual friend Rebecca, throwing dinner parties at her big, fancy house. But…that's a story for another time.

Q: What's one line or scene in this book you're most proud of?

A: This book was the hardest one yet (until *A Fool's Game,* where I had to take not two but THREE people through emotional arcs, and it nearly killed me). I was pushing out books really fast when this one originally came out and decided to do the launch at the Smut Lovers event in Orlando. I had launched Ben and Victoria's book at a Portland event the spring before, and it was so fun that I thought I'd do it again. But it was much less fun—and way more stressful. Flying to these events with books is no small task. Smut Lovers that year was my first big, cross country signing event and pulling off the whole operation all by myself was already too much. So, to add a book release—in person at the event, as well as online—shut me down. I didn't have the energy to give this book the release it deserved. I'm really excited I have the opportunity to do it better this time. I've learned a lot over my years of publishing and let me tell you—less is more. That's my mantra now. I whisper it to myself when I'm stacking my calendar with way more things than I'm ever going to be able to do in a month. Less is more. Less is more. And I see now that this isn't even really an answer to this question, but there you go. I'm proud that this book exists. Thanks for reading!

The best place to find the most current info about my books and events is here:

linktr.ee/authorloretownsend

www.loretownsend.com

Join Lore Townsend's Romance Club

www.ingramcontent.com/pod-product-compliance
Lightning Source LLC
LaVergne TN
LVHW040214110826
845146LV00005B/1285